GUENEVERE
THE QUEEN OF THE SUMMER COUNTRY

Also by Rosalind Miles

Fiction
Return to Eden
Bitter Legacy
Prodigal Sins
Act of Passion
I, Elizabeth

Non-fiction
The Fiction of Sex
The Problem of Measure for Measure
Danger! Men At Work
Modest Proposals
Women and Power
Ben Jonson: His Life and Work
Ben Jonson: His Craft and Art
The Female Form
The Women's History of the World
The Rites of Man
The Children We Deserve

GUENEVERE

THE QUEEN

of the

SUMMER COUNTRY

a novel

ROSALIND MILES

POCKET
BOOKS

LONDON · SYDNEY · NEW YORK · TOKYO · SINGAPORE · TORONTO

First published in Great Britain by Simon & Schuster UK Ltd, 1999
This edition first published in 2000 by Pocket Books
An imprint of Simon & Schuster UK Ltd
A Viacom company

Simon & Schuster UK Ltd
Africa House
64–78 Kingsway
London WC2B 6AH

Simon & Schuster Australia
Sydney

A CIP catalogue record for this book is available
from the British Library

1 3 5 7 9 10 8 6 4 2

ISBN 0–671–01812–4

Typeset by Palimpsest Book Production Limited,
Polmont, Stirlingshire
Printed and bound in Great Britain by
Caledonian International Book Manufacturing Ltd, Glasgow

For the One Who Walks the World Between the Worlds

FAMILY TREE

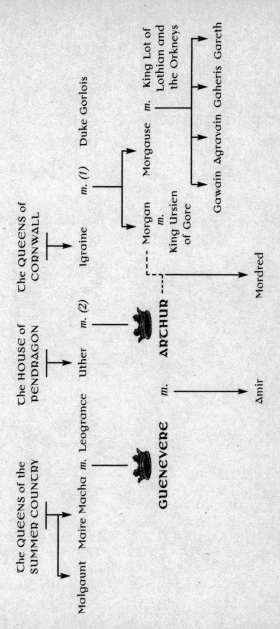

The QUEENS of the SUMMER COUNTRY

Malgaunt   Maire Macha *m.* Leogrance

GUENEVERE *m.* → Amir

The HOUSE of PENDRAGON

Uther   *m. (2)*

ARTHUR

The QUEENS of CORNWALL

Igraine   *m. (1)*   Duke Gorlois

Morgan *m.* King Ursien of Gore

Morgause *m.* King Lot of Lothian and the Orkneys

Gawain   Agravain   Gaheris   Gareth

Mordred

IT BEFELL IN THE DAYS *of Uther Pendragon* when he was King of all England, that he loved a fair lady by the name of Queen Igraine. But she would not give her assent to the King.

So for pure anger and great love King Uther fell sick. Then Merlin said to him, "If ye will fulfill my desire, you shall have your desire. And the child you get on Igraine you shall deliver to me."

"I will well," said the King. Then he came with a great host to Cornwall and laid siege and killed Igraine's husband, Duke Gorlois. And Merlin raised a great mist, in which Duke Gorlois was slain, and afterward he brought Uther to Queen Igraine in the likeness of Gorlois. That night Uther lay with Igraine in her castle at Tintagel, and begat on her the child called Arthur.

Then he took Queen Igraine as his wife, and willed King Lot of Lothian and the Orkneys to wed the Queen's daughter Morgause. Her other daughter, Morgan Le Fay, he put to a nunnery, because he would have it so.

Then the Queen waxed great with child, and when she was delivered, the child was given to Merlin out at a postern gate and placed with a faraway lord to nourish as his own. Within two years King Uther fell sick of a great malady, and his enemies usurped his lands and slew his people to right and to left. And so he died and left the realm in great jeopardy.

And after many years, Merlin called all the lords and kings and people to London, to show who should be rightwise king of this realm. And so it happened that a good knight called Sir Ector came from his far estate along by Wales, with his son Sir Kay and the young Arthur that was brought up as Kay's brother, and they came upon a sword set in a stone . . .

MORTE D'ARTHUR

CHAPTER 1

The old man shivered, and leaned forward to warm his hands on his horse's neck. White fingers of mist were feeling their way down from the mountains ahead, and the short April day was drawing towards night. Already the grass was damp with evening dew, and soon there would be rain. London lay far behind, and they were miles from shelter and food. It would be another wet and hungry night.

No matter. A white light flickered in his yellow eyes. When they reached their destination, every man would eat his fill.

'Merlin?'

He started. 'Yes?'

The young man riding beside him stirred uneasily. His grey eyes were troubled. 'When you called all the kings and lords together to proclaim my right – how did you know they would accept me as king?'

'They were promised a sign.' Merlin stared off into the mist, avoiding his companion's gaze. 'And we gave them one.'

The younger man ran a hand through his thick fair hair, and gave an embarrassed laugh. 'What, the sword in the stone?'

'What else?'

If the young man heard the rising irritation in Merlin's tone, he did not care. His broad shoulders went back as he spoke. 'But that was not a true sign from above. You made it happen, you brought it about.'

'It was the sign they needed.' Merlin turned on him. 'And it has made you king!'

Merlin's eyes blazed. He could still hear the cheers echoing round the churchyard, as the crowd had roared for Arthur till the heavens rang. So what if the petty kings and jealous lords had slunk off vowing war? The boy had won over the rest of them with his simple honesty and shining faith.

Sourly he eyed what he secretly doted on, Arthur's open gaze, his boyish smile and thoughtful air. 'King Arthur now!' he snarled. 'What more do you want?

'Ha!' Arthur laughed ruefully. 'A king without a kingdom.'

'Not so!' The old man angrily tossed his head. 'Your lands may lie in the hands of your enemies. But when we reach Caerleon, all the people will rally to your flag.'

Arthur smiled faintly. 'All of them?'

'All your true subjects!' came the sharp reply. 'And they will fight for you against those who carved up your kingdom when your father died.'

When Uther died—

A shadow of old pain crossed Merlin's face. Long ago, many lives before this, he could remember the land sliding into anarchy when the Romans left, and the legions marched away. But that was nothing to the darkness that came down when King Uther fell.

Merlin's chest heaved, and his breath wheezed in his throat. 'The Christians say, "Woe to the land where the king is a child." The Middle Kingdom has belonged to the

House of Pendragon, time out of mind. If your father had lived till you were grown, no man on earth would have dared to usurp your right. We would not have to fight to reclaim your throne. We would not have to take Caerleon by storm to bring you into your own lands again.'

'The Christians.' Arthur's thoughts had taken another turn. 'Our people here follow the old faith. What are the Christians to us?'

Merlin's eyes grew opaque. 'They are the coming men. We must have their support.'

'But the Old Gods will never die.' Arthur glanced up in awe at the mossy oaks by the wayside, the black mountains ahead, and the arch of the sky encrusted with the first faint glistening stars. 'And—'

'—the Great Mother, who was here before them all?' Merlin cackled harshly. 'Never fear, boy! Like all true females, the Goddess has a weakness for young men. If you smile on the Christians, she will forgive you. And a king must be king of all his people, not of one faith alone.'

A light drizzle was beginning to fall. Arthur looked round at the small column of men following behind. 'We must make camp,' he said heavily. 'The men have had no proper sleep for days. They are exhausted, we must rest now.'

He was aware of the old man's cruel glare. 'Your enemies will neither rest nor sleep. Every delay allows them to grow strong.'

Arthur took a breath. 'They are strong already, sir. After twenty years, a day or two can make no difference now.'

Merlin ground his teeth. 'Push on, I say! Strike hard and fast, to drive them from the land!' The old man passed a hand over his eyes. 'Strike without mercy, smash them to a pulp!'

His pulse raced. Yes, pulp and bonemeal, food for crows and dogs. And one, above all, must pay a hundredfold. King Lot of Lothian should feel his wrath like fire.

Lot of the Lothians, King of the Orkneys, Lord of the Isles.

Lot the loathsome, Lot the loathed.

Merlin's sight faded, and a broad, black-bearded face rose up before him, set on a beefy neck. Now Lot and all of them would eat hot iron, and drink their own blood.

With a sensuous pleasure he pictured himself plunging his sword-point into Lot's throat, watching the black eyes bubble till they burst, hearing the last gurgling blood-choked scream. It would be good, so good—

Arthur's voice cut across his waking dream. 'If the men aren't fit to fight, we can't strike at all.' He smiled an apology, but his tone was firm. 'Forgive me, Merlin. You shall command everything else, but I must lead the men.' He threw a glance behind. 'They have left their lords, their kings, their lands to follow me. I must take care of them.'

Merlin turned his gaze up to the indifferent stars. His thin frame shook with the effort to master his revenge. 'Well, after twenty years, I can wait for King Lot.' His laugh was shrill. 'When he drove me out, I swore I would return. He will be there when I come for him.'

'Where? In Caerleon?'

Merlin shrugged his thin shoulders. 'His vassal kings rule your land for him there. He'll be in the north, in his own distant realm. Where he lived well enough on the territories he had, till your father's death left your kingdom undefended and a prey to greedy rogues like him.' His teeth flashed yellow in the evening light. 'But we shall draw him south, I have no fear.'

Arthur nodded. 'And beat him in a fair field, man to man. Only so will I reclaim my kingdom and my lands.'

Merlin's eyes gleamed. 'And only so will you make yourself High King!'

Arthur paused. 'I know my father made himself High King when all the other kings agreed to follow him. But he fought many wars to give them peace. I only want what I can call my own. If I can bring the Middle Kingdom back to the rule of Pendragon, I shall be content.'

The veins knotted on the side of Merlin's head. 'Pendragon means High King, ruler of all the Britons!' he ground out. 'Don't fool with your destiny, boy! You are called to fulfil it now!'

'If it is truly my destiny, it will fulfil itself,' Arthur said quietly.

Merlin struck his forehead with his hand. 'You will be High King! I have proclaimed it in the face of the whole assembly when I declared you king!'

Arthur gave a loving smile. 'Dear lord, if it is to be, then it will be as you say. But now I have to face the task at hand.' He grew serious again. 'From what you say, I have harsh wars to wage at home before all those who have claimed a piece of the Middle Kingdom are driven out. Attacking Caerleon can only be the start.' He laughed self-consciously. 'And such war-work is not all that I must do. A king must have a queen. If I am to be a true lord to all my people, I must have a wife.'

Merlin's eyes flared. So the boy's mind was already turning that way? 'One day, yes, of course. But you're young yet, boy – there's plenty of time.'

'Men of my age are married with children.' Arthur's voice changed. 'And I met a lady, a month or two ago.'

'When you went to the tournament? The girl at the castle?'

Arthur stared. 'You knew about that?' His fair skin coloured as if he had been slapped. 'How did you know?'

Merlin met his angry glance indifferently. 'I knew.' Of course he knew. It was his business to know. He gave an unpleasant laugh. 'And I know that she will be nothing in your life. A fine young man can have any girl.'

'She was not any girl!' Arthur coloured again. 'She—' He broke off, and looked away.

Merlin watched him without sympathy. How young he is, he thought.

Arthur could feel the force of the old man's sulphurous glare. 'She wasn't just any girl,' he said stubbornly.

But Merlin did not care. 'No girls!' he pronounced, with ferocious emphasis. 'In time we shall find a royal princess for you, virtuous and well-bred—'

'Like Guenevere of the Summer Country?' Arthur leaned forward eagerly.

Merlin tensed. 'Guenevere?'

'She's brave and beautiful, they say, and she will be queen.' Arthur glanced at Merlin. 'When we win back the Middle Kingdom, they'll be our closest neighbours, and we shall need them as friends.' He paused. 'We're passing very near their borders now. Should we turn aside to pay our respects?'

Not a chance, boy, Merlin cackled to himself. He waved a skinny hand dismissively. 'Forget her!' he ordered. 'Later on, we shall make a treaty with them, to keep our borders safe. But the Princess Guenevere is not for you.'

The grey eyes fixed on him were curious now. 'Why not?'

Why not indeed? Merlin hugged his thoughts to himself. He kept his voice light. 'She's spoken for, that's why. She's already betrothed, she's to be married soon. But it's no loss to you. She's born to be a trouble to her husband, that one.'

He looked round casually, and pointed between the trees. 'You wanted to call a halt, and make camp for the men? This looks a good place, here.'

He reined in his horse, and sat for a moment brooding heavily. 'I must leave you for a while. Tomorrow I shall return. We shall meet again by nightfall, in the woods above Caerleon.' He smiled, and gathered up the reins. The dying sun lit his hooded eyes. 'Wish me well, then, for I have much to do.'

CHAPTER 2

Why have I never been like other girls?
She always knew that she lay in a queen's arms when her mother told her stories of the Fair Ones who watched out from their hills and hollows for little princesses like her. And she knew that she rode out beside her mother to greet the people all in white and gold because all the queens of the Summer Country had done so too.

When her nursemaids said, 'Hush, do not trouble the Queen,' her mother would smile and say, 'Let her come to me. One day she will be queen.'

When her father frowned and said, 'Guenevere is a grown girl now, she must be married one day soon,' the Queen would laugh and say, '"One day" is soon enough for her to choose.' And all the tall knights round the Queen's throne would smile at her, and agree.

Childhood was one long summer in sunlit meadows clad in white and gold, daisies and celandines spangling the grass like stars. At midday the sun blazed down on silent glades and lofty forests, living green cathedrals roofed with fire. Of all the kingdoms of these islands, her mother said, summers were longest here. That was why, when the Old

Ones made the world, they called this the Summer Country, the sweet green south-western kingdom by the sea.

It was an enchanted childhood in a land of summer sun. And though the autumn winds were blowing that would turn her world to winter, she saw nothing, and felt nothing, until suddenly it was gone.

Why is it all so very different now?

'Guenevere, where are you? Hurry, darling, do!'

She could hear her mother calling as she slowly climbed the stairs. In the wide gallery as she reached the top, the Queen stood in the midst of the crowd surrounded by her knights. Radiant in her light gown and crown of gold, she shone like a flower in the forest among the tall men.

So many men, so many watching eyes—

Guenevere moved towards the group of knights, willing herself to avoid their curious gaze. Laughing, the Queen took her hand, and drew her towards the rail. 'See, they're all here, which one shall I choose?'

Below the viewing gallery, a handful of horsemen were already out on the jousting field. Like dolls on their prancing steeds they curvetted about, the spring sun flashing from their armour of shining steel. On the meadowland beyond, the bright pavilions of the contestants dotted the grass like flowers. Between the tents, squires and pages hopped to and fro like crickets as they worked furiously to prepare their knights for the fray.

In the distance the white towers of Camelot shimmered in the sun. Clad in their holiday best, crowds of the towns-folk were pouring out of the gates and over the meadows towards the jousting field. With a loud peal of trumpets, the heralds were making their rounds. 'Move along, there! Clear the field, make way!'

Guenevere breathed deeply, savouring the sweetness of the new-mown grass. She smiled at her mother's joyful

face and dancing eyes. The first tournament of spring was
always the Queen's Championship, and the Queen showed
her pleasure openly, like a child. Indeed, she still was a child
in many ways, Guenevere thought fondly, not like a queen
nearing forty with a grown daughter now.

'Oh, Guenevere!' The Queen touched Guenevere's hair
with a loving hand, and brushed the silken sleeve of her
new gown. 'So fair – darling, you're so lovely today.' She
was looking around the gallery as she spoke. 'Has one of
my gentlemen caught your eye at last? Your father thinks
someone has—'

Yes, Mother, someone has—
But how do I catch his?

A dull sense of defeat dampened Guenevere's soul.
She willed herself to meet the playful gaze. 'The King
sees husbands for me everywhere,' she said levelly. 'But,
madam, this is your special day, not mine.'

The Queen's face clouded. 'My special day—' She gave
an odd, small laugh. 'It's the feast of Penn Annwyn, did you
know that?'

Guenevere shook her head. 'The old Lord of the Underworld?'

The Queen nodded. 'This is the day, they say, when the
door of the year opens the way to the world between the
worlds. When the Dark Lord comes for those he has chosen
to take home.' She shivered, the silk of her dress rippling like
sunlight over water, and tried to smile. 'Old superstitions
from the Welshlands, where old things die hard. We have
had word that Merlin has been seen.'

Guenevere gasped. 'Merlin?'

She always knew it as a name of fear. The countryfolk
went in dread of strangers, because Merlin could take so
many different shapes. Once her nurse had snatched her
up and run from a child with staring eyes, certain it was

the old enchanter himself. But that was childish nonsense, long ago. She steadied her voice. 'Is it so?'

The Queen looked away. 'The old man of magic is about again, it seems.'

Guenevere grew cold. 'But that means—'

The Queen raised her hand, and shook her head. 'Where Merlin goes, dreams, rumours, phantoms always follow him. We have sent messengers to London and to the Welshlands, and our scouts are everywhere. Whatever happens, we shall know of it.'

Suddenly the Queen's spirits lifted, and she touched Guenevere's cheek. 'Never fear! Whatever is coming is already in the stars. And tomorrow will be soon enough for that.' She smiled her sweetest smile. 'Be happy, my love!'

She called to the chamberlain. 'Are the knights ready for the tournament?'

He bowed. 'Ready and waiting for the royal word.'

'Why then,' she beamed, 'begin!'

In front of the gallery the heralds and trumpeters lined the grassy field, their coloured tunics as bright as playing cards.

'All who challenge for the title of the Queen's champion, come now into the field!' cried the chief herald. 'Enter now, or all depart in peace!'

The Queen stepped to the edge of the viewing gallery, arms upraised to acknowledge the cheers of the crowd. She stood for a moment revelling in the applause, then dropped her handkerchief. The scrap of white lace fluttered through the air like a drowsy dove. The chief herald's baton fell, a fanfare of trumpets split the air, and the best knights of the land rode out before their queen.

'Look, Guenevere, look!'

Guenevere smiled. She knew her mother would miss no detail of the glittering armour and elaborate trappings as the twelve knights took to the field, their horses strutting out stiffly one by one. In their bright plumage of red and white and black, blue, green and gold, they were gorgeous beyond compare. But, with their helmeted heads and tall nodding plumes, there was something sinister about them too, more like birds of prey than men. Guenevere shivered. Why should such thoughts darken this sunny day?

'Leogrance the King, the Queen's first champion!' the heralds bawled.

Into the ring rode a tall shape encased in golden armour, a gold coronet encircling his helmet, attended by knights bearing banners of cloth of gold. *First champion and first love*, the Queen told Guenevere, in the white and gold wonder of their early days, when the glow they shared brought her into the world. Uneasily Guenevere eyed the heavy form still straight in the saddle, but stiff and unbending on a none-too-willing horse. *Why do you do this, Father, every year*, she wondered unhappily, *taking the field with knights young enough to be your sons?*

The Queen sat bolt upright, staring ahead. Do not ask! commanded her rigid back. See only that he has to do it, and that he needs our love.

Now all the challengers had made their bows, and still the people had not seen the man they craved. A clamour began and was carried round the field. 'The champion! Give us the champion!'

Once more the bellowing heralds split their lungs. 'Give welcome to the Queen's knight who comes here to brave all challengers – welcome the Queen's champion and her Chosen One—'

'Lucan!'

The crowd roared its applause. From behind the wooden walls of the knights' enclosure at the far end of the field bounded a huge black horse with evil in its eye. Mounted on its glossy back, standing up in the stirrups, was a tall, lithe, laughing figure in red and gold.

The newcomer dragged the furious beast to a standstill before the gallery, and bowed to the Queen. 'Your servant, Majesty, in life and death!' he cried. Deftly he sent something spinning through the air. One of the knights reached down to catch it for the Queen.

It was a heart-shaped posy of roses and pinks, with trailing strands of honeysuckle scenting the air.

'A bleeding heart!' Guenevere said, entranced.

The Queen's glance flashed towards Lucan and away again. 'A weeping heart,' she corrected, her tremulous fingers playing with the honeysuckle as if it were Lucan's hair. Her eyes were very bright, and the smile she gave him was for him alone.

The heralds were trumpeting the next lord into the ring. But after the laughing knight in red and gold, all the challengers were shadows in his sunlight, doomed to fade. Lucan would win, he knew it, all those around him knew it, and even the dark and ugly monster that he rode seemed to know it too. With each challenge the black beast charged down the field in a frenzy, bent on destroying what lay in its way.

But for all its boldness, Lucan's horse did not please the Queen. 'That new creature Sir Lucan rides, what is it?' she demanded, and back the answer came: 'A black stallion he sent for out of Wales, when he heard of its spirit from a lord who owned it there.' The Queen nodded, but the faint frown did not leave her face.

The sun beat down, hotter than usual for the time of year. Lucan was clad now in deep black armour gleaming like his horse, and his opponents had no more chance than men of tin. One by one they galloped down the lists, and one by one he knocked them all down. At last the sun stood half-way down the sky, and Lucan held the field alone.

'So, now, which shall I choose?' The Queen's face was pink, almost girlish, and lit again with that special smile.

'Madam, you know that you must choose the victor,' Guenevere said fondly, 'if you want the best of your knights to defend you to the death.'

Once more the strange shadow crossed the Queen's face. 'Don't talk to me of death!' She closed her eyes.

Guenevere stared. This was the woman who never admitted fear, the queen who had faced death in battle, fighting from her chariot like the queens of the Summer Country from the ancient days. *No tears, no fears*, she had soothed Guenevere from childhood as she schooled her to be strong. Faint strands of fear entangled Guenevere's heart. What was haunting her? Was she enchanted? Was she ill?

'The Queen's champion!' The herald's chant was howling round the ring. 'The Queen will choose her champion and honour him.'

The Queen opened her eyes, and gave Guenevere her best smile. 'No tears, no fears, little one,' she whispered, squeezing Guenevere's hand. 'I must go.' Guenevere could not speak. She sat without moving as the Queen's knights and attendants parted the crowd, and ushered her below.

In the centre of the field, the men-at-arms had raised a low platform for the Queen. Guenevere watched as her mother lightly crossed the trampled grass and mounted the dais, all happiness now, her quicksilver soul at ease again. Others followed with tasselled cushions bearing the rewards for the victor, rich gifts of gold made ready for many months.

In front of the knights' enclosure, Lucan stood waiting beside the King. Enraged at being kept standing, his horse was shying violently, till it was all the champion could do to hold the brute down.

At last the heralds gave the signal to move forward to the Queen. Flanked by the King, waving to acknowledge the wild cheers on all sides, Lucan set off in triumph down the field. On the dais ahead, the Queen waited for him with starlight in her eyes.

The sun was low in the sky now, the heat of the day no more than a memory lost. A sly wind sprang up, whipping the heavy trappings round the horses' legs, and the air grew cold. The sun sank behind a livid bank of clouds, blue, black and purple swelling from the east.

The two riders drew up before the dais.

'Your Majesty,' cried the King, 'I declare the victor of the combat to be your knight Lucan, who has held the field against all challengers, and won in fair fight.'

The Queen stepped forward to meet him, the gold chain of victory in her hands. 'Well fought, sir knight!'

'My lady and my queen!' Still astride the snorting horse, his face wreathed in a grin of triumph, Lucan leaned down towards the Queen. She smiled, and reached up to place the chain around his neck. Neither of them saw the horse's evil eye fix her in its glare. With a loud scream the great beast reared up, its front legs pawing at the dying sun. Then like heaven falling, it plunged down to strike the Queen and crush her into a broken, bloodstained heap beneath its feet.

With a cry of horror, Lucan leaped from the horse and dragged it away from the pale shape lying motionless on the grass. Still howling, he tore his sword from its sheath and struck straight and true into the horse's heart. As the monster beast keeled over, bucking and heaving, a laughing, snorting spirit burst out through its mouth, and took to the sky. The last echoes mocked the hollow air and died as the horse's life-blood sprouted in great red blossoms, soaking the earth where the Queen's body lay.

'He has come!' A low cry swept through the horrified crowd. 'The Dark Lord, the Lord of the Underworld has come, he is here!'

CHAPTER 3

Gods, it was cold! And sure to rain before night. Blowing on his hands, the guard shouldered his pike and stamped up and down. Dubiously he eyed the dark armies of full-bellied clouds massing in the west. But even on the best of days, Caerleon was a bad place to defend.

With a jaundiced eye he surveyed the rugged walls of the old castle, the low battlements, the shallow moat. Standing at the head of the valley, it was girdled with thick woodland that a shrewd defender would have cut back by a mile. A spy could look down from the hills behind, and see all he wished to know. But whoever built Caerleon had cared more about presenting a handsome face to visitors than repelling attack. And since King Lot seized the land, the puppet kings who ruled the place for him had never had to defend it at all.

In fact, they'd probably forgotten how to fight. The guard cocked an ear to the drunken sounds of revelry in the Great Hall, and shifted his numb feet. Come tomorrow, none of them would be fit to lift a sword.

Yet kings must know what common people knew. And everyone knew that Merlin was about.

Some reckoned he'd been seen above Caerleon, but

others swore he was in the Summer Country now. He had been in London when he called that great assembly there only days ago, that was a fact. Then he had vanished again, most likely back to the Welshlands where he lived with the wild pigs in the forest, rode a horned stag under the full moon, sang to the stars, and drank rock water for his wine. That was true too, everyone knew that.

But no one knew if it was true about the new king. A king for the Middle Kingdom, they said, where there had been no king since old King Uther died. Or, rather, where they had had too many, ever since King Lot's vassal kings had arrived. The guard grinned mirthlessly to himself. Six of them all told, and every one a coward or a fool.

But a Pendragon now, that was different. Uther Pendragon, he had been a king. The ghost of the dead king rose before him, and the guard remembered him with pricking eyes. A man to rejoice in, lusty and full of life. Hands made to swing a sword in battle, and arms as strong as a bear. Built like a bear too, big and broad and rough, but a man through and through.

The guard dwelt tenderly on Uther for a while. Strange that a man like Uther had never had a son. His queen had had children from a marriage before, but there never came one of the marriage that Uther could call his own.

Yet Uther had taken his plough to the field often enough if gossip spoke true, the guard chuckled to himself. Both night and day, men said, he had had his heifer in the barn. But she never threw a single calf for him. Well, only the Gods knew why.

The shade of Uther faded into the glimmering dusk. A nameless sadness overtook the guard. Everything had been better when the High King was alive.

He turned and stamped his way back to the shelter of the gatehouse, kicking his boots against the stones to warm his feet. Would the red dragon ever fly from the topmost turret of Caerleon again? The first Pendragon had claimed this land a thousand years ago. If Merlin had truly found a king who was a Pendragon, or a Pendragon who could be king, then every man jack would rally to his flag.

A burst of bellowing laughter came from the Great Hall, and once again the sound of wild carousing filled the air. The six kings were in their cups, there was no doubt of that. Gods above! They'd be brawling soon, wasting the fight they'd need to meet an attack.

An attack – hopelessly he gazed around. The guards on the battlements were drinking and playing cards, while the look-out dozed openly in his box. But what could you expect of the lads, when the lords were drunk already, and calling for whores in the Great Hall? Even a small band of raiders would go through them like a knife through butter.

Well, serve them right.

If only—

His eye quickened. If only Merlin had found a new king for them. A king of the people, as old Uther used to be, to put down evil and restore the good. A young king who would take a queen, and sire more sons of Pendragon to reign. A man whose name and honour would never die.

Pendragon.

If only the King would come again—

Alone in the shadows of the castle, cold and wretched and without hope, the guard allowed himself to dream.

In the Great Hall of Caerleon, the torches had burned out. King Carados groaned, and raised his pounding head. The table was sticky with spilled beer and wine, the hall full of sweating bodies, most of them asleep. They had started at noon, and it must be past midnight now – twelve hours and more of low debauchery.

In every dark nook or corner a knight huddled down with a half-dressed serving girl. On the benches round the walls some of his men were still drunkenly availing themselves of the women of the town, rutting like stags. Well, knights would be knights. They were no worse than their lords.

Better, most of them. His stomach lurched as he remembered the fat slut he had toyed with earlier, when his blood ran high. Thank the Gods he had thought better of it, and sent her back to the kitchen where she belonged!

He turned in his chair, in a spasm of disgust. And there she was, sprawled across the table in a drunken sleep, her body shamefully exposed, her nipples swollen and red. Now he remembered taking her from behind like a dog, punishing those plump breasts, pinching her nipples savagely as she knelt before him on the table, to the loud applause of all. One thought possessed his mind. Ye Gods, why did I do it? And why now?

Painfully Carados raised his eyes. What time was it? By the fading stars, the dead hour before dawn. Beside him lay another victim of last night's revelry, his breath whistling through his drink-slackened throat, a trickle of thin vomit running down his chin. Carados eyed the loose body with something close to hate. Gods above, if they had to rely on Rience, they might as well give up now!

Still, Rience was no worse than the other four. And thank the Gods, there was no cause for alarm. Six kings would be more than a match for anything. They were all in this together, each sworn to King Lot for his portion of the Middle Kingdom, each ready to defend it to his dying breath.

Carados caught himself up. Gods above, why talk of

dying now? In twenty years, they'd never had to fight for the Middle Kingdom, and they never planned to die for it, then or now.

Still, this threat of Merlin's boy had to be faced.

'Lights!' he roared, booting the nearest servant boy awake. 'Get me some lights here, or I'll have your hide!'

Further down the table, another of the drowsing shapes stirred and came to life. 'Carados, you devil, is that you?' It was King Agrisance, the hardiest of the six vassals of King Lot. 'You and I must be the only ones still alive.'

'We won't be alive for much longer, unless we can rally them!' Carados jerked a thumb down the table at the sleepers beyond. 'Rience will sleep till noon, and Vause is no fighter at the best of times. Nentres and Brangoris are puking-ripe to take to their beds for a week. If this boy of Merlin's comes, you and I will be facing him alone!'

Agrisance broke into a roar of drunken laughter. 'He won't come! And if he does, tell me, what can he do? Make six kings bow to a bastard of no blood? Yield up our swords to a beardless boy?'

'He does not come alone,' Carados muttered. In spite of his head, he found himself reaching for more wine.

'No.' Agrisance chuckled. 'He comes with that mad old warlock Merlin and a ragged army of boys and fools, marching with their arses hanging out of their breeches, and half dead for lack of food.' He burst out laughing. 'Think of it, man, would you attack a dunghill with a force like that?'

When Agrisance cackled, the old sword scar on his cheek puckered till it swallowed up his eye, making him look like a death's head grinning for its prey. Carados averted his gaze. 'Laugh if you like,' he said sourly. 'But they've succeeded in getting Lot's son on their side.'

'Lot's son?' Agrisance was still laughing, but the joke was fading fast. 'What are you talking about?'

'Lot's son!' Carados persisted. 'The eldest, Gawain. He was at the assembly in London when Merlin proclaimed his boy. And he was so taken with this Arthur that he left his lord to follow him.'

Agrisance's mouth formed a silent whistle of disbelief. Carados noted with satisfaction that he was not smiling now. 'In fact, Gawain was the first to swear his allegiance to Arthur, and offer up his sword. And the self-styled king was so delighted that he knighted Gawain there and then. Quite a stunt, eh? Rience and Vause said Merlin must have staged it all.' He took another pull of wine, and felt it burn his throat. 'But bad for Lot, and no mistake, his son and heir to leave the camp like that.'

Agrisance nodded. 'It'll end in blood, as soon as Lot gets to know.' Slowly he groped in his wine-sodden brain. 'But Lot's in the Orkneys eight hundred miles away. If we don't kill Merlin's rabble, the cold and hunger will. So the lad'll be dead before Lot gets to hear. Then all he'll have to do is to bury the shame.'

There was a heavy silence before Carados spoke. 'Unless it's Lot's fate to fall . . . to pay for the wrong – if he did wrong – years ago.'

Agrisance stared at him. 'What are you talking about?'

Carados could not shake off a growing chill. 'Lot. And Uther. If they wronged the Mother-right—'

Agrisance could not contain his irritation. 'Great Gods, man, spit it out! How on earth—?'

'Remember when Uther was making himself High King?' Carados drew a deep breath. 'He seized Cornwall, then he took the Queen of Cornwall against her will. She had two daughters, and he gave them both away. He wanted the Queen to belong to him alone.'

'Well, so would any man!'

Carados shook his head. 'Uther meant to break the

Mother-right. To make sure that neither of the girls would come to her mother's throne.'

'Well, there was sense in that.' Agrisance vaguely remembered it now. Uther had wronged the Queen, he had to admit, and yes, her daughters too, but war was war. 'But where does Lot come in?'

Carados found himself shivering. 'Uther gave the older girl to Lot.'

'To Lot? She could have done a lot worse. A lot!' Agrisance laughed, delighted with his own wit. 'What happened to the younger one?'

'Morgan, she was called. If she'd been twelve, she could have been married off. But she was just too young. Uther put her in a nunnery till she was grown.'

Carados paused.

An old memory lit the fire behind his eyes.

Morgan, yes.

Child or no, he'd have taken her himself.

He could see her now, the tall thin body well sprouted for her age, the lean flanks, long thighs a man could take his time between, and sharp, high, pointed breasts that could take a man's eye out if he moved too fast. And her eyes, that look they had! His flesh stirred. Eyes to drown in, black pools of midnight, pure enchantment – Gods above, young as she was, the girl had been more witch than a nun! He could feel the heat in his groin. Yes, he'd have had little Morgan, any time.

He glanced back down the table. The kitchen maid was still there, her fat breasts spilling from her bodice, her skirts around her waist exposing her all. Memories of last night returned to Carados, and he felt himself thicken and throb.

Agrisance's voice reached him from far away. 'So Uther put her in the nunnery for life?'

But Carados had lost interest. He reached for the wine,

and swallowed half a flagon down. The rest he sluiced into the kitchen-maid's open mouth, and over her bare breasts.

'Whaa—?' She came to cursing, then fell into a simper as soon as she saw Carados. 'Oh, sir—'

'And the older girl, the one who married Lot,' Agrisance was still droning drunkenly on, 'what was she called? Morgause, wasn't it?'

Carados closed his ears. Fate, blood, death, it was all with the Great Ones now. If Lot had done wrong, then he would surely pay. And if Lot's fate was hanging in the stars, then theirs was too. If Lot went down, so did his loyal vassals, all of them. Time to take action, before it was too late.

'Oh, sir—' The maid giggled, a wet look in her eyes. Her mouth opened as she looked down, and saw her wine-soaked breasts. She struggled to sit up. Her nipples glared redly at him through the blue-black lees of the wine, like devil's eyes.

'The light you ordered, sir?'

Carados turned. The page set the burning torch in a nearby sconce. A shaft of light illuminated the Great Hall, and a last impulse of reason coursed through Carados's mind.

Merlin was coming with his motley crew. The ragged army could have reached Caerleon by now. The bastard Arthur could be camped in the woodlands above, only waiting till dawn for the signal to attack. He should order the guard to be on full alert, call up the garrison, and set special watches on each of the four towers.

And he would.

Afterwards.

He heaved the slut further up the table, and threw her on to her back. One hand found a fat purple nipple, while the other ground away at the hairy triangle below.

His mind was spinning.

Afterwards, yes, he would—

The girl opened her legs. An acre of white belly, hips and thighs spread out before him, and he let go of thought.

CHAPTER 4

One guard dreaming on the gate, a score or so idlers on the battlements, and a sentry half asleep on the watch – Caerleon could certainly fall to a surprise attack. From his vantage-point in the woodland above, Arthur methodically studied the castle's defences, and memorised what he saw. It would not be easy, and he had too few men. But it would not be the suicidal enterprise he had feared.

He stood for a while drinking in the early evening air, absorbing the life around him until he could have been one of the broad oak trees that covered the hilly bluff. When the outlying troop of men saw him walking back into the camp some time later, they nudged each other with an understanding air. Already they had learned that their leader, young as he was, had a way of moving beyond mortal preoccupations when he chose.

'Arthur! There you are!'

Arthur raised his eyes to the short figure hurrying towards him and stifled a sigh. He loved Kay dearly, but the tension engraved on his foster-brother's sallow face would not be denied.

'He's not here,' Kay began abruptly. 'There's no sign of him!'

'If Merlin promised to be here, he will come.'

'Why did he ride away last night when we made camp?' Kay fretted. 'Where did he go?'

Arthur smiled. 'He is Merlin. Who knows?'

'You ought to know, he should tell you, you're the King! And the commander of our forces, such as they are.' Kay gestured sourly to the men huddling over their camp-fires in the dank air. 'It's three days now since they had any food. They'll find some game and such in the forest here, but it can't support us long. What if Merlin doesn't come?'

Arthur paused. It was hard for Kay, he knew. All his life Kay had been the son of a noble household, Arthur the child from nowhere taken in to be his squire. Kay had had the best of knighthood training to serve his father's overlord, King Ursien of Gore. Then suddenly the unknown boy had leaped over him to a higher destiny.

But Kay had risen to the moment without hesitation, and loyally thrown in his lot with Arthur when the call came. He had earned the right to be answered now.

Arthur took his arm. 'Merlin will not fail us,' he said confidently. 'But today is the feast of Penn Annwyn, a great day in the Welshlands where the Dark Lord still reigns. Merlin is a Druid of the highest rank. Of course he will be needed for those rites.'

'Ah!' Kay's sardonic laugh showed what he made of this. 'So our man of might is away with his spirits at this crucial time?' He leaned forward urgently. 'But we can't wait for ever! Any minute now they'll get wind of us in the castle, and send a troop up here to flush us out.'

'Never fear. I've given orders that we attack tonight before dawn, just as we planned.'

'So!' Kay's face sharpened, and his eyes lit up. 'Well, if we go in fast enough, one strike should do it, even without his help.' He did not need to voice the thought that struck them both: with or without Merlin, one strike is all we have.

'Courage, brother!' Arthur broke the silence. 'I have seen how the castle lies. It will be ours.'

'Hmm.' Kay was not convinced. But there was no point in dwelling on the fear. He tried to lighten his tone. 'Well, if we lose, we can always make a run for the Summer Country and take refuge there.' He stole a look at Arthur. 'Their queen's a wonder, they say, and a rare fighter too. And her daughter—'

'We will not lose.'

Kay pursed his lips. 'So we win then, brother, you've decided that. And then?'

'First let us deal with the six kings below, the scoundrels who dare to call my kingdom theirs,' Arthur said levelly. 'And then we have a far worse threat to face.'

'You mean the Saxon hordes?'

Arthur's eyes lost focus, seeing terrible things. 'Someone has to deal with the men from the north, and the terror they bring from across the sea.' He ran a tense hand through his thick fair hair. 'And perhaps the Gods will say it must be me. But it cannot be yet. They will not send a half-fledged king, who is not yet lord in his own kingdom, against men driven by the Horned One to destroy and kill.'

Around them the evening mist seeped from the ground. On all sides the forest darkened towards night. A faint sound of movement caught Kay's ear. 'Who's there?' he called.

Two figures were approaching through the trees, laden with harness that jingled as they walked. Arthur rose to his feet. 'Gawain and Bedivere!' he cried. 'You've settled the horses for the night?'

The bigger of the two men raised his arm in acknowledgement. From his broad fist dangled a brace of pheasants, while his companion shouldered a stick bearing a clutch of plump rabbits for the pot.

'Look, sire!' Gawain roared. 'They ran into our nets, as if by magic!'

'Magic, eh?' Arthur glanced humorously at Kay. 'Do you still think Merlin is not with us tonight?'

Smiling, he turned away. He moved through the camp, and retraced his steps back to his vantage-point on the high hill. Only hours now before his courage, strength and good fortune decided his fate. Before the Great Ones unfolded his destiny.

He paused on the bluff, soothed by the cool night air. The castle lay below, veiled and secret as it waited for the dawn. Sound asleep still, Arthur mused, and ready to drop into his hand.

He bowed his head, and allowed his thoughts to drift. Breathing deeply, he drank in the wholesome sweetness of the living world. The towering oaks and soaring pines had been here when time was born. Every gnarled root, every lofty crown of leaves, every low branch waiting to waylay the careless traveller was as old as the stars, and as uncaring too.

Here, in the heart of the forest, he was soothed with a sense of littleness in the grand scheme of things. Dimly he could feel the mighty whole of which he was only a part. His call had come, and he had followed it. He was ready to die for it too, if it was required. The Great Ones had decreed what was to come. The word of it was already written in the skies.

Then he frowned, all his senses alert.

What was that?

Surely not?

Gods, above, no!

And there it was again, there was no mistaking now.

Down below, a light was flaring in the Great Hall. Fresh torches had come in. Early as it was, they were awake, and stirring for the day.

Well, so be it. Arthur watched calmly enough, but his stomach set like a stone. If the revellers in the Great Hall were rousing themselves, there was no hope of surprise.

And without that . . .

His small, untrained force against a whole garrison. His men, hungry, wet and cold, fighting on hopes and dreams against soldiers with full bellies who had slept in warm beds. His raw skill as a leader against the might of King Lot's allies, even if the great king was not there.

So be it.

A light breeze blew gently through the trees. Beside him, the night air shivered and took shape, and Merlin appeared. He nodded to Arthur. 'It goes well?' he said.

'Not as well as it might.' Arthur pointed to the light in the Great Hall below. 'I hoped they'd still be sleeping off last night. But, by the look of that, they're on their feet again, and ready to go. No matter.' He turned to Merlin. 'How was the feast of Penn Annwyn? Did it go well?'

Merlin let out a high cackle, crowing like a cock. 'Well enough, well enough!' He rubbed his withered hands. 'I have done good work, boy, since I saw you last!'

Arthur knew better than to question the old man. 'I thank you, sir,' he said courteously. 'And I am pleased to see you back. My knights have missed you – Kay above all. He did not see how we could attack Caerleon without you.'

Merlin's head swivelled like a hawk's. 'But you did, I trust.'

'Yes, I did,' replied Arthur equably. 'Still, I am glad you're here.' He made his voice sound firm and confident. 'We'll give a good account of ourselves today, even though we've lost the element of surprise.'

Merlin peered curiously down at the light in the Great Hall. 'Perhaps, perhaps not.' He did not seem concerned. 'You attack at dawn?'

'Earlier, to take advantage of the dark – the men are making ready now.' Arthur gestured towards the camp. Sounds of quiet movement reached them through the dark. 'D'you hear that? I must go.'

He turned to Merlin, and tenderly put out his hand to take the old man's arm. 'Let me help you, sir, the going's not easy here.' He raised his eyes to the stars, absorbing their cool, indifferent stare as they gazed down. 'And when the men are ready, will you call on the Great Ones, and say a prayer for our success?'

Merlin shook his head. 'You do not need my prayers,' he said brusquely. 'And I must go too. There is still much to do.'

So much to do . . .

Merlin raised his hand to his head, and covered his eyes. A great weariness assailed him. Still so much to do, and only he to do it, such as he was. Gods above! His old bones protested, and his soul cried out. When would he be free? Free of the burden of Arthur's destiny, free of foreknowing what was to come?

Nausea filled him. 'Never' was the answer, he knew. But he could spare the boy some of the worst of it. The girl from the Summer Country, above all.

Merlin's face grew pale with suppressed thought. That girl was Arthur's evil fate: he must never marry her. No, she would have to be entangled in a dark fate of her own. Then she would be beset by troubles, assailed by enemies, and dragged down before Arthur had time to think of her again.

Yes, that much was plain. He nodded feverishly. A hard rain must fall on the Summer Country, the bad seed must flourish, and the Mother-line decay.

He muttered to himself in time with the chanting of his inner voice. No more queens. The girl must come into her own, and then just as speedily pass out of it. No more queens. New powers must triumph over the Mother-right now. Only so would he keep her from Arthur, and save Arthur from himself.

Well, he had made a good start. It would not be hard to weave another thread of darkness into the loom of destiny, to change the fate of the Summer Country and its queens. Not hard, but hard enough, and thankless too. Merlin gritted his teeth, and braced his old frame for the fray.

One day the boy would know all he had done. One day his work would be finished, and his old flesh and bones could escape to the place of pleasure, where he could be free.

Pleasure – Gods, yes! How he longed for it! Spring was coming, and with it the old hunger, that sweet itch.

But not yet. He schooled his twitching muscles and rebellious soul. Not yet, there still is work to do. Another shape, another form, another task. He looked with a lover's longing at Arthur's concerned face, the big body arched protectively towards him, the hand outstretched in kindness to lead him on. He shook his grey head, and turned his face away. 'I must go,' he said.

CHAPTER 5

In the Queen's apartments, the air was cool after the heat of the sun. The musky scent of patchouli, which had been her mother's favourite for as long as Guenevere could remember, still hung sweetly in the air. But the silent figure propped up on the great bed would have no need of such things now.

The chief of the Queen's doctors was a healer so venerable that the hands that gently probed this way and that were translucent with the passage of time. 'She was alive when you picked her up – that gives us hope,' he murmured. 'Yet it is strange . . .'

Guenevere roused herself from a waking dream of pain. 'Sir?'

'Here, Lady Guenevere.' The doctor's fingers parted the Queen's bright hair. One gleaming wound showed where the horse's hoof had slashed through to the bone. 'But otherwise . . .' He shrugged, and spread his hands.

Slowly Guenevere followed his train of thought. Serene upon her pillows, her fiery cloud of russet hair unbound from its long plaits, the Queen seemed unmarked by her ordeal. Her body was soft and white, her face was calm, and she looked like a child asleep in her mother's arms. 'Yes,' Guenevere murmured, 'it is strange.'

'The Dark Lord, Penn Annwyn, he came from the Underworld . . .'

In the shadows of the low arched chamber, an old crone of the household was knocking her head against the wall. 'The Dark Lord sent his spirit to do his will,' she moaned. 'He is coming, the Dark Lord—'

Goddess, Mother, spare me, spare her this—

'Call the guard!' Guenevere burst out to the woman nearest the door. 'Have them take this woman to her quarters, and admit no one, except those I allow!'

'At once, lady.' The woman was hurrying forward as Guenevere spoke. 'And the King is here. Will you speak to him?'

Guenevere approached the door. Outside in the corridor King Leogrance stared out unseeing as he kept a silent vigil, his face still grimed with the dust of the jousting field, clutching his helmet in the crook of his arm.

'Goddess, Great Mother, save her, save the Queen!' Further off Lucan was waiting too, crying out and beating his forehead to blood as he roamed up and down.

She could hear the old crone wailing as the guards led her away: 'He came for her, the Dark Lord . . .'

Trembling, she stepped back into the quiet of the chamber, and shook her head. 'Tell the King as soon as there is any news he will be the first to know.'

She hurried back to the Queen's bedside, and caught at the healer's sleeve. 'Will she live?'

He shook his white head. 'Only a fool would say.'

'Be a fool then!' she said fiercely. 'We have gold enough, if that will help!'

The old healer's smile came from very far away. 'You must find another fool then, Princess, for my thoughts are not for hire.'

He bowed and moved away. Guenevere clasped her

hands and pressed them to her eyes. *Goddess, Mother, help me now—*

Another of the Queen's women crept up like a cat. 'Madam, Lord Taliesin the Chief Druid is here. He wishes to call all the Queen's knights and lords to meet with you, to take counsel what to do. Will you consent?'

Taliesin here? Goddess, Great One, thanks—

She could not remember a time when the wise old man had not been there to advise her mother, and warmly encourage her. All Druids had been warriors once, she knew. But, to her, Taliesin had always been the very soul of peace. She looked at the young woman at her side. 'Tell him – forgive me, I have quite forgotten your name.'

'It's Ina, lady.' The girl with the spotless headdress and white collar was on the verge of tears. 'Oh, lady, bid me do anything to help the Queen! I'd die for her, if that would bring her back.'

'Thank you, Ina.' Guenevere took a breath. 'Send to Lord Taliesin that he has my consent. See that the King and Sir Lucan are informed, and say that I shall meet them all in the Great Hall.'

The woman dropped a curtsey, and was gone. Guenevere crossed to the bed, and leaned over the motionless form. All around her now lay the quiet of the sickroom, the clean scent of rosewater and herbs, and the soft hum of the Queen's women as they moved to and fro lighting the chamber lamps as evening drew in.

She took her mother's hand, seized by a sudden fierce reluctance to leave. She called to the nearest of the women, 'Send for one of the bards to sing for her till I return.'

The woman curtsied. 'Who shall we call, lady?'

Guenevere paused, and one name filled her mind. She tried to steady her voice as it passed her lips. 'Call Cormac, she always loved him best.' Her heart lurched. 'And tell him

– ask him to wait for me afterwards. Beg him not to leave
till I get back.'

The woman smiled sadly. 'As you will, lady. But the
Queen will not hear.'

Fool! Of course she will hear, who dares say otherwise?
Swallowing her anger, Guenevere turned away. She took a
last look at the figure on the bed, the strong face still so luminous, the long red hair without a thread of grey. Stooping,
she brushed the smooth forehead with a kiss. As she did so,
the Queen's eyes opened and looked straight at her.

'He is coming,' she said clearly. 'Through the fires, he
comes.'

After the glow of the Queen's chamber, the Great Hall struck
cavernous and dank. Overhead the high stone arches were
lost in the soaring gloom, despite the torches flaring up the
walls and the fires blazing on every hearth. As she came
in, Guenevere caught sight of the knights' bright shields
and coloured banners hanging from the walls, and her skin
crawled. Could she ever bear to see a tournament again?

At the far end of the room, set proudly on its dais of
dressed stone, was the Queen's throne. In the centre of the
hall stood the Round Table, its vast surface glowing with
inner light. Around it stood the great wooden chairs the
knights called their 'sieges', each with its high back and
carved canopy bearing their name in gold.

The knights themselves clustered nearby, talking unhappily. She could see the iron-grey head of old Sir Niamh,
one of the Queen's earliest champions, deep in conversation
with Sir Lovell, the champion who had succeeded him after
a heroic fight. Behind them stood a clutch of the younger
knights, Sir Damant, Sir Cradel le Haut, Sir Epin of the
Glen, and a dozen others – yes, there were more than she
had expected here.

As she came in a tense figure detached itself from the nearest group, and Sir Lucan, the Queen's champion, bore down on her.

'How is our lady?' he demanded roughly.

His eyes were red with weeping, and Guenevere's heart strained to tell him what he longed to hear. Yet what was there to tell? After those few strange words, the Queen had closed her eyes again and said no more. And if that was news, then King Leogrance, her father, should be the first to hear. Guenevere nodded. 'The Queen is well enough.'

Across the hall, King Leogrance was waiting stiffly by the hearth. Beside him stood a tall, spare figure robed from head to foot in white, his hands folded inside his flowing sleeves. At the sight of him, Guenevere felt the first comfort her sore heart had received. She hastened towards him. 'Lord Taliesin!'

The Chief Druid made a slow and formal bow. His face was grave beneath its crown of white hair. 'Princess Guenevere, I am glad to see you well – and sad beyond measure at what brings us here today.'

'My lord—' A rush of sorrow blocked Guenevere's throat and she could not speak.

'Shall we proceed?' asked the Druid gently. Before she could reply, he took her hand and led her towards the throne. With a start, she drew back, but Taliesin pressed on. 'It must be, my lady,' he murmured softly, as he seated her.

The steps to the throne were firm, and the arms of the great bronze chair were cool beneath her grasp. Standing on the dais beside her, Taliesin raised his arms like wings. 'My lords,' he called. He leaned down to whisper in her ear. 'Princess, will it please you summon them to begin?'

Guenevere spread her hands in greeting, and swallowed hard. 'My lords,' she began, trying to sound as her mother always did, 'welcome to this council. May I ask you all to take your seats?'

There was a general murmur as the knights bowed and obeyed. King Leogrance took the place of honour as the Queen's first champion and her Chosen One. Taliesin moved to the seat at his right, and Sir Lucan, the new champion, to his left.

As soon as all were seated, Taliesin rose to his feet. 'Forgive us this hasty council, lords. Not all your number can be present, as so many are out on knightly errands for the Queen. But they have all been sent for by the swiftest horse, and those nearest home should be with us soon.'

Seated beside the Druid, King Leogrance cocked an eye. 'Malgaunt?' he said dully.

Taliesin bowed. 'Prince Malgaunt was the first name in our minds. He should be with us any moment now.'

Malgaunt.

Guenevere shifted uneasily on her throne. 'Where is he?'

Taliesin smiled. 'On the same errand that the Queen gave to me. She directed us to find out Merlin's plans, as soon as she heard the rumours that he had been seen. Prince Malgaunt went to London at her bidding, to attend the gathering that Merlin summoned there.'

'And?' A note of irritation sounded in Leogrance's voice.

Taliesin sighed. 'Merlin still dreams of his days of glory, when Uther ruled, and he sat at the King's right hand. We should never forget that he was Pendragon born.'

'Pendragon born?' Leogrance stirred in anger. 'Merlin? He was no more than a bastard in the female line! It's true his mother was one of the daughters of the royal house. But his father was never known, and the wench covered her shame with some mad tale about being raped by a devil, and never knowing a man! Merlin was the by-blow of all that. He has no claim to power!'

'That never stopped any man from seeking it,' Taliesin said quietly. 'Least of all one like my old Druid friend. And now, at last, Merlin thinks his time has come. He is playing for high stakes here – no less than all.'

'So!' One of the knights swore softly under his breath. The rest exchanged glances, and looked away.

A heavy silence settled in the room. Outside the window the white ribbon of the highway wandered off through the purple dusk. As Guenevere looked, the dark green hills shimmered before her sight, and a tramping filled her ears. Through the haze she saw kings in red robes and coronets riding towards London, proud princes in furs and velvet, great lords in silver mail, and rough chiefs with their battle-hardened warriors tramping behind. Newly made knights freshly come to chivalry, ladies on fine horses, and pink-cheeked squires eager for adventure were all riding to hear the word of Merlin, rallying to see his sign. The road to London lay choked with the dust of countless feet.

And in London itself—

Nothing.

The scene faded, and she came to herself again. Her sight cleared and she drew a deep breath. 'What can we do?'

'No more than we have done, until we know what Merlin plans,' Taliesin said. A shaft of piercing sorrow crossed his face. 'The Queen's ailment is a grievous blow.' He paused, then held Guenevere in his pale stare. 'Are you prepared, Princess? All our hopes lie with you now.'

Guenevere shuddered. An answering frisson ran round the table as the knights gazed expectantly at her. King Leogrance turned on the Druid angrily. 'With Guenevere? What are you saying, man?'

'Guenevere will be queen.'

Guenevere forced herself to speak. 'My mother is still queen. When she recovers, she—'

'Hear me, Lady Guenevere.' Taliesin's voice sang in her ears like the sea. 'Time out of mind, your mother has held this kingdom, and the Sacred Isle, and the white towers of Camelot itself. She had it from her mother, and her mother had it from her mother, back to the days of the Old Ones, from the One who is the Mother of us all.'

He paused. 'Elsewhere it was not so – not in the north or west, nor in our neighbouring country of the Middle Kingdom after the Christians came. They set their faces against the Great Mother, and where they found her worshipped, they tore down her shrines. But here, in the Summer Country, we have kept the old ways. You are the only daughter of a ruling queen. This is your country, lady, and this is your time.'

'Yes, yes!' Guenevere cried in agony. 'One day, but not yet.'

Taliesin held up his hand, and his voice took on an incantatory tone. 'Remember Avalon. That is why the Queen sent you there.'

Avalon, Avalon, sacred island, home—

Guenevere's senses swam. She saw the beloved landscape once again, the island floating in the pearly air, the green hill rising from the dark, still waters, its rounded slopes drifting with apple blossom, its woodlands loud with birdsong and the flutter of white wings in every tree.

Avalon, Avalon, home—

Taliesin's chant went on. 'The Queen your mother lies in the land of waking sleep. Until she wakes, you are queen here by the ancient Mother-right, and all men of the Summer Country are yours till they die.'

He rose to his feet, and motioned Lucan to stand. Lucan obeyed at once, grieving and deathly pale. Taliesin moved towards the throne, and beckoned Lucan to follow him. As they reached the dais, Taliesin turned to face the younger man. 'You are the Queen's knight and her champion, hers in life and death. Do you swear to follow the Lady Guenevere as you would the Queen, until the Queen recovers, or the Princess is queen indeed?'

Lucan reached for his sword. Kneeling before Guenevere, he lifted his swollen eyes to hers. He held his weapon by the blade, and laid the heavy jewelled hilt between her hands. 'By the Goddess-Mother of the Land, by the faith of the Summer Country, by the order of our knighthood and my honour as a knight, by the Old Ones who made the world and all the new Gods waiting to be born, I swear.'

Taliesin waved Lucan to his feet. 'And now, my lady, shall we conclude our debate, or wait till Prince Malgaunt returns? He has been sent word to hasten back at once.'

Malgaunt? she wanted to say. *Let him stay away, we do far better without his dark face and sardonic smile.* But the time had passed when she could be governed by her own desires. She had to think as her mother would have done. 'If Merlin has been active in London, should Malgaunt go on there, as the Queen my mother planned?' she said at last.

King Leogrance shook his head. 'No, Malgaunt must return. We must have him here, ready for whatever comes.'

'Until we know what is coming, Father, we do not know how to prepare.'

'Child, we need men in a crisis. Malgaunt is one of the best fighting men we have!'

Guenevere leaned forward passionately. 'Surely we need to know what Merlin means to do?' She groaned under her father's angry frown. *Why does he not see?*

Taliesin turned to Lucan. 'You are the Queen's warlord, sir. In your advisement, what is it best to do?' Then he broke off, listening, and smiled. 'Our dispute is resolved, I think. He comes.'

A Druid's ears can catch the sound of fishes whispering

under water, and the small thoughts of snakes as they slip sideways through the grass. Guenevere waited with the rest until she heard the far-off tramp of approaching feet and the sharp cries of the guards outside.

'Ho there – within!'

'Prince Malgaunt comes! Make way for the Prince and his knights!'

Guenevere turned. A shaft of light split the gloom at the end of the hall. The high bronze doors groaned on their hinges, the torches flared, and looming against a bank of swords and shields, the man she feared was there.

CHAPTER 6

As he came in, Guenevere saw the dogs on the hearth growl and back down – no creature loved Malgaunt except himself. Yet his bold gaze and hard brown body always drew women's eyes, and he never lacked a bedmate when he wished.

Why did she fear him so? He was neither tall nor strongly built, and the clothes he wore hung on a wiry frame. The lines on his face showed a man of thirty or so hard years, but she knew that his restless moods were those of a wilful child. Now his tawny eyes were dark with meaning as he bore down on her, ignoring the greetings of the other knights. At a glance he took in Lucan and Taliesin standing before the dais, and Guenevere ensconced on the throne. 'So!' he hissed.

Slowly he twitched his travel-stained cloak from his shoulders, and held her gaze as he let it drop to the floor. 'So, Princess! Or should I call you Queen? No kiss for your cousin, then, no welcome for the traveller gone on the service of the realm?'

'Good evening, Uncle.'

Uncle, cousin, too near kin for me—

His hot eyes on her, there it was again, the old blend of resentment and lust. Guenevere nodded as lightly as she could. 'Welcome back to your country, sir, in the Queen's name and my own.'

Malgaunt flung his mud-caked gauntlets to the floor. 'My country, you say? Only under the Queen my sister, and now, as it seems, under you.'

Guenevere closed her eyes. *Do not mind him,* her mother used to say, when Malgaunt's cruelties were too much to bear. Fate had made him a puny, late-born child always lagging far behind the Queen, and for that he would never forgive the cruelty of the Gods. He was the son of a lesser, later union too, not like the Queen his half-sister, who was born of her mother's marriage to her first champion and Chosen One. But Malgaunt had a fiercer quarrel with the Great Ones, Guenevere knew. Why had they made him male in a land where women were born to rule? Why was he born her kinsman, when the heat of his loins drove him to look on her quite another way?

Yet kinfolk could be married—

He would have thought of that—

He was taunting her now, determined to draw blood. 'Under you, Lady Guenevere?' he sneered. The lingering emphasis made his lewd meaning plain. 'Indeed, any man who served under you would find himself well rewarded for his pains.' His eyes raked her up and down. 'You have your mother's beauty – do you have her other tastes as well?' He glanced at Lucan with an insulting stare.

She would not let him rile her. 'I sit here, sir, only until the Queen resumes her place. You went forth at her bidding. Will you tell us what you know?'

Malgaunt laughed bitterly. 'Oh, it is true. The sword in the stone, everything the madman Merlin claimed!'

Merlin again.

Guenevere's stomach turned.

'What?' Leogrance stared. 'You mean the assembly Merlin called took place?'

'It did indeed!' Malgaunt snorted. 'From far and near, kings, lords and chieftains came to answer Merlin's call.'

Taliesin raised his eyes. 'And the miracle he promised, the sign of the new King?'

Malgaunt grew pale. 'There was a sword set fast in a block of stone. It stood in the churchyard of the Christians, by the great new place of worship they have built for their God. Whoever should be rightful King of all the Britons would draw it out, Merlin declared. Many tried, and every one of them failed. Then up stepped some great lout and pulled it out, while Merlin grinned like a gargoyle and looked on.'

'King of all the Britons?' Lucan leaned forward urgently, gripping the handle of his sword. 'So, then, it will be war.'

Malgaunt nodded, his rage breaking through. 'It cannot be avoided. In the face of the whole assembly, the boy from nowhere was proclaimed High King. Merlin declared that he is Arthur, son of Uther Pendragon, the lost heir of Uther's kingdom, and so, by descent, king over us all.'

King Leogrance gave an angry gasp. 'But no man can be High King by descent!'

Old Sir Niamh hotly backed him up. 'The title only comes by making war!'

Sir Lovell nodded. 'Just as Uther won it long ago, when all the lesser kings agreed to follow him.'

'But London has had no king since Uther died,' Leogrance put in. 'There's not a soul there to challenge his so-called rule. All they've had is a poor people's militia, a bunch of stall-holders and merchant-men. They'd follow any man with a sword in his hand!'

'And Merlin's boy is special, so he says.' Malgaunt grinned like a wolf about to strike. 'Given away into Merlin's care at birth.'

Guenevere stirred 'Taken from his mother? Why?'

'To save him from Uther's enemies, is the tale,' Malgaunt

sneered. 'Merlin says he had the boy brought up in secret, till the time came for the truth to be revealed – as the whole world now knows.'

'The whole world?' queried Taliesin mildly.

Malgaunt turned on him. 'Druid, you know as well as I do that one of your kind can call the birds from the trees. Every petty king and lord turned up, every would-be baron or knight.' He looked round the table with a sarcastic laugh. 'Believe it or not, Merlin has bewitched the Christians too! They lent their great church for the so-called miracle. And there the boy pulled out the sword from the stone, so proving him the rightful king over all Britons – and allegiance to be sworn on the way out!'

'But the kings, the great lords?' Lucan demanded. 'Surely they vowed to fight to the death to keep what they call theirs?'

'Do you doubt it? They all threw their gauntlets at his feet, and left breathing fire and sword. And so it must be war.'

Malgaunt dropped his head, and silence fell.

War.

Guenevere felt herself trembling and sick with fear. After all the years of peace, so hard-won by her mother, must they face war, blood and death for the dreams of one half-crazy man? 'Who is this boy of Merlin's?'

Lucan's eye lit up. 'A poor pretender should be easy to expose,' he agreed. The muscles tightened in his scarred brown sword-arm. 'And easier still to kill.'

Taliesin folded his pale hands upon his wrists. 'Only if he truly is an impostor, as you say. And only the Great Ones know the truth of that.'

'But the Christians?' Guenevere persisted, fighting a nameless sense of dread. 'Why would they welcome this Arthur to their own sacred place?'

'Ha!' snarled Lucan. 'They'll welcome any man who'll fight for them against the Old Ones and the Mother they have sworn to overthrow.'

Taliesin demurred again. 'Perhaps they hope, as we do, that this youth can bring peace.'

King Leogrance snorted with disgust. 'More likely their hothead monks, the so-called soldiers of Christ who never held a sword, are hoping for war!'

Sir Niamh laughed sarcastically. 'Either way, the lad will do well to beware the embrace of the Christians. They fight by their own rules!'

Lucan was still thirsting for the kill. 'Where is he now?'

'Seizing his hour of glory!' Malgaunt snorted. 'Gone to Caerleon to claim the Middle Kingdom as his own. He and his rabble must be hoping for victory from a surprise attack. But Caerleon won't give up without a fight.'

'Caerleon?' King Leogrance gave a disbelieving laugh. 'It's hardly worth a fight!'

Sir Damant agreed. 'Not since Pendragon died and left the dogs to scrap over the bones.'

Sir Lovell rolled his eyes. 'Dogs who won't willingly go back to their kennels again!'

'Yet if this youth can settle the Middle Kingdom, what a blessing for us all!' Taliesin urged. 'A strong leader could drive out the lawless, and unite the warring factions just as Uther did. If this Arthur is the Promised One, then we of the Summer Country should be the first to wish him success. We have prayed so long for peace in that ravaged land!'

Lucan suppressed a furious start. 'You pray, Lord Druid, some of us fight! Only the Severn Water has protected us from the same fate as the Middle Kingdom and her petty kings. We have endured their conflicts on our borders, we have paid with our lives for the peace we now have. You say this upstart will bring peace? I swear he'll stir them up again to war!'

Outside the wind was howling louder now, and the logs of the fire were spitting like snakes on the hearth. The sour smell of damp wool seeped out of Malgaunt's clothing, and a grim foreboding hung in the stale air. Guenevere took a breath and tried to sound assured. 'Why should we fear the worst? This is not the first tale of the king who was to come, nor will it be the last hope of another strong High King.'

'Gods above!' King Leogrance burst out. 'Try to think like a sovereign woman, daughter, not like a girl led by her foolish hopes! If this young upstart wants to make himself High King of all the Britons, of course we are in danger! The Summer Country will be vital to his plans!' A wide sweep of his arm took in the world beyond the night-time walls. 'With our strong fortresses, our horses and fighting men, our rich acres and good people, he must seek to make this land his own.'

Lucan gestured to his companions round the board. 'Not forgetting what any king must covet, the order of our knighthood, sworn to our Queen even in the ranks of death!'

Malgaunt bared his teeth. 'Spoken as befits the Queen's champion, sir knight!'

Lucan rose to the bait. 'Do you quarrel with that?'

'Lords, lords!' Taliesin frowned as the two knights snapped and glared, bristling like dogs. 'No, sirs, there is a greater thing than that! The most precious of all we have in the Summer Country is our Holy Isle of Avalon, the seat of the Lady, and the Great One she serves. The home of the Goddess is the key to the kingdom.'

'Yes!' Guenevere said passionately. 'The key to the kingdom.'

Avalon, mystic island, home of my dream-time, it is not the

*key to the kingdom, it is the kingdom. It is all I want and all I
ever wanted, since I knew it was mine.*

Avalon, Avalon, always calling—

Avalon, Avalon, Mother, Lady, home—

'Come, my lords, come!' Taliesin's strong voice broke
in on her thoughts. 'The stranger King may come to us in
peace. We must not be the first to offer war.'

Lucan scowled, tensing again for action: 'There are
times when peace is only won by making war.'

Malgaunt eyed him jealously. 'Do we need the Queen's
champion, sir, to tell us that?'

'We need all the champions we have,' came the hot
reply. 'Above all, men who fight with swords, not words!'

Malgaunt flushed with rage. 'Do you call me a coward?'

Goddess, Mother, spare us.

Guenevere rose angrily to her feet. 'If war comes, then
we fight!' she broke in. 'Till then, I beg you, no more hostile
words!'

Too late she felt the force of Malgaunt's malice switching
towards her. 'And if war comes, my Lady Guenevere,
what happens to a country without a leader, without a
queen?'

'We are not without a queen!'

'Without a queen to lead us, while my dear sister is
away with the Fair Ones in the twilight land, and you, her
heiress, ignorant of war.'

'Not so ignorant, Uncle!'

'In which case, you must have a champion,' Malgaunt's
harsh voice went on. 'If war comes, a man must lead on your
behalf.' A slow smile split his face. 'And who better than your
own blood and kin?'

My blood and kin—

Not if you were the last man on earth.

She nerved herself to face down his inky gaze. 'If I need a champion, sir, I will choose my own!'

Malgaunt grinned. 'What will the people say to a queen who has no champion, one who thinks to rule alone, like the Lady of Avalon herself, taking her partners as she wills, answerable to no man?'

Guenevere was in agony. 'The queens of the Summer Country have always chosen their partners, and changed them as they wished. If I choose to live my own life, Uncle, and be mistress of my own body, who are you to say me nay?'

'So as Queen then, Guenevere—'

But Lucan could take no more. 'Our Queen still lives, let me remind you, Prince!' he burst out. 'And the Queen of the Summer Country will always have a champion!'

'But the Queen's champion will not always be you!'

And suddenly their hands were at their sides, their chairs thrust back, their half-drawn swords dancing in the flickering light.

'My lords, for shame!' Taliesin rose and stepped between them, his pale eyes on fire. 'Dangers surround us, sorrows rush in, and our Queen lies on the very edge of life. Is this a time for vile and vicious brawls?'

He paused, his face darkening as he spoke. 'Hear me, for I hear what I would not hear, and see what I never thought I would have to say. The old moon is waning, and tonight she dies. I see a new moon rising among other stars.'

He passed a hand over his eyes, and turned his gaze within. A great stillness settled on him, and the weight of his sadness reached out to them all. A faint high noise thrummed through the chamber, the humming of a thread stretched out to the full, singing its heart out in the moment before it breaks. In the air all around, there came a deeper note, the still, sad sound of all life's loss and grief.

Taliesin's voice was part of the concert now. 'The feast of Beltain comes with the new moon. Let us pray that holy things may come at this holy time. And when the ceremonies are done, when the Beltain God has come to the Mother, and She has blessed the Summer Country, then the future will be clear.' He sighed. 'A future that is fast upon us now.'

There was a slight sound behind them like a small thing dying, or the last whisper of a departing soul. Taliesin turned his head. From the shadow behind the throne, a dark figure moved out into the flickering light, throwing a black shape high up on the wall. Guenevere felt herself drowning in fear and grief. Only an intimate of the palace knew the private way from the Queen's chamber to the place behind the throne.

King Leogrance stared at the newcomer like a wanderer from the Otherworld. 'Why this coming? What is happening now?'

'Speak,' Taliesin said quietly. 'We know the word you bring. Do not fear to break it to us now.'

Before them stood the Queen's bard Cormac, a pale image of living grief. 'The Queen,' he murmured, 'the Queen—'

CHAPTER 7

'Pendragon!'
'Arthur! Arthur!'
'Pendragon à moi!'

King Carados awoke with an ugly start to the sounds of an attack. Ye Gods, he was having nightmares of Arthur now! Hurriedly he levered himself off the rank, sticky body of the kitchen maid to set Caerleon on full alert. And only then did he realise that it was too late.

'Pendragon!'

Silent among the loud cries of his men, Arthur led the attack straight over the drawbridge, through the archway and into the central court. In the east, the sky was lightening towards dawn. On the wooded bluff high above, Merlin was raising all the power of Pendragon to throw in on his side. Gawain, Kay and Bedivere were flanking him, and his other knights ran behind. Caerleon lay open to them now, castle, towers and keep.

So far so good – better than he had hoped. The sleeping watchmen might have been under a spell for all the alarm they raised. Now he could see the guards on the battlements, frozen in a parody of surprise as he called up to them, above the shouts and screams, 'Throw down your weapons, and you'll come to no harm! I am Arthur Pendragon, come to claim my own. Yield now, and you will live!'

They did not know, Kay reflected sourly, as he ran with Bedivere at Arthur's side, that Arthur had ordered all lives to be spared, whether they yielded to him or not. 'We take no prisoners!' Kay had argued forcefully. 'We can't afford the men to guard them when they yield!'

Gawain had supported him, oddly enough, Kay thought, since he and the rough Orkneyan agreed on little else.

'When they're stone dead, they don't argue,' Gawain agreed, with relish. 'I was at the siege of Bel Rivers, when my lord was fighting there. When we took it, we killed 'em all, and not one of 'em came back for more!' He looked round to approving nods and grins from most of the other knights.

But Arthur had gone pale, Kay noted, and he knew that the point was lost. 'These are my people,' Arthur said quietly. 'I have been called to serve them, not to bring them death. I would not have a hair harmed on their heads.'

And so it had to be.

But the captain of the guard now leading a determined charge from the guardhouse seemed unaware that he was among Arthur's cherished ones. 'Follow me, lads!' he bellowed. 'Stick it to them, get the leader first!' Behind him ran a solid square of men.

As he ran, the captain took in his opponent, the leader of the band. So this was the King, was it? Tall, and his armour – what? Ye Gods, he had only a breastplate and light helmet, no defence at all! Yet still he looked as merry as the month of May. He might have been in his own castle, welcoming his friends. Not a beardless boy then, the captain noted, with a tug of something he did not recognise as anxiety, but a bastard right enough, a big bastard, and useful-looking too.

Still, the bigger they were—

'Now!' he roared, as they bore down on the invaders, a paltry clutch of men only half armed like their master. A bunch of peasants he told himself, like killing sheep – still, it had to be done. Sword at the ready, he braced himself for the trusty one-two-three of close-body killing. Stab, rip, up, stab, rip, up, he could have done it in his sleep.

Afterwards he could never quite say how it happened, he'd practically had the great oaf dead on the end of his sword. But heavy as the stranger was, he'd somehow floated to one side, then feinted to the other, and come up under the attacking sword with a dagger at his hand. The big bastard was close enough to kiss when he grinned and cried, 'Pendragon!', but his dagger was even closer, and that was that.

'Pendragon!'

Gods above, but Arthur could fight! Gawain thought fervently, as he ran along the battlements, his men howling on his heels, inspired by the defeat of the captain below. May all their battles be as easy as that!

But ahead of him guarding the first tower was a warlike bunch who did not look easy at all. A sergeant-at-arms and a group of seasoned men, they were the sort to sell their lives hard for no better reason than that they were soldiers, and that was what soldiers did.

'Arthur! Pendragon!' Gawain bellowed, thirsting for the kill. Much as he loved Arthur, he had little time for his leader's policy of peace. To a son of the Orkneys, it wasn't a fight without a good show of blood, well-hacked bodies piled around the walls, and a few heads to kick around the courtyard as footballs when all was done.

And, from the look of the opposition, this would be a doughty battle, with plenty of cruel blows. In the event, it was enough to satisfy Orkney honour as far as the farthest isles. It did not end until Gawain had split his opponents' shields, shattered his own short sword, and seen blood, real blood, drawn on either side.

At last the beaten defenders knelt at his feet, sullenly awaiting their fate. 'Kill them!' arose by habit to Gawain's lips. Then the face of Arthur swam into his mind. He waved aside the forest of hungry swords, and gestured towards the wall.

'No need to kill them, lads,' he said magnanimously. 'Chuck 'em in the moat! Sing out for Pendragon as you sling them over the wall. And make sure they can say "King Arthur," before you let them back in to dry!'

Goddess Mother, and all Great Ones, blessings on your name.

Arthur leaned heavily on his sword in the centre of the inner courtyard, and raised a prayer of thanks. On the battlements above, Gawain had made a clean sweep of the guard. His other knights, too, had fought like heroes, as bravely as if they did not care whether they lived or died. Young Sagramore had proved worth a dozen men, and as for Griflet and Ladinas – well, there would be time to praise them later on. For now, most of the defenders had thrown down their arms, and the rest were being marched off to custody to think again.

He glanced around. Each of the four guard towers had been taken now, the drowsy watchmen stumbling down sheepishly to join their fellows under lock and key.

'That's it, then, sire,' grinned Gawain, appearing at Arthur's side. 'The place is ours!' His face felt tight from the dried blood on his skin, and he could smell his own rank sweat and the stink of others' blood. Arthur had fought as hard as he had, Gawain knew. Yet, damn him, how did he manage to look so clean and fresh?

Arthur turned his head. 'Not quite.' He nodded across the courtyard towards the Great Hall looming through the grey dawn light. 'We have one last ceremony to perform. Let us make our hail and farewell to King Lot's six vassal kings.'

Inside the Great Hall King Carados coldly surveyed the ruins of the feast. Without self-pity, he eyed the grim-faced knights who held them prisoner, and prepared himself to die. For folly on the scale he had shown today, he expected no mercy, and allowed himself none.

But he'd die resigned at least, if the fates would grant him one last wish. It was not for a sight of his faithful wife of twenty years, his six daughters, the prince his heir, nor even the joy of his life, his youngest son. It was to slit the throat of the fat slut who had made him betray himself, and watch her bleed to death like the pig she was. To die for her, to throw his life away for that sodden, snivelling, naked lump of flesh – a wild disgust raged like vomit in his gut.

At least the other five were acting like true kings now. He had despaired of Vause when Arthur's men first burst in, seeing the soft face crumpling like a schoolboy, the gaping mouth, the gibbering 'Whaaa—?' And Rience had woken up fighting drunk, and done his best to get them all butchered on the spot. But Agrisance and Brangoris were old soldiers, schooled to the fortunes of war. Nentres, the youngest of them all, was wisely taking his lead from them.

The doors opened at the end of the hall. Carados heaved himself up in his seat, and switched his attention to the figure coming in. So here he was, Merlin's boy, the living miracle at last! A good fighting man by the look of that powerful body, and he had full command of his men as soon he came through the door, there was no mistaking that. But the look he wore, that air of luminous authority, that – what the devil would you call it?

What was it Arthur had? For the hundredth time, Carados cursed the drink that had stolen his brain, even as he knew that this rare encounter gave promise of something he would long for all his life, and search for ever afterwards in vain.

Gods above, but it was vile! The smell of drink and sex, the reek of stale bodies and long hours of debauch, struck Arthur in the stomach till his gorge rose. He ran his eyes over the slouched bodies, some still too drunk to cover their nakedness, others sprawled among the empty hogsheads and spilled wine on the floor. Now the dogs were nosing around between the rushes, sniffing the splashed vomit and licking the dark pools of liquid puddled in the stones underneath.

What a scene in such a place as this! High overhead, a tracery of fine beams soared through the airy void to support the massive roof. Around the walls long mullions of stained glass let in rainbow shafts of red and blue and gold. Sorrow overwhelmed Arthur, and a strengthening anger too. This place was his royal birthright, not a common stew. He never thought to see it used like this.

At the far end of the hall ran a raised dais with a dining-table, where the royal revellers sat. Arthur's voice rang down the room. 'Bring them to me!'

Kay nodded to his men. All the occupants of the high table, the six kings and their companion knights were brought to their feet, and herded down the hall. Carados found himself transported from a stoic resignation to a state of seething fury. A king to be called before a bastard upstart like this?

Rage overcame his judgement. 'Whoever you are,' he ground out, 'beware—'

'You may not speak to me,' came the calm reply. 'I am king here, and you have usurped my place. For twenty years you have possessed my land. I have come to reclaim it from you now.'

'Darkness and devils!'

Arthur raised his hand to stem another furious outburst, from King Rience this time. 'I understand that you held this land from King Lot. I know you believe that he took it by right. But that is over, and your reign is ended now. You may go in peace, for I am here to rule.' He signalled to Kay and Bedivere, and the whole party shuffled under guard to the door.

'Farewell, kings!' Arthur called. He raised his right arm in a royal salute. 'Go in peace, and the blessings of the Great Ones on you all!'

And that might have been that, King Vause later told his wife, if the great fool had been content to leave it there. It was all taken care of, the maids dispatched to their sculleries, the whores sent back to the town hardly able to believe that they had not been made spoils of war, and all the knights allowed to join their lords. No one had been killed, though it was plain from the faces of Arthur's knights that they would not have been as magnanimous as their king. At last every man was safely mounted, ready to ride out.

But who would believe it? Vause shook his head. At the last minute, the would-be king had blown his own peace apart. His face glowing with that look of his, as if the Gods had granted him some special grace, he'd raised his long arms and waved them in the air. 'Peace to you all!' he cried. 'And pray to the Great Ones to guide this kingdom now! Give thanks that this land is returned to the rule of Pendragon at last!'

And that, as King Vause observed sorrowfully to his wife, his plump face dissolving in fear, he might have known the other five would never do. Pray for Pendragon? Rejoice that a bastard had put them off their lands? That was the insult they could not pocket up. That was the challenge that had to be avenged.

So that was why Carados had sent messengers flying north to King Lot. That was why they were all madly rallying, calling for men, for arms, to rendezvous for war. And he had no choice, he told his weeping wife through his own tears, but to honour his pledge. So that was that, war on this Arthur, if it meant death for them all.

So the boy had done it!

Well, he had known he would.

From his vantage-point in the highest watch-tower of Caerleon, Merlin smiled down upon the scene beneath. He knew that he had not needed to return in body here. His spirit shape had sufficed to keep watch on what was happening, and to let Arthur know.

Let him know what? Merlin chuckled to himself. All that the boy needed to know.

A movement in the distance made him look up. The black bird was no more than a dot on the horizon as it flew down. But it landed on the wall beside him with a clatter of heavy wings, and its harsh crow came from another world than this. Merlin cocked his head. 'So?'

He listened intently as the bird clacked in his ear. 'So?' he cackled gleefully. 'Dead, eh? Good, good!'

Pleasure suffused him as he felt his own power. Now the Summer Country must make a new queen. And the new queen would be an irresistible prize to her kinsman

Malgaunt. With war in the Middle Kingdom threatening their borders, her countrymen would demand she took a champion. Malgaunt would seize his chance, and she would have no choice.

Yes, yes! Let her fall a prey to her uncle, who had spent his life lusting to possess her and the land. Then she would be well out of Arthur's reach! Merlin's old skin crackled, and he rubbed his dry hands together with a sound like sticks. The girl had always been a danger, he had known that since she was a child. Now that she had grown bold and beautiful, she was a threat to be crushed without mercy, at the risk of all. If Arthur had one sight of her, he would be lost.

And they must never marry! The old man shook in the grip of his inner rage. No daughter of the Goddess would make a bride for his boy! No girl from the Summer Country could forget her Mother-faith, her body-hunger, her woman's will. She would come between him and Arthur, and between Arthur and his destiny. And she would break his heart. This way she would be crowned and dethroned, wedded and bedded by Malgaunt, while Arthur fought on here to hold his own.

Merlin nodded tensely to himself. Yes, the six kings would keep Arthur occupied. Carados and the others would return again, they must. Indeed, they were gathering now, beating up men from the fields, from the farms and towns, to come again with a mighty host. They would send to King Lot for his aid as well, and Arthur would look out from Caerleon to find the earth black with his enemies as far as his eyes could see.

And then?

Merlin shook his head furiously, trying to clear his sight. But the darkness was coming down now, blinding his thought and sight. All his life, all his many lives, it had been so.

He moaned in misery. And when it came, it eclipsed everything. He had to feel what was going on, because he would see things, then not see them any more. Yet darkly, darkly, he could see things slipping away.

Merlin's spirit sighed like the wind in the trees, weeping aloud. He could feel himself being drawn back to the place where he had left his body, in spite of his will. Gods, how he suffered in these times of trial! Why was he fated to feel his old body mutiny against its decay? Why was he forced to feed the lusts of his withered flesh?

Why?

He moaned again. For a lord of light as he was, to carry within him this darkness was a punishment beyond pain.

'One more task!' he cajoled the demanding flesh. 'One more shape, one more form, let me complete one more task! Do not call me back yet, I beg of you, for I have one more thing to do. Let me leave word for Arthur to direct him in my absence, for he is young and headstrong and may easily go astray. Grant me a little time to tell him what he should know. Then I am yours, do as you will with me!'

'One more task, then,' came back the mocking reply. 'One more task if you must, old fool, and then you are mine to do with as I please!'

CHAPTER 8

Jesu, Maria, what a land this was! What a wretched people, and this London of theirs, what a town! The Abbot clutched his worn black robe as tightly as he could round his thin frame, and plunged head down across the churchyard into the driving rain.

Faint wisps of thought tormented his absent mind. For a few moments he felt again the warm streets of Rome beneath his sandalled feet, saw himself moving towards the great Mother Church in all her glory, St Peter on his rock—

A sudden gust of sleet slashed across his face.

Dear God, this place!

And this news from the Summer Country, what would it mean? The Queen struck down – good, good, he prayed passionately, let her die! So perish all those who stand in the way of Our Lord! But with a grown daughter poised to succeed, the Mother-right was strong, it would be reinforced. And that could only work against God's purpose here.

Furious, he puzzled on. Till now, we have made great gains in Your name, Lord God. Slowly but surely we were bringing this land to You. And now this! Had she ruled on into a feeble old age, the pagan queen might have been overthrown by one of the other petty kings here, forever coveting her lands. Or by a nearer enemy, the brother, cousin, whatever he was to her, whose jealousy was well known.

Yet now—

Now a young queen, bold and beautiful. Doubtless a shameless pagan as her mother had been, revelling in her freedom, flaunting her band of knights. Knights? He gave vent to a savage inner laugh. Paramours and bed-warmers, male concubines, warrior thugs to kill or pleasure her at her command. And this – this thing of iniquity to become queen?

We must bear witness, there is no other way. We must send one to declare the Word of Christ. They must not continue in their wickedness unopposed. Think, think! he urged himself. There must be a way to disrupt the succession of queens. To turn these savages against each other, to feed their greed and envy till they destroyed themselves. Yet who to send into the heart of the Mother land? Who would be canny enough to weave this web for God, and brave enough to oppose the Mother-right?

He picked his way grimly through the gloaming dusk. Ahead of him loomed a dark square of stone, squatting like a living thing beside the churchyard path. Another grievance burst upon his mind. Lord have mercy, that thing still here – still standing where Merlin had left it that day!

Yet would not any man leave standing the memorial to his finest hour? Let alone the great miracle Merlin claimed.

Merlin's miracle.

The Abbot's soul scorched in the flames of disgust.

How could I have allowed this devil-play to be taken for holy work? he tormented himself. I who have seen the miracle of God's love, who have felt the wonder of Christ's resurrection and His life after death. Help me, Lord, he implored for the thousandth time, ease my troubled mind.

When I agreed to Merlin crowning his boy on our ground, did I do right to accept these pagans here?

For how could this be a miracle, this trick with the sword in the stone? A true miracle showed forth the glory of God. This had brought nothing but a great youth who thought he should be King.

And for sure, that meant war, warfare with famine and the sword, death and suffering that would not spare the kingdom of God in this land, the struggling communities, the cells of holy men. Leaning into the shafts of wind-blown sleet, the Abbot pulled up his hood and tried to shelter his shaven head. Did I do right, O Lord?

And what an evil thing it was, this stone of theirs! As he drew near the stone, he could see a sickly fern beginning to sprout from the hole where the sword had been. Yellow lichen was spreading like venom down over the sides, where knight after knight had braced himself in a vain attempt to draw the weapon out. Yet surely evil could be turned to good, or what was the point of their whole mission here? The good Christian had no choice but to start with the works of Satan, if he wished to bring this land to God.

And nothing should be beneath their notice here. They were warriors for Christ, not dainty diners at His feast. No chance should be neglected, not even this. If Arthur perished, then there was no loss. But if he came to good, the Christians would be foremost among those he had to thank. Proclaimed on Christian land, welcomed and honoured by men of Christ, how could he refuse them permission to build their churches, to preach the Word, to grind the Old Faith and all its wickedness into the dust?

And the youth might win. The Abbot's thoughts lightened even amid the gathering gloom. Young or not, he had shown a rare power, even a spiritual grace. In time, he could well be brought to God.

For a brief moment, the Abbot indulged himself with a vision of what might come. A Christian king, ruling a Christian land, would mean that a great church could be built here, ten times finer than this first poor attempt. The Abbot's fancy took flight. There could be a church for each city, perhaps even one in every town. He dreamed on. A king who would bring all his people to the knowledge and love of Christ. A ruler who would impose Christian virtue and morality on his disordered flock in place of the filthy customs these people followed now.

A shudder seized his fastidious frame. How these people lived! It was vile, beyond vile, to ignore the rule of God. To permit women to choose their own partners, when God had shown that women should be chosen and ruled by men. To allow them, young and old, to bed men without marriage, and even when married too – to take and discard men in love and lust, to practise their so-called 'thigh-freedom' even when they were the mothers of young, or matrons of many years. It was loathsome, animal, vile.

Yet it was all that a Christian had to work with in this place. And God would forgive them what they had to do. Averting his gaze, the Abbot hurried past Merlin's stone, along the side of the long low church ahead, and ducked down a flight of steps through a small door into the gloom of the crypt. When the brothers had more time, when more money came from Rome – for the thousandth time he choked back the desire for better buildings, a better space that was large enough to meet.

Yet the brothers looked easy enough sitting among the tombs. And the underground burial place was out of the wind at least. It was bitingly cold, but never plagued by draughts. The lone candle burned steadily in the centre of the group, like the light of faith. There was much to thank God for in this stony space.

Jesu, Maria, bless what we have to do.

As he came in, the monks rose to their feet and bowed. Briefly he sketched a hasty blessing in the air and signalled them all to resume their seats. He hastened to the vacant chair at the head of the rough table where they sat. As he sat down, a door opened at the far end of the room and a young monk led a bedraggled figure in.

'Is this the man?'

The young monk bowed. 'It is, Father Abbot.'

The Abbot stared at the creature with Brother Boniface, and a weary disfavour seized him, body and soul. Was this truly God's instrument? 'What does he want?' he said.

'He told the porter, service among the men.'

'So.'

The Abbot scrutinised the newcomer with disdain. Service among the men? What kind of man did he call himself? With his strange squat body, stubby arms and pelt of damp black hair, the visitor looked hardly human, not made in God's image, as the blessed were.

Cold as it was, the Abbott sensed a new chill, and smelt the dank odour of standing water hanging in the air. Without reason, he felt the mist rising off the mere, and heard the mournful cry of waterfowl. His soul congealed. Is this Your doing, Lord? Show me Your will—

Seated at his right hand, Brother Gregory seemed to read the Abbot's mind. Born into a labouring family, Gregory made up in practical wisdom what he lacked in mystical grace. 'They're strong, these Lake-dwellers,' he grunted quietly. 'He'd be a good worker if we took him in. In God's house, even the beasts of burden have their place.'

A murmur of assent ran round the group. The Abbot nodded. 'But do we really need a beast like this?'

He turned back to Brother Boniface still standing patiently alongside his strange charge. 'And why here with us? Why has he come all the way to London from the Summer Country when there are other cells of brethren along the way?'

Brother Boniface nodded. 'He says that he heard you made a new king here. That you and Merlin between you will bring in the rule of men.'

Men again, the Abbot noted. 'Why did he leave the Lake?'

The young monk suddenly flushed a vivid red. 'I could not say, Father. He speaks the language of the Old Ones, and I did not truly understand the things he said.'

The Abbot softened. The young monks often hated the customs here. Striving to be pure, they felt contaminated. 'You have not been with us long, Boniface,' he said courteously. 'I am sorry that you must find it so far removed from the ways of Rome.' He turned back to the creature squinting in the shadows, watching the proceedings closely, his black eyes on fire. 'You!' he addressed him roughly in the coarse accents of the Old Tongue. 'What are you doing here?'

The creature shuffled the dank skins round his shoulders and a grin broke over the darkness of his face. When he spoke, the sound he made was like an otter's bark. 'I saw it, up there!' He gestured to the churchyard overhead. 'The great stone.'

'Yes?'

'The sign of the new king!'

The Abbot sighed. 'It is true that God in His mercy gave us a miracle here,' he said, with as much patience as he could muster. 'The lost king of the Middle Kingdom was revealed to us by the Druid Merlin when he drew a sword from the heart of that great stone you saw. But what's that to you? You come from the Sacred Lake. Your Lady there is far from our way of thought.'

The man's lips twisted in a snarl. 'She sent me away!'

'The Lady banished you from Avalon? For what?'

The guttural voice deepened with pure rage. 'In the Lake village, we serve the Lady on the island, as our people have done since time was born. We ferry her people as they come and go, we bring them food and wine, we keep the causeways clear and the boats and barges in repair. On the island, she is the Lady, and all obey. But in the village, we are our own men.'

False, all of it, thought the Abbot, already wearying of the man's coughing whine. Other people besides the Lake villagers brought offerings to the island, and many faithful souls provisioned the dwellers there. The Lady's rule was not confined to Avalon: the Great One she served had been Mother of all the godless world till Christ was born. And what kind of men can call themselves their own masters when they permit their women the freedoms enjoyed in the Lake village, or on the Sacred Isle?

Yet God, to do Thy will—

He stifled the harsh words rising to his lips. 'Continue.'

The Lake-dweller shuffled his feet. 'Beltain comes.'

'We know of it.' The Abbot did not hide his distaste.

'My wife meant to go to the feast this year, and seek a partner of the fires.' The sound he made was half a coarse laugh, half an angry grunt. 'I told her no. She said my no was nothing, she would go.'

The Abbot nodded. 'So you beat her.'

'I was not the first! Other men in the village keep their wives in line.' He chuckled nastily. 'But their women know better than to complain.'

'But yours?'

The Lake man gave a high resentful grunt. 'She fell and broke her jaw.'

'She did? And then?'

'She went to the Lady.' The small black eyes grew inflamed. 'And the Lady declared me outcast from the Lake. She – she—'

The thick body began to shake with rage. A torrent of abuse fell from his lips. Witch – whore – great sow – no right to tell men to come and go—

Praise God, the Abbot thought, that Brother Boniface does not know this tongue. Still, when all the men in this land were of this creature's mind, the Lady would be no more.

And then, Lord God, oh then—

With a start he was aware that the Lake-dweller was addressing him again. 'I knew you were against the Lady too, so I came here.'

The Abbot paused for thought, suspending both judgement and disgust. Slowly his eyes passed round the assembled monks, absorbing the message of their nods or shaken heads. At last he held up his hand. 'Enough. We shall admit you to serve the brethren here.' He fixed the Lake villager in a commanding gaze. 'Look that you obey their every command, or you'll be whipped and turned away again.' He raised his voice and called to the end of the room. 'Ho there!'

A shaven head popped instantly round the door. 'Pass this man over to the brothers in charge of the household today,' the Abbot ordered. 'Have them feed him and find him a bed, and put him to work.'

'At once, Father. This way, man.'

The Abbot inclined his head. 'Go in God, brethren. Boniface, a word?'

The Lake-dweller padded swiftly through the door. One by one the monks rose and followed him. The Abbot sat for a moment in silence, then turned to Boniface with a disenchanted smile. 'You came to learn from us, and share our ministry. You see from this the struggle that we have here.'

Brother Boniface's delicate features registered a complex play of thought. 'Sir?'

'You heard him talk of Beltain?' He paused for the young monk's nod. 'You know what time of year we are approaching now.'

'Nearing the end of April.'

'As it gives way to May.' The Abbot waited while comprehension flooded Boniface's mobile face. 'Yes. The old feast of the Great Mother through all the pagan world. Almost forgotten in Rome since our Lord Jesus Christ came to save us from such things. Dying out now in these islands, in every place where our faith has taken root. But still alive in the Summer Country, where they keep the rule of queens.'

'So.' Once again a slow flush disfigured the young monk's fair skin.

'Yes,' the Abbot repeated, with grim emphasis. 'Three days of dark magic from the great North Circle to the lands of the distant east. One long feast of fires and flowers, when these souls in darkness believe that the Mother calls the Sun God back to life after his winter sleep.' His voice took on shades of deepening contempt. 'When he comes to her as her lover – as the young God Bel – to renew her with his force.'

He stopped, observing Boniface intently, ready to stamp out any signs of shame. Purity or no, the youth had to learn. 'You follow me?' he demanded brutally.

Boniface nodded with downcast eyes.

'So,' the Abbot pressed on, 'they rally to the highest hills to aid the renewal of the Mother with their own efforts on her behalf.'

'So it is true?' Boniface whispered fearfully, 'that they—'

'—that they act out the deed of the Great Mother with

her golden lover, yes,' said the Abbot with savage sarcasm. 'The women become the Goddess, and may bid any man to bed them at this time. Then these gods and goddesses rut like animals, for three days and nights. And they call this copulation holy work!'

'Holy Mary, Mother of God!' muttered Boniface aghast, crossing himself. 'They profane the purity of womanhood!'

'Their Queen herself changes her consort at will. And they are aided and abetted by the profane women who lead this evil cult,' the Abbot agreed grimly. 'Above all by their so-called Lady, their priestess as they think, the great whore who lives like Jezebel on her island in the Lake.'

Boniface fumbled to cross himself again. 'May God in His mercy show them the error of their ways,' he said fervently. His fine-featured face glowed with concern.

'Yes,' said the Abbot slowly. He looked at Boniface. Even with the shaven crown that proclaimed him a monk, he was a handsome youth. His large eyes had a tender, trusting look, and his well-shaped face and chin invited a woman's caress. 'Yes,' the older man said absently again.

His mind went spinning away into realms of gold. The lord of gold, these pagans called their god, the handsome youth who came to bed the old whore, their ancient goddess. He smiled mirthlessly. No crone so ancient, no old slut so decrepit that she could hardly open her legs, but they all, every one of them, loved a golden youth. Boniface had that shining quality. The Lady would admit him and listen to him, when his seniors would be driven from the Isle.

And once a Christian foot was in the door—

He stepped forward to place his arm around the young man's shoulders in a fatherly embrace.

'May God show them the error of their ways, you say?' he murmured. 'Oh, He will, He will. Their sacred island is a holy place. We shall win it from them, never fear. We shall pluck down the ungodly from their seats, we shall enthrone Our Lady where their great witch reigns now. I see a church rising on Avalon, I see the cross of Christ atop its so-called Tor.'

'Truly, Father?' Boniface turned up his large eyes like a hopeful girl. 'When?'

How young he is, the Abbot thought. 'We have made a beginning,' he said heartily, 'but more must be done. Think what it could be if we made this island sacred to our rites, not theirs.'

'Yes!' Boniface breathed.

The Abbot made up his mind. Send me others like Boniface, gracious Lord, he prayed silently, and I shall deliver their Avalon into Your hand. And, in the meantime, I shall begin with him.

'So, Brother,' he resumed, 'this Lake-dweller, the man I just admitted to our ranks, see that you check his progress constantly. Befriend him, learn from him all you can about the Lake, the island, and the people there. Above all, get from him the secrets of their ritual, and all he knows about this Lady, God's enemy. It is as well you glean from him all you can. It may be,' he eyed Boniface carefully, 'that God will call you there one day.'

'Ohhh—' Boniface's eyes were like full moons. He was almost too entranced to speak.

The Abbot waved his hand. 'Well, we shall see.'

From the church tower above came the faint insistent calling of a bell. The Abbot nodded at Boniface. 'Time for vespers. Be off now to your prayers.'

Brother Boniface knelt to clasp the Abbot's hand and bring it to his lips, then disappeared through the back door to the church. Deep in thought, the Abbot retraced his steps to the outer world. The stinging sleet that met him in the churchyard went almost unnoticed as he paced back to the cold cluster of dormitory cells.

His mind returned fretfully to the question that had occupied him on the way. Who to send to the Summer Country to bear witness there? Of all our fellowship in this benighted land, who, Lord, who? The cold numbed his brain and the weather was getting worse. Names, faces, revolved hopelessly in his mind.

Jesu, Maria—

Then a harsh voice, a bullet head and a pair of angry eyes rose up before him through the driving hail. By the time his hand fumbled for the wooden latch of the low dwelling he sought, his mind was clear. Thank You, Lord Jesus, he prayed humbly, and thanks to Mary the Blessed Mother above all. I have the man.

CHAPTER 9

'You say – the Queen is dead?'

'Just now, my lady.'

Cormac fixed his deep-set eyes on Guenevere, and her heart constricted in her chest. *How pale you are in your cloud of shining hair*, his look seemed to say, *how beautiful in your pain*. She looked away. 'How did she die?'

'She smiled, and said your name. Will you come to her?'

She lay just as she had when Guenevere last saw her, with the same serene air. Standing beside her in the chamber, Guenevere's soul made its last farewell. *How could your spirit have left you, in the short time I was away? If you had lived, I would have tended you night and day. And now you have slipped away to join the Old Ones in the Otherworld, and I did not say goodbye.*

But she would not weep, for she was queen now, and queens do not weep. Only alone and silently, just as her mother had departed, her shining soul going out to the Plain of Delight, where all new spirits, free of the chains of their bodies, in the star-eyed world-beyond-worlds for ever laugh and play.

*   *   *

'So now – the Queen is dead?' Malgaunt's eyes were on Guenevere, like those of a ravening wolf.

Guenevere fell back in dread. Malgaunt saw her fear, and smiled. But then she heard her voice ringing round the room: 'I claim the Mother-right! This land is mine, and whoever steals it from me, I will repay!'

The mountain range was shrouded in ice-cold mist. Slowly the line of chariots wound uphill. Guenevere gripped the chariot rail and stared out through the rain. In a cruel April they were bringing her mother home, home to the Mother who had given her birth.

The going had been bitter all the way. Ever since dawn, great weeping clouds had darkened the earth, and sleet as sharp as elf-arrows whipped their flesh. Standing beside her father in the chariot, Guenevere burned with unshed tears. How could they leave her here in the cold like this?

Ahead of them Lucan drove the leading chariot dressed for battle, his sword and shield hanging by his side. With his pale face set like marble and washed with rain, his neck garlanded with the champion's chain of gold, he looked like a creature from the Otherworld.

Behind him Guenevere could see the body of her mother reclining on an ivory couch, dressed for war. She wore a silver breast-plate, and a white robe girdled with gold. A silver helmet adorned with wings of gold crowned her head, and her long red hair flowed out loosely below. Deep bangles of ivory and ebony covered her arms, and at her feet lay her ceremonial sword and shield and spear.

And suddenly Guenevere was a child again in her chamber, touching the dread regalia half in fascination, half in fear.

Mother, will you go to war?
Hush, nonsense, darling, no, we are at peace.

But if there is war, Mother, will you fight?

Yes, little one, but with real armour, not with this.

When I grow up, will I fight too?

Warfare is changing now. When you grow up, you will lead battles from a high hill-top where you can command, not from the front.

Will I have a champion?

Yes, but he will fight for you in the field, not beside you in the war chariot as mine does.

And knights? Will I have knights?

A queen will always have her knights.

Guenevere glanced around. Yes, she would always have her knights – they were with her now. On all sides marched the Queen's champions, each with his own band of men. Some were knights of recent years, others grizzled warriors who had fought in tournaments long gone by. Some were disfigured by great scars and wounds, others still handsome, though old and greying now. Sir Niamh, one of the earliest, was weeping openly as he marched along. In a short lifetime, Guenevere saw, her mother had won herself an eternity of love.

How did a woman make men hers for life?

Guenevere cast a sideways glance at her father, following the Queen as he had done all his life. 'Father?' she ventured. He nodded impassively, and stared straight ahead.

Why was he so cold? When she was a child with hair like sunlight, he had her always by his side. While her mother was in council or busy with affairs of state, he would take her roaming the meadows at dawn, or riding all day long. At owl-light in the Great Hall he would teach her the ways of chivalry, how to meet and greet even the finest lord, how to kiss and dismiss. She was his golden child, and he loved her like his life.

But as she got older, he liked her less and less. If she

questioned him, he would snap, 'D'you think you know better than your father now?' He spent more and more time at feats of arms, while the challengers grew younger every year. Guenevere was glad when he lost the Queen's championship, because he would have more time for her. But then he was always angry, and she did not want to be with him any more.

And he never stopped telling the Queen that Guenevere should be married now she was full grown. And when Guenevere would not agree to speak of this, in time he would not speak to her at all.

But now? She could not bear it. 'Father, when we get to the Hill of Stones—'

'Beyond that ridge, not far,' he broke in curtly, pointing with his whip to the rocky outcrop ahead. As she looked, a shape flickered between the rocks and was gone. A moment later, there it was again, the figure of a wild, aged man dodging along the topmost edge of the ridge. Outlined against the sky, his skinny body was wrapped in a ragged cloak, and his head was covered by worn and dripping furs. The glittering stare that flashed from beneath the hood had more than a hint of madness, and the knife he brandished could have killed them all.

His thin scream reached them from far away.

'Make no queens here!' he cried out, in a voice like the undead. 'Let your Queen sleep in peace, do not put her daughter in her place! For I bring you word from Merlin – mark what I say!'

He was chanting now, low and rustily, with his eyes closed. His bony arms, blue-black with dirt and bruises, waved round his head. 'Make no queens here in Camelot, for there is one coming who will sweep you all away! He is the King you have longed for, all the years of your life. From the Welshlands, from the north, from the east where the terror of the invader reigns, he has come to set you free. He will purge the land of your enemies, and bring the peace you have sought in vain. Merlin has shown him forth in the great church in London, and he will be High King!'

He opened his blank yellow eyes, and threw his arms in the air. 'No queens, then, no Queen Guenevere, before God and the Gods!' he screamed. Then he turned on his heel, and raced shrieking out of sight. 'For he is coming, he is coming, and he will soon be here!'

His mocking cackle lingered in the air. Guenevere could hardly speak. 'Father!' she began huskily. 'What does it mean?'

Leogrance shrugged. 'Madness, foolery, nothing, pay no heed! This is Beltain, remember, when strange things walk. He won't be the only wild wanderer out on the mountainside tonight.'

Beltain.

Another trouble surged into Guenevere's mind. 'Father, after the funeral, Taliesin says the wine will flow and the fires will be lit, and the people make ready to welcome down the God. What happens then?'

King Leogrance angrily tossed back his wet hair. 'If your mother had listened to me, you'd know all this by now! You'd have come to the feast of Beltain long ago, and found a partner of the fires to champion you through what lies ahead.'

Something in his voice chilled Guenevere worse than the wind. 'What lies ahead?'

'That!' Cracking the whip, King Leogrance laid savagely into the backs of the horses, and pointed ahead. The chariot juddered as the horses strained to pull forward through the mud. 'The Hill of Queens!'

And there it was, the great hill rising up through the mist, a halo of weak sunlight gilding its crest. Its vast greenness seemed to float above the watery valley like a landscape seen in dreams.

At the top of the hill Guenevere saw a circle of standing stones, ancient grey giants brooding in the mist. Further down stood a clutch of low stone barrows, all facing east, aligned to the rising sun. Here every Queen of the Summer Country had been laid to rest since time began. They had brought her mother home.

At the bottom of the hill a great crowd of villagers and countryfolk clustered about the grass, some weeping silently, some crying out in grief. Further off were huddles of the shy, dark people they called the Land Kin, the ancient folk who lived hidden in the hills and forests and secret places everywhere. They were the true guardians of the land, Guenevere knew, descended from the first dwellers in these isles who had mated with the Old Ones long ago.

The slow procession straggled to a halt. And there he was, appearing before she was aware.

'Lady Guenevere, permit me?'

Cormac put out his hand. Beads of silver hung on his dark blue robes, and jewelled his black hair. His eyes, burning like charcoal, wore a distant air. Guenevere did not trust herself to speak. Her hand trembled in his hard, indifferent grip. *Why was he so cold?*

All around, the mourners were climbing down from their wagons, easing stiff limbs and rubbing frozen hands. With a muttered word, King Leogrance left her to cross to Malgaunt, and the two fell at once into a conversation she could not hear.

'Lady Guenevere?' Taliesin nodded towards the largest of the burial chambers. The dark interior showed a pinpoint of light. 'The Lady has come to welcome your mother home.'

'The Lady has come from Avalon?' Guenevere was astonished.

'She loved your mother,' Taliesin said gently. 'This is her farewell.'

As he spoke, a chanted melody began inside the chamber, a song without words. Yet it spoke of the beauty in the heart of the flame, of the passing glory of the white bird on the wing, and the blossom of the sea spray under the shining prow. It sang of a mother with her baby, of the hard love between men and women, and the gentle rest that comes at last to all.

The doorway of the chamber was beckoning them in. At Lucan's sign half a dozen of the Queen's knights lifted her body down from the chariot, and carried it across the hillside into the chamber.

Guenevere followed with King Leogrance and Malgaunt, nerving herself to plunge into the earthy darkness within. Down they went and down until they came out into a low, domed space dimly lit with dragon-lamps. In the centre of the chamber stood a funeral chariot cast in solid bronze. The six knights set the Queen down on the chariot, and withdrew.

Beside the chariot waited the Maidens of the Lake, girls destined to become priestesses, robed in white and gold. Deftly they arranged the Queen's war regalia, and raised her battle standard above her throne. Beside her they set her silver mirror and comb, and her beloved cosmetics in their bowls of coloured glass. In her lap they placed her jewel box brimming with amber, turquoise and pearls, all her treasures from this world to delight her in the next.

'Hear me!'

Guenevere's heart leaped in fear. Silhouetted against the entrance stood the wild shape of a giant black and white bird, its wings outstretched for flight. It was Taliesin, arms upraised in his singing robes, a great cloak of swan and raven feathers, half man, half god.

Cormac was harping passionately at his side. Taliesin cried again, 'Hear me! I sing of a princess born to rule, of a young queen who loved her first champion, and made him her king and Chosen One. I tell of her courage in battle, her frail form fearless against spears and arrows, her chariot always in the thick of the fray! I hail her strength in peace, and her wisdom in war.

'And weeping, I praise the beauty of a soul that made the Old Ones take her before her time!'

The dying cry hung trembling in the air. Nothing stirred in the singing, shimmering gloom. Then a radiance grew and filled the pulsing dark. In the heart of the brightness stood a lofty figure veiled from head to foot. Guenevere's eyes burned. The Lady had come to bring her mother home.

The muffled shape raised her arms, fluttering her gauzy draperies. The sound that filled the chamber was the deep music of the earth itself.

'Great Mother of us all, you are life, you give life, and to you all life returns. You danced on the white foam of the waves, and divided the sea from the sky.

'From your body flows each sparkling stream, and from you all waters make their way to the sea. In the starlit sky, you come to us as the Moon. And when the Sun goes down and your children fall asleep, you are here to take us home.'

Now the haunting chant swelled up to ecstasy.

'O Mother, Goddess, Great One, take to yourself this child who was your servant, this queen who loved her people, take this woman's body, and let her soul sweetly slip its unwanted shell!

'Ease her journey to the Plain of Delight, speed the passing of her spirit through the world between worlds, and bless her steps to come to us again!'

'Be it so!' cried the Maidens with one voice. 'Be it so, be it so, be it so!'

Suddenly all the dragon-lamps went out, plunging the burial chamber into night. In the black silence Guenevere felt a man's breath – whose? – on the back of her neck. A scream rose in her throat and she choked with fear.

Then a voice she knew sounded from near the door. 'Come!' called Taliesin. One by one the mourners turned, and stumbled towards the light.

Outside on the hillside the roaring crowd was calling on the Goddess and all the Gods. But faintly above the clamour came an unfamiliar noise. Guenevere blinked in the sudden sunlight, and stared about.

And there it was again: '*Domine, domine, miserere—*'

'He hath put down the mighty from their seat,' rose the thin drone. 'He hath punished the ungodly in the imagination of their hearts.'

Round the side of the hill came a column of chanting monks, led by a black-robed figure brandishing a cross.

'Christ-worshippers!' Lucan swore. 'How dare they come here?'

Malgaunt calmly surveyed the approaching troop. 'Perhaps they have come to pay their last respects.'

'Respects?' Lucan exploded. 'When they call the Old Ones idols, and destroy our shrines? These men respect no faith but their own!'

And on they came, swarming like black beetles up the grass. Their shaven heads shone red and raw in the cold, and their coarse gowns and rope girdles made them look more like swineherds than holy men.

Guenevere stared. *Goddess, Mother, why do they dress like that?* Cormac's bardic silks were dyed with indigo from the East, and Taliesin's everyday gowns were woven from the whitest wool. Anything less was an insult to the Great Ones, who gave us beauty for our delight. Why did the Christians make themselves so ugly for their God?

Taliesin emerged from the burial house, something glinting in his hands. 'This is the ancient sword of all our queens,' he said with a bow. 'Take it, my lady, for it is yours now.'

Trembling, Guenevere looked down. The sword lay across her hands, heavy with slumbering power. In awe she stroked the sheath of jewelled gold and felt the antique gemstones pulsing with inner fire. Their force flowed into her, and she gripped the weapon like a talisman as the line of monks drew near.

'God be with you!' the leader cried, planting his cross in the ground. 'I am Brother John, and these are the servants of Christ. We come to bring a blessing on the Queen who has gone.'

Guenevere forced herself to speak. 'Welcome, sir. We take your blessing with thanks.'

'And we come to know,' he went on, thrusting his coarse red hands deep in his trailing sleeves, 'who rules the Summer Country now?'

Taliesin drew up at Guenevere's side. 'The Summer Country obeys the rule of queens. And the queen-making of our Lady Guenevere takes place tomorrow, at the feast of Beltain.'

Brother John pursed his lips. 'This queen-making . . .'

'It is the ceremony at which the Queen makes her mystical marriage with the land,' Taliesin's mellow voice went on. 'Her sacred union with her country, in the sight of all her folk, when the people come to the fires, when the Sun comes to the Earth, when the God comes to the Mother, and all life begins anew.'

'New life?' Brother John let out a contemptuous snort. 'There is no life but in our Saviour Jesus Christ, nothing but death in following false gods!'

False gods? Guenevere felt the rage rising up her throat.

How can they hate so much, these Christians, and still call them-selves good? Why do they hate, when religion should be love?

'False gods?' Lucan was at her side, hungry for blood. 'Do you insult our worship? You lousy dog, if you were a man and wore a sword, instead of making yourself a eunuch for your God—'

The monk's face filled with blood. 'We are warriors for Christ, you heathen slave, and we bring death to those who will not hear our truth!'

'Sirs, sirs!' Guenevere held up her hand. 'Brother John, your kindness is welcome on my mother's death. But I beg you, do not disturb our sacred rites. Hear me, sir—'

'Hear you?' he broke in violently. 'No, madam, you hear me!' His eyes were bulging with a furious glare. 'What you do here is against the laws of God! God has forbidden women to have authority over men. Men were made in His image to fulfil His aims. Your queen-making is the work of the devil, and against God's will!'

How dare they? 'Yet I am Queen here in spite of you!' Guenevere raged. She tore the sword from its scabbard and waved it round her head.

Brother John snatched up his cross and flourished it in her face. 'Get thee behind me, Satan!'

Lucan could take no more. 'Get out! Leave this place as you came, or you'll find yourselves head down in a ditch to feed the crows!'

'Go!' Guenevere ordered, at the top of her voice. 'You heard our champion – go!'

'I curse you, demon woman!' the monk screamed. 'Leave off this queen-making, or you'll burn in hell!'

There was a slow but unmistakable ripple through the crowd. Lucan leaped towards the nearest group, farmers and villagers by their open look. 'You heard these men!' he called. 'Will you defend the Queen and the Mother-right?'

'Will we not, lord?' A clutch of brawny youths and sturdy men and women cheered and surged forward at Lucan's call.

'Get back! Get back!' Brother John brandished his cross and began jabbering a Latin curse, *'Maleficia maledico—'*

Lucan sprang at him, and levelled his sword at his throat. 'Get out of here!'

The monk was pale, but with fury not with fear. 'We go!' he shouted, mouthing down his bile. 'But, like Our Lord Himself, we shall return! Your late Queen has died young, struck down before her time. It's a sign from above! Your Gods are failing, ours will give us victory!'

Brandishing his cross with a final flourish of defiance, he turned to descend the hill. Behind him his black tribe trooped on his heels. Guenevere watched them with a sinking heart. They spoke no more than the truth. Like their Lord, they would return.

CHAPTER 10

The sound of chanting slowly died away. The column of monks wound down the hill, and was lost in the fading light. High overhead the first star of evening appeared in the sky. And Guenevere breathed deeply in the damp, sweet air, and looked around her with new eyes.

Below them, the watchers on the hillside were settling in for the night. One by one their camp-fires bloomed in the dusk as they made themselves at home. Others were lighting the Beltain fires, the great bonfires that would make the crest of the hill as bright as day, and create welcoming pools of warm darkness for those who would creep into them together later on.

The fires—

Guenevere paused. Her mother had spoken of fires with her last words on earth.

Through the fires, she had said, *through the fires he comes.*
Who?
When?
Tonight?

Tonight the Queen would already know the answer as she passed through the Beyond, crossing the astral plane on the wings of their prayers. Unless the hatred of the Christians had hindered her journey, and ruined their last farewell?

Beside her Taliesin sighed. 'Fear not, Lady Guenevere. Your mother is already walking in the world where the wind and stars are one.'

'No thanks to the Christians.'

Guenevere started. Like Taliesin, Cormac was answering her thoughts. He stared at Malgaunt. 'And the Christians are the coming men, it seems.'

Malgaunt nodded, a smile playing round his lips. 'So it seems.'

'They were there in London, you say, to welcome Merlin's boy?' Cormac went on, his eyes fixed on Malgaunt's face. 'And today they were here again for our Queen's farewell?'

'They wish to spread their faith.' Malgaunt shrugged. 'There is no mystery there.'

Guenevere tensed. 'But why here, today?'

Malgaunt smiled. 'Ask them.'

Lucan stirred angrily. 'They want to destroy everything we hold dear!'

'Yet their leader, the old man on Iona, is said to be wise and kind, and not given to the sword.' Taliesin raised his head, and deep lines of tiredness marked his face. 'But it grows late, my lords. Shall we bring the Lady Guenevere to her rest?'

The royal pavilion was bright with rugs and rich hangings and great standing braziers warming the chilly air. To and fro went the Queen's women in the candlelight, plumping up cushions, setting out hot wine and honey-bread, and casting sweet herbs upon the glowing coals. As Guenevere came in, a dozen hands helped her out of her wet garments and into fresh clothes.

Now she was seated in the Queen's great chair, with her feet on a padded footstool, and a hot goblet of spiced wine in her hand. Outside a troop of the Queen's knights kept guard, ready to perform her every whim. Yet she would have traded it all to be free of the fear that dogged her now.

The Christians want to overthrow the Goddess, and bring in the rule of men. But only one man here would gain from that. A man born into second place, learning to hate the rule of women. One man hungry for power, and determined it should be his—

Guenevere leaped to her feet in fury, clapping her hands. 'Send for the King! Say the Queen his daughter begs a word with him.'

The Queen his daughter?

She gave a bitter laugh as the attendant ran to obey.

Not if my loving uncle has his way.

Goddess, Mother, Great One, help me now!

Outside, the Hill of Queens slept its primeval sleep. Through the walls of the tent, the camp-fires glowed like fireflies in the night. Where the countryfolk were camped, the funeral games and songs had been going on for hours. Now their chants took on a different note as more urgent rhythms stole through the dusky air.

Guenevere shivered. The children of the Old Ones were celebrating Beltain with all the power at their command. Could she harness the force of their earth magic to her own cause, as they laboured to draw down the Golden One?

A solitary drum-beat cut through the night air. Inside the tent, a sound fell softly like the evening dew. *'He is coming—'*

It was her mother. Guenevere stood quite still, and let her come.

'—through the fires he comes—'

Slowly the wisps of thought wove through her mind.

He is coming—

The night fires—
Beltain and the coming of the God—'

Was he the one she awaited, the Goddess's Chosen
One?

The voice came again: '*—he comes—*'

Covering her face, she closed her eyes and wept.

'My lady!' It was one of the attendants. 'The Queen's champion is outside, craving a word.'

'Admit him.'

'My Lady Guenevere!'

Lucan's smile reminded Guenevere how he had won
her mother's love. He was freshly groomed, and handsomely
turned out in a red tunic and white shirt, fine dark wool
breeches and sleeveless leather over-mantle, and perfumed
with heavy musk. At his neck he sported the massive gold
torque of knighthood, glinting with jewels as bright as
animals' eyes.

'My lady.'

Bowing low, Lucan kissed Guenevere's hand, and smiled
into her eyes. The joy of his own power coursed through the
knight's veins. She was half-way his already, he could feel
it. Tonight he would do well.

Guenevere's skin prickled, and she moved away.

Why does he look at me like that? 'Will you take a cup
of wine?'

He shook his head. 'I have news that you must hear.
When the Christians left, my men waylaid the leader and
loosened his tongue. It seems they were encouraged, lady,
to disrupt our rites.'

Guenevere caught her breath. 'Who encouraged them?'

'A great lord from Camelot, the monk said.'

'Who?'

'Who knows?' Lucan turned his head and looked away.

Guenevere gritted her teeth. Well, only a fool would name Malgaunt without proof. 'What are you saying, sir?'

'Madam, you need a champion, to defend you against such as this!'

Guenevere studied the handsome, confident face. 'Yourself, by any chance?'

He smiled his winning smile. 'Who else?'

'But you were my mother's champion.' She fumbled for the words. 'And her – Chosen One.'

His eyes flared. 'The Queen of the Summer Country takes a Chosen One for the good of all. She must maintain her vigour, when her vital life is the life of all our tribe.' He grinned with all the confidence of youth, revelling in his unchallenged animal strength. 'As queen, she marries her country, not one man. One man alone cannot sustain a queen. Men grow older, they tire, and their flesh fails. So the Queen takes a new consort to renew herself. It is her duty to renew the marriage of the Sovereignty with the land. And more – it is her right!'

He laughed, showing strong white teeth. In the enclosed area he seemed to fill the space with raw manhood, prowling like a tiger, smiling, cruel, bold. 'You do not like me, lady.' He stepped towards her, reaching for her hand. 'That would change as soon as you are Queen.'

He was very close now, and the musky scent of him was dangerous and strong. Slowly he turned her hand in his hard grip. 'Your mother took your father as the first of her Chosen Ones. She made him King, and the father of her child. He never lost these rights, though the Queen took younger men when the time came.'

Guenevere could not move. His fingertips brushed her palm. 'Lady, your mother was wise, as well as beautiful.' He looked away, and for a second Guenevere saw his loss pass over his face. 'Any young queen would be wise, too, to take a proven champion.' He raised her hand and touched it to his lips. 'Especially one who offers himself to her freely, body and soul.'

'Ha!' The spell was broken. '"Freely" you say, Sir Lucan? Even young women know that few things are free.' Guenevere stepped back, and pulled her hand away. 'What is your price?'

'Truly you are the daughter of your mother!' Lucan laughed in delight. 'And the man who has loved one will be doubly blessed in the love of the other.' He caught her hand again, and brought it to his lips in a fervent kiss.

'But your love, sir?' Guenevere persisted. 'What does it cost?'

'You wrong me, lady, my service has no price!' He laughed again. 'But you would naturally reward the champion who helped you to the throne. You would make him King, and the father of your child.' He paused, his eyes flaming in the candlelight, his voice dark. 'And he would make you love him, in ways you do not know.' He slipped his hand inside her sleeve and touched the soft skin of her wrist.

Guenevere could feel her face growing hot, and her breasts pricking inside her gown. 'Not so fast, lord,' she said huskily. 'You are offering me your service, if I make you my King?'

'My service – and my life.' She's coming, Lucan rejoiced to himself, she's mine—

'But surely I can already command you to do anything I like?'

Lucan paused. 'Lady?'

'You swore your service to me before all our knights, when I took the throne on the night my mother was struck down. To the death, I believe – if my memory serves me right.' Guenevere moved in for the kill. 'So if I want a champion, you are already mine.'

'But I thought – now you are Queen—'

Lucan's dismay was so comical that Guenevere had to smile. 'Now I am Queen, I must do the best I can. Goodnight, my lord.'

'Ha? So!' Lucan took his dismissal with good grace. 'Then I bid you goodnight, my lady, and a good dawn tomorrow, on your day of days.' He laughed. 'And Lucan's sword is still at your command!'

Guenevere raised her hand and gave him a warm farewell. 'Good night, Sir Lucan, and a good dawn to you too.'

Malgaunt—
    The Christians—
    So, both of them working against me now—

There was a tense footfall, and a tall rigid figure came thrusting through the door. 'So, Daughter, why the summons? I had gone to Malgaunt's tent to take a cup of wine.'

She stared at her father's frowning face. 'You were with Malgaunt?'

'You should be glad I was.' Striding over to the wine mulling on the brazier, King Leogrance gave a short, angry laugh. 'Don't you know that Merlin and his mob will have reached Caerleon by now? And when Lot's six kings beat them bloody and send them running for their lives, where d'you think they'll come?' He took a swig of wine. 'If this would-be King of theirs lands on our doorstep, what will you do?'

The same sneer again, you are nothing without a man, the same unanswerable demand, you must take a champion – Guenevere's soul shrivelled with impotent rage.

King Leogrance reached for more wine. 'You cannot rule alone,' he said stubbornly. 'Your mother was a warrior, battle-trained. She was descended from our queens who fought against the Romans, and her foremothers laid all England waste. But you have seen no blood.' He smirked. A glint of former triumphs lit his eye. 'And your mother had a champion when she came to the throne. I was the greatest fighter of my day. You must have a champion too.'

'But why?' Guenevere cried out. 'All I do tomorrow is to claim the Mother-right!'

'Daughter, when war looms as it does now, the people will want a war-leader before they'll make you Queen! You'll need a champion to win their acclaim. And when you do, take him for life, and forget the old ways.'

Guenevere gasped. 'Forget the old ways of the Mother Herself? But our women have had the right of thigh-friendship since time out of mind! It is the freedom of the Mother to give love where She chooses.'

'The Christians do not permit it.'

'The *Christians?*' She was blazing with anger. 'By what right do they dictate our customs now?'

'Malgaunt says we must work with them. He sees the boy Arthur as powerful in their hands.'

Guenevere could not bear it. 'Malgaunt says!' she cried. 'Who is he to say? He wants to take my throne!' She was weeping with passion now. 'Father, you must stand for me! You must be my champion, and defend the Mother-right!'

'Now, Guenevere . . .' Leogrance was playing with his goblet, staring into the wine. He tried not to meet her eye. 'Listen to me!' he said heartily. 'Malgaunt's your kinsman, you have nothing to fear from him. And he's right, you need a champion.' His voice hardened. 'But the man who fights for you by day should lie with you by night. You need a partner of bed as well as sword.' He looked away. 'My day is done. Follow the rising star. Heed Malgaunt now, for he will have his way.'

'Oh, Father . . .'

She saw it all now, the whole story, in his rigid carriage and shifting eyes. The years spent watching and waiting in the shadow of a queen, a lifetime in second place.

Always in second place – like Malgaunt.

Her father and Malgaunt—

The two in council tonight—

Guenevere raised her head, and managed a fair smile. 'Thank you, Father, for your help and advice. And now goodnight, for I must go to bed.'

As he left, the great bonfires on the hillside above made the night as bright as day. The air was sweet with woodsmoke and the first warm breath of spring. Under a full-bellied moon, April was ripening into May as hope and expectation filled the air.

Other soft sounds and sighs came trembling through the dark. A great yearning gripped her, as sharp as any pain. At Beltain, her nurse told her, all the doors of the Otherworld were opened wide for love.

And as the barriers dissolved between the worlds, the Otherworldly Ones themselves came to the revels, to partner whom they would. Many a girl went to the fires and encountered a dark stranger, a man of no country, tall and unspeaking, shining in the night. Many a man found himself taken by the woman of his dream, strange, lovely and silent, and afterwards would search the length and breadth of the land for her in vain.

All were here to celebrate the life the Goddess gives, to add their vigour to the struggle of the earth. As these lovers were doing now, from the soft laughs and cries and moaning in the dark.

Goddess, Mother—

Why am I alone, when I may choose too?

The night wind was rising, and with it her hopes. And

there he was, in the very heart of her hope, the long shadow of his slender frame, the clever, bony hands, slate-blue eyes and hard, questioning stare—

She drew a shuddering sigh, and sent a messenger speeding through the night.

Goddess, Mother, tell me, will he come?

CHAPTER 11

The line of monks plodded on into the dusk. At the head of the column the leader surveyed the sky, anxiously snuffling at the damp air like a lost child. If they could bring Brother John to shelter by nightfall, he would thank God on his knees, he would kiss the threshold as they entered it. After what they had suffered, another night out of doors would be too much to bear, even for His sake.

No, that was wrong. A good Christian bore all suffering joyfully, and turned it to the praise of the Lord. The Lord must be praised. Praised be the Lord. He closed his eyes, and his lips mumbled a prayer.

Praise the Lord that the good soul in the village had parted with her donkey to help them on their way – they'd have taken days to get here if they'd had to carry Brother John themselves. It was bad enough getting him away when the pagan soldiers had finished with him. And, of course, he wouldn't rest where they found shelter, he had to push on, being Brother John.

But the Lord's mother, the Blessed Mary, had inspired the old donkey-woman's heart with compassion for their beaten brother and his sore injuries. And tonight, God willing, they would reach the convent where Brother John was Father Confessor. There the good nuns would receive them with the love and the kindness of the Blessed Mary again. Praise be to Mary, from whom all blessings flow.

Salve, Mater, salve, Regina, his tired heart sang. Hail, Mary, Mother of God, Queen of Heaven, Mother of us all. The first notes of the familiar chant fell from his lips, and the brothers took it up.

Salve, Mater, salve . . .

At the back of the column, snatches of the great hymn to the Mother reached Brother John as he swayed on the back of the donkey, clutching the pommel of the saddle with broken hands. His mind, clouded by pain, seized with a terrible fervour on the well-loved name, and his swollen mouth struggled to shape a prayer. 'Hail, Mary, who has brought me to this hour! As Thy Son had His Calvary, so I had mine. May I not be spared the whips and thorns that scored His precious flesh . . .'

'God be praised! In the valley, look, there's a light!' The voice of the leading monk betrayed something like a sob. 'It's the convent! We'll make shelter there tonight!'

Brother Peter had broken his vow of silence, John noted dispassionately, and he must be scourged for that when the time came. But, for the moment, things were well enough.

He thought again. No, they were better than that. Careless of his pulped cheek and split lips, his bleeding back and the agony in his flanks, John raised a smile. He had fulfilled the task he had been ordered to do. He had sown the seed of doubt, he had sent forth the necessary falsehood to fight for the truth. Contentedly he turned his battered face up to the heavens, and began his prayers again. 'Hail, Great Mother of God, Mother of us all . . .'

In the Convent of the Holy Mother, the Abbess Placida prided herself on living in devout accordance with her name.

But the Holy Mother herself could hardly have listened to the story of Brother John without distress.

'So you fell among the heathen, did you, Father?' she murmured, settling her large moist eyes on him sorrowfully.

Brother John adjusted his aching bones, and felt that the state of his injuries excused him from any reply. Thanks to the attentions of the pagan band, it would be weeks, rather than days, before he could move without pain.

But from the daybed in the cloister where he lay, he could see the sunny convent garden spread out before him sweet with herbs and flowers. Yellow tansy and blue banks of lavender, white camomile and nodding foxgloves romped away in the shelter of the high stone walls. On the paths between the flower-beds, white-robed novices fluttered to and fro like doves as they tended the plants.

It was a sight to soothe any pain of body or soul. And he was blessed in his attendant, for the clever hands attending to his hurts had a rare skill. She cared, did Sister Ann. He did not need to look up at the pain in her huge black eyes, the tension in the lean, black-clad body hunched over him, to tell him how much she felt his sufferings.

'God have mercy!' The Abbess stared with horror at Brother John's varicoloured wounds as Sister Ann parted his robe to expose his shoulder and chest. 'Pagans and heathens! And their warlord must be a devil, to send armed men against a brother of the cloth!' Then her Christian propriety got the better of her. 'May the Lord forgive them,' she murmured piously.

Brother John gave an unexpected laugh. 'Oh, He will – for indeed they do His work. He used them for His ends. Our mission was to warn their Princess Guenevere that she has no right to call herself a queen. And when we strike at their so-called Mother-right, we make way for our God!'

The Abbess nodded, concealing her awe at the marvellous workings of Brother John's mind. Their Father Confessor could be a bishop soon, even Archbishop in time, she thought with pride, a great man like him.

Her simple fancy soared and took flight. Even the sainted Augustine, the first archbishop in this heathen land, austere as he was, had recognised the role of women in the church. When Brother John ascended to Canterbury, perhaps there might even be a place there at his side for a woman of proven authority and spiritual grace.

'Well, the Lord be praised, if this creature is not made Queen!' Her plump face sharpened. 'So may He put down all the daughters of unrighteousness! But what will become of her? Perhaps this young woman of yours would be grateful for a good home here with us?'

Brother John's mind roamed back to the last confrontation on the Hill of Stones. That sword-swinging harridan a nun? Lord, give me strength, Brother John cried in his heart. 'She will marry her uncle,' he said heartily. 'And serve the will of God just as well in submission to her husband as she would do in silence and service here.'

Brother John smiled. With Guenevere's dismissal still scalding his ears, it was good to know that she would be punished for her shrewish tongue. A virago like her would take some beating before she would be tamed. But, by the look of him, her kinsman would not shrink from such a task.

Still, it was a pity that the girl would not come here. John looked at the Abbess with sardonic eyes. For all her piety, her soft wet spaniel's gaze, John knew she ruled the convent with a rod, and loved her work. Every one of her novices was whipped and whipped again, her buttocks soundly belaboured for the sake of her immortal soul. They entered the convent as hopeful brides of Christ. But to the

Abbess they were all sin-laden daughters of Eve, tainted with the Fall that had brought Christ to His death.

He glanced up at Sister Ann, still patiently tending his wounds. Her long white face, pale and remote, was the picture of sainted sisterhood. Yet she, too, would have been forced to kneel before the Abbess, confess her sins, and bare herself for the rod.

A sudden evil possessed him before he was aware, and a tantalising image flickered across his mind. Through veils of scented darkness he saw the long body of Sister Ann naked and dancing, her high, sharp breasts pointed straight at him, her belly quivering, her hips writhing in an ecstasy of desire. Later he was to scourge himself mercilessly for this one lapse in a lifetime of blameless dealing with women and girls. But a more immediate punishment was at hand.

'Aagh!' Brother John screamed, and raised his fingers to his neck. Fresh blood was seeping from a cut in his neck, where Sister Ann's probe had jabbed deep into the already mangled flesh.

'Father, forgive me!' Sister Ann wept, her eyes dark with distress. 'I did not mean to hurt you, it was an accident!'

'What are you doing, Sister?' The Abbess rose in fury to her feet. 'That's enough, leave us, get out!' She watched the nun hurrying off with a resentful glare. 'What's to be done with her? I sometimes wonder about God's purpose for Sister Ann.'

Why are even Christian women prone to jealousy? Brother John wondered for the thousandth time. He debated with himself whether or not to tell the Abbess what he had heard. Here, in this holy place, would she need to know? Yet strange events had a way of breaking in on quiet lives.

He inclined his head. 'Yet He has favoured that sister with good fortune now – or bad, perhaps, as it may turn out.'

'Good news for Sister Ann?' The Abbess took it as a personal affront.

'You have not heard recently from London, then, I think? Nor from the Middle Kingdom?'

Furious, the Abbess shook her head.

'A young man called Arthur lays claim to King Uther's crown. With the backing of Merlin, he styles himself King of the Middle Kingdom, and he may succeed.'

'And if he does?'

'King Lot will make cruel war. And the terror may sweep through the rest of these islands too.'

A flash of clarity seized the Abbess, who knew that her house of women was more vulnerable than she cared to think. 'But already the Saxons fall like sea-wolves on our shores. And, on top of this, you say all the kingdoms will be fighting each other now?' Her wimple trembled with the horror of it all. 'We will pray to God. He will ensure that this Arthur fails in his monstrous claim!'

John shook his head. How obtuse this woman was! He began again. 'But Sister Ann—'

The Abbess froze him with a dignified regard. 'Forgive me, Brother, but what has this to do with Sister Ann?'

'Nothing, perhaps. But if he wins . . .'

Brother John paused, beginning to think again. Was it wise to tell the Abbess how a victory for King Arthur would affect Sister Ann? After all, it might never come to pass. The new King would have much to deal with if he ever won the throne. Would his rule ever reach out as far as this quiet convent, where the reverend sisters lived so blamelessly in the worship of God?

Already the Abbess had a reason to hate Arthur for

the danger he posed to her. And she needed no more encouragement to punish Sister Ann, even if the nun had now outgrown the whip. No, let the story come here by itself. And if it did not, well, who would be any the worse?

'So, boy, King Arthur now!'

Standing in the courtyard of Caerleon, Arthur heard the words of Merlin echoing inside his mind, and smiled and shook his head. Nothing had prepared him for the glory that would be his when the ancient citadel fell into his hands. If I had a queen now, he caught himself thinking, this would truly be a castle fit for a king.

Like boys on a lark, he and Kay, Gawain and Bedivere explored Caerleon from top to bottom when the six kings rode out. Trunks of fine garments showed that Lot's faithful vassals had come with a whole summer of frolics and feasts in mind. From the magnificent suits of armour, much of their time would have been spent in jousting or on the tournament field. And their leisure hours, too, had been well provided for. The Queen's apartments were far from queenly now, reeking of whorish scents and littered with bright trinkets and gaudy shoes and clothes. But in the right hands they would soon be fine again. And once more the odd refrain went through Arthur's head: If I had a queen, a woman to help me now . . .

One like Guenevere of the Summer Country, tall and beautiful and unafraid. But she was already betrothed, Merlin said. If only she were free, their two countries could be joined as one to make a dazzling kingdom for them both. How firm was this betrothal, he wondered suddenly. He must ask Merlin as soon as he returned.

And where was Merlin? All he wanted was Merlin to share this precious hour of triumph, and Merlin was not here. Yet he had to believe—

'My lord!'

It was one of the castle servants, falling to his knees. 'Rise, sir,' said Arthur courteously. 'What is your errand?'

'A message from Merlin, sire, left at the gatehouse by an old beggarman.'

Arthur took the proffered scroll. 'Where is he now, the beggar?'

'We put him in the gatehouse, and gave him food. But when we looked again, he was gone.'

Arthur nodded bleakly and opened the scroll. Merlin's wild writing capered before his eyes.

> *You have done well, sir King. I knew you would. Boy no more, eh, but truly King Arthur now! I shall soon be back to raise a cup to your victory. For now I have gone to seek alliance with the Summer Country, to secure peace on our borders there. I shall be back before you know that I have gone.*
>
> *But beware yourself, my son, while I am away. Beware the darkness that is coming, that awaits us all. Make good your army, set your look-outs, and never let your guard sleep on the watch. Prepare for an attack. For the darkness is descending, it comes without a doubt. I feel it, though I know not when it comes.*
>
> *Merlin the Bard*

Silently Arthur passed the scroll to his companion knights.

Kay gave his sharp laugh. 'So he's off to the Summer Country, is he, making peace for us there?'

'The Summer Country, yes.' A wisp of memory passed through Arthur's mind. 'We passed by their borders on our way here. We talked of a treaty then, to keep them safe.' And not only of a treaty, he remembered silently.

'Isn't Merlin taking too much on himself, acting for you like this?' Kay said disagreeably. 'A king should make his own treaties. And as for the rest of it—'

'Yes, what's all this nonsense about "the darkness"?' glowered Gawain. 'Why does he spoil our victory with such thoughts?'

Kay nodded, his face sour. 'As if he needs to tell us to set look-outs, and keep a watch.'

'The six kings,' said Arthur tensely. 'He is saying they will return. He is warning us to beware.'

But Bedivere watched Arthur's face, and read his eyes. He was from the Welshlands too, and he knew what Merlin meant. 'And to take heed of the darkness,' he said quietly, in his firm, rhythmic lilt. 'For every man has his darkness, and the greatest has most of all.'

Oh, it was dark now, it was a great darkness, darker than ever, yet better than ever too!

Merlin groaned till he felt his ribs crack.

She rode him hard, this spirit woman, and she changed shape every time. Yet it was always the same woman, and it always had been, at least he knew that now.

He cried out, and tried to shift his aching loins under the abiding torture of her jabbing frame. When had it started, the darkness and desire?

Long, long ago, too long ago to recall. Once, he knew, he had been like other men. Oh, he had been granted the gift of tongues, and the making of music too. Above all, he had had the power, but in the Welshlands that was nothing strange.

The power had been with him from childhood, when his Pendragon mother taught him all the magic that she knew. Then as a man he became a mighty bard and in the end a Druid of the seventh seal, one of the lords of light, the masters of the earth. Yet even then he had been like other men.

But one by one the ropes had frayed that bound him to this world. All his male kin except Uther were lost in a great battle, butchered one by one when the power failed him, and he could not turn the tide. Not a man was left standing on all that field of blood, and he had to watch them all slaughtered, one by one. After that he ran mad, harping from high hills and singing to the stars.

So he took a young wife, to bind him to the earth. He loved her, and she had given him a son. But his wife had caught a fever that made her as mad as he was, and burned up her sweet body to a crisp.

When she died, she took their son with her to the Otherworld, because she loved him far too much to leave him behind. Then Uther, his great kinsman, as big as a bear and as brave and beautiful, he had wasted too and died, though Merlin had used all the power he had to hold the life in him for days afterwards, and even made him move and speak and cry out too.

And then they were all gone, and he was driven from Caerleon, hunted like an animal, till he became one too. And it was then, when he lay buried in the deepest part of the forest, huddled in a black cave in the heart of the living rock, that she first came to him. A night-riding beauty, a princess of the air. A spirit for sure, but his body felt her flesh and knew it, his ancient organs trembled under her fingers, her touch brought back his fire.

Since that first time, she had come again and again. Always in the spring, though she came at other times too. Sometimes she came as a pure young virgin with a lascivious sideways glance above a starched white collar and a forget-me-not blue gown.

Most often she was a wanton woman, who lured him to

make free with her, then scorned and derided and punished his withered flesh. Sometimes she was a haughty matron, and he had to take down her arrogance, and the pleasure then was in her pain, not his. She had even been an old woman with soft, loose, crumpled flesh, well worn in the ways of love, and none the worse for that.

But always she came to him out of the darkness of his lust and desire and despair and fear of death. Indeed, she brought the darkness, she was the darkness, and always she left him in a worse darkness than before.

Yet still he craved her coming, and was powerless when she came. He knew the price of pleasure was a blindness that prevented him from seeing what he should, when he was in the grip of it as he was now.

'Gods above, I beg you, let me be free!'

He cried out, and opened his eyes. Above him on the bed rode a woman with a fox's head and bared white gleaming fangs, and instead of nipples, burning orange eyes. Her white hands ended in claws as red as blood, and her feet had claws too, tearing the flesh of his legs as she straddled his groaning pelvis, gripping his hollow flanks with her iron knees, digging the spurs of her claws into his bleeding thighs.

He cried out for mercy and she laughed aloud, he screamed and she rode him harder, he begged for relief and she pulled herself off him to leave him raw and unsatisfied, laughing at his throbbing misery now a hundred times worse than before. He could not reach his suffering to relieve it, for she had tied his hands. He could not escape, for his feet were bound too.

And only she could release him from her poison, touch him and stroke him with her hands or breasts or belly till the release came that would leave him humbled, clear and chastened – until she came again.

He could feel his whole being bursting towards this point. How long would she hold him here, condemned to bear the painful standing of his juddering flesh – hours, days, weeks?

He shook his head frenziedly as the darkness gathered once more. There was still something he should think of, something he had to do.

Something about Arthur in Caerleon – about the Summer Country, and the queen-making there—

Something he must see to, take care of, before he could enjoy—

He gathered all his fading mental forces for a final act of will. One more visit to the Summer Country. One brief effort to send forth his spirit shape to do what it must. And then he could embrace the darkness, go with her where she would.

Then he could take this beauty with her pulsing lips and all-devouring mouth. Or be taken by her till the darkness drowned him at last, drowned her, drowned all of them.

CHAPTER 12

*G*oddess, Mother, tell me, will he come?

He came at midnight, stooping through the hangings, his dark-dyed robes sweeping the ground. Behind him the moonlight glimmered on the black sheen of low-lying distant waters, and further off still lay the cloudy shape of Avalon, framed in its inland sea. His thick hair was bound back, Druid-fashion, and his white skin and blue eyes shone with unnatural brightness in the candlelight.

Guenevere stepped towards him, her heart in her mouth.

Cormac, Cormac—

When had she first noticed him? She did not know. He had been there all through her childhood, a lanky youth too old to play, yet always patient with a little girl. She was there as he grew to manhood, learning the mastery of horses and men. When he proved a ferocious fighter, she was first among the maidens who crowded round to applaud. Like his boyhood friend Lucan, he seemed destined to challenge for the title of Queen's champion when the time came.

But then he took to walking in the woods, and it was whispered that his spirit was turning away from war. At court he shunned the feasts, and would not dance when the minstrels played. He was seen haunting the Stone Circle, the great temple of the Mother, seeking Her aid. At last he vowed himself to Her to serve life, not war and death. Now he was foremost among the young bards in the College of Druids where Taliesin was chief. And Guenevere had looked at him, and dreamed of him, for many weary months.

'Lord Cormac, you are welcome.'

'Good evening, lady.'

His sombre face softened as he came in. In his hand he carried a small silver lyre inlaid with gold. Her joy at seeing him vanished at once. Did he think she had sent for him to sing a lullaby?

She had forgotten he could see into her mind. 'You do not wish for music?' he said sharply. 'How can I serve you, then?'

Guenevere pulled herself up. 'I need your counsel. Tomorrow I fear my kinsman Malgaunt plans to tell the people that I cannot rule alone, that he will try to overthrow me, or install himself beside me on the throne.'

'So—' He broke off, his face alive with thought. 'And your father?'

She laughed bitterly. 'My father sees the future in Malgaunt, and the rule of the Mother as passing from us now.'

His eyes sought hers with burning urgency. 'Tell me, then, where do you stand?'

The blood rushed to her face. 'I stand on my right! I am Queen here, by due descent. And all true men should love and serve me now!'

He gave an unexpected laugh. 'Oh, they will, lady, they will!'

She was suddenly, foolishly happy. 'Will they?'

'You are our Queen! And for tomorrow – listen!'

He strode to the entrance of the tent, and threw back the

hangings at the door. From the warm, spark-filled darkness, low groans of joy, small cries and whispers, and noises of content floated through the fiery air. The night was full of acts of love and worship, the joy of bodies doing the Goddess's will.

Guenevere felt herself grow hot. Cormac lowered the door-covering and looked at her, a smile of great sweetness on his lips.

'It is good to celebrate the life the Goddess gives,' he said gently. 'These are your people, lady, and there lies your right. Tomorrow when their desires are sated and their love-duty done, they will raise you to the Stone of Queens. Prince Malgaunt must present you, according to custom, as the Queen's blood kin. And Taliesin and all the servants of the Great Ones will be there to confirm you in your place. What is there to fear?'

'My father says that I must have a champion.'

Again his burning eyes were fixed on hers. 'Lady, you will never lack a champion.'

'But tomorrow,' she persisted. 'Who will stand for me tomorrow?'

He smiled again. 'Why, so will I, and so will Taliesin and all your men. We live only to see you enthroned.'

'You,' she said, trembling, 'would you champion me?'

'I have said so.'

A sudden joy was singing in her veins. 'Then I call on you, Cormac, for I need you now.'

He gasped. 'What?'

'If Malgaunt moves against me, I want you to fight for me, and help me to the throne.'

He was very pale. 'I have given up the way of death.'

'But you would take up your sword again if danger threatened something you held dear?'

'I – I would.'

'But not for me?'

'Lady!' He threw back his head in pain. 'You need a warrior, not a poet and a dream-weaver!'

He moved away, and began roaming round the tent. 'In times gone by, the finest flower of our young men was sacrificed for the life of the tribe, hung on the tree till the third day when the heavens opened for them, and the sky turned black. Today we believe in a faith of love, not killing, of life, not suffering and death. So now, those who hope for the highest must sacrifice themselves, and give their lives to the Goddess. I have made that vow. I have sworn to make the journey to the Island of the West, and live there in holy worship of the Great One all my days.'

She knew she must not weep. 'And tomorrow?'

'Tomorrow you will have many knights. Choose one of them, and leave your bards to serve you as they can.' He reached for his harp and bowed as if to go.

Guenevere could not bear it. 'So you abandon me to Malgaunt? You throw me to the wolf?' Her resolution crumbled, and the hot tears flowed like rain.

At once he was by her side. 'Lady Guenevere,' he said urgently, 'what do you fear?'

His robes were heady with incense, and his body was very close. *Oh, why does he not take me in his arms?*

'Tomorrow is nothing,' she moaned. 'We will live long after tomorrow. I am young and unpartnered, and I need your love!'

He recoiled, his eyes wide with shock. 'All this has been too much for a young girl,' he said slowly. 'You are still in grief, Lady Guenevere, you do not know what you say.'

'Goddess, Mother!' she wept. 'When will men see I am a woman grown, Queen of my country, and of my body too?' She turned to him. 'I know what I am doing, don't you see?'

'But – why do you choose me?'

She seized his hand and looked deep into his eyes. The blood rushed to her head, and she felt herself grow strong. 'Lord Cormac, I have loved you all my life. Be my champion now, and I will call you to the fires before all the folk tonight. I will take you as my King and consort, I will make you the father of my daughter, I will not change you for a new champion but love you always!'

His face was glistening with pain. 'Oh, lady, lady,' he groaned, 'truly those who made you made you lovely among women. Whoever shaped your flesh was a master of his art.'

He reached up to touch a strand of her hair. 'The Gods made this from moonbeams,' he said, with a breaking sigh, 'and the evening star put the light in your eyes.' Like a man in a dream he moved his hands down her body. 'Oh, you are ripe for love! And you would grace the life of any man.'

For a long moment he held her like a lover, then pushed her away. 'Oh, Gods, you torture me – how have I sinned?'

He was weeping now like a warrior, denying the grief. 'I cannot break the vow that I have sworn! I cannot choose you above the Mother, for Her anger would kill us both.'

He made a faint farewell. 'I will not say forgive me. But when your champion comes, let him help you to forget.' With a last glance, he stepped weeping into the night.

The night was very long. But she was ready when they came for her, ready for Malgaunt, ready to be Queen. She had dressed with care in a fine gown of poppy red, and a cloak of cloth of gold from out of the East – the people should see her, even from the furthest hill. At her neck she wore a gold collar studded with rubies, glowing with deep fire. The Queen's women – still she could not think of them as hers – had treated her face with the Queen's colours and rubbed her temples with sweet patchouli to calm her nerves. Now her lips were as red as her gown, her skin glowed, and no trace of last night's weeping marked her eyes.

The chief of the women deftly dressed her hair and fixed in place the Queen's gold diadem, its great pendant moonstones encircling her brows. 'There, my lady!' she said proudly, holding up the mirror.

Guenevere looked, and hardly recognised what she saw. The face that looked back at her was both older now and harder, the cheekbones high and unyielding, the dark-eyed stare that of a woman who, if she could not have what she wanted, was determined to take what she could get.

It was the look of a queen.

Queen Guenevere.

Trembling before the mirror, she swore in the darkness of her soul that it would be so.

They came for her as the sun soared in the heavens, pouring down rays of gold from a clear blue sky. As she stepped out of the Queen's pavilion, Malgaunt was the first to meet her eye. 'Good greetings, Guenevere.' He smiled. 'We come to call you to the Hill.'

Guenevere's gorge rose. Yet he looked no different from her father, Lucan or Taliesin, all finely arrayed and armed to the hilt. Where were the signs of treachery? What was brewing in Malgaunt's subtle mind?

Even in daylight the Hill of Queens still basked in the warmth of last night's feasting, wearing the smiling face of a woman who has been well pleasured, and looks for more. They climbed the hill through the great crowds of sated onlookers, past the still-smouldering fires and flattened beds of bracken, over the shining grass. Lucan led the way with a troop of the Queen's knights, and the Queen's women and attendants brought up the rear.

As they mounted, the crowds thinned out towards the top. Below them lay the Summer Country, ageless in beauty, drowsing under the kiss of the sun. Guenevere looked down on the vast primeval forests crossed by their ancient greenways, hidden tracks made by the Old Ones long before the Romans came to make roads. Across the flat-lands wandered countless little farmsteads, each with its wattle pens, bee-hives and chicken runs, and a cherished pig or cow. The silver streams wound in and out of dark, brooding pools, and the rivers fed green-black lakes gleaming like glass. All along the riversides were groves of creamy hawthorn, and weeping willows trailing their fingers in the water like lovesick girls.

At the top of the hill stood the great Stone Circle, and at its centre a massive square of black rock as tall as a man. Once a queen was raised up there before all the people, she would rule the Summer Country till her dying day.

In front of the Queen Stone stood a carved wooden throne plated with bronze, glittering in the sun. On its high back were scenes depicting the Great Mother inviting all to drink from her loving cup, feeding the hungry from her dish of plenty, succouring the weak with her sword of power and spear of defence. They were the sacred relics of Goddess worship since time began. Guenevere's heart leaped as Taliesin led her towards it through the throng. *Goddess, Mother, make me worthy of this place!*

But the mere sight of Malgaunt taking his seat was a sick reminder of how far it still was from hers. And all around him were those who could block her path to the throne, the people of the Summer Country from high and low. In the first ranks sat rows of the greatest lords and knights, their velvet robes, gold collars and sleek silver mail proclaiming their status to the world. Behind them were the strangers she had first seen yesterday, short, sturdy, warlike men in rough pelts and furs, their swords lying ready on their knees as they watched the proceedings with fierce unblinking stares. They were the chiefs of the Land Kin, the dwellers in these islands from ancient days. These were the men, King Leogrance had said, who would not make her Queen unless she could give them a champion and war-leader too.

Guenevere looked around. In the centre of the seats facing the throne Malgaunt, King Leogrance and Lucan were plain to see. Shadowed by the Queen Stone, Cormac stood ready in front of a band of dark-clad Druids, holding his harp. His drawn face showed that he had slept no better than Guenevere last night. But his haunted gaze never once turned her way.

Now a trumpet called for attention, silencing the crowd. A cry rang through the hushed assembly till it echoed round the hills: 'Hear me! And through me, hear the words of Her I serve!'

Taliesin stepped forward from the shadow of the Queen Stone, his pale face blazing, his eyes in a trance. On his head he wore the priestly crown of gold, and his long robe flashed with discs of gold that sang sweetly as he moved. His voice echoed through the standing stones. 'Great Goddess, Mother of us all, bless this new Queen. Raise her up to the Queen Stone, and honour her as the leader we now choose!'

Behind Taliesin, the massed ranks of Druids swelled his prayers with a deep, heartfelt chant. The cry passed to the people as more and more voices took up the call.

The day wore on. As Guenevere watched and listened, the power of the ritual stole over her, and her dread began to fade. Lulled by the chanting, cocooned by the warm air, she fell into a trance. Now she could hear the secret music at the heart of things, and feel the breath of the mystery brushing against her cheek. Her senses swam in a pearly light like Avalon, and a great sweetness filled the air.

Suddenly she was touching the world between the worlds. Somewhere near, she knew, her mother's spirit was passing among the stars. *What is there to fear?* Cormac had said. Resting her back against the throne, feeling the weight of the Queen's diadem, Guenevere dared to believe that it might be so.

Taliesin was coming to the end of his song. 'I am old, I am young, I am dead, I am alive, I am Taliesin!' he cried. 'From the cold, from the fire, from the land of the dead, from the world-to-be, I bring you your Queen!'

'So be it!' came Cormac's strong response.

'So be it, so be it, *so be it!*'

The chanting of the Druids and the cry of the harps were blending now with the rising of the wind and the sinking of the sun in the sky.

'Here is your Queen!' Taliesin cried to the echoing hills. 'I call on the Queen's kinsman to bring her to the Stone.'

Malgaunt rose from his seat and moved to stand before the throne. 'Hear me, people of the Summer Country!' he cried, pitching his voice to the far rolling hills. 'I come to bring you Guenevere. She is your true ruler by descent, and we are here to make her our Queen.'

I come to bring you Guenevere . . .

She wanted to laugh, to weep, to break into a dance. How she had wronged Malgaunt! All along he meant to give her the people, as he knew he should. He was going to make her Queen!

She stumbled to her feet and tried to speak. 'Good people—' But her voice failed in a rush of happy tears.

And Malgaunt was still calling to the crowd. 'You all know that war threatens us now. So I pledge myself to you as the Queen's companion in arms, her war-leader and champion, to guide and direct her through what lies ahead. Take me when you take her, make me her consort, and I dedicate my life to her service – and yours!'

With a triumphant cry he tore off his mailed gauntlet and threw it at Guenevere's feet. Then he turned on her, smiling his whitest smile. 'So, Guenevere, what is it to be?'

CHAPTER 13

Already the cheers were roaring through the crowd. Guenevere was faint with fear and anger, gasping for breath. 'You cannot – dare not do this! I will denounce you – I will refuse!'

'You may not refuse.' Malgaunt did not even look at her as, wreathed in smiles, he raised his arms and stepped forward to acknowledge the applause. 'Thank you, my good people!' he bellowed jovially. 'My dearest thanks to you!'

His good people?

A voice Guenevere did not know tore from her throat: 'Father!'

So Malgaunt thought he was the only one who could present the new Queen? But a father was a kinsman too, his voice would serve! 'King Leogrance!' she called. 'Father, propose me now!'

From the ranks massed round the throne, King Leogrance rose to his feet. As he stood up, the whole assembly quietened to hear what he had to say.

And there it was. Dully she shook her head. *No, Father, no!*

'Guenevere must take a champion for the sake of the country. And who better than her kinsman Malgaunt?'

Oh, Father, Father, where is the man my mother loved?

'Malgaunt then has my voice. With Malgaunt as her champion—'

She felt sick with dread. Suddenly there was a furious flurry at her side.

'Malgaunt for champion? Never!' Lucan's howl of fury was ringing round the hillside. 'The Queen's champion stands here!'

Malgaunt's eyes bulged with shock. 'What, Sir Lucan?' he snarled. 'Do you dare to challenge me now?'

'Dare?' scoffed Lucan, grabbing for his sword. 'I dare, Prince Malgaunt, any time you choose!'

'Hear me, profaners of our ritual!' Taliesin's rage blasted them like a winter storm. 'Do you forget, lords, why we are here? This is Beltain, when we bring back the God! We shall invoke his presence now, at once. When the God comes, we shall settle your dispute!'

Guenevere closed her eyes. Oh, it was loyal of Taliesin to buy time like this! But he could only put off her defeat. And what good could it do, deferring the evil hour? She clasped her hands in prayer. *Goddess, Mother, help me now—*

And the answer came.

The Land Kin – if I can make them mine, they will make me Queen.

'Sirs!' She turned to the dark-faced chiefs. 'Hear me!' she cried.

The leader rose to his feet. 'You are the Throne Woman,' he said, in the rough tongue of the Old Ones. 'What is your will?'

'Go!' Guenevere urged him furiously, tears in her eyes. 'Go to your people, bid them enthrone me now! Say I will not leave them undefended if war comes. But I will choose my own champion, as a queen should – by the laws of the Mother and the ancient freedoms of this land!'

The chief inclined his head, and his men rose to their feet. 'We go.'

Malgaunt stepped forward, laughing in his throat. 'They will not save you, Guenevere. In other times, they would cling to the old ways. But now they want a warrior, not an untried girl. And as your champion,' his teeth flashed in a venomous grin, 'I can wait, my dear.'

And so they waited as the golden day faded, and the fires of evening sprang up all around.

'Great Bel, golden God, Lord of the Fires, Son of Heaven, Only Beloved of the Mother, come to us now . . .'

In the shadow of the Queen Stone, Taliesin had returned to his prayers. The sacred smoke rose in blue and purple gusts as he began the ceremony to draw down the God to earth. Outside the circle of the stones, the people were clapping and singing, some dancing, some threading the sacred fires. Already the bolder women were approaching their chosen men, and the sounds and scents of earth magic hung heavy in the air.

Time passed without a trace. The low chanting of the Druids lingered in the gold and rosy dusk. Without warning an attendant appeared at Guenevere's side. 'A stranger bard has come to honour our feast, he says,' he declared. 'Will you hear him?'

Guenevere hardly cared if the standing stones themselves had offered to dance a jig. 'Admit him,' she said monotonously. 'Let him sing his song.'

Into the firelight came a tiny boy carrying a harp as tall as himself. Leaning on the child's shoulder, the aged bard walked behind, moving with blind deliberation, using the boy for his eyes. He was richly clad in a long green velvet robe, its silken sleeves brushing the ground. On his head he wore a tall bardic headdress over his long grey locks, and beneath the hair matted on his forehead, one yellow eye stared blankly out. As he took up his place at the centre of the arena, his sightless gaze swept the assembly and, to Guenevere's troubled mind, seemed to fasten on her like a hawk.

But soon she found where his real interest lay. Taking his harp from the boy, the bard struck a loud chord, and began.

'Lords, knights, chieftains, I sing of a hero and a man of might!' came the rhythmic, wailing cry. 'The Gods themselves will set him at the right hand of Queen Guenevere, to guide her to destined things!'

Malgaunt! The bard was promoting Malgaunt against her! *Seize this old villain, silence his song, and cast him where no man ever sings!* her soul cried out. But it was too late to stop his tribute now.

Across the grass she could see Malgaunt frozen with delight at his good luck. Could he have sent for the bard, she wondered frantically, ordered his attendance, commanded this song of praise?

No, it was impossible – bards were Druids, they served the Great Ones, and their voices were not for hire. Had this bard, then, seen something in the stars that foretold Malgaunt's success? If he had, she was defeated, and might as well yield now.

She could have moaned aloud. *Goddess, Mother, what wrong have I done? Why do you punish me now?*

And still the chant went on. 'Prince Malgaunt is the hero of my song. He will rule this land, he will reign for many generations as the Queen's consort and her Chosen One. He will be lord of many battles and father of many children, he will live through war and death, and die at peace in his bed. He will be King, when all men raise him now!'

Already the word was passing among the people, racing down the hillside from fire to fire. 'Malgaunt for champion, Malgaunt for King!' And now the chieftains were returning through the gathering dark, bearing the verdict of their folk – would they say the same?

Taliesin stepped towards them. 'What news?' he cried.

'We took the word of the Throne Woman to our people,' called the chief, 'and we bring their answer now.'

'Say on!'

The chief paused. 'They say, "We will take the Lady Guenevere as our Queen."'

So!

Guenevere's heart burst with joy. She had triumphed, she had—

'We will take her with the champion, who has come forward for her, now, here, tonight. We take Prince Malgaunt to be her lord and consort – now, here, tonight!'

At last!

Ohh, it was sweet—

So sweet—

Malgaunt let out his breath in a long hiss of joy. Taliesin stood motionless, and Lucan screamed and beat his head with his hands. The fiery twilight spread across the hills, and a great darkness settled on Guenevere.

'Goddess, Mother, call down the Lord of Gold! Show us your sign, before we raise up the Queen!'

It was Taliesin, making one last attempt to hold back Malgaunt's triumph, and save her from her fate. At the altar, eyes closed and head thrown back, his face upturned to the full moon, the chief Druid was praying as he had never prayed in his life.

'The God, Great Mother! Give us the God! Bring down the Lord of Gold!'

All the crowd was hushed by his terrible cry. The wind was rising in the brightness of the dark, passing softly between the standing stones. Behind Guenevere rose the voices of the Druids, 'Come to us, Lord of Gold, great Bel, come!'

'Come, come!'

From the hillside a thousand voices echoed the call, their yearning cries drowned by the howling wind.

'Come!'

'Come!'

'*Come!*'

A wild scream pierced the darkness at the foot of the hill.

'He comes! He comes!'

Outlined against a camp-fire, one of the women of the Land Kin stood pointing into the darkness, her voice shrill with terror and joy. 'There!'

'There!'

The groups around the fires broke and scattered in dread. A howling clamour swelled up through the night, 'The God is here!'

'He comes!'

'The God comes!'

A crowd had gathered round the unseen thing. Now the whole group was surging up the hill. Inside the Stone Circle Guenevere rose to her feet, craning forward, eyes straining to penetrate the dark. A wild hope knocked at her heart – *could it be?*

And suddenly there it was, a massive shape in the midst of the swirling mob. Broader than a bear, taller than a man, it towered head and shoulders above the rest.

'He comes! He comes!' The wailing intensified.

Fear gripped Guenevere, but a mad excitement too.

Who was coming?
The God?
Could it be the Golden Lord Himself?

She covered her eyes, then forced herself to look. A huge bear-like figure, armoured in gold from head to foot, was making his way through the crowd. Behind him were three others, lesser Gods in gold and silver too, coming up the hill. The leader was covering the ground with mighty strides, forging through the camp-fires in his way, scattering sparks as he went.

The crowd howled in ecstasy, their cries filling the air. And on he came cresting the flames, fire on his golden helmet, fire on his breastplate, sparks of fire on his spurs and thighs, flashing through the dark. He swam towards her, armoured and helmeted, a creature with no face, as she stood breathless, almost lifeless, waiting for him. In the silence at the heart of the clamour, she heard her mother's voice: *He is coming – through the fires he comes.*

'The God!' howled the people, and the whole hillside shook. 'The God! Bel comes!'

Opposite her Malgaunt stood frozen in rage and dread, his face grey-green in the fire's red light. King Leogrance stood as still as the standing stones, Lucan beside him staring like a child.

Now the noise was deafening, rending the night sky. Then a deeper cry rang out above it all. 'The God! The God! Bel has come to champion the Queen!'

Leaping to the centre of the arena, Cormac threw his voice to the furthest hills. 'Hear me! You wished for a champion for the Queen, and lo, here he comes! You called him forth, and he has come to her!'

What?

Malgaunt's head snapped back, and his lips parted in a wordless snarl.

'Stop him – stop Cormac!' But the moment had passed.

'The God comes!' ran like wildfire through the crowd. 'The Queen has a champion. Bring her to the Stone!'

Guenevere stood quite still. The gold-clad stranger entered the ring around the Stone Circle and made straight for her.

'Raise the Queen to the Stone!'

For one long moment the newcomer faced her, his gold and silver knights on either side.

Then the strong mailed hands of his knights were gripping her by the elbows, and she was lifted above their heads on to the top of the great stone. As her feet found a purchase she steadied herself, then turned to face the people. Gripping the edges of her golden cloak she raised her arms like wings, offering herself to the land, to the night, to the Gods, and the Goddess of them all. There was a groan from the hillside like the shrieking of the earth: 'The Queen! The Queen! Guenevere the Queen!'

Below her she could see Malgaunt, white with the shock of defeat. Beside him Lucan fell to his knees, his eyes raised in adoration, his hand on his heart.

But nearest of all was the unknown stranger, the lord of gold. His three knights converged on their leader and vaulted him up to the Queen Stone at her side.

Guenevere faced her saviour. 'Who are you?'

He knelt before her, and took her hand in his gold-mailed fist. Reverently he touched it to his forehead, then brought it to his helmet's cold metallic lips. Then he clenched his fist, and placed it on his heart. I am your champion, his actions said. Your champion and your servant, for as long as I live.

Half mad with fear and joy, she leaned down to him: *'Who are you?'*

The gold-clad figure shook his armoured head. But from

somewhere within the helmet came the soft chuckle of a man. Guenevere closed her eyes. And through the falling air, her mother spoke for the last time: '. . . *through the fires he comes.*'

CHAPTER 14

High overhead, birds wheeled and sang in the cloudless sky. Beside the track, yellow coltsfoot and white moon-daisies tossed in the passing breeze, and all around them the grasslands rolled away like a green sea. Now they were coming to the outskirts of the forest, passing under the shadow of the trees, the horses picking their way delicately through the pale pools of sunlight on the leafy floor. The woodland lay hushed and dreaming as it welcomed them in.

Guenevere fixed her eyes on the cool green shade ahead, and tried not to look at the man riding by her side. Tall and broad-shouldered, he handled his horse with the air of one born to master his world and all the creatures in it. Beneath his armour he wore a royal tunic of glossy red silk edged with gold, and loose breeches of fine wool. His leather belt was inset with gold, and at his side hung a sword of kingly magnificence and a dagger inlaid with gold dragons chasing each other down the blade.

In front of them rode a band of knights, behind came a troop of marching men. At the head of the procession a red dragon fluttered on the stranger's banner, bold against a background of pure white. His wrists were blue with tattoos of twin dragons locked in fight, half concealed by

wristlets of heavy gold. And Guenevere was still wearing
her coronation dress of yesterday, and furiously wishing
that she had something else. For she was Queen Guenevere
now, riding back to Camelot with a guest of equal royalty – Arthur, High King of Britain, for so he said he
was.

Queen Guenevere, and every inch a queen, both queen and
woman, the woman of the dream—

Arthur made himself sit his horse quietly, holding the
reins loosely so that the horse did not feel the trembling of
his hands. He knew that he was holding his breath, and
schooled himself to try to breathe normally.

Queen Guenevere—

Guenevere my love—

He dared not look at her. But now he knew what force
had drawn him here, against reason, against all sense. Only
days ago he had been fighting in Caerleon against enemies
on all sides. Yet here he was, riding out on a May morning
in search of love.

No, not love, that was not it, he told himself, trying to
order his thoughts. He had come to find Merlin, because he
needed his mentor now. He had pardoned the six kings, and
sent them away, sparing all their lives. And that, as Gawain
had forcibly reminded him, was to have turned loose an
angry wounded beast, hungry for revenge. They would be
sure to come again. Soon he would face the greatest battle
of his life.

But where was Merlin?

Merlin had come here.

I have gone to the Summer Country, his letter had said,
to secure our borders there. But if a treaty was to be made,
and this was Kay's sharp contribution to the debate, then
as King, Arthur should be there too. What could be more

important than good relations with his kingdom's nearest neighbour and potential ally, even friend?

Determinedly Arthur had turned his mind to the objectives to be achieved. And, equally determinedly, he had closed his mind to the dream he had had the night before he came – of an unknown woman, never seen before but recognised on sight, her form veiled in a cloud of bright hair, her eyes the eyes he had only seen in dreams.

Who was he?

Whoever he was, Guenevere owed him her throne.

For the stranger's appearance, armoured in gold from head to foot, had swayed the people to her side. All night she had sat enthroned with her new champion, while all came to swear their allegiance to her. Only Malgaunt held aloof, pale-mouthed with fury, but powerless to resist.

Behind them the three stranger knights stood on guard, living statues of gold and silver in the dancing light. Outside the ring of stones, the Beltain bonfires made night into day. The hill was alive with drumming and dancing, feasting and drinking and joy without end. All night long the cries and moans of lovers filled the darkness as maids and wives called their chosen ones aside into warm beds of bracken, to honour the Goddess with the gift She gives.

At last the sky lightened in the east, and Guenevere felt the wind of dawn. A thought stole through her mind: *The Gods of night are never seen by day.* As if he heard her, Guenevere's faceless champion rose to his feet. With one mailed hand he signalled his knights, with the other he raised her up and led her from the Stone Circle, downhill and away.

At the foot of the hill, his banner fluttered in the air, flaunting his huge red dragon to the skies. Around it clustered a train of knights and soldiers, serving men and maids, dogs and horses, pack mules, boxes and chests. The rising sun lit the whole world with gold, but brighter still were the waiting faces when they saw their lord.

Beside the road the three companion knights were ready with a troop of horses. Gravely Guenevere's unknown saviour helped her to mount a pearl-white mare, then swung himself up on a stallion of royal height. Seizing his reins, he turned the horse's head towards Camelot, pushing up the all-concealing visor of his helmet at last. And only then did she see his face.

'Who are you?'

It was the question that had haunted her all night. She could still feel the shock that had run through her when he first took her hand, the burning where his hands had circled her waist as he helped her to mount. And then the first sight of him, as he looked into her eyes.

Who was he?

She tried to read his face as she waited for him to speak. Bright and open, it glowed with youth and trust, high ambition and the will to change the world. His thick fair hair was tousled now that he had taken off his helmet, but still he had the natural dignity of the finest lord. His grey eyes held a visionary gleam, and an age-old sense of the sadness of the world.

He looked to be in his twenties, no more than a few years older than she was. Yet he wore signs of sharp experience too, and an air of hard-won authority beyond his years. There was a weary set to his shoulders, and deep lines of resolution round his mouth. The same look could be seen on the faces of his knights, she thought, all men newly battle-scarred, hard and wary, with hands never far from their swords.

He turned his clear gaze on her, and something shifted around her heart.

'Who am I?' The strong fair head went up. 'I am Arthur, son of King Uther of the House of Pendragon, Lord of the Middle Kingdom and her City of Legions, born to be High King of Britain and Dragon King of these isles.' He paused, then gave her a light smile. 'Or so the Lord Merlin insists that I am called.'

Guenevere found herself oddly annoyed. 'Why does your Druid tell you what to say?'

'Because only he can tell me who I am,' Arthur replied. 'He took me from my mother when I was born, and had me brought up in secret by a knight of the King of Gore.'

'He took you from your mother? Why?'

'It was all to make me King when the time came. Merlin helped my father to win my mother's love, and in return, Merlin demanded me.'

Guenevere gasped. 'Merlin told you this?'

'And more.' He took off his gauntlet, clenching and flexing his fist so that the tattooed dragons fought and snarled around his wrist. 'He showed me that I bear the mark of kings. These signs denote the House of Pendragon. Indeed Lord Merlin bears them himself, for he claims kin to my father on the female side. I have borne these tattoos all my life, and never knew before now what they meant.'

Pendragon.

I am one of the House of Pendragon.

Arthur paused. Could any listener, even this queen hanging on his every word, understand what this meant for him, after a lifetime as the boy with no name? Doggedly he went on, 'Those who fought with my father say that he was a lion. But I think of him as a dragon, and this was his sign.' He smiled, but there was a question in his eyes: *Is this foolish? I beg you, do not think I am a fool.*

Guenevere felt a pain that she could not name. And suddenly, behind the great bear-like figure at her side, she saw the spirit shadow of another king, older and greater, more luminous, yet bathed in dying light.

His father?

Or Arthur himself, as he was to be?

Who are you? her soul cried to him again. Yet if what he said was true, how could he know?

She made herself try again. 'We heard that Merlin proclaimed you in London. They called you Merlin's boy.' She found herself colouring to remember Malgaunt's taunts. 'How old are you?'

He smiled, but his colour rose a little too. 'Older than I look,' he said quietly. 'And older than you are, Queen Guenevere, as I hear.'

She felt herself grow hot, and hurried to change the subject. 'When Merlin proclaimed you—'

'Yes?' He laughed, a young and happy sound.

'He told you that you were the chosen ruler of the kingdom, born to be King?'

His face was shining with conviction. 'He did.'

'How did he prove it?'

Arthur's eyes glowed. 'He said that I would draw the sword out of the stone before all the people, and foretold that they would make me King.'

'But how did you do that?'

Arthur burst out into open, boyish mirth. 'Why, when I was a boy, we did it all the time! We tried our weapons out on everything, on rocks and stones and trees!'

'What?' She did not understand.

'To test them for battle,' Arthur explained. 'Swords have to hack through armour, and split helmets like rotten apples – and heads too!'

'But this sword, this stone?'

Arthur fixed her with his large, honest eyes. 'There is a knack to it, finding the vein of weakness, sinking the sword into the stone in a way that only you can know. I had put the sword in the stone among many tests of strength, so of course I could draw it out. Merlin says that my father often made such proofs of his prowess.'

Merlin said, Merlin says. 'What else did Merlin say?'

If Arthur heard the sharp note in her voice, he gave no sign. 'He said that we should march at once on the Middle Kingdom,' he replied. 'He foretold that we should take Caerleon, and we did. He has also promised to bring the leader of the Christians to crown me there.'

Guenevere started, and a shadow fell across her path. 'Merlin wants you to have a Christian coronation?'

Arthur turned his fearless gaze on her. 'Yes,' he murmured. 'Is that wrong?'

'I fear the Christians,' Guenevere said hotly. 'They hate the Great Mother, and religion should be love!'

'Yet they love their own Lady, the Mother of their Christ.'

'All the worse that they put down the Goddess, and destroy Her worship among our people!'

'Yes, the people,' said Arthur thoughtfully. 'Do you not think that the faith of Christ may be good for them, and easy to understand? One life, one salvation, one God?'

'What is hard about the love of our Mother?'

'Ah, lady,' he said slowly, 'where I grew up, the rule of the Goddess has passed away. We cannot make enemies of the Christians, Merlin says. I shall need their help in establishing my rule.'

Did Merlin make all the plans, Guenevere wondered, with another spurt of annoyance. Yet Arthur did not look like any man's puppet. She was at a loss. 'Why have you come here?'

'Your country is my country's nearest neighbour. My first concern must be alliance with you.'

'And mine with you.' Guenevere smiled at him more sweetly than she knew. 'I will always be in your debt. Your arrival came most luckily for me.'

'It was an honour, madam, to be the man who raised you to the Queen Stone!' he said fervently. 'I only hope your kinsman Malgaunt is not angry with me for usurping his role!'

Malgaunt angry, defeated and pushed aside? Guenevere savoured the thought. 'It is true,' she said carefully, keeping her face straight, 'that Malgaunt did not expect you to be here. He did not think you would win back your lands. He was sure that all the petty kings and lords who carved up your kingdom would band together to drive you out.'

Arthur took a breath. 'And so they did,' he said heavily. 'Oh, the common people rallied to me at once – they had not forgotten my father, who gave them peace and upheld the rule of law. And I had a small band of friends, who swore to follow me as soon as I was proclaimed.'

He broke off, and turned in the saddle to Gawain, Kay and Bedivere riding behind. 'Come, sirs!' he cried. 'Let me present you to the Queen!'

At once the three broke ranks, and rode up, Gawain in the lead. At last a chance to meet this gorgeous creature, the big knight thought excitedly, struggling to hold back the wrong response. Gods above, with that face, that hair – he dared not think that body – Arthur must go for her, or he had no blood in his veins! And if he did not, Gawain vowed, he'd be tempted to try for her himself.

'Gawain!' cried Arthur.

'My lord?' The big knight looked at Arthur with something close to love.

Guenevere smiled at Gawain, taking him in. As well built as Arthur, he rode with the same rough style, and his big beefy face was bright with the same hope.

'Sir Gawain was the first of all those in London to offer me his allegiance,' said Arthur fondly. 'I knighted him there and then, though he was young for the honour, because he left his lord to follow me. He was my first companion, and he swears he'll be the last.'

'Not if fate spares me!' came a tart interjection from the second knight. Guenevere turned her gaze. A sallow, sharp-faced man a few years older than Arthur, small and well shaped, he sat his horse like a knight, and held the reins in knowing, quiet hands.

'He rides well, no?' said Arthur merrily, following her gaze. 'But, then, Sir Kay had an excellent training in knighthood. I should know – I used to be his squire!'

Kay smiled uncomfortably. 'The King was brought up by my father,' he explained. 'We learned all our battle skills together from childhood on.' He gestured to Bedivere riding at his side. 'As this knight did too. He came to us from the Welshlands as a boy, also to undergo his knighthood training with my father.' Kay laughed ironically. 'Little did we know whose knights we would become!'

Bedivere smiled and nodded. Dark-haired and slight, he had the look of the Old Ones, Guenevere decided, like all those born on the Marches, that misty borderland between their world and ours.

'You are from the Welshlands?' she asked. Was he another of Merlin's changelings? Or was she seeing the hand of the old enchanter everywhere?

'Born just outside the Middle Kingdom, lady,' he replied. The lilt of his birthplace was unmistakable. So was the glance of devotion he turned towards Arthur as he spoke. 'They call me Bedivere, and I serve the King.'

'And these loyal souls were with me when we took Caerleon, against an alliance of six kings!' Arthur said.

'Six kings?' Guenevere said fearfully.

'Six,' he repeated sombrely, 'each with all his lords and knights, horses, weapons and men. All vassals of King Lot of Lothian and the Orkneys.'

'King Lot!' Guenevere shuddered. Only the invading Saxons, who crucified their captives, were crueller than this king. 'How did you prevail?'

'I hardly know. We were outnumbered a hundred and more to one. Merlin had read the skies, and saw a great victory written in the stars. He proclaimed in London that I would reclaim my right. But many there laughed at him as a dream-reader, and called me a fool. They had no thought that we might win.' His voice darkened. 'But at dead of night I and a hundred knights made a blind sally into the castle, and sent them running for their lives.'

As he spoke, a mist rose before Guenevere's eyes. Through the gathering gloom she could hear the thunder of horses' hoofs bearing down on sleeping troops, the screams of those awakened at sword-point, and the howls of dying men. Now the scene ran with blood and she saw a bleak dawn, and a lone figure weeping on a corpse-logged battle-field, with crows and ravens circling round his fair head.

She shivered through and through. Slowly Arthur's voice came back to her through the mist. 'So all six kings were defeated . . .'

'And were sent packing, leaving everything they had!' Gawain crowed. 'Horses, armour, even the finest weapons thrown down in the heat of the fight.'

Kay laughed. 'Bag and baggage too!'

So that was it, Guenevere smiled to herself. That was where all the finery had come from – the royal armour, the great swords and horses, probably even the tunic Arthur wore – they were all spoils of war, abandoned by fleeing kings! Well, now she knew how a boy from nowhere had made himself a King, how an unknown youth became a golden God.

Yet still he was a man, and a man above men, a man like no other, a man who—

Goddess, Mother, what was she thinking of?

Visions moved before her eyes. Guenevere gripped the reins, and forced herself to sit still. Slowly the swirling images faded into the air. What was happening? How did this Arthur have the power to stir the sight in her, moving her to thoughts she never chose to have?

All at once she could not look at the long, well-breeched leg lying along his horse's flank, the great size of him, the strong brown soldier's hands. 'One more question,' she said, suddenly conscious of a husk in her voice. 'What now?'

He made a graceful bow. 'Now I must come to you in state, and sue for the friendship of you and yours,' he said confidently. He paused, and his eyes met hers. 'I have good men,' he flashed a loving glance at his knights and the troop marching behind, 'but they need—' He broke off in sudden confusion. 'In truth, they and I both need – we need – I want—'

He stopped again and looked away, forcing a sudden laugh. 'Well, time enough for that.' He gave a signal, and Gawain, Kay and Bedivere fell behind.

'Camelot!' came the cry from the head of the line.

And suddenly Guenevere was as miserable as she had been happy before. The journey was ending, and they would never have this time again.

And there it was, the ancient citadel of queens, the precious stronghold of the Summer Country, looking as small as a child's castle in the valley below. It lay deep in its wide green hollow, its towers and battlements white in the golden sun, banners fluttering from every slender spire. Around it flowed a ring of bright water edged with reeds and marigolds.

Arthur did not try to hide his admiration. 'A fine place, Your Majesty.'

Guenevere smiled at him, delighted with his praise. But he was scanning the whole place systematically with a warrior's eye. 'When were you last attacked?' he asked casually.

'Attacked?'

His eyes continued their restless search. 'Where the castle sits, raised up on a walled mound in the valley, that's a good position. And your whole city below the castle is walled too. But all fortifications can be breached. I was wondering how easy it was to defend.'

Guenevere stared at the grim set of his jaw, and grew cold. Her rescuer, the High King, the golden God, might have won one battle, but he was still in danger of his life.

Oh, Arthur, Arthur—

Guenevere's heart quailed, and her soul cried out.

Arthur, you came to my aid when you cannot yet call any place your own. You spare time for me, when your own task looms so large that no ordinary man could face it alone. Widows and children are driven from your lands to seek refuge in ours. Your orphans hide in our forests, living on roots and acorns like wild swine. Your countrymen, brutally beaten, stumble across our borders, barefoot and bloodshod, only to die in the first kindly arms. And you have taken it on yourself to right these wrongs, when you do not know if you can sleep safely in your bed at night?

Her senses stirred as her mind wandered this way and that. *His bed at night—*

What was she thinking of?

She was trembling, her body burning, her face and hands like ice.

Goddess, Mother, help me now.

With an effort she forced her thoughts back into orderly grooves. Arthur was her guest. His bed tonight would be in Camelot, and there she would defend him from all foes. All Camelot would honour King Arthur, son of Uther Pendragon, as if he were High King of Britain now.

And these were her orders as they crossed the causeway and rode through the crowds of cheering townsfolk into Camelot. Dismounting at the gatehouse, they were offered water in jewelled goblets, and honeyed wine. 'Conduct King Arthur to the royal guest apartments,' she told the goggling servants, 'and see to it he has everything he needs.'

Arthur bowed. 'If it please Your Majesty, events are pressing in the Middle Kingdom, and I cannot be long away. When may I meet your council to propose our treaty and discuss our needs?'

Above his wide cheekbones, she saw now, great bruising shadows darkened his grey eyes. He looked sick with tension and fatigue. Guenevere nodded. 'I will command a general council at once.'

'My warmest thanks.' He bowed and turned to go, then turned back, frowning strangely.

Guenevere searched for words. 'So, when we meet, sir, you will tell us what you want?'

He fixed her with his clear gaze of command. 'Oh, I know that already,' he said calmly. 'I want you.'

CHAPTER 15

'Y ou and your force of arms.' Arthur's voice rang out round the Great Hall. 'My dearest wish is to come to terms with the Summer Country, and with all of you here.'

Seated on her throne, Guenevere listened impassively. *Is that all?* her heart cried. *Of course,* her reason chided harshly. *What else?*

Arthur paused and glanced around, feeling for a response. But the knights and lords of the council were stone-faced as he pressed on. 'I want you as our ally, and I ask for your military help against our joint enemies.' His voice echoed round the vast space to the vault above. 'I want a pledge of mutual aid against hostile attack, each to support the other in case of invasion or aggression, whatsoever it be.'

He was making a good impression, Guenevere noted, there was no doubt of that. Standing between her throne and the council table he looked entirely at ease, and his urgent sense of purpose filled the hall. His tall, powerful bulk put him head and shoulders above any man there except Sir Gawain at his side. And he was royally dressed in a blue tunic of fine velvet and kidskin breeches as soft as silk, with a gold fillet round his brows, and gold at his neck and wrists. But the kings who had lost all this finery must be planning a royal revenge. Arthur was well advised, Guenevere thought with a sudden chill, to make as many friends as he could.

The gifts he had brought would win hearts, she knew. Great plates and bowls of silver, and goblets and ewers of gold spilled from a chest borne in by four strong men. For the late Queen, now for Guenevere, he had brought a bolt of wild silk the colour of an April evening, and a crown of amethysts. From a pouch at his waist he drew out pearls and rubies, and a great tourmaline shining like a star veiled in a cloud. He cast them all before her feet, and the setting sun bathed every one in fire.

As he offered the gifts, the members of the council and the knights standing around were slowly weighing him up.

'The pledge of our aid?' demanded King Leogrance. 'A troop or two of our fighting men in time of need? Words and promises of good will? Is that your desire?'

Arthur bowed. 'It is.'

'Well, lords?' Guenevere asked, glancing round the room.

How strange that so much had changed, while so much had not. Glittering in his finest array, Lucan had boldly stationed himself at the right hand of the throne, as if he were still the undisputed champion of the Queen. Her father the King, grim-faced as ever, still shifted irritably in his seat while Taliesin waited calmly, his hands in his sleeves. Also in attendance were the other lords that a full council like this required. And lurking in the rear, Guenevere noted with a start, was one she had never thought to see hanging back like this.

But Malgaunt's defeat at the queen-making had cost him dear. Looking grey-faced and sick, he held himself aloof from the rest of the council, his hand restlessly playing with the hilt of his sword. His only companions were two of the lesser knights. A pang of pity swept Guenevere as she watched. She had to try to reconcile Malgaunt now.

But if Lucan noticed Malgaunt's misery he did not care. 'As your warlord, my queen,' he began with a flourish, bowing to Guenevere, 'I second King Arthur's request. Any peace in the Middle Kingdom will bring peace to us too.' He flashed a brilliant smile. 'And the sooner we give the King the assurances he needs, the sooner he will be free to return to his own lands. For it seems he has much to do there, and we must all wish him well.'

King Leogrance nodded darkly. 'Yes indeed.' He turned on Arthur. 'Surely the wars you face will drain all the strength you have? How do we know our men will be deployed only to protect our borders with your land?' He laughed harshly. 'We don't want blood of the Summer Country shed to make you High King!'

'A fair concern, sire,' Arthur said stiffly. 'But my sole desire is to regain my father's lands. I do not think of making myself High King. If I can win and hold the Middle Kingdom, my life will be well spent.'

Guenevere shook her head. 'If we make alliance, King Arthur,' she began, 'and—'

My sole desire, he said. *If I can only win the Middle Kingdom—*

An idea of such raw violence took hold of her that it stopped her breath.

Goddess, Mother, is that why you sent him here?

She could not speak. With a swift glance, Taliesin came to her aid. 'I think our men know who they fight for, sire.' He smiled at the King. 'And if we offer King Arthur the promise of border patrols, I believe they will remain just that.'

'My lady?' It was Sir Niamh, once the late Queen's champion and her first Chosen One, then one of her wisest counsellors and a trusted friend. He gestured towards Lucan and Taliesin. 'These lords speak for us all, I think. Let us make treaty with the Middle Kingdom to hold our borders safe. That is the way to bring peace to all.'

A chorus of approval followed his words.

Guenevere found her voice. 'So, lords, is this your wish?' She turned to the King. 'Does this meet with your approval, sire?'

'It must,' he nodded moodily, 'if all are agreed.'

'Then let a scrivener stand by,' Guenevere announced. 'We will proceed to treaty tonight.'

'My warmest thanks, Your Majesty.' Arthur's face was a study in delight.

A general sense of satisfaction warmed them all. Then a voice like the wind off the graveyard cut through the air.

'And is this all?'

It was Malgaunt, thrusting forward from the back of the group, his face deformed by an inhuman smile. 'Something tells me that we have not heard the last of our visitor's demands.'

From the look in Arthur's eye, Guenevere could see that Malgaunt had hit home.

What did Malgaunt know?

Malgaunt, Malgaunt, will it never end?

Arthur raised his eyebrows in acknowledgement, and smiled. 'No indeed, sir,' he returned courteously. 'We seek your friendship too to learn from you. The Summer Country was loved by your late Queen like her own child. But my poor land has been a prey to cruel scavengers, where the evil have grown rich. I must have men pure-hearted enough to drive them out, men who won't shrink from vengeance, but who would not tread the path of evil themselves.'

He bowed to Guenevere, and once again she saw the flame of purpose in his eyes. He gestured towards Lucan and Sir Niamh. 'Your knights of the Summer Country are famed far and wide. Your order of chivalry is the finest known. The brotherhood of the table where they meet has become the ideal of all.'

He raised his arm in homage. On the wall high above their heads hung the Round Table of the Goddess, where it had been since life in Camelot began. Heavy with power it smiled down on them all, its great face as lambent and inscrutable as the moon. Beneath it stood a hundred great chairs lining the wall, each with its own finely carved canopy bearing a knight's name inscribed in gold.

Arthur moved between them, speechless with awe. He reached out his hand towards the gilded lettering. '"Here sits Sir Lucan,"' he read under his breath. His tracing fingers moved on down the line. '"Sir Niamh", "Sir Lovell the Bold".' He breathed like a man entranced, his eyes never leaving the stately row of seats. 'So each knight has his place, his and his alone?'

'Just so, my lord,' Guenevere agreed. 'And if any knight is absent,' she indicated the deep red squares of tasselled velvet lying folded on the seats, 'a cover protects the canopy and keeps his name bright till he takes his seat again.'

'So!' Arthur sighed. 'And how did it come here?'

Guenevere paused. It was a favourite tale of the Summer Country, one she had first heard in her mother's arms. 'It was a gift to us from the Goddess herself. Long, long ago, the Great Mother lived with the Shining Ones here in the Summer Country. Then there were more worlds for Her to rule, and She had to leave us to take care of them. The Shining Ones went with Her to the astral plane, to dwell for ever in the world between the worlds.'

A sudden memory of her mother made her catch her breath. She paused for a moment to compose herself. 'But She left behind the boldest and fairest of their maidens to be our first Queen here. The bravest young men also chose to stay, to be the Queen's knights and defend her to the death. She took the best of them for her first champion and Chosen One, and from them all our queens have descended since. And ever since then too, our leading warriors become knights of the Queen. They have the right to sit at the Round Table, and do battle to become Queen's champion. But their true lives are vowed to service and chivalry. They live to fight against cruelty, to defend the right, to protect all women, and uphold the weak against the strong.'

Arthur approached the Round Table, his face alight with his dreams. *I have knights who are ready to move on to another plane. Kay, yes, he is worthy. Bedivere has a secret inner grace, and Gawain is the bravest soul alive. Sagramore, Griflet and the others, I can bring them with me too. If I can shape this rough force that I have, if I can raise the ideal of what we might be, and if this sweet queen will make some of her country's fine horses over to me, for there is no knighthood without chivalry . . .*

Guenevere watched the dreams fleeting over Arthur's face with something approaching a mother's tender joy. *See how the hope takes him, how the vision struggles to be born.*

And once again her own white thought bloomed in her head. *Arthur, Arthur, I have had sight of the future, hear me.*

Malgaunt's vicious laugh shattered the dream. 'You want the Round Table of the Goddess, sir?' He jabbed a contemptuous finger at Guenevere. 'That Table is the dowry of our queens. Only the man who marries Guenevere will get his hands on it!' He leaped forward to crow in Arthur's startled face. 'A challenge to any knight! For she is pledged already, married to her own will and desire!'

A mortal silence fell on all the room.

'And for you, young sir,' the taunt was unmistakable, 'I fear that even the Round Table of the Goddess cannot help you in your quest.' Malgaunt rasped on, glaring at Arthur like a maddened dog, 'At Caerleon you beat six kings, that's true. But let King Lot rally all his vassal kings, and next time you will face twelve of them and more, all hungry for your head.' He gave a cruel, cracked laugh. 'And you'll need more than any Round Table, sir, to save you then!'

Malgaunt.

Shaming yourself and me, dishonouring a guest, insulting a king?

Is there no end to your hating, hateful man?

Guenevere surged to her feet. 'Where is the scrivener?' she cried imperiously. 'We will make the treaty at once! This meeting is concluded. Conduct King Arthur to my apartments for refreshments while we wait. Thank you, my lords, for your attendance here!'

She raised both her arms as she had seen her mother do. 'Go! Go with the blessing of the Great One. May She bring you all safely on your way.'

Arthur shot her a glance, and strode stiffly out. One by one the others bowed and withdrew, and Guenevere was alone. Only her servants and attendants, she noted drearily, lined the walls in silence, awaiting her will.

Her will?

Married to her will?

What did Malgaunt mean?

Yes, on Avalon, for sure she had thought she would never marry – that she could live the life of the Lady and all the women there. *I wanted so much to own my own soul, to rule my body, to do as I choose, to enjoy the freedom that married women have to forgo.*

But now—

Now Arthur waited for her in the Queen's chamber to finalise the treaty they had agreed. And with Malgaunt's foul insults and innuendoes poisoning the air, how could she look him in the eye?

Married to her will?
Was that true?
No.
But now this man is here—

A flood of sensations seized her, and she burned from head to foot. Slowly she left the Great Hall, slower and slower she paced the long corridors with her women silently following till she reached the Queen's quarters where Arthur awaited her.

In the corridor outside, Gawain, Kay and Bedivere stood awkwardly around. Avoiding her eye, they bowed as she approached, and saw her in. Inside the chamber Arthur stood alone before the fire on the hearth. 'I have dismissed the chamber attendants,' he said coolly. 'Can these women with you wait outside too?'

Wide-eyed as rabbits, they shot off without a word. Guenevere gasped with rage. 'By what right, my lord, do you order my servants now?'

'Hush, lady,' he said absently. He was very pale. 'You and I have things to discuss alone.'

'The treaty will be ready just as soon as—'

He came nearer, raising his hand as if to place a finger on her lips. 'I do not mean the treaty.'

Guenevere pulled back furiously. 'Not the treaty? Then what?'

In the low chamber, his fair head seemed to knock against the beams.

'Why, I told you before,' he said simply. He looked into her eyes. 'Merlin has told me much. But I must ask for myself the things I want to know.'

Through the casement window, the sky round his head was spangled with bright stars. He took another step towards her now. 'Tell me one thing, lady. Prince Malgaunt, your noble kinsman, when do you marry him?'

Guenevere's heart thundered in her breast. '*Malgaunt?*'

'Merlin told me that you and he were betrothed to wed. And tonight he said you were pledged, married to your choice, though in truth I did not understand what he meant.'

'*Malgaunt?*' She could not contain her rage. 'I would not marry Malgaunt to save my life!'

He beamed with joy. 'Then, Lady Guenevere, will you marry me?'

CHAPTER 16

'Will you marry me?'

Guenevere could not breathe.

Gods, speed my words, Arthur groaned inwardly, let me not stumble now. 'You promised the people a champion, and a queen needs a warlord with a strong right arm,' he urged tensely, his eyes fixed on her face. 'For my part, a king must have a queen. My people long for a wedding. All my knights and lords in Caerleon will want me to marry to consolidate my rule.' He gave a rueful smile. 'Even Merlin agrees, though Kay teases me that Merlin will always expect to come first in my heart.'

Outside the dusk was falling, and a waning moon rose slowly in the sky. All the stars of evening shone round Arthur's head as he came closer and took her by the hand. 'And you – oh, lady, the whole world has heard of your loveliness, and you come of a brave line. Your mother was called "Battle Raven", was she not? And her beauty, too, was sung in every hall.'

He laughed self-consciously, and his colour rose. 'I am no poet, but the very thought of you stirred my soul. Then Merlin told me to put away such hopes. You were betrothed to your kinsman Malgaunt, he said, and the two of you were to wed. He said that you were born to love another man.'

Guenevere shuddered with dread. In a dark corner of the chamber she could see a shadowy shape of a man half turning towards her, then turning his face away.

Merlin?

Her unknown lover?

Who?

A chill of fear invaded her to the bone. 'Merlin – where is he?'

Arthur frowned. 'I do not know. I thought he would be here. He was coming ahead to make a treaty with you. So I set out to follow him, and somehow overtook him on the way. Which left me the honour of calling first on you.'

He reached for her hands, and brought them to his lips. 'Lady Guenevere,' he stumbled over her name, and his voice was thick with feeling, 'I'm a poor wooer, but I offer you a heart as true and valiant as your own. Will you marry me? Two lands like ours, two rulers like ourselves, could we not build a kingdom together, the like of which has never been seen?'

She could hardly speak. But once again the white vision bloomed inside her head. 'A kingdom, my lord?' she said huskily. 'Why not a world?'

To marry Arthur—

To be his queen—

Guenevere set little store by the stormy council meeting the next day when Arthur made his offer known. She informed them all that she had not yet made her choice, and sat back to hear the worst of what could be said. She was prepared for her father's resistance, Lucan's stunned disbelief, and Malgaunt's spite. Nothing mattered to her as long as Taliesin blessed her with his smile. And only one other voice counted with her at all.

She turned to Arthur as they left the Great Hall. 'Will you go with me to the Lady of the Lake?'

He smiled tenderly. 'Lady, I will go with you anywhere.'

Malgaunt stood aside as the rest of the lords and knights left the Great Hall. At the last minute he leaned forward to pluck Lucan by the sleeve. 'Sir,' his white teeth gleamed at the champion, 'may I beg a moment of your time?'

Pale and sweating, numb with shock, Lucan knew that the time had come to lay aside old feuds. 'For sure, Prince Malgaunt,' he forced out. 'I am yours to command.'

'This will surprise you, lord. But I think that for once, our interests coincide.' Malgaunt stared at Lucan broodingly. 'It seems that our Queen means more by this youth than we thought.'

Lucan clenched his teeth. 'When he appeared at the queen-making, I thought it was all a trick of the Gods.'

'Or of that old wretch Taliesin,' Malgaunt agreed sardonically. 'Like you, he only wanted to keep me out!'

'I thought the Old Ones had sent a spirit shape, or even the God himself, to aid the Queen in her time of need. I never thought he'd still be there in the light of day.'

'And when he'd vanished, she would choose one of us?' Malgaunt grinned. 'Yourself, perhaps?'

'She had to choose me, I was sure of that!' Lucan swept on, careless of giving offence. 'And even when we knew who he was, I thought the only thing he wanted was to get back to the Middle Kingdom with the promise of extra men.'

Malgaunt nodded. 'I knew that he might want her. I did not think that she would consider him, when—' When she should be mine! his shrivelled soul cried out. Mine by right, by blood, by the hunger of my loins! Furious, he glanced at Lucan ready to spring to the attack if he had betrayed himself.

But Lucan was lost in his own outrage, his sense of insult swelling like a wound. 'You are a lord of the Summer Country, a prince of our blood. I could have borne to lose out to you. But this – to *him*?' He paused, breathing heavily. 'And will she marry him? Will she make him father to our future queens?' He paced the floor in mounting rage. 'An unknown bastard to seed our royal line?'

The smell of panic fury filled the air. Malgaunt's index finger played thoughtfully on his lip. 'Hear me, sir. Let us make a truce till we see how this goes. Guenevere may simply be trying her new-found strength.'

A spark of hope sprang up in Lucan's eye. 'Letting us feel her power, reminding us that she has the right to choose?'

'And that she has a choice other than us. Surely she will see reason in the end. But we should have a course of action if the foolish girl is minded to persist. Agreed?'

'Agreed!' Lucan swore.

Malgaunt broke into his most infamous grin. He threw a glance at his two companion knights hanging behind. 'Then the only question is, do you kill him or do I?'

They set out the next day, in a cool shining dawn. Soon Camelot lay behind, as they threaded their way through the woods by tracks hardly known to man. Guenevere had not travelled these hidden greenways since she was taken to the Sacred Isle as a girl. Then she had ridden in a litter, pampered, but still treated as a child. Now she was flanked by the knights and men of her own guard, their banners dancing, and lances glittering in the sun.

Arthur's three companions, Gawain, Kay and Bedivere, rode with them too, their air of suppressed excitement showing that Arthur had told them of his hopes. Arthur himself hung on her every word. Was it this that made the May blossom gleam so bright, and the meadowsweet bless every verge with gold?

'See, madam!' he called merrily, as the lapwings flashed up from the ground, or the startled hares went racing for cover at the sound of the horses' hoofs. At every turn of the road she could see how much he loved the land, from the loftiest oak to the speedwell by the way.

'Where do these old tracks cross the Roman roads?' he asked curiously. He told her of all the main highways of the land, all the routes an army could use. He had grown swiftly into kingship, she could see, knowing that when war loomed, there would be no time to lose.

But as they drew near Avalon, and the sweet mist of the holy waters began to reach them through the trees, he grew more subdued. By the time they came down through the forest to the plain of the Sacred Lake, he was tense and silent, straining for his first glimpse. And there it was, hovering above the water, the island in the lake that the Old Ones called the Isle of Glass. Before them waited the boatmen of the Lady to ferry them across.

Beside the lake, the yellow kingcups and blue forget-me-nots dabbled their leaves in shallows as clear as glass. The midday breeze ruffled the shining water, and silver fish drowsed in the sunlit depths. Far off, beyond the island, the water grew dark and brackish, overhung with trees and clogged with bulrushes and water weeds. Shrouded in mist, the far reaches of the mere were home to the village of Lake-dwellers, the followers of the Goddess who lived out of their hooded skin canoes, and hid from sight. But where Guenevere stood, the kiss of the sun felt like the Mother's welcome home.

Leaving the rest of the troop on the shore, she and Arthur embarked with Kay, Bedivere and Gawain. The island lay before them like a dream. Along its shore, weeping willows trembled in the midday breeze, and above them drifted the blossom of a thousand trees. And rising proudly over the orchards was the great Tor of Avalon itself, the high hill shaped like the Mother lying at rest, hiding her secrets beneath her grassy flanks.

Standing beside Guenevere in the flat, slow-moving boat, Arthur pointed towards the Tor. 'The Welshmen call this the way to the Otherworld,' he said thoughtfully. 'They say the hill is hollow, the home of Penn Annwyn, the Dark Lord, King of the Underworld.'

The Dark Lord who came to take my mother home.

She could not let him think it. 'The isle is sacred to the Mother, and her love brings life, not death.'

At the island's edge a rough stone jetty thrust out into the lake. Waiting to greet them was the small, taut figure of Nemue, the chief priestess of the Lady of the Lake. Her eyes glimmered in greeting as they stepped ashore. 'This way,' she said, in the rusty voice of those who rarely speak. 'The Lady foresaw your coming. She is waiting for you now.'

In silence they followed Nemue up the winding path from the jetty, through the white apple orchards and the dark groves of ancient trees. At last they stood before the

Lady's House, a delicate frontage of carved white stone built into the side of the hill. At a sign from Nemue, the doors opened without a sound.

'Only Queen Guenevere and the King may be admitted,' Nemue said to Kay, Gawain and Bedivere. 'You will wait here.'

A brusque sign from Arthur silenced Gawain's protests. Wordlessly the two of them approached the door. Guenevere watched Arthur grow pale as he gazed into the darkness within. When she had lived on Avalon, the girls in the House of Maidens used to whisper that the Lady's House was not a house at all, but her enchanted way down to the Lake below. Now as they crossed the threshold the air felt humid, and she thought she heard the sound of water far beneath.

But as the great doors clanged behind them, they were in a warm, well-lighted place. They stood in a round chamber with a low domed roof, its walls plastered with soft honey-coloured loam. Rich woven rugs in all the colours of the East covered the floor, and a tiny glowing dragon-lamp crouched in every niche, casting a pool of gold.

A rich and heady fragrance filled the air. Arthur stood staring about him like a man entranced. His eyes were fixed on a tall, strangely made throne set against the furthest wall. At its foot lolled a pack of large sleek water-hounds, their gold collars glinting dully in the light. Guenevere watched as Arthur moved towards them, his fingers clicking in command. Then from behind them came a voice from her childhood, from the time before her dreams.

'These dogs are trained to my hand, King Arthur. They will not come to yours.'

Out of the shadows came a tall majestic shape veiled in

soft draperies from head to foot. One floating arm pointed towards a pair of low stools by the throne.

They settled at her feet as she took her place. Above the gauzy veil she wore a moon-shaped diadem of palest gold, its face encrusted with pearls. On her second finger she wore the Goddess ring, and in her hand she held an orb of polished crystal bound in gold. 'Welcome back, dear Guenevere,' she said fondly. 'And welcome, my lord King.'

Guenevere knelt forward eagerly. 'Lady, this king seeks your help. He faces many dangers. Can you tell what lies ahead for him?'

The Lady nodded. 'It is already written in the stars. The King who hates him . . .'

'King Lot, it must be!' breathed Arthur.

'. . . this king of darkness broods now in his castle, calls his astrologers, browbeats his Druids, and does not sleep at night.'

Arthur's face was bleak. 'He plans his revenge. He will come for me.'

The shrouded shape nodded slowly in agreement.

A terror gripped Guenevere. 'And what then?'

'All men must flourish and vanish in their time. The only truth is the everlasting dark.'

She could not bear it. 'But will Arthur be High King?'

A soft sigh came from behind the Lady's muffling veils. 'Ask that question of the right High Queen.'

'The right queen?' Arthur breathed.

The great veiled shape slowly inclined her head. 'You are young, sir, and you long to feel your power as King. But women are the givers of all life. It is for women, then, to rule both life and love. If you hold fast to this truth, you will gain both life and love. And when you lose it, you will lose Queen and all.'

Arthur grinned with relief, and shot Guenevere a

glowing glance. 'Believe me, Lady, if I win this Queen, I will never lose it, or her, or anything!'

'No? Never? Are you sure?' There was a sigh like the sadness of the world. Then the Lady rose to her feet. 'Come!'

Behind the throne, the dragon-lamp shone on the first steps of a wide stone staircase plunging down into the dark. 'Follow!' came the command.

Eyes wide, Arthur reached for Guenevere's hand and carefully helped her down the slippery steps. Above their heads the void whispered with unseen wings, and the soundless call of creatures who dwell in the dark. Step by step the blackness deepened till they might have been descending to the Land of the Dead. At last their feet hit softness, and the sound of water filled their ears. Out of sight in the shadows, small nameless things scurried away to their lairs.

Suddenly the dark space was ablaze with light. They stood in a vast stone grotto, roofed with glistening crystals in red and white, walled round by curtains of primeval stone. Unseen above their heads loomed the great mass of the Tor. All around them treasures richer than any dreams hung from the ceiling and clustered against the walls, gold plates and bowls of silver, jewelled weapons, gold chains, ropes of precious stones, vast cauldrons of copper, and drinking cups of bronze.

At the centre of the chamber the Lady stood erect and motionless, like a pillar of stone in her pale, sculpted robes. On either side, bubbling up into two deep hollows carved into the rocky floor, rose the waters of two springs, one white, one red.

'The Body of the Mother,' the Lady crooned, spreading her arms to embrace the echoing space. She pointed to her left and to her right. 'The blood and milk of the Mother, the red spring and the white. The love of the Mother as it pours forth to the world.'

She whirled around, caught up a lamp from the wall, and turned into the darkness behind. 'Come!'

As she raised the lamp, the light fell on an altar at the back of the cave. Arrayed on its black surface were four huge shapes of antique gold. Guenevere stood stock still. She had seen them before, in the scenes carved on the back of the coronation throne.

'The Hallows of the Goddess!' hissed Arthur, falling to his knees.

The Lady answered, in a voice ringing with pride, 'Yes, lord, the sacred treasures of our worship from the time before Time.' Setting down the lamp, she took up a massive gold dish, heavily embossed around the edge. 'The great dish of plenty, from which the Mother feeds all who come to Her.' She reached for a two-handled goblet patterned with strange symbols, big enough to send round a Great Hall. 'The loving-cup of forgiveness, with which She reconciles us all.'

Now a long gold blade circled through the air. 'The sword of power.' In her other hand the Lady brandished a slender golden lance. 'And the spear of defence!'

Reverently she replaced them on the altar. 'These are the treasures of our Goddess, my lord King. Will you swear to defend them if she grants you this Queen?'

Arthur's eyes were shining with reflections of milk and blood. 'I will!'

'And what of the Christians?'

Arthur started. 'The Christians?'

'They seek the death of the Goddess, so that they can claim the Hallows as their own.'

Arthur shook his head. 'The Christians say that they bring life, not death.'

The Lady's low musical voice throbbed with scorn. 'What use are fine words on the lips of those who hate? Religion should be kindness. Faith should bring us love.'

Arthur nodded gravely. 'And in that love, we all can become one. As King of all my people, I may not act against men of good faith. But I swear to defend the faith of my Lady Guenevere to the last breath I have.'

'So then, King Arthur.' Her voice was warmer now. 'If you win Guenevere, do you swear to love and honour her all your days?'

Arthur tore his sword from the scabbard and raised the hilt before him, gripping the blade with both hands. 'I swear!' he cried.

'And will you defend the Goddess, and be strong in Her defence?'

'On the honour of a king!' Arthur cried. 'On my sword, on my soul! And if I break this oath, may I lose life and honour too!'

Guenevere's soul was dissolving. *Oh, Arthur – Arthur, my love!*

The Lady's sigh came from very far away. 'Remember this! You have pronounced your own doom if you break your word. You are bound to this Queen and our worship now, and have thereby promised to defend every woman against the power of men. And, in token of this, the Goddess will send you a sign.'

Now her spirit grew till it filled the echoing space. 'On one condition. You must return this gift to the Goddess when the time comes. If you do not, your soul will not find peace. Swear to abide by this!'

'I swear!' Arthur's oath went rolling round the cave.

The Lady bowed. 'And now, Sir King, you must go back to the world above.'

'Now?'

'And leave your sword behind.'

'Leave my sword?' Arthur was aghast. 'Lady, no! A knight cannot go unarmed!'

'All who come here must make offering,' the Lady intoned. 'Either to me in place of the Mother, or else by casting their treasure into the Lake.'

Arthur hesitated, at war with himself. Then he stepped forward, kissed his sword, and laid the weapon at the Lady's feet.

'Farewell, my lord.' The hand in the gauzy draperies pointed him to the stairs. Then the Lady's posture softened, along with her voice. 'We shall meet again, King Arthur, do not fear,' she said tenderly. 'At the last crossing of the water, I shall see you there.'

CHAPTER 17

T he lone figure of Arthur climbed up to the world above. The Lady sighed. 'And now, little one, let us talk.' She raised her hand to her head, and unveiled her face.

A radiance filled the chamber, almost too bright to bear. At first Guenevere thought she saw the face of her mother as she remembered her, the starlit eyes, the same undying smile. But then she saw more than could belong to any woman – something more than human, a face alive with the wisdom of the ages and the freshness of the dawn.

'So, Guenevere?'

The Lady smiled her thousand-year-old smile, and the words fell from Guenevere's tongue. 'Oh, Mother, King Arthur has asked me to marry him, and I'm afraid – but why? What do I have to fear?'

'Ah!'

The Lady rested her chin on her hand, and thought for a long while. At last her deep, musical tones filled the air. 'The dance of life is the rhythm of rise and fall. When we fall, we are returned to the earth from which we came. Then we come forth once more from the womb of our Mother the Earth to live our dance again.' She leaned forward. 'We have many lives to live, and women may dance more than once in the course of their days. One man alone cannot make all the music of the world.'

She looked at Guenevere shrewdly, her large, luminous eyes searching her upturned face. 'Ah, Guenevere! You are not fated to be like other women. Ahead for you there lies a great and mighty love, a love you do not hope for, cannot dream.'

'Oh, Lady.'

Guenevere was weeping with joy. She would know love, love would come to her. Arthur would fill her heart, she would look at him as her mother looked at Lucan, shining with delight. And she would build a life, a great kingdom, an undying world with Arthur, just as her vision said—

'Bless you, Lady!' Laughing and crying, Guenevere kissed her hand.

The Lady smiled. Why did she look so sad, when she had foretold so much joy? 'Ah, Guenevere,' she sighed, 'we are only the keepers of the dream. Fate spins as it will, and even the Mother cannot turn back the wheel.'

Sighing again, she stood up. 'Go then, in grace and strength.' Leaning forward, she brushed her cool lips against Guenevere's face. 'Go with the blessing of the Great One herself. Those who follow the Goddess can always enter the dream. May you awake from yours, and become that which you have dreamed.'

Blinking, Guenevere stumbled out into the light. Nemue was waiting to lead her back through the orchard to the water's edge. There in the same large, flat-bottomed boat as before, Arthur stood pale-mouthed and transported, while Gawain, Kay and Bedivere clustered anxiously round their lord. He seemed to be trying to tell them about the Otherworld and the Lady beneath the lake. But as Guenevere approached he sprang forward, shouldering the boatmen aside to grip her fiercely and draw her to himself.

A single look passed among Gawain, Kay and Bedivere, and the three knights withdrew to the furthest end of the boat. The stolid boatmen set to with a will until they were moving at speed across the water. But Arthur was oblivious. 'We are foreordained, Guenevere!' he mumbled thickly, crushing her hands. 'We have the blessing of the Goddess, and the love of the Lady herself. Merlin himself must smile upon our choice!'

Merlin, Merlin – why always Merlin?

'My lord! My lord!'

Crouched in the prow of the boat, Gawain was pointing wildly at the lake ahead. The early evening light glimmered on the water, and the sudden flash of silver in the dusk ahead looked like a fish leaping, or a water-bird landing in a shower of spray.

But there, rising from the surface of the water, was a woman's hand holding a shining sword. Tall and tapering, its silver shaft seemed to draw all the light of the lake, thrumming softly to itself with hidden power. It was a gift from the Otherworld, made for a hero by one of the Gods.

From her days on Avalon, Guenevere knew of the great treasures cast into the lake as offerings to the Goddess. She knew, too, which of the Maidens were trained to swim up from the depths to catch them, and bring them back to safe-keeping in the rocky caves beneath the Lake.

Yet it was more than human skill that held the great sword above the water now. It was a more-than-human form below the surface, swathed like the Lady in gauzy white. And no human lungs could have breathed so long underwater as the unseen figure awaiting Arthur's approach.

For there could be no doubt who the gift was for.

'The sign!' Arthur was beside himself. 'The Lady promised me a sign to defend the right!' He turned a blind gaze on Guenevere. 'And to defend you, my queen!'

Leaning forward, he reached out and seized the sword. The hand that held it sank beneath the surface. In the dusk of evening, they could not see who or what moved below the glassy surface of the lake. But the gift had reached its destination, without doubt.

The sword lay quietly across Arthur's lap. Awed and speechless, Gawain, Kay and Bedivere gathered round Arthur to admire the prize. Even in repose, the long silver blade flashed fire, and the massive hilt of gold with its smooth gemstones was made for a warrior's grip.

Down the blade ran a line of ancient runes. Arthur turned to Guenevere. 'Can you tell these marks?'

The sword was light and strong within her hands. The runes leaped in the half-light like living things. Guenevere turned the blade this way and that as she struggled to make them out. '"She Who Is and Was, Made Me For Your Hand,"' she spelled out at last. '"They call me Excalibur."'

'Excalibur!'

Arthur breathed out in bliss, and fell to his knees. Reverently he grasped the blade and brought the hilt to his lips. 'You are mine now,' he whispered, 'and you and I shall never part, till the last battle on the last day on earth.'

Guenevere could not hold back. Gently she reached out to the great form kneeling in the bottom of the boat. Arthur looked up, and set Excalibur down to reach for both her hands.

'You too, my lady!' he cried passionately. 'From now on, you and I will never part! For me you will always be the sun in winter, the light in the darkened hall.' He was weeping now, dashing away great tears. 'Marry me, Guenevere! Take me for your love!'

She was shuddering so hard that she could scarcely stand. Now the vision that had come to her in the council meeting could no longer be contained. 'Hear me, Arthur,' she said tremulously. 'You spoke of your one desire to win back your father's kingdom. Now we talk of uniting your lands with mine, to make one greater kingdom of the two. Have you thought . . .' she paused to breathe, and let her soul take flight '. . . have you thought that together we could build something greater yet? That it lies in our power to turn back the tide of lawlessness that threatens our land, and bring back the glory it once knew?'

Arthur's face was very white. He did not speak.

Guenevere surged on. 'That we could make all these scattered kingdoms into one, and turn this country into an Island of the Mighty once again?' Now she could hardly speak. 'That we are destined to become High King and Queen?'

Now Arthur felt the force of what she saw. 'You are the Throne Woman,' he breathed. 'Take me to your throne, and I will deliver this whole country into your hands. You say I might be High King of these islands? I will make you High Queen of all the world! You and I shall so rule that our names will never die!'

Guenevere seized his hand, and the blood sang in her veins. 'Let us make the sacred marriage then, not as our mothers made it, changing with the years, but in a new mating, to become for ever the mother and the father of this land!'

'And of many children!' Arthur cried, with shining eyes.

And suddenly she was trembling, and something caught around her heart. She could feel the cold wind of death and the breath of sudden loss, but of what, she did not know.

'Children?' she said faintly. 'If the Mother blesses us. If the Great Ones permit.'

But that shadow passed with the moment, and Guenevere was in high spirits again as they rode back to Camelot. Arthur's gentle kiss as they pledged their love gave Gawain, Kay and Bedivere the signal for whoops of delight, much back-slapping, and uproarious mirth all round. The hours on the road seemed nothing as they hastened back joyfully to make nightfall and home. At last they crossed the causeway, gained the outer courtyard of the castle and threw down their reins to the grooms who came to their aid.

Flushed with laughter, Guenevere turned to Arthur and took his hands. 'My lord.'

'Your Majesty?' It was the stately figure of the chamberlain. 'A stranger arrived, only moments ago. We have not yet enquired his business here. Will it please you greet the man?'

She looked at Arthur, smiling into his eyes. 'A visitor for you or me, my lord?' she murmured happily. 'Well, we shall find out.'

Inside the gate-house, a different air breathed from the low stone roof, brick floor and clammy walls. A group of knights and men formed a crowd around the roaring fire on the hearth.

'Make way for the Queen and King Arthur!' cried the guard.

The group around the stranger parted at once. In its centre stood a wild, aged man, richly clad. His thick grey hair flowed down to his shoulders and beyond. He had the golden eyes of the Old Ones and a smile as old as time. He stood like a shadow of darkness in the green twilight of the room. As they came forward, his gaze raked both of them and pounced like a hawk on Guenevere.

'Merlin!' cried Arthur, in ecstasy.

And Guenevere found herself looking into the mad yellow glare of the strangers who had haunted her days and stalked her waking nights.

CHAPTER 18

He was dressed like a king in a velvet gown of forest green and a travelling coat of thick furs that swept the ground. Gold earrings writhed like serpents in his ears. His hair was held back with a circle of silver, and his fingers flashed with jewels as big as thrushes' eggs. As he raised his arms the torches leaped up the walls and flickered with a blue and yellow light. Everything about him was strange and wonderful.

'Merlin!' Arthur cried.

'So, boy, so!'

The old man's thin lips split in a cackle of delight. Arthur sprang forward and crushed him to his chest. Merlin returned the embrace, clapping Arthur on the back in a pantomime of joy. But over Arthur's shoulder, the fierce unsmiling eyes never left Guenevere's face.

She was numb with shock. *Merlin here, Merlin the enchanter, the old Prince of darkness himself?*

Oh, I have seen you before, sir, though you must think I do not know who you are.

Fragments of remembered voices rang in her head.

Make no more queens, for there is one coming who will sweep you away – yes, you were a beggar-man then, old sir, 'Merlin's messenger' you called yourself.

For a second the crazed old derelict reared up before her in her mind's eye. A moment later another shape took his place. A stately bard, pacing towards her on the Hill of Stones. Another soothsayer, miraculously granted a vision of a future that excluded her. Another voice, speaking against her right. *The Gods themselves have sent Malgaunt to Guenevere. He will rule this land, he will be the father of many kings—*

Merlin, Merlin, oh, I know you now—

He saw at once that she had recognised him. Another yellow smile split his ancient face as he released himself from Arthur's clasp. 'Madam, forgive us!' he declared, with an old-fashioned bow. 'My lord, will you present me to the Queen?'

Arthur was like a puppy as he bounded around them both. 'With all my heart!' he cried ecstatically. 'For you two must be friends! Give Merlin your best welcome, my Lady Guenevere.'

'Greetings, Lord Merlin.' Guenevere forced a smile. 'Tomorrow we shall feast your arrival here.' *And tomorrow will be soon enough,* she prayed, *to tell him of our plans.*

But Arthur had no thought of holding back. 'Oh, Merlin, so much has happened!'

A quick alert awoke in Merlin's eyes. 'Tell me, my lord.'

Arthur waved his arms self-consciously. 'The Queen and I – that is, I and Queen Guenevere . . .'

'Sire?'

Arthur turned colour, and grinned. 'Confound you, Merlin, you came too late for what has happened here!' His eyes sought Guenevere with a look of shining love.

The old man's smile vanished like snow in spring. 'Too late?'

And suddenly Guenevere saw him clad from head to foot not in furs but creeping toadflax, his long crooked fingers straining towards her like briars, his eyes darting poison, and the tongues of serpents hissing from his mouth.

Then her sight cleared, and understanding came to her in a flood. *He never thought that his boy, his puppet Arthur, would act for himself. He thought he had time to promote Malgaunt's claim, and dispose of me.*

He was so intent on forwarding his own schemes that he never thought to look behind. And Arthur was coming behind him to find me.

Arthur—

A surge of joy filled her from head to foot. *Arthur proved to be his own man, after all.*

'So, then, the Queen and I have agreed. We're going to be married, Merlin!' she heard Arthur say, and her heart overflowed.

'This is good news! Joy to you both, my lord!' Merlin stood smiling broadly, clasping Arthur's hand. He reached out towards Guenevere, and she forced herself to clasp the cold leathery fingers between her palms.

'It grows late, sir,' she said, 'and you must be longing for your rest. I will give orders that you are lodged near the King.'

Merlin bowed. 'Yes, he and I have much to discuss.'

Guenevere looked at Arthur, and tried to put her heart into her eyes. *Arthur, beware, he is not as he seems. There is more here than you and I can know.* But her mouth said only a few cool words of farewell. 'Blessings on your counsels then, my lords. And may they bring peace and comfort to us all.'

Merlin!

Gods above, what is he trying to do?

Dismissing the servants, Guenevere paced the Queen's apartments to think.

Merlin—

First the wild wanderer who cursed her path to the throne. Then the blind Welsh bard, Malgaunt's champion.

Merlin's malice in action against her. To make her marry Malgaunt as the price of her throne. To ensure that she and Arthur would never meet, or fall in love. But why? What lay behind it? And where would it end?

She came to with a start, cold and terrified. While she pondered, the fire had burned out. She sank on to a couch, covered her face, and wept. *Oh Arthur, Arthur, where is the joy we had together, only hours ago?*

'My lady?'

It was one of the Queen's women, leaning over her. Above the white collar her face was full of concern. A faint memory stirred in Guenevere. 'You were here when my mother was struck down?'

The young woman smiled sadly. 'You sent me running for herbs and salves.'

'And I did not know your name.'

'It's Ina, my lady.' She moved lightly to the cold hearth, and set to work on the fire. 'The Queen took me in when I was ten years old, and my mother died of the plague. She would not want to see you now, so sad and alone.'

'Oh . . .' All Guenevere's anxieties surged up afresh. 'I have much on my mind, Ina, the treaty with the Middle Kingdom and its king.'

A flame leaped up on the hearth, and Ina stepped back to admire her handiwork. 'Well, then, my lady.' She had the face of a clever little cat, her broad cheekbones and slumbrous eyes giving her an unmistakable look of the Otherworld. 'If you have worries, why not ask the King?'

Guenevere stared at her in amazement, and began to laugh. Why not, indeed?

Joyfully she found her voice. 'Send at once to the King's

apartments. Say the Queen would like to see him at the first
convenient hour.'

'King Leogrance, lady?'

'No, Ina, King Arthur, send for him!'

But seconds later, she was in agony.

'Ina, I can't see the King like this. I've been on a horse
all day – I must smell like a horse, or worse!'

'Let me call for another gown, my lady.'

'Call for two! Four! And for someone to attend to
my hair!'

'Yes, madam – and refreshments for the King?'

Swift as a bird, Ina darted to and fro, calling up the
page-boys to take care of the fire, and the chamber-maids to
perfume the apartments and make them sweet and clean. In
between she oversaw the waiting women as they freshened
Guenevere's skin and dressed her hair, and slipped her into
a pale blue chamber gown with a great collar of white fox
fur. Then with her own hands she touched Guenevere's
wrists and temples with patchouli, the fragrance from the
East that her mother had loved so well.

'There, madam!' she cried proudly at last. 'Fit for a
king!'

But the King did not come. When the knock came at the door,
it was a red-faced Sir Gawain who stepped through with Sir
Kay and Sir Bedivere to confront Guenevere's disappointed
stare, shifting his great bulk from foot to foot.

Gawain had never been so uncomfortable in his life.
Gods above, what an errand for a man who lived by the
sword. He'd rather face an army single-handed than fool
around in a lady's chamber like this!

'Your Majesty, the King begs your forgiveness,' he said
awkwardly, 'but he cannot come.'

Dear Gods, Kay thought, what an oaf Gawain was,

he was only making matters worse! Sighing, he stepped forward to try to smooth things over. 'Lord Merlin came with many affairs of state. The demands of the kingdom press in on the King now.'

Then it was Bedivere's turn. 'Lord Merlin bows to your displeasure too, Your Majesty,' he said, in his quiet tenor, his soft brown eyes pleading for favour again. 'Only for the good of the country, he declares, would he dare to come between a king and his queen.'

Guenevere smiled graciously. 'Thank you, sirs. Will you take some refreshment? I will be with you shortly.' Then as calmly as she could, she withdrew to the inner chamber, where it was all she could do not to roll on the floor and howl.

She threw herself into a chair to think.

Merlin!

Always Merlin!

He had not been here an hour before he had taken Arthur from her, flaunting his power, twitching Arthur's chain! But why should Merlin come between her and Arthur now? He knew that they planned to marry – surely he would not try to change Arthur's mind?

Why should he?

Why not?

Suddenly she saw it all. Kay had said that Merlin would always expect to come first in Arthur's heart. So when Arthur married, Merlin would want some simple-minded girl for him, a devout princess of the Christians, say, schooled in silence and submission to men. No wonder he wanted Arthur under the sway of the monks in black!

Yes!

Guenevere sat bolt upright. And no wonder he planned to get her out of the way. No wonder he had tried to make Malgaunt King in her place. No wonder that he had lied to

Arthur, telling him that she was pledged to Malgaunt, and not free to marry him!

So – now that she saw the game, she could play too.

Calmly she returned to the outer chamber, where Sir Gawain, Kay and Bedivere stood awkwardly drinking wine before the fire. 'My compliments to the King,' she smiled, 'and tell him that I shall wait for him, however late he comes.'

It was past owl-light and almost dawn, as the palace yawned and stirred and made ready to begin the day, when Arthur came at last. He looked like a ghost, pale, stiff and old, from the hours of dealing with Merlin's demands.

'You are tired, my lord.' Guenevere's heart yearned. Gently she drew him to a seat by the fire, knelt at his feet, and took his hands in hers. 'Soon, my king,' she told him tenderly, 'when night comes, you will sleep your fill. But before then, when the court gathers in the Great Hall, let us announce our betrothal to the world.'

Arthur nodded, and smothered a great yawn. One tired finger gently touched her temple and traced the line of her jaw. Absently he framed her face in his hand and turned it upwards for a kiss. 'And how soon after that, my love, can we be married?'

When Arthur kissed her, Guenevere knew that, whatever Merlin had said, Arthur was still hers. He wanted her, she could tell, as he had never wanted anything before.

And she wanted him. His first kiss in the boat on the lake at Avalon had felt like a flower against her lips, or the downy flutter of a newborn bird. But now he had taken her mouth, and the fire he lit in her was something new. She laughed softly to herself. Had she thought she loved Cormac, when all she loved was the idea of him? Now she knew Arthur, she was longing for his touch, and more – for the embrace that would make her a woman, and the love that would make her his.

'Guenevere, Guenevere . . .'

Gods, she was lovely! He longed to touch her as she knelt there with her body warm against him, and held himself back with a groan. Could this all be true? Or was it the heat of the fire, the heady spiced wine she had pressed into his hand, or the deathly fatigue of recent days deluding his senses now?

Arthur felt he was a lost soul, a soul lost yet found, a man who had yielded himself up to the mists of an endless dream, only to stumble on something that he did not know. But he knew this was no dream. The soft arm pressing trustingly against him now, the promise of her full yet slender form, were real enough to banish all his tiredness and all dreary thoughts of state.

And soon he would make her his, soon he would possess the woman of the dream in reality. Soon they must marry, he told her, breathing hard after that endless kiss. Tonight they should announce their wedding to the world. It must be within the week, for a king could not leave his kingdom unattended for long. And besides, he murmured, kissing her again, why else should they delay?

CHAPTER 19

'Make way for the Queen!'

Guenevere always loved the evenings in the Great Hall when the wine went round by torchlight, and all the court came in its finery to gossip and rejoice. But as she came in that night, she knew that the glow she wore owed nothing to the soft bloom of the candles or her royal gold and pearls.

'The Queen!' bawled the attendants at the door. 'Make way for the Queen!'

'The Queen!' came the reverent murmur from the crowd. 'The Queen!' And as they spoke, she saw herself shining in white and gold, a woman clothed in love, reflected in the mirror of all eyes.

Oh, Arthur, Arthur my love—

And there he was, waiting for her by the entrance, surrounded by his knights with Merlin at his side. In his rich red tunic and white cloak he looked pale and deathly tired, but there was a glitter about him that matched her own. His fair hair was crowned by a wreath of gold, and a collar of jewels glinted at his neck. As he held out his hand, gold bangles shone round his wrists. But the smile he gave her was brighter than them all.

'Queen Guenevere!' Glowing like a boy with a secret, Arthur bowed and kissed her hand.

Behind him Merlin stood robed in a long gown coloured like thunder and lightning, now flickering blue and white, now brooding and grey-black. Its high collar seemed to elongate his neck, and the long sleeves dropped like rainfall to the floor. In his hand he carried a slender wand of polished yew murmuring to itself in a high, fretful whine. Like Arthur he wore a royal coronet, and all around were treating him like a king.

'Lord Merlin!' Guenevere made him a fulsome bow.

His yellow eyes looked sick, but he had to smile at her. 'Your Majesty!'

Slowly Guenevere led Arthur round the hall. Love is an open secret, and theirs seemed to be known by all. Laughing knights in silver mail, solemn lords in their rich dark velvets, Druids in their familiar blue-purple robes and court ladies blooming like flowers, all beamed and nodded as they drew near.

Even Malgaunt, Guenevere saw to her relief, seemed to wish them well. Lurking by the door with a group of knights and men, whispering to his grinning companions, he frightened her at first.

But then she saw that he was dressed in purple and gold, and decked out with his ceremonial weapons, ready to take his place at the feast. So he would accept Arthur as her champion, for the sake of the country, if not for Guenevere herself! Her heart surged with joy. As they came up to him, she gave him the warmest greeting of her life. 'Blessings on you, Uncle! You are welcome here!'

'Your Majesty!'

Now it was Taliesin's turn to bless them with a smile. From Cormac came a solemn bow, a fervent kiss on Guenevere's hand and a heartfelt, 'May the Mother bless you both!'

His eyes said, 'I wish you joy of your love with all my heart.' Even the King her father, Guenevere thought, looked cheerful tonight.

'Thank you, thank you all.'

Beside her Arthur smiled, and bowed to lords, and kissed ladies' hands as if he had been doing it all his life. But soon he whispered lightly in her ear, 'Lady, let us speak our love now, for I am weary of all this.'

Guenevere turned, smiling into his eyes. How could she deny him? In a mist of joy, she led him towards the dais at the end of the hall. As they mounted the steps, the trumpets pealed, and the noise of the court died away.

'Attend all here!' the chamberlain cried. 'Hear and obey your Queen.'

Guenevere stepped forward to face the sea of eyes. 'Good people,' she began, 'I promised you a champion, and I have made good my word. Here is the man who will fight for me and for our country, to defend us in war and bring us lasting peace.'

Her voice grew until it filled the hall. 'Arthur Pendragon, son of Uther the High King, lord of Caerleon and ruler of the Middle Kingdom, is to be my champion and my Chosen One. Soon we will marry, and he will be my king. And I give him to you now!'

Laughing and flushed, she stepped back to enjoy the applause.

'No!'

The howl of rage split the air and echoed round the hall.

'No foreign king shall champion our Queen, while a man in the Summer Country can lift a sword! No stranger wins the right to lie beside our lady, when a lord of the Summer Country lives to say him nay!'

Lucan!

Guenevere could not move. Thoughts of pure terror almost drowned her mind. *Why did I never take account of this? Why did I not see that he would defend his position as the champion to the death?*

For Lucan wanted blood, it was plain. Feet apart, eyes glaring, he was advancing crab-wise through the crowd armed with sword and dagger, a figure like death itself.

'King Arthur, will you fight?' he ground out, through gritted teeth. 'I ask no quarter, and I will render none!'

'A challenge, a challenge, *à l'outrance*, to the death!' yelped the chamberlain, hardly able to voice the age-old words. 'Your Majesty, do you say yea or nay?'

'Nay!'

After days on the road, after the Battle of the Kings, after sleepless nights here and on the Hill of Stones, if Arthur was forced to fight now, he was as good as dead. And for Lucan to challenge him here, to defy her Chosen One in the face of her own court, was not to be allowed. 'I will not permit it!' Guenevere raged. 'The Queen's word is nay!'

'The word is *yea*, Lord Chamberlain.'

Drawn up to his full height, Arthur was pale, remote and terrible. 'Forgive me, madam.' He took her hand and touched it to his lips. 'This is your court, your kingdom, your command. But this is a challenge that may not be denied.'

Oh, my love, my love—

Tears blinded Guenevere's sight. Through a scalding mist she saw Arthur lying prostrate on the ground, swathed in black. His great frame was supported by three black-clad women, and the whole scene was framed in blackest night. Standing beside Arthur was Lucan, leaning heavily on his sword, his body gaping with open wounds.

Blood pounded in her ears. Lucan would kill Arthur before she even held him in her arms—

Arthur, my only love!

Arthur leaped from the dais, and landed lightly in the space in the midst of the crowd. In one swift movement he drew his sword and plucked his dagger from his belt. 'Lay on.'

'So!'

Lucan drove at Arthur from above, his sword slicing the air in a vicious curve. Arthur jumped back heavily, stumbling and catching his breath. Shifting his sword in his hand, he tried a clumsy pass as Lucan leaped forward again with a mocking laugh.

Guenevere clasped her hands and brought them to her lips. *Goddess, Mother, help him, help my love.*

Lucan moved in and out, taunting Arthur, wearing him down. Like a dog in the ring he nipped away at the great frame, and Arthur took all the punishment he gave with the blind dignity of a tormented bear.

Goddess, hear me now!

But Arthur was calling on Gods of his own. Planting his feet on the ground, he turned his eyes upwards and reached into his soul. Then he braced his broad shoulders, gripped his sword, and moved on to the attack.

'Pendragon!'

Now it was Lucan's turn to dodge and weave, to stumble and sweat. And as Arthur found his strength, Excalibur danced in its master's hand as it kept Lucan at bay without ever striking home.

For Arthur would not hurt Lucan, that was clear. Now the strain showed in Lucan's bulging eyes, his reddened face, and the sweat running like blood from his brow. It maddened him not to win.

'Come on, sir!' he snarled, whirling his sword round

his head. His every stroke was growing wilder now, his eyes inflamed and blinded by sweat. At last with a scream he leaped forward to thrust at Arthur's heart. And swiftly, smoothly, Arthur took him off balance and sent him crashing to the floor, his sword finding Lucan's throat.

'So, Sir Lucan!'

Lucan was a warrior. He knew how to die. 'No quarter!' he gasped. 'I offered none, and I ask none.' His pale lips moved in silence as he gave his soul to the Old Ones, and asked the Mother to take him home. Then he braced himself: 'Strike home!'

Arthur raised Excalibur. The mighty blade cried out for blood. A silence like death fell on all the hall. Sick and faint, Guenevere turned her head away.

'No, not today,' Arthur's voice said softly, 'not today, my dear.' He kissed the sword tenderly and put it away.

The crowd let out its breath in a huge collective sigh. Arthur looked round, the battle-magic falling from him like a cloud.

'Arise and live,' he said quietly to the figure on the ground. 'It would be a poor gift to Queen Guenevere to take the life of her finest knight!'

Unsteadily Lucan struggled to his knees, his breath straining in his throat. Then he lifted his eyes to Arthur, crossed his arms on his chest, and bowed his head. 'Accept my service, sire,' he said huskily, 'till the end of my days. From now on, this life of mine is yours.'

He lowered his head, and kissed Arthur's hands. Arthur placed one hand on Lucan's head, and with the other struck him lightly on one shoulder, then the other, once, twice, three times.

'It is done, Sir Lucan,' Arthur said, with the ghost of a sigh. 'You are my knight now.' He raised his head. 'Gawain?'

'My lord?'

The three companions tumbled forward as joyful as dogs when their master returns safe from war.

'Go, all of you,' Arthur said fondly. 'Give this knight all the assistance he needs to recover himself, and bring him back here as soon as you can.'

'Yes, sire.'

The three companion knights led Lucan away. Slowly Arthur turned to the still hushed and fearful crowd. 'And now,' he called into the depths of the hall, 'we are here to celebrate my betrothal to your Queen. No more sadness then! Let the rejoicing begin!'

A wild hum of delight ran through the court. Slowly Arthur turned back to the dais, his eyes searching for Guenevere.

Tears filled her eyes.

Oh, my love, my love—

Arthur, Arthur, my love—

The harsh sound broke in like an evil dream. *Goddess, Mother, what—?* Guenevere searched the hall in torment. What was that noise?

'King Arthur, a word!'

Again the clash of weapons sounded through the air. Malgaunt strode forward, his sword and dagger ringing in his hands. At his back were the two knights he had been whispering with before.

Malgaunt struck his weapons together again. 'A new challenge, sir!' His eyes were bright with mischief, and he was wearing his serpent's smile. 'And this time, to your honour as a king!' He pointed his sword at Guenevere. 'You should know that this fair field of the Summer Country, this virgin soil you so desire, has been under the plough before!'

'Under the plough?'

Arthur slowly turned towards Malgaunt. Guenevere could not move.

Malgaunt raised his voice, and his words echoed round the hall. 'Your queen-to-be has known men before. Will you marry her now, King Arthur? Your Guenevere is unchaste!'

CHAPTER 20

*U*nchaste?
'Yes, unchaste!' Malgaunt's sneering voice went on He indicated the two men by his side. 'As these knights will tell.'

'Arthur?' Guenevere cried, holding out her hands. But he was staring at Malgaunt, refusing to look at her.

Malgaunt.

What had he paid these men? What would they say? What did it matter, now the harm was done?

'Unchaste?' Thrusting furiously through the stunned and silent crowd came a warlike figure, stooped and greying now, but still a man to be feared. 'Take that word back, Prince Malgaunt, before you shame us all!'

Suddenly Guenevere was on the brink of tears. *A queen will always have her knights,* her mother had said. And here was one, championing Guenevere as he had fought for her mother before.

The newcomer came to a halt before the dais, planted his feet, and gave Arthur a sturdy bow. 'They call me Niamh, sir, and I serve the Queen. I was her mother's champion and Chosen One, and I will not stand by to hear the daughter so abused! In the country of the Goddess, we honour the gift

She gives. And She gives all women the right to treat their bodies as their own!'

'Yes, indeed!'

It was the tart voice of Brangwen, Niamh's wife of many years. 'The Mother's love for men is the source of all life. Without that, there is nothing! So all women have the right of love with the men they choose, and no man may say them nay.' She paused to throw a glare at Malgaunt standing by. 'And when a woman takes a man in thigh-freedom, she is still mistress of her body, and not property of his!'

'All this is true.' Taliesin's voice rang strongly through the hall. 'But hear me, King Arthur, Queen Guenevere has never taken a Chosen One, nor shown thigh-friendship to any man.'

Strong murmurs of agreement ran through the anxious court. But Arthur seemed deaf and blind to every sound.

And with a sinking heart Guenevere saw another figure gliding towards the stage. Merlin was moving up to be with his boy, ready to drop his poison into Malgaunt's brew.

For Merlin had chosen to have Arthur brought up as a Christian in the kingdom of Gore, where the worship of the Mother had failed long ago. In the Middle Kingdom where Arthur was now King, the rule of the Goddess had also passed away.

By the laws of Christ, only men had the right to rule. By those self-same laws, women belonged to men. The old Mother-rights of womankind were loathed and despised by them.

Merlin must have fostered these beliefs in Arthur, Guenevere knew. And now that she was accused of what they called a woman's greatest sin, Arthur must reject her, for his own good name.

Goddess, Mother, help me now.

'So, sire!' It was Malgaunt's voice, reeking with malice and delight.

'So, Prince Malgaunt.' At last Arthur stirred. 'The Queen is unchaste, you say.'

Malgaunt grinned lasciviously. 'Ask the Queen if she has a mole inside her left thigh.'

A mole inside her thigh?

A rush of shame left Guenevere scarlet from head to foot. *Malgaunt, you only know of this from our childhood, when all summer long we played in the sun. How long have you planned to use it against me?*

Already Malgaunt was in full flow with his tale, crooking his hand to summon one of his men. 'These knights will confirm all that I say against the Queen. Myself, I was the first man in her bed. But, for all I know, there have been many more than these.'

Why did Arthur say nothing, do nothing now?

Guenevere turned heavily towards him, avoiding his eye. 'My lord—'

'Prince Malgaunt.' The great bear-like form stirred again at her side. 'You say the Queen is unchaste.'

'I do!' Malgaunt scented triumph, he could scarcely contain his glee.

Slowly Arthur lifted his tired head. 'Then prepare to defend yourself, sir. For I am the Queen's champion, my task is to defend her, and a queen can do no wrong.'

It was almost worth the pain Guenevere had suffered to see the shock in Malgaunt's eyes. 'Fight, my lord? No, not I!' he stuttered.

Arthur shook his head. 'We must fight, sir,' he said, almost absently. 'And to the death, I think. For such things must not be said about a queen.' The smile he gave her now held all the sweetness of their love. 'Take courage, my lady,' he said quietly. 'I will not let this pass.'

When she spoke, it sounded like a sob. 'Arthur, no, don't take on this quarrel! You are exhausted – I beg you not to fight!'

He stepped towards her and laid his finger on her lips. 'Sweetheart, I must.' Wearily he signalled to the chamberlain.

Guenevere turned to Malgaunt. 'Give up this advantage, if you call yourself a knight!' she cried. 'It is against all the rules of chivalry to do battle with an over-battled knight! You gain no honour if you defeat the King!'

Malgaunt laughed in her face. 'Too late for courtesies! The King has challenged, I may not refuse.' He turned swiftly on Arthur where he stood. 'On guard!'

In an instant Malgaunt's sword and dagger were slashing down. Doggedly Arthur blocked the sudden assault. Stroke by stroke he withstood the shining hail of blows. With sudden burst of power, he succeeded in driving Malgaunt back. But Malgaunt returned to the onslaught, and again Arthur thrust him away.

And so it went, backwards and forwards, and Malgaunt could not break Arthur's guard. Yet every minute that passed was draining Arthur's strength.

'Ha!'

Arthur stumbled, and fell back with an oath. Grey-faced and sweating, he was having the worst of it now. Even Excalibur had lost its lustre, the great sword swinging weakly in his hand. Malgaunt was winning by wearing Arthur down, drawing out the agony to prolong his opponent's pain.

Guenevere watched, frantic. At every thrust of Malgaunt, Arthur would block and parry, parry and block again. He seemed to have no thought of going on to the attack. Was that to spare her kinsman, or his hatred of taking life? *Oh, Arthur, Arthur, he would not spare you!*

Malgaunt would have spared no man now, Arthur least of all. 'Gods above, drive my sword into his heart!' he prayed exultantly. He could smell blood, he could taste it, it filled his nostrils as they flared for the kill. Then a violent spasm crossed his face, and he screamed out with pain. His sword dropped from his nerveless hand as he fell on one knee.

'The Prince!' cried one of his knights. 'Save the Prince!'

Arthur threw down his weapons, and rushed to Malgaunt's aid. Guenevere saw him bend forward anxiously over the kneeling figure just as Malgaunt's dagger flashed up towards Arthur's heart.

'*Arthur!*' she screamed.

Arthur leaped backwards like a cat. The dagger missed its mark, and slashed low across his side. Blood blossomed on his tunic, and like a man awakening, Arthur came to himself at last.

Seizing Malgaunt's wrist, he tore the treacherous weapon from his grip, and forced Malgaunt face down on the ground. As Malgaunt fell, spattered with Arthur's blood, he felt his own dagger pricking the back of his neck, its point lodged in the soft hollow at the base of his skull.

Throughout the hall there was no sound but the drip, drip, drip of Arthur's blood. Malgaunt lay pinned to the floor, his face empty of everything except defeat.

'So, Your Majesty.' Arthur looked up at Guenevere. 'What is your will? Shall he live or die?'

Malgaunt dead? The thought was almost too good to bear. *But to take a life?* She hovered in an agony of mind.

Below her Malgaunt stirred. 'Let me die standing,' he screamed. 'Let me see my death!'

'Rise then!' commanded Arthur, picking up his sword.

Slowly Malgaunt clambered to his feet. 'Let me live, Guenevere!' he called, with a show of his old assurance. 'And I will swear allegiance to you till I die!'

Malgaunt's allegiance? Guenevere was seized by a wild urge to laugh. His allegiance was only to himself. No, with this last act of treachery alone he had forfeited the right to live. *Let him die!*

But would her marriage be ill-omened, bathed in Malgaunt's blood? If Arthur came to her bed with the life of her nearest kinsman on his hands?

In the Great Hall, the clock of life stood still.

Guenevere leaned down to Arthur. 'What do you say, my lord?'

He shook his head, his eyes on Malgaunt. 'You are Queen here. The word is yours.'

Still she hovered in an ecstasy of doubt. Yet Arthur had spared Lucan, he must want Malgaunt spared too. She raised her voice to sound all through the hall. 'Let him live!'

'On your knees, then, Prince Malgaunt!' Arthur ordered. 'Withdraw the charge you made against the Queen. Then let us hear you swear your oath to her.'

Malgaunt could not kneel or swear fast enough, as he jabbered out the words. Then he leaped to his feet and made for the dais to kiss Guenevere's hand.

Too much, too much!

'Do not come near me, Malgaunt!' she exploded. 'Your life is spared, but you are banished to your own estate till I send for you. If you stir from Dolorous Garde, your life and all are forfeit. Any defiance will be paid with death!'

For a second, the old Malgaunt flashed in his eyes. But he dropped his head, bowed in silence, and was gone. And gone indeed, she realised, trembling with relief. Malgaunt's lands were far distant, by her mother's deliberate choice. Guenevere had never been there, and now she knew she would never pass through those gates. Malgaunt was as good as dead to her from now on.

As he left, a silver mist rose before Guenevere's eyes.

Suddenly the whole hall filled with a faint sweet scent. She saw the castle of love fulfilled rising in the air. Arthur had defeated Malgaunt and overcome Lucan, he had triumphed over them all! Trembling and overwrought, she could feel the foolish tears pricking her eyes again. She reached out her hand. Nothing and no one could come between them now.

'Come, my lord!' she called rapturously.

Arthur smiled. The torchlight glinted on his hair as he came towards her, turning to face the crowd. 'The Queen stands before you without a stain on her name,' he called out. 'And nothing now bars the marriage that we shall make.'

A roar of delight spread through the excited crowd. The one lone voice rising above them all strained to make itself heard.

'A king must look to the future. And the stars tell a different tale.'

A pale-faced Merlin stood before the dais. His robe flashed thunder and lightning, and his yew wand hissed in his hand.

'Merlin, what now?' Arthur looked stunned. A thin sheen of panic broke out on his forehead, and his grip on Guenevere's hand tightened as he spoke.

'King Arthur, I must tell you that your will is no longer your own,' Merlin intoned. 'This Queen has already set contrary events in train.'

Arthur spoke with a great effort. 'What do you mean?'

Merlin pointed his writhing wand at the open door. 'You wanted to kill Prince Malgaunt. Instead the Queen has sent him away in peace.'

Guenevere looked at Arthur in horror. 'Arthur, surely you would not have killed Malgaunt? I only spared him because I thought it was your wish!'

'You were wrong.' Arthur was very pale. 'I would have killed him. He fought treacherously, and he deserved to die.'

'And you will live to regret this, Arthur,' Merlin went on, his voice growing shriller with every word. 'For Malgaunt is fated to destroy your peace! He will rob you of your best jewel, and leave a gaudy imitation in its place. All this he will do, because you spared his life!'

Arthur's face gleamed with a strained and unnatural light. 'On my head be it, then.'

'But there is more,' Merlin's high voice sang on. 'When you take her as your wife, you put your life at the mercy of this Queen. And she will have no mercy.'

He was chanting now, both hands outstretched, his wicked wand quivering towards Guenevere.

'I could have found you another, a damsel of beauty and simple goodness, one who would please you and love you all her life. This Queen is one of the fairest women alive, and you will not turn from her now your heart is set.' His eyes were flashing fire with every word. 'But she will be faithless to the marriage bed. She will betray you with one of your own knights!'

CHAPTER 21

Merlin's high-pitched cackle died away. The only sound was his harsh panting as he regained his breath.

Arthur gasped in pain, clutching the wound in his side. 'Merlin, for the sake of the Great Ones, have a care what you say! I have sworn to marry Queen Guenevere, on the oath of a king. Would you have me dishonour my vow?'

'I have seen it!' hissed Merlin blindly. 'I have seen it in the stars!'

'What have you seen, old man?'

It was Sir Gawain, his broad face burning with anger, his big body poised for a fight. 'You accuse the Queen with one of the King's knights? Then you accuse us of treachery to our lord!'

'It is written!'

'Written of me, or any of us here?' Furiously he indicated Kay and Bedivere. 'Or these?' He jerked an angry thumb at the dumbfounded Griflet and Sagramore.

Merlin shook his head reluctantly. 'No!'

'Who then?' demanded Gawain.

'My sight has not shown me! I do not see the face!'

Gawain laughed in relief. 'Then your sight is not worth much!'

Merlin screamed in rage. 'I can call spirits from the Otherworld!'

Gawain could not resist making sport of the old man. 'But do they answer when you call to them?'

An uneasy laugh ran through the crowd. Merlin rounded on them, blind with fury. 'I have seen it!' he shrilled. 'A tall knight, with his visor down, a stranger to the Queen, coming to her aid!'

A strange shudder seized him, and his body convulsed. Thunder and lightning racked his skinny frame, and all the air grew dark. Now his eyes were as blind as the night of the queen-making when he sang as a bard.

'He comes to her aid against Malgaunt!' he gasped, as his inner vision burst painfully to life. 'Malgaunt will take her – force her – but her knight comes, he comes to save her now!'

A deep groan escaped him as another sight was born. 'And in gratitude, she takes him to her bed!' He was shaking now as men do in a high plague-fever, when they know the end is near. Yet he would speak, or die in the travail. 'All this I have seen! And I see the truth!'

'Dear lord, you do indeed!'

Arthur leaped towards Merlin, and held him till the convulsions subsided and the old man grew calm. 'Never have your visions failed you, Merlin,' Arthur said tenderly, 'and they do not fail you now. But what you see has already come to pass!'

He threw back his head in a loud laugh of triumph. 'You saw the story of the night I met the Queen! You saw her under threat from her kinsman Malgaunt, as she was in truth. And I was the stranger knight, coming to her aid – I myself, not one of my own men!'

He turned towards Guenevere with a sudden, violent blush. 'And now I hope to come to the lady's bed. For I have wooed and won her, and I will marry her.'

Goddess, Mother, be thanked—

Guenevere could not hold back her tears.

So, Merlin, are you answered?

Yet Merlin had one last card to play. 'Why rush your nuptials, sire?' he wheezed, his voice creaking like the last leaf on the tree. 'A queen like yours deserves a royal wedding, with all the honour we can give. Delay the ceremony till you have pacified your kingdom, and you can lay your victory at her feet. Then the Queen can come to Caerleon for a great wedding there.'

Guenevere gasped. *Delay the wedding? And marry in Caerleon, when every woman, let alone a queen, rightfully marries from her own hearth and home?*

'Hear me, King Arthur!' The words broke from Guenevere before she was aware. 'In a true marriage, a man comes to a woman and she takes him, body and soul. That is the sacrament of union, and so it has always been.'

She shook her head in pain. If Arthur did not understand this, there was no hope. 'A man enters the circle of the Goddess when a woman admits him to her virgin body out of love. Men know this place only three times in their lives, once when they are born of their mothers, when they take a woman in first union, and when the Mother folds them in the last embrace. A woman offers this love only once. And it is not to be delayed!'

'So!' Merlin gasped for breath, passing his hand over his eyes, but from beneath it watching Arthur like a snake.

Guenevere paused before Arthur, trembling from head to foot. 'If you choose me, choose now. And if you choose to wait, then you must choose again. For I will not go to Caerleon to be married, and if you return for me, I will not be here!'

There was an endless pause. Then Arthur shook his tired head, and his clear grey eyes met hers. 'My love, I have chosen.' he said, with infinite sweetness. 'And I ask you again, how soon may we be married?'

That night all Camelot slept a deep and dreamless sleep, and next day the work began. For this must be the feast of a lifetime, Guenevere knew. It would be the start of her life with Arthur, and their first act as King and Queen. Not even her mother, entertaining six kings and queens at a banquet, had ever done as much.

At dawn, messengers were sent galloping far and wide. The list of wedding guests stretched throughout the kingdom and beyond. The fastest riders took the road west to the Middle Kingdom to summon Arthur's knights and barons, while others went north towards Gore to King Ursien who had sheltered Arthur as a child, and the foster-parents, Sir Ector and Dame Arian, who had brought him up. Guenevere saw that a special envoy was sent to the Lady too, though she knew that the ruler of Avalon had ways of knowing faster than any horse.

In the palace Ina ran to and fro, ordering dress-makers and milliners, shoe-makers and flower-girls, to her heart's content. 'White and gold, lady, white and gold!' she breathed. 'These are the colours you must marry in. And I know who must make your wedding gown!'

The next day she brought a withered old woman to the palace, a crone from the poorest end of the town, her crooked frame clad from head to foot in black. She might have been Ina's kin, Guenevere thought, for she had the look of the Otherworld often seen on Ina's cat-like face. She examined all the silks in the palace chests, and pronounced that they would not do. But in three days, she swore, the Queen would have a gown.

Three days would bring them to the feast of high midsummer and the night without dark, when the doors of the Otherworld stand open for love. Taliesin would marry them in the heart of the woodland, Guenevere told Arthur, close to the Mother and the source of life. Then they would feast all night in Camelot, till the last revellers crept to their beds in a rosy, laughing dawn.

And then—

In truth, she did not know what happened then.

Her mother said, *When love comes, you will know. And when you know, you will know what to do.*

Well, love had come – Arthur would know what to do.

Goddess, Mother, smile upon us now.

As the wedding day drew near, events took on a rhythm of their own, and the work proceeded with more than human aid. The maids came down at dawn to find the floors sanded, the pewter and copper shining, and all things sweet and clean. By day, all Camelot was in the grip of a flaming June. Around the castle, roses and honeysuckle bloomed as they had never bloomed before. And every evening Guenevere and Arthur would walk together entwined in each other's arms, whispering softly through the purple twilight as night fell.

In all this time, Merlin was nowhere to be seen. He was resting, Arthur said tenderly, exhausted by the sight he had had. And he had to build up his strength for the ride to Caerleon as soon as the wedding was done.

Of course, said Guenevere, and was there anything she could do? Would Arthur give him her greetings, and assure him of her regard? *And would the old meddler kindly keep to his bed?* she found herself thinking, though the thought made her blush.

But in truth there was little time to think of Merlin now. Wavering between happiness and blind fear, Guenevere had

to prepare for her new life as Arthur's Queen. With only
days before the wedding, suddenly half her gowns and
jewels and cloaks and shoes, half her books, even half
her mother's face colours and pots and lotions must go
with her to Caerleon. What to take, and what to leave
behind? Ina enrolled all the Queen's women in the impossible task.

And every day now brought new arrivals to grace the wedding feast. Though time was short, Arthur was determined
to be married like a King. So the crown of Pendragon
was sent for post-haste from Caerleon, brought by the
remainder of Arthur's band of companion knights – fourteen
all told, making their numbers up to twenty with those
already there.

　'Tor! Helin! Oh, it's good to see you here!' Sagramore
rushed forward, whooping like a boy, to greet his fellows,
while Griflet and Ladinas ran up behind. 'And Erec!' He
hailed a brawny figure with a long fresh scar on his neck.
'Where did you get that?'

　Arthur watched ruefully as the newcomers rode clattering into the courtyard, and dismounted to loud cheers
and hurrahs. 'You see why I envy your Order of the Round
Table,' he said lightly to Guenevere, 'when a hundred
knights sit there under Lucan's command. We are so few
– may the Gods send us more!'

　'My lord?' Guenevere pointed towards the castle gate.
Riding in was the kingly figure of an older man. Beside him
rode a fair youth, and with them a standard-bearer and a
troop of knights. Arthur stared at the banner fluttering
overhead. On an azure ground, a white swan soared proudly
through the air. He seized Guenevere's hand in a painful
grip. 'Listinoise!'

　'King Pellinore of Listinoise greets the Queen,' cried the

standard-bearer with a courtly bow. 'And he comes to lay his sword before the King!'

The newcomer dismounted, attended by the young man at his side. Together they approached Arthur, and knelt before him on the cobblestones. The King lifted his head. 'Sire, I was the first to swear for your father King Uther, when he made himself High King. I was at his side through every battle, and with him when he died.' A hard hand passed briefly over his eyes. 'When I heard you had returned, that Pendragon had come home to Caerleon again—' His eyes flared, and he scrambled to his feet. 'I would have rallied to you then, sire, had I known, to help you drive those weevils from your father's lands. And when they come again, my sword is yours!'

Arthur fell forward, and folded him in a bear-like hug. Then he turned to Guenevere, tears in his eyes. 'My lady, bid this good King welcome, for he promises to be a dear friend to me.'

But King Pellinore would not hear Arthur's praise. His grey eyes sought Guenevere with painful honesty. 'Your Majesty, this is no more than any man would do.' He gestured to the young man standing tensely at his side. 'I and my son will only be the first. Countless others will stand for King Arthur as soon as they hear of his struggle against King Lot. The memory of Uther will draw thousands to your side. The name of Pendragon is greater than all of us.'

Guenevere eyed him carefully. Lean, grey and reserved, King Pellinore would never take credit simply for doing right. Wherever he placed his faith, he would be loyal all his life. The same would be true of the fair young man by his side, who blushed and trembled as he kissed her hand. Lucky the woman who won the love of Pellinore's son, she thought smiling, for young Lamorak's Chosen One would have it till she died.

Guenevere favoured both father and son with her best smile. 'Welcome, sirs. You are welcome, in the King's name and my own!'

She must have said these words a hundred times as the guests poured in. For the first time in years she saw again chuckling old men from her childhood, and bright-eyed dames with tales of her mother when she and they were girls. With Arthur at her side she welcomed lords from the mountains, and yeomen from the valleys, and the short shy chiefs of the Land Kin she had first seen at the queen-making. They had to be encouraged to draw near Arthur to kiss his hand, and they bowed and squinted before him as if he were the golden god Bel indeed.

All had the warmest welcome. But to Arthur, one group meant more than all the rest. As the trumpets sounded and the heralds cried 'Give welcome to King Ursien of Gore!' Guenevere saw great tears standing in his eyes.

'See, Guenevere!' was all that he could say.

First to dismount was the King himself, a bluff old soldier who clapped Arthur on the shoulder, and forbade him to kneel or bow. 'We are brother monarchs now, boy, not king and knight any more.' He threw a glance around. 'And if your Druid Merlin's dreams come true, the time will come when I will kneel to you.'

Arthur laughed in confusion. 'If you say so, sire!'

'I do.' He waved a hand. 'But High King or no, you must honour your foster-mother Dame Arian here!'

Blushing and bobbing in King Ursien's shadow was a small neat woman fondly shaking her wimpled head. She looked at Arthur, chuckling with delight. 'Gods above, to see you here, a king! Still, I always knew that you would come to good. And you were always as dear to me as my own son!' Then her head turned sharply, like a hen seeking her chick. 'Where's Kay? What have you done with him?'

With a knightly flourish, Kay stepped forward to take his mother's hand. 'The King has done nothing with me, madam, I'm here! I might as well ask you where's my father, what have you done with him?'

'Kay!' Careless of his dignity, Dame Arian reached up with a cry of joy to plant a smacking kiss on both his cheeks. 'Your father was delayed as we came through. He stayed on in Caerleon, to bring dispatches for the King.' She dropped a curtsey to Arthur. 'So he sent me on with King Ursien here. But he will be with us for the wedding, sire, have no fear of that.'

'I have no fear of Sir Ector's loyalty.' Already Arthur was laughing at her busy, bustling ways. 'And all shall be as you say, Dame Arian, as it always was!'

The night before the wedding, an army of men and maids scoured the Great Hall, then decked the roof and beams with green boughs, ferns and flowers like a woodland bower. The high table on the dais was draped in white damask, and laden with bowls of white lilies for the bride and red poppies for the groom. A hundred places were set with silver knives, and cups and plates of gold. In the centre of the hall stood the Round Table, where the knights alone would dine. And up and down the length of the hall ran rows of stout wooden trestle tables for the guests.

In the kitchens the cooks had toiled for days, thrown on their mettle by the sudden demand. A thousand and more would sit down to eat, all the court and people of Camelot, all the lords and knights who kept their own castles and manors in the country beyond. Those who could not be seated in the hall would be fed on the grass outside, served by armies of attendants with food and wine.

And there would be meat and bread, eggs and cheese, an abundance of all good things. Every home farm for miles had been raided for its stock. 'Pay the best prices, give them what they want,' Guenevere ordered, 'but we must have every table groaning with good food!' None who came would go hungry, Guenevere swore, if they had to feed five thousand there. Everyone would share the glory of the feast.

On the eve of the wedding, Guenevere told Arthur that they would not meet that night. They would not dine together, nor walk in the twilight as they had. The last hours of her maidenhood she wanted to spend alone. But now, as the night wore away, she sent for him.

Deep underneath the castle lay a cavern, in the heart of the living rock. Some said it had been the first war-stronghold of the palace itself. Others said it was a sacred place of the Mother, one of the wombs of the earth, which the old Land Kin made into a shrine to worship Her. At its darkest end it still held the ancient black stone of the Goddess, sister to those on Avalon and the Hill of Queens.

In other castles, chambers such as this were reserved for dark tortures, or as living graves. But this was used as the treasure chamber of the palace, bright with heaps of gold and silver piled up on long stone tables, loving cups and great dishes, and trenchers a yard across and more. Royal crowns for queens and kings, gold collars a hand's span deep, and ropes of gold sparked in alcoves round the walls.

Further down, fine jewels spilled out of silk-lined chests, and glowed in boxes of sandalwood and shell. Here were the royal rubies and the amethysts Arthur had brought, with all the pearls and garnets, coral and amber, turquoises and tiger's eyes that the Queens of the Summer Country had treasured since time began. Here, too, slept all the country's finest weapons of war till their time came to awake. And here on the altar lay Guenevere's wedding gift.

Arthur, my love—

Her heart leaped with a painful joy as she saw him shouldering through the torchlit darkness of the low passageway, ducking his fair head into the chamber, his sword Excalibur as always by his side. In the world above, she knew, the air was warm in the June night, glittering with fireflies, heavy with all the sweetness of the earth. But here the rock sweated like a living thing, and the torches guttered in the thick damp air.

In silence Guenevere drew Arthur down the room. On the altar where she had placed it lay the regalia of her mother, the Queen's sword and shield and spear. She took up the sword, drew it from its scabbard, and laid the weapon down again. Facing Arthur, she passed the jewelled sheath into his hands. He started, and a look of wonder passed over his face. 'Why, Guenevere!' He sighed. 'It's like a living thing!'

She nodded soberly. She could hear her mother's voice as she used to tell this tale. 'There was a Queen of the Summer Country who was so beautiful that the King of the Fair Ones fell in love with her. After long wooing, she took him for her love. Though she was a mortal, she made the sacred marriage with this man of the Otherworld so that all her children and all the Queens of the Summer Country after her would be like him, tall and fair with shining brows.

'And he loved her so much that he made this magic thing. He wove a charm into the gold and silver of the casing, and whispered his will into the stones and jewels that adorn the sheath. The spell he cast was to keep her safe. Being mortal, she could lose her life with one blow. But when she wore this in battle, even if she was wounded, she would shed no blood. The spell still holds today. And this is my gift to you, Arthur, because I love you so.'

His hand flew to the place where Malgaunt had wounded him. His eyes met hers, wide with love and desire. 'You know what it means if you give me this?'

Guenevere nodded. 'I know that I will never lead an army in battle as my mother did. She would not train me up for it, because she said that warfare was changing now. When the Romans came, they brought new ways of death. Soon even our war chariots will be things of the past.' She pressed his hand. 'But that is not why I am giving up my birthright to you. It's because there is a life now that is dearer to me than mine. You are my life. And tomorrow when we marry, you will be mine, and I yours, for ever and a day.'

Arthur took the scabbard and raised it to his lips. 'So be it,' he said huskily. Tears of deep feeling were welling in his eyes. 'I have sworn to protect you, and now you show your care for me. May this gift shield us both from evil to come. May I never betray this tribute, or prove unworthy of your love.'

Oh, Arthur, Arthur . . .

She never loved him more than she did then. But as he spoke, a gust of air brushed her cheek, and she heard the shadow of a sigh.

It was the sigh that had breathed through Avalon when Arthur swore his undying faith to her. It was the voice of the Lady, and it whispered of all the sorrow of the world. In it she felt the wind off the desert, the chill of the place beyond Eden, the grief of all vows shattered, broken hearts, and faith betrayed.

But a moment later she was shaking the tears from her eyes and laughing joyfully as Arthur kissed her and crushed

her to his chest. And she shook the moment off, and they
hastened back to their chambers to make ready to step out
gaily on their wedding day. For they were young, and knew
nothing except that they were in love.

CHAPTER 22

B ack in her chamber, Guenevere still carried with her the memory of Arthur's face. She saw his high forehead with its prominent brow-bone and thick eyebrows of glinting gold. She saw his broad cheekbones and strong nose, and his fearless laugh as he threw back his head. She saw his kind eyes, and his wide mouth approaching for a kiss. How could she ever be good enough for him, she moaned to Ina, roaming the chamber in spasms of dread as the dawn birds cried.

'Never fear, madam, you will!' Ina soothed. Her Other-worldly face was alight with its wild-cat gleam. 'He should ask himself if he is good enough for you. Come, now, your gown!'

Ina was purring with pride, as well she might be, marvelled Guenevere, her eyes out on stalks. For the old dress-maker had created a wonder to behold. With her crooked fingers she had spun a gown out of gossamer and moonbeams, floating in a magic of its own. She had fashioned a headdress and veil as delicate as the blossom on Avalon, and a train made of morning hopes and sweet evening dreams. The whole creation whispered and sang to itself as it waited for its time, dazzling and shimmering in its own reflected light.

From another of Ina's kinfolk came a pair of little slippers as dainty as foxgloves, with silken heels. Her stockings were cobweb-fine, held up by garters of white lace. Gold bracelets set with moonstones circled her wrists, and a moonstone collar clustered round her neck. And, like her bridegroom Arthur, she too wore the crown of her own country, the great diadem of queens, gold and moonstone, set with crystal and pearl.

At dawn they rode out of Camelot, Arthur on a bay stallion and Guenevere on a mare of silver-white. The grooms had bridled the horses with reins of silk and gold, and plaited tiny bells and rosebuds into their manes and tails. The women of the town had fashioned arches of greenery to hold above their heads, and the children ran before them, strewing leaves and flowers under the horses' hoofs.

Carolling and dancing, a long train of townsfolk followed the couple down from the hilltop where Camelot floated above the valley, across the causeway over the ring of shining water, and into the woodland beyond. The town piper made merry music, and sweet bells and cymbals sounded from every hand.

Arthur rode beside Guenevere, chastely clad in a tunic of pure white. But his cloak was a vivid scarlet and his soft leather boots and breeches were ebony black. Deep clasps of gold encircled his wrists, and his wide belt was inlaid with gold. At his side Excalibur hung sleeping in its new jewelled scabbard heavy with old gold. And on his head he wore the great gold crown of King Uther, surmounted by the beast of Pendragon made all of emeralds, with great rubies flaming from its dragon eyes.

On they rode, and into the woodland's heart, through hidden greenways and tracks hardly known. Now the laughing, dancing crowd fell silent as it followed them into the temple of green trees, hushed by the spell of the Mother as they entered Her domain.

With a proud smile, Arthur caught Guenevere's eye and glanced at his knights riding behind. At the head of the band were Gawain, Kay and Bedivere, glittering in their finest mail. Behind the bright banners of the knights came King Ursien and Merlin, escorted by both King Leogrance and Lucan, splendidly arrayed. As Guenevere looked back, she met an unblinking golden eye. Riding on a white mule bridled with silk, resplendent again in all his woodland hues, Merlin could have been the lord of the forest, the Horned One himself.

On they went, and on. Above the green roof of the woodland, the noonday sun burned down. Shafts of sunlight burst through the trees as they passed, and flecked their path with fire. A languorous warmth hung under the canopy of leaves, and the rich scent of foliage filled the air.

The heart of the forest was crowned with burning sun. Through the trees the red and gold light beckoned them into the green grove ahead. And there Taliesin waited with his Druids, a white-robed choir humming a chant of love. At the sight of them, he raised both his arms, and began.

'Guenevere, Queen of the Summer Country, and Arthur, King of the Middle Kingdom, I bid you draw near . . .'

As they made their vows, a cloud of doves burst cooing from the trees and hovered overhead, a living, fluttering canopy of white. In the west the love-star bloomed in the eye of the sun, then gently faded into the evening light. How she made her responses, what Arthur said to her, Guenevere did not know. But she saw she was lovely to him, and beloved beyond compare. She saw it as they stood at the green altar in the forest, and she saw it, felt it, rejoiced in it, all the way back to Camelot.

For now they were married, now she wore his ring on

her finger and he wore hers. Now the singing, drumming, dancing, laughing and crying was redoubled as the townsfolk escorted them back through the woodland over the hills and valleys, and down to Camelot where the revels lay.

As they came into the Great Hall hand in hand, roars of approval rang to the roof-beams. It was the signal for the minstrels to pipe up in the gallery, for the jugglers and tumblers in the hall to spring to life, for the choir of children to begin their wedding song.

'Courage, my love!' breathed Arthur, as the people pressed in from all sides.

'See how they love you!' she whispered back. The heady scent of the bridal lilies enveloped her like a caress, and the leafy boughs decking the hall breathed a green woodland air.

'And I you!' he murmured, his heart in his eyes. 'But all the world loves us as we love each other now!'

Somehow they made their way towards the dais, as the joyful hubbub increased. Behind them King Leogrance and Lucan struggled to bring Merlin and King Ursien through the crowd. Arthur's twenty knights and Lucan's hundred were of little help. For knights like Lucan were heroes to the people, and each had his own band of admirers impeding him.

They had reached the steps to the dais when they heard the flurry at the door. It was the chamberlain: 'Your Majesties! A messenger from the Lady, come from Avalon!'

The figure who stepped into the hall was robed in shining silk, her head veiled, her sweet face grave. In one hand she carried a wand of applewood, in the other she held the Lady's crystal globe bound round with gold.

A slow hiss of breath came from Arthur's right. Guenevere turned to see Merlin staring at Nemue as if he had seen the vision of his life. 'A messenger from the Lady?' he breathed heavily, his eyes glittering. 'Who is she? Who?'

Guenevere eyed him coldly. 'Her name is Nemue. She is the chief damsel of the Lady of the Lake.'

'Queen Guenevere!' cried Nemue in her strange husky voice. 'And my lord King Arthur! The Lady sends you joy on your wedding day. She calls down the blessings of the Mother on your bed. And she begs you to accept these gifts of love.'

She raised her hand. Through the door came four of the Lake Maidens, lustrous in their gold and glossy green. The first led a dainty white bitch on a gold collar and lead. 'For the Queen!' she called, and bowed.

The second had a white hart on a chain and collar too, a tame doe who calmly looked around, and fastened her great liquid eyes on Arthur. 'For the King!' the Maiden cried.

On a green velvet cushion the third carried a massive torque of twisted gold. 'For the King!'

And gleaming on its own cushion lay a crown of moonstones cool in the burning sun. 'For the Queen!'

'The Queen thanks you, for herself and the King!' Guenevere cried in delight.

Merlin leaned towards Nemue, and crooked a withered hand. 'Come to me, my dear!' he beckoned, grinning with an odd familiarity. 'Sit beside me. I dare swear that you and I have much to say to one another – and much to learn!'

What?

Would the old man dare to try to impose himself on a priestess of the Goddess, their most honoured guest? Guenevere felt herself flushing with anger and shame.

Nemue looked at him with eyes as clear as the waters of the Lake. 'Forgive me, Druid,' she said coolly, 'but I am sworn to the Mother, and I only keep company with men of my choice.'

Merlin cackled with delight, rubbing his hands. 'And what must a man do to win your choice?'

Nemue's voice grew colder and clearer still. 'I do not choose men by what they do, but by what they are.' She turned to Guenevere. 'May I take my seat with my Maidens, Your Majesty? We have travelled long to be with you today.'

'Certainly, at once!'

Turning her back on Merlin, Guenevere ushered Nemue through the ranks of joyful revellers, some already the worse for the freely flowing wine. In the central aisle of the hall, the people were cheering the tumblers and jugglers and village clowns. Yet none of the capering fools grinned and nodded as Merlin did, Guenevere thought angrily, or looked at Nemue with such wild eyes.

He was watching them closely now, his withered forefinger raised as if to beckon Nemue to his side. Gods above, what was he trying to do? Guenevere could not suppress a sharp unease. Could Arthur speak to his old mentor, and take care of him?

But across the hall she could see Arthur in deep discussion with Sir Kay and his mother Dame Arian. Kay's sharp face was troubled, and Dame Arian showed signs of evident distress. 'Have no fear, lady!' Arthur was reassuring her. 'Sir Ector will not miss my wedding day.'

Kay nodded. 'He may have been delayed at the Severn crossing,' he said slowly. 'The water can be rough there, even in June.'

'I do not doubt it. Come, let the feast begin!'

Laughing and jostling, court and countryfolk queued to find places at the long tables in the body of the hall. Good humour and good wine were flowing in equal measure, and it was a long while before all were settled and ready to begin.

At last the trumpets sounded, and Arthur stood up to speak. 'My Queen, ladies and lords, knights and revered Druids and people of Camelot—'

'Gods above!'

There was a loud commotion outside the hall.

'Your Majesty, forgive me!'

It was the chamberlain crying at the door. Leaning on his shoulder as he staggered in came an old man covered in blood, raw with the wounds of great falls from his horse.

Arthur's throne crashed to the floor as he started up. 'Sir Ector!' he cried in horror.

The old man fell to his knees, spitting blood, then raised his battered head. 'To arms, to arms!' he rasped. 'King Lot has raised eleven kings against you! Their armies are massing, many thousands strong. He challenges you to meet him in the field. He has sworn an oath to kill Merlin's boy!'

CHAPTER 23

*A*rthur attacked – *on our wedding day?*
Guenevere stood drained of all thought but one.
*Goddess, Mother, is this Your will? Your punishment?
What is our sin?*

Beside her Arthur drew in a long ragged breath. 'Caerleon attacked?'

'Not yet, my liege. But the hosts of King Lot are on the march.'

'To horse, to horse!'

Gawain leaped into action, bellowing orders at the servants by the door. Kay and Bedivere sprang to follow his large ungainly frame. 'I will order the horses, sire!' he threw urgently over his shoulder. 'Do not fear, they will be ready sooner than you can think.'

'Gawain, *no!*'

The stern command cut through the silent court. Arthur took Guenevere's hand, and turned to face the crowd. 'Tomorrow at dawn we ride to Caerleon, not before.'

'Sire!' Gawain was aghast. 'They're massing against you, marching on Caerleon now!'

'They will not reach Caerleon overnight. And I will not go to war on my wedding day.'

Sir Ector raised his bruised and battered head. 'Thousands,

many thousands are coming,' he said hoarsely. 'All whom Lot can rally to his side.'

Kay hastened forward. 'My lord—' he began. Behind him Sagramore, Griflet, Ladinas and all the rest of Arthur's companion knights were pressing forward too, eager to be off.

Arthur held up his hand. His face was set, and his voice remote. 'Tonight is sacred to the Queen-Goddess of this land. I have married her, and I will fulfil her rites.'

When lovers married in Camelot, all the court would bring the bride to bed, laughing and dancing, with candles, songs and flowers. But there would be no revelry tonight. Alone with her women, Guenevere waited for Arthur to come.

In the cool of the Queen's apartments, she would not let them undress her – she was not ready to lay aside the beauty of the day. But she was glad to feel light hands lifting off her crown, and bathing her face and hands before she sent them away. Their silent care lifted her sombre mood, and at last her heart revived. The sky might fall tomorrow, but tonight would be for love.

He came at last, and she ran towards him to relieve him of his cloak. But he laid his finger on his lips with a mischievous smile, and took her by the hand. 'Come!'

His eyes were dancing like a wild creature of the wood. Together they stole unseen through the depths of the palace, down, down into the heart of the rock, till they found their way outside into the wood. And soon they were lost in the great green depths again.

High in the sky rode a moon as white as buttermilk, attended by a thousand twinkling stars. Beneath the trees the woodland lay warm and still, and the scent of night hung heavy in the air. Within a grove of hawthorn blossom, a thick fall of honeysuckle made a natural bower. And there

Arthur took her in his arms, and kissed her as a man kisses the woman he means to make his. 'Oh, my sweetheart!' he murmured brokenly. 'My little love!'

Inside the palace, Guenevere knew, the bright candles and torches that brought the bride to bed made every woman shine like a queen of the night. Here only glow-worms hung in the bushes, and the pale moon smiled down. But Arthur shone on her like one of the Lords of Light who had walked in this forest before the world was born. He was as fair as the Shining Ones who had made the world.

'Arthur, Arthur, my love!' She reached for him, and wrapped her arms round his neck. Gently he stroked her face, and kissed her again. She clung to him, drowning in his touch. His body was hard against hers, and the hair on the back of his neck was as soft as down.

'Guenevere!'

Arthur drew in his breath in bliss. He might have been born for this minute, and he wanted to hold the joy of it for the rest of his life. His hands slid blindly down her back, and with a sigh of wonder he took her by the hips. Her body was warm and full, more real than he had dreamed. 'Such a little waist!' he said.

Guenevere laid her head upon his chest. The scent of him was mingling with the sweet airs of the night, honeysuckle and violet and vernal-grass. All around them the living woodland breathed in its sleep.

'Come!' Arthur whispered. He threw his cloak over the bed of ferns, and drew her down to lie by his side. Overhead the wild honeysuckle made a natural canopy, and the white moon gleamed through the lattice of pink and cream tendrils on to Arthur's face. Suddenly he had lost the soft look of boyhood, and taken on the spirit of the wild. Now she could see the desire in his eyes, and feel the heat of his body pressed the length of hers. And a heat she had never known before rose to answer him.

Trembling, Arthur fumbled with her gown, his great hands baffled by the tiny pearl fastenings in the front. With a drowsy laugh, she lay there till the last one gave way. Her gown moved like moonlight on water as he parted its shimmering folds.

Arthur could hardly breathe. Never had he seen anything so lovely as Guenevere's naked form. Her body was white in the half-light, glowing with the pale moon's midnight fire. And she was giving all this to him?

Yes, Arthur, Arthur my only love . . .

Guenevere lay lost in ecstasy. She was floating now, above her body, above the forest, above the roof of the world.

Arthur shook his head like a man in a dream. 'Ohh . . .' he breathed. Roughly he stroked her breast, and the warmth at her centre blossomed under his caress. 'Oh, my love!' he moaned.

He reared up and tore his tunic over his head. Naked, his body gleamed with a golden light.

'My queen – my wife!'

He entered her, and she felt a shaft of pain. Then a triumphant burning grew in her and spread till her whole frame throbbed with fire. A raw cry burst from her throat.

Arthur cradled her in his arms and gentled her tenderly, stroking and soothing her with a thousand little sounds and soft caresses as if he had been doing it all his life. Then he gripped her hard, and plunged and reared and cried out in throes of his own. Afterwards he laid his head on her breast and wept. Then he folded them both in his cloak, and they lay entwined in their ferny hollow, and watched the stars dancing till they fell asleep.

*   *   *

Guenevere awoke the next morning in the Queen's great bed. Arthur was standing fully dressed at her side. 'Awake, my love!' he said urgently. 'We ride for Caerleon now!'

All Camelot heard them as they thundered out of the castle and down through the narrow cobbled streets of the little town. Ahead of them rode Arthur's knights, while behind came all the Queen's knights with Lucan in the lead. In the midst of Arthur's knights rode Merlin with King Ursien, King Pellinore, and last night's messenger Sir Ector himself. Forbidden by Arthur to ride, the old man had ordered the grooms to hoist him on to his horse, tied himself into his saddle, and declared that he would go with them, or die.

'To Caerleon!'

Arthur's cry roused the birds from their trees. Guenevere took one last look at the white battlements of Camelot, their glimmering turrets bright with flags in the dawn, and turned her face away. The Summer Country would be safe in the hands of Taliesin and her father, she had no doubt of that. But when would she see her beloved land again?

'Onward!' Arthur cried, standing up in his stirrups, his upraised arm cleaving the air. 'To Caerleon!'

To Caerleon—
Onward to Caerleon—
Onward—

Those who saw them pass said they rode as if all the devils of the air were on their trail. Four, six, eight hours after they left, the round-eyed observers were still wondering at their furious pace.

From Camelot they made straight to the Severn Water, pushing on mile after dreary mile. Darkness overtook them before they reached the ferry, but they dared not stop to rest. On the other side of the water, a final gallop brought Caerleon into their sights.

Caerleon—

Dimly Guenevere traced the looming outline of the great castle on the rock, its back against the mountain, its four high towers encircling the mighty keep. But they crossed the moat in darkness almost before she was aware, raced at full pelt up to the citadel, and there, without pausing to change their travel-stained clothing, swept into the nearest chamber for a council of war.

Inside the castle it was colder than the night outside. The room where they sat smelt fusty, the hangings were worn and faded, the air stale with dust undisturbed for many months. The corridors they traversed were dirty and rubbish-strewn too, with cracked flagstones and cobwebbed beams proclaiming their neglect. The six kings may have descended on Caerleon for sport and revelry whenever they desired, Guenevere saw, but the place had not had a chatelaine's care in years.

And who were all these grim, unsmiling men? Why did Arthur not command more torches, to brighten the room and put heart into them all? Guenevere sat in silence, her senses bruised by the strangeness of her surroundings, and tried to follow what was going on.

Could this be Caerleon's ruling council, this handful of sad old men huddled by the light of one dim candle round the end of the council board? And surely she and Arthur must have been hurried into an unused antechamber? Vast as it was, this musty room, with worm-eaten panelling, cracked windows and worn baize, could never have been the council hall of kings!

Yet here they were, half a dozen greybeards with furrowed brows and lined faces, clad in ancient gowns of spotted velvet smelling strongly of better days. Sir Baudwin, an old knight of King Uther and lord-lieutenant of Caerleon, bluntly broke the news. His large plain face was carved

with deep concern, and he tugged restlessly at the forks
of his iron-grey beard. 'King Lot has declared war, and is
marching on Caerleon. But let me tell you, sire, that old Sir
Ulfius, your father's wisest counsellor, has gone hot-foot to
him with urgent terms of peace.'

'So!'

Across the table Merlin sat bright and attentive, showing no trace of the long hours on the road. Guenevere eyed
him with sharp distaste. Did he know that his actions had
stirred up this hornet's nest? Was there no way to reclaim
Arthur's birthright without inflaming King Lot? How could
Merlin so blithely have ignored the malice of the man who
thought he should be High King?

'Where is King Lot now?' Arthur sounded calm.

'On his way down from the Orkneys, rallying his allies
as he comes,' said Sir Baudwin heavily. 'He rewards all who
join him and kills all who refuse, making them sacrifices
to his cruel Gods. Eleven kings have joined the league
against you now. Some see the whole country coming under
his sway.'

'The whole country?'

Sir Baudwin groaned. 'The whole island, sire! King Lot
commands more territory than you think. He holds lands in
Cornwall as well as his Orkneys terrain. So he claims the
right to rule in the north and in the far south, with our
kingdom, sire, lying conveniently in between.'

Arthur looked baffled. 'Cornwall? How?'

A low whine escaped from Merlin's yew wand as
it leaned against his chair. But the old man sat smiling
strangely, staring out at them all. Guenevere glanced round
in fear. Had anyone else heard the wand cry out?

Arthur seemed oblivious. Another of the old lords
round the table took up the tale. 'Sire, when your father
was making himself High King, he needed King Lot as an

ally, to hold northern territories for him. But Lot knew his price. He wanted King Uther's eldest daughter as his bride.' Baudwin bowed down the table in apology. 'At the time, my lord, the girl was all that Uther had in the way of kin. Your father kept your birth secret, so no one knew that he had had a son. In Lot's mind, then, marrying Uther's daughter made him the High King's heir.'

'What?'

The blood drained from Arthur's face. 'Lot married King Uther's *daughter?*' He gripped the edge of the table, his eyes bulging with shock. 'I thought I was my father's only child!'

Again the yew wand made its grumbling complaint as its owner smiled, and smiled. 'You are indeed, my lord!' Merlin agreed. 'King Uther, your father, married only once, and had one child, yourself. When you were born, he sent you away in secret under my care, because he feared that his enemies might capture you; he wanted to save your life. But the Queen your mother had been married before. She had two girls by her first husband. It was the elder who was given to King Lot.'

Arthur was still struggling with it all. 'There were two daughters when I was born – half-sisters to me, then?'

'Hardly that,' said Merlin brusquely. He waved a withered hand. 'The Queen and her daughters have no meaning in your destiny.'

Guenevere stared. A ruling queen dismissed out of hand like this? A mother to have no place in her son's life?

Arthur was very pale. 'Why did you tell me none of this before?'

Merlin opened his eyes wide, and gave a smiling shrug. 'There has been little time for family history, sire!'

Sir Baudwin nodded. 'But you see from this, my lord, why King Lot thinks fit to challenge you now. He had thought of himself as the premier king of these islands for many years. Already he rules Lothian and all the Orkneys in the north. Until you came, he thought he held the Middle Kingdom as his own. And through his wife, he claims Cornwall too.'

He inclined his head courteously to Guenevere. 'You must know, Your Majesty, that like the Summer Country, Cornwall has kept to the old ways. Her queens, like yours, rule in their own right. The daughter who married King Lot is her mother's natural heir. Already Lot uses his power and his marriage to her daughter to try to bully and dictate to the old Queen. When she dies, King Lot expects to claim the land in his wife's name, and rule it as his own. With all these territories under his control, King Lot would be set fair to call himself High King.'

A hollow silence settled on the room. Guenevere had to speak. 'Lot is married to King Arthur's half-sister, you say?'

Every grey head round the table nodded in response. Guenevere leaned towards Arthur. 'Then King Lot is your kinsman, my lord. Why not send him a strong brotherly overture of peace, to back up the treaty offered by Sir Ulfius?'

Arthur laughed bitterly. 'Guenevere, I'm no kinsman in his eyes! If he declares war now, that means he denies my claim. To him I'm no more than a bastard King Uther gave away!'

'My lord! My lord!'

It was Gawain, clamouring at the door. 'The embassy to King Lot has returned!'

'Ha! Sir Ulfius, did you say?' Arthur leaped to his feet. 'Now we shall see how our peace terms were received!'

And they saw indeed. Thrown into the castle gatehouse by

King Lot's horsemen lay the body of old Sir Ulfius, covered in blood. The peace treaty was pinned to his chest by a knife buried in his heart.

Arthur leaped to pick up the battered form. Serene in death, his grey hair tumbled and his face smudged with dirt, Sir Ulfius lay in his arms like a sleeping child. Arthur raised his head and stared out into the night as the sound of galloping hoofs slowly died away. 'So, Lot!' he breathed, his eyes dark. 'We offer peace, and you return us death. Look to it, then, for we shall pay you back! You will feel our vengeance a hundredfold!'

CHAPTER 24

Above the cloister, the sound of the angelus bell faded on the evening air. The chant of plainsong rose to take its place. Cramped into a corner of the low sleeping space, Brother John allowed the glorious melodies to weave their way in and out of the chambers of his heart. Oh, to be one of this community!

But that would only be if he proved worthy of the call. Brother John struggled to contain his soul in due humility as he shifted his body gingerly on the hard wooden chair. He was still sore enough from the beating he had taken at the hands of Lucan's men to think twice before he moved. But the news that had brought him to the Abbot could not wait.

'Married?' Seated opposite John in the small cell that served him for office, dormitory and living space, the Abbot pressed an index finger to the side of his aching head, and tried to think. What now, O Lord, what next?

Brother John frowned. 'As they call married. By their pagan rites.'

'Spare me.' The Abbot waved a weary hand. 'I know their filthy ways.' His mind recoiled. A crusty silence settled in the room.

'So,' the Abbot resumed after a while, 'their two kingdoms

now will be one. But will both lands now come under the Mother-right?'

'The Middle Kingdom is ours!' protested John. 'Or, at least, it was. We had driven their Goddess into the furthest hills. We even built a chapel in the stronghold of Caerleon itself. If Arthur wins this kingdom from King Lot, surely he won't throw it all at his concubine's feet?'

The Abbot sighed. Brother John was a man of virtue, to be sure. But a monk could be too upright for his calling, when it blinded him to the lower impulses of other men. What was wrong with all these Britons, he asked himself. Did dishwater run in their veins, not blood? For the hundredth time he found himself wishing that all their young men were forced to spend part of their novitiate in Rome, the city of love, the smiling city of sin. Did they not know here, did they never observe, that for the whore who pleased him a man would do anything? He groped for an inoffensive way of putting it. 'The Queen of the Summer Country may bring him under her influence, and win him to her ways,' he said at last.

'And the succession!' John fretted on. 'Their offspring will inherit a united land. But will a child of theirs be for us or against us, Father? Can you see that far?'

The Abbot brought his fingers to his lips. 'That all depends upon the child God sends. If the pagan queen throws only females as her litter, then the people will likely cling to the old ways.'

John's eye quickened. 'But if she has a son . . .'

'Then God will have shown us that this land is ours. That He has sent one to carry out His will.'

Brother John nodded eagerly. 'This Arthur can hardly call himself a man if he will not fight for his own son to succeed!'

'Just so.' The Abbot paused, and a slow smile broke

over his cavernous face. 'And if he fails – or even if the
Queen bears him ten daughters and rears them all in the
faith of the Mother of Evil herself – there is another fighting
on our side.'

'Ha! Of course!'

Brother John had taken his meaning in a second, the
Abbot saw. Well, it was plain enough. 'Merlin will not suffer
the daughters of Guenevere to triumph over one of Arthur's
sons. He will move heaven and earth to hold Arthur to his
destiny, just as he held the spirit in Uther's body for three
days after the life had died. The old devil will do anything
to advance Pendragon power. He will spare no one, least of
all a foreign woman or her child.'

Brother John looked at the Abbot with reverent eyes. It
was plain to see why their leader held his place. But even as
he basked in this thought, the Abbot was speaking again.

'Our other task must be to see that there is little or
nothing for a daughter of the pagans to inherit when the
time comes. We have destroyed the Great Mother in many
places now, country by country, shrine by shrine. We have
other kingdoms in these islands under our rule. If we turn all
the force we have under God against the Summer Country,
how long can it hold out?'

Brother John gazed at him wonderingly, and shook
his head.

'No longer than it takes to get a toe-hold on Avalon. To
wrest their relics and rituals to Christian use.' The Abbot
leaned forward and tapped Brother John on the knee. 'A
renegade from Avalon, one of the Lake villagers, has come
to us. His tales of the gold objects of their worship, I confess,
inflamed my desire. The Goddess has a loving-cup, it seems,
from which she succours all who come to Her.' His thin face
took on a sacral gleam. 'Imagine, Brother, if we had such a
relic of Our Lord!'

'The cup He used at the Last Supper, say!' Brother John breathed ecstatically. 'The blessed Holy Grail, which God has promised we shall regain some day!'

'We shall. We must! When these pagans are dazzled with the gold of other Gods, we must have trophies of our own to wave before their eyes. So Avalon must be our goal.' He paused, and the face of Brother Boniface swam before his mind. 'I have already given thought to this. I have sent to Rome for assistance with my plan.' For a handsome youth, as dark as Boniface is fair, he wanted to say, but refrained. For a lusty lad with that special light in his eye. Who may be vowed to Christ, but whose purity can be sacrificed to win us Avalon. Who will spend the rest of his life under the whip, in tears and penance for his broken vows, but who will give us the way to the Lady that we need. Either he or Boniface should catch the old whore's eye. After that, it will be up to others to drive the advantage home.

'There is also the King,' Brother John broke in on his thoughts. 'This Arthur, if he survives. We supported his proclamation, we should be able to gain some help from him.'

'We will, Brother, we will. We have done much in this benighted land, and we shall reap our reward.' The Abbot folded his hands. 'And God is with us,' he said confidently. 'He will deliver these pagans into our hands.'

On the day of the battle, the sun was slow to rise. Roaming about the tent, Arthur went to the entrance again and again, searching the heavens for the morning star. From the camp bed where she lay, Guenevere watched him wearily, and felt again a soreness around her heart. *Death and war, war and death, instead of new love and the first sweet steps of their life together – why did this have to be?*

'Arthur!' she called.

He turned and came to her, leaning over the bed. She stroked his chest, her body still remembering the strained and hasty love he had offered her last night. She took his face between her hands and drew him down to kiss his anxious eyes. 'Fear not, my love. What will be is written in the stars. And we are ready to meet the will of the Great Ones, whatever they decree.'

Now, as she looked down on the battlefield, Guenevere asked herself again, were they right to march out to meet King Lot, or should they have drawn him south and waited for him to attack?

Arthur had sworn that he would not let his enemy set foot in the Middle Kingdom. Still less should they fall back to the Summer Country and find themselves cornered in Camelot. So they had rallied their troops and marched due north to the kingdom of Gore. On his borders, said King Ursien, lay the plain and Forest of Bedegraine. There on the plain, with the forest at their back and a range of hills ahead, they could take their stand, and do battle with King Lot.

Long days of marching and nights of broken rest had brought them here at last. Soon the scouts were bringing back warning of King Lot's approach. An army was coming, so vast, the out-riders said, that all the earth shook under their tramping feet. Then their torches had burned late into the night as they hammered out their campaign.

When you are grown, you will lead battles from a high hill-top where you can command, her mother the Queen had said. *And you will have a champion, but he will fight for you in the field, not beside you in the war chariot as we used to do.* So Guenevere had armed Arthur with her own hands. She had strapped on her mother's scabbard to keep him safe, and as she buckled Excalibur to his side, she had offered a prayer for victory and a long-drawn-out kiss. Watching now from her chariot on the hill, Guenevere would command more of the battle, she knew, than those fighting on the plain below.

Now their forces were assembling, in the precise formations they had planned out, hour after weary hour. To her left and right, a dozen gallopers stood poised to carry her orders to the commanders in the field. Below her, Arthur, Lucan, King Ursien and King Pellinore commanded the four main divisions of the attacking force. But many others had rallied to their banner too. When the messengers had ridden out, sounding the trysting horn to the cry of 'Pendragon!', kings, lords and fighting men had answered the call.

They came from the north, south, and west, lords, knights and men-at-arms. They came from the far islands of Man and Wight and Mona, to fight beside silent Shetlanders and bands of laughing giants from the Islands of the West – laughing only until battle began, Arthur said, and then even their looks would kill. Men came from the east too, even from the threatened Saxon shore. They abandoned their fight against the invading Northmen in favour of Arthur's war against the enemy within. All came for the memory of King Uther, to honour his dead name.

And then there were Uther's old allies from France, King Ban and King Bors from the kingdom of Benoic. These two brothers had crossed the sea from Little Britain with their three young sons to honour their former bond of friendship with the High King. Lean, handsome men speaking broken English in the endearing accent of the French, they made one bow to Guenevere with their bright eyes and quicksilver smiles, and she warmed to them for life.

King Pellinore had raised his forces too, and five divisions took to the field under the banner of Listinoise. And from the far northern kingdom of Terre Forraine came King Pellinore's brother Pelles, with all his men.

With his son Lamorak at his side, King Pellinore had

presented Pelles to Guenevere with rough pride, but a certain constraint too. 'Greet my brother, Your Majesty, I beg?'

Guenevere had stepped forward smiling, but at the sight of King Pelles she had felt a sudden chill. Lean as a skeleton, his bony frame seemed to rattle inside his armour, and his sunken face and bloodless skin had the clammy pallor often seen in men on the point of death. In his moribund body, only his eyes showed any signs of life. Buried deep in their bony sockets, they blazed with a fanatic's fire.

'Welcome, my lord,' Guenevere said heartily, 'for your dear brother's sake. King Arthur and I are most grateful for your aid in this war. And may all your Gods fight with you under your banner, and protect you in the field.'

'There is only one God, and Jesus is His name!' the King responded, glaring into her eyes.

'Now, Pelles,' said Pellinore, with a warning cough. He turned to Guenevere. Embarrassment was written on his face. 'My brother has had a great trial to endure, my lady. It was given to him to love only one lady in all his life. She died giving birth to their only child.' The loving glance Pellinore threw at Lamorak here told Guenevere the rest of Pelles' tale: he had never had a son.

'My wife was sainted among women!' Pelles cried, in the same high tone. 'Her father was the first king in these islands to declare for the one God. She was silence and submission and virtue itself to me. But, for my sins, God chose to punish me with her death. And I have lived in prayer and fasting ever since.'

'But the child survived, a beauty, like her mother,' Pellinore went on warmly. 'Her name is Elaine. And, through her, my brother believes that he will have a destiny higher than that of other men. It has been foretold to him that his grandson will be the noblest knight in all the world.'

'But only if she comes untainted to the bridal bed!' King Pelles interjected feverishly. His pallid face took on an unhealthy flush. 'She must be known to no man except one. The best knight of our time will come to her, and father her Christ-given son. This boy is fated to do the work of God. His name shall be called Galahad, the servant of the Lord!'

Guenevere felt a spurt of wild distaste. So Pelles refused thigh-freedom to his daughter, in pursuit of this mad dream? 'Where is she now?' she said, watching King Pelles with mounting unease.

'Safe in my castle of Corbenic!' He laughed, an unpleasant sound. 'She lives like a princess in a golden chamber, inside a silver tower, within a wall of bronze. She is secured behind three locks, each with a different key, each in the care of a different lord of mine, until the knight comes who is fated to father her peerless child!'

'How so?' Guenevere queried grimly. 'How can her child become the noblest knight in the world? How can he be nobler than all we have here? And how can she meet the knight who will be her love?'

'It shall be as it has been told to me!' Pelles insisted wildly. 'Hear me, Your Majesty—' He was still protesting as Pellinore led him away.

Guenevere repressed a shudder of anger and shock. 'The poor girl's a prisoner!' she had said to Ina afterwards. 'And all for the sake of her wretched virginity!'

Ina had nodded vigorously. 'That's what comes, madam, when the rule of the Mother is overthrown, and women find themselves under the sway of men. Why, the girl could be with us now, riding to war in a silver chariot, instead of being locked up to wait for the mystery man!'

The mystery man.

Would a lover ever come for poor Elaine? Or was she doomed to live for ever as a virgin in a tower?

'Benoic!'

'A moi, Benoic!'

A flurry of sharp cries from below brought Guenevere out of her reverie, and staring down at the plain she saw the blue and white banner of Little Britain, and three tall youths on fiery horses charging and wheeling as they rehearsed for the fray. They were the sons of the French kings, Ban and Bors. If men could bring their sons to battle, why should daughters be forced to stay at home?

The three sons of Benoic fell back into the ranks and were lost to sight. Guenevere shivered in the raw early-morning air. On the plain below, dark shapes were moving through the remains of the night. Beyond the forest, she knew, the army of King Lot was rousing itself for the kill. All the forces of death were massing for bloodshed now.

From her hill-top vantage-point, the battlefield stretched away, miles of green grass that would soon be red with blood. How would they fare? The six kings who had turned against Arthur had swollen to eleven, fielding more than three times the forces of Pendragon, the scouts reckoned, a monstrous total of a hundred thousand men. And this evil host had sworn to destroy Arthur and all who fought with him.

Goddess, Mother, be with us, do not fail us now.

Closing her eyes, she bent her head to pray.

How thick the darkness is just before dawn! A clammy mist swirled about them, enveloping the hill-top. Guenevere shuddered, gripped with a sudden malaise. Suddenly all the world was sick and out of joint.

'My lady?'

'It's nothing, nothing to worry about!'

Brusquely she brushed aside Ina's anxious stare. But the

sickness remained. All around them the Queen's guard were shivering uneasily too, their weapons and harness clinking in the dark. A light breeze swept past them with a graveyard kiss, and the air grew very cold. Guenevere sensed something like impending fate, and cast wildly around. But there was nothing to be seen. Then the curtains of mist lifted languidly and parted, and there, wreathed in white drifts, they were.

Shapes of menace, but of enchantment too. She saw tall women, queenly and veiled in black. She saw spirit children laughing and singing as they danced towards her, holding out their arms. She saw a little child, a boy, watching her sturdily, standing foursquare amid the shifting mists. Then coming towards her was a tall, serene, floating form that Guenevere would have known anywhere.

The Lady of the Lake come from Avalon, veiled from head to foot in black.

I will be there, Arthur, she had said, *at your last battle I will be there.*

The Lady had come to take Arthur home.

Guenevere stared till the blood burst in her brain.

There was a roaring in her ears, darkness closed her eyes, and she knew no more.

CHAPTER 25

'Goddess, Mother, save the Queen's life! You took her mother, do not take her too!'

Guenevere opened her eyes. She was lying on the damp, chilly grass, with the dawn light streaking the bowl of the sky overhead. The mist still writhed around her like a living thing, but the shapes she had seen were nowhere in sight. Ina hovered over her, praying and weeping, her tears turning to joy as Guenevere opened her eyes. 'Oh, my lady!' she wept. 'Whatever ailed you there?'

Guenevere struggled to sit up. 'Nothing – a sudden faintness, that's all.' Whatever this sight meant, there would be time enough later to wonder about the cause. 'Hurry, Ina, help me up.'

From below came the sudden roar of war-horns sounding the start of the fray. The high-pitched snarl of trumpets rose above the battle-cries of a hundred thousand throats. The two great armies began moving across the plain. The war of the eleven kings had begun.

'Pendragon!'

Arthur's battle-cry rang round the field as the two forces met. Those in the front died with the light of dawn. Before the sun had risen, many more lay dying on the ground. From Guenevere's vantage-point, the knights and men looked like toy figures struggling in the world below. But the hideous clash of arms, the shock of iron on flesh, the cries of anger and pain rose with terrible clarity to her ears.

Arthur's banner marked his progress through the fray. Guenevere watched with dread as the red dragon plunged here and there, wherever the fighting was at its worst. But everywhere Arthur went, Gawain was at his right hand, Kay on his left, and Bedivere guarding the rear. The four of them cut a wedge of death into the enemy troops, leaving the dead and dying on either side.

Under a dull and bleeding sun, the work of death went on. On Arthur's left flank, King Pellinore slashed and slew like a lion while on the right his brother King Pelles did the same. Lucan commanded a wheeling counterattack from the side, taking the massed armies of the kings on their undefended flanks and wreaking cruel havoc. When her mother said that queens must command from the top of a hill, did she know, Guenevere wondered, what it was simply to watch and endure?

Mother, Goddess, must I suffer this? She shifted her stance, and the thought beat through her brain, *Oh, to be a man now, or a warrior queen!*

'Goddess, Mother, rain down fire like blood, hail your fury on the heads of our foes, give strength to our swords, bring our warriors safe home.' With tears pouring down her cheeks, Ina kept up a running prayer for victory. Guenevere echoed her in silence, and growing dread.

For all their enemies were now afield, and the stoutest heart would have looked on them with fear. King Carados of Northgales commanded the right-hand block, while to his left was King Nentres of Garlot. She saw the banners of King Agrisance and King Vause, and the kings of North Humber, of Solise, and the Castle on the Rock. All the traitors to Arthur were there, King Rience, King Brangoris and the King of the Western Isles.

And then Guenevere saw the black banner of Lothian with its sign of the raging bull. Below it fought a giant of a man, clad in black armour plumed with red and gold, and red and gold trappings on his black-armoured horse. Even from a distance she could see a massive body, and above it a gross black beard on a broad beefy face. Arthur's most fatal foe had taken the field.

Guenevere caught her breath. No visor to his helmet? King Lot was so confident of killing Arthur that he had armed himself as if for war-play, rather than real combat, man to man. Instantly she saw why. Surrounding King Lot in a solid block rode his knight companions, all men as heavy and huge as he was, all with one aim. From above, the steady progress towards Arthur of the black-armoured wedge of death was plain to see. But surely Lot's execution squad would not get within a yard or two of Arthur before he was aware that they were near? Her stomach lurched with fear. *Goddess, Mother, save him, save my love!*

Meanwhile the battle raged. The two forces advanced and gave ground, wheeled and returned to the fray. Yet boldly as they fought, the sheer weight of numbers began to tell against Arthur's men.

If we lose—

It was a fear that they had never voiced. Guenevere looked around, desperation fraying her self-command. In the forest on the edge of the plain, the two French kings and their sons waited in ambush, she knew. How long would Arthur struggle to turn the tide? When would he give the French the signal to break cover, and attack?

On Arthur's right, the flank under King Pelles was beginning to crumble and give ground. And still King Lot and his knights continued their deadly progress through the ranks. A sudden fear flooded Guenevere, with it a certainty. *Arthur had lost sight of the overall command. He would wait too long to signal the kings to attack.*

In a frenzy she scanned the field, and called a scout to her side. 'Ride to the kings in the wood! Order them not to wait for Arthur's signal, but to launch their ambush now!'

'Ride to Sir Lucan!' she cried to another. 'Say the Queen orders him to redirect his force. Attack on the left-hand side. At all costs save the King!'

Goddess, Mother, too little, too late!

A passion of fear and grief ran through her frame. Weeping, she wrung her hands and searched the field again. There on the outlying flank flew the banner of King Pellinore, Arthur's most loyal friend. She looked around. 'Ride for your life!' she cried to a flying scout. 'Tell King Pellinore that King Lot is threatening King Arthur, and the King will die!'

Now all her messengers were racing downhill to the plain, clods of earth flying up beneath their pounding hoofs. On the battlefield, Arthur's banner had moved again. Now he was fighting another knight in close combat, laying about him with furious power. Above the turmoil Guenevere caught the strains of Excalibur's song, high and clear. But as Arthur swung and hacked, a lance from another knight pierced his mount to the heart.

The poor beast convulsed. Its scream rose above every other sound. When its agony ceased, Guenevere knew, its knees would buckle, pitching its rider head first to the ground. Impeded by his heavy armour, a knight on foot was lost. Arthur himself spared every knight he unhorsed, disdaining to strike a man when he was down. But who would show him such chivalry?

Arthur, Arthur, my love—

Guenevere screamed as the horse had, one long dying cry: '*Pendragon!*'

*   *   *

'For Pendragon! For Pendragon!'

With a ringing shout, Gawain forced his horse towards Arthur, and plucked him from the saddle by main force. Kay caught a riderless charger at loose in the mêlée, and dragged it alongside. Bedivere drove forward to assist Gawain, fending off an attack on his fellow-knight's undefended back as he came. There was a wild confusion of men and horses, flailing arms and legs, then in a mighty scramble, Arthur was newly mounted, safe and unhurt.

'The King! They saved the King!'

Ina screamed in triumph, but Guenevere's heart was numb. How long could they fight against such overwhelming odds?

Now the dead were everywhere, hampering every move, bringing down the living under the horses' hoofs. Men fought with split helmets and shattered shields, with hands and faces sliced and hacked away, with heads, necks and bodies cut through to the bone. Above the soldiers' cries and dying moans the horses were screaming too, kicking out in agony from slashed guts, gaping throats and broken knees.

And still King Lot worked his way towards Arthur, nearer, ever nearer, his wedge of black knights carving a path of death. The sun glinted off his broadsword as he raised it in both hands, and prepared for his moment to strike.

King Lot!

Arthur, beware King Lot!

Hear me, Arthur, he is upon you now!

Guenevere was choking on her screams, almost vomiting with dread. Where were the forces she had commanded to attack? Where were the men who would save Arthur's life?

'Pendragon!'

'Benoic! A Benoic!'

On the edge of the mêlée, she could see Lucan's troop wheeling to change the direction of their attack. At the same time, the French kings Ban and Bors and their sons burst out of ambush from the wood, a small but deadly force thundering across the plain. But they could not, would not save Arthur now.

Lot's hoarse bellow rose above the fray: 'Die, bastard boy!' With a terrible slowness, his sword parted the air. Guenevere threw back her head, and spread her arms to the skies. 'Goddess, Mother!' she howled. 'Do not let this be!'

Then suddenly she saw him, one lone rider with a squire in his wake. A king, not a knight, for he bore a gold coronet round his helmet, and no other crest. The banner borne by the squire was fluttering so feverishly that she could hardly read its sign. But then Guenevere saw the white swan of Listinoise, and knew who it was.

Welcome this king, Arthur had said, *for he is a loyal friend to me.*

The newcomer's words rang again through her mind: *I have done no more, lady, than any man would do.*

Pellinore!

As Pellinore charged, he carried his lance light and low by his side, and did not raise it till the last. So King Lot never saw the silver spear that flashed through the air to pierce his open visor, shattering his coarse black beard and red, grinning face. He died, laughing a laugh of triumph as his sword carved towards Arthur to split his skull. Then he fell like a mighty tree, toppling out of his saddle to plunge head down to the earth.

'Goddess, Mother, praise and thanks to Your name!' Again Guenevere threw back her head, and a triumphant ululation burst from her throat.

Within moments the cry was resounding round the field.

'King Lot! King Lot is dead!'

'Death to the tyrant! King Lot is dead!'

'Benoic! Benoic! A moi!'

Now the assault of the French kings broke like a tidal wave upon the enemy host. And king by king, man by man, they began to lose heart. King Vause was the first to flee, trailing his golden banner in the mud. After him, all the others were beaten back one by one, or followed Vause and took to their heels in flight.

And as their leaders quailed, the rank and file threw down their weapons and ran for their lives. The defeat turned into a bloody rout as the victors hunted down their beaten foes, and chased them from the field.

At last the red dragon flew in solitary grandeur over every other flag. The harsh cawing of trumpets signalled the end of the fray. Guenevere brought her clasped hands to her forehead and bowed her head. *Goddess, Mother, praise and thanks for this victory over those who would deal us death.*

'Your Majesty!'

Guenevere opened her eyes. It was one of Arthur's scouts, his face aglow. 'The King is coming to lay his victory at your feet!'

She raised her head. And there he was, surrounded by his victorious kings and knights, picking his way towards her through the injured lying groaning on the ground, and the bleeding mounds of dead. Relief overwhelmed her, then a trembling joy. They had won the day, and Arthur was alive!

'Blessings on you, my lord!' she called ecstatically as he came within earshot of her call. But the man who drew near was a stranger to her now. The face in the shadow of the helmet was black with blood, baked by the heat to a fearsome sheen. The eyes were set in a strangely bright stare, the whites bloodshot, as if he were exalted by battle, drunk on blood and death.

Guenevere was shaken with an impulse of pure dread. Where was her Arthur, the loving husband, the gentle, generous man she thought she knew? This was the red ravager of whom the old folk talked with bated breath, the dragon whose fury laid waste the land so that nothing would ever grow there again.

'My Queen!' Arthur cried, in a strange high voice, waving a gauntleted fist encrusted with dried blood. 'We have won the day. Give thanks to these kings who turned the tide for us!'

Under their fluttering banner of blue and white, the two French kings from Little Britain laughed and bowed as gaily as if they were revelling at Camelot, in the Great Hall. Arthur looked at them and his red eyes lost their glare. His pent-up breath escaped him in a sigh. Slowly she could see him returning to himself again.

'We kiss your hands, Majesty, in joy to meet again!' cried the taller of the two. 'I am Ban of Benoic, and this is my brother Bors. And we thank the King your husband for a good day's sport!'

Guenevere looked at King Ban's dark dancing eyes, and had to smile too. 'Good sirs, we are for ever in your debt!'

'We would wish that you should also greet our sons,' spoke up King Bors in the same attractive accent as King Ban, 'but you see the boys are otherwise engaged!' Merrily he gestured to the edge of the field.

Across the open grass before the wood, three racing figures were chasing the fleeing enemy, rounding up the stragglers as they ran. In the front the tallest rode standing up in his stirrups, with the two other youths spurring to keep up.

'My son Lancelot,' announced King Ban, proudly pointing out the leader, 'with his cousins Lionel and Bors. He has a noble heart. He has fought well today. He will not rest till the evil are hunted down.'

'Lancelot, you say?'

Lancelot . . .

In the sultry heat, Guenevere felt a breath far off, sighing like a wind from Avalon. In the soft heart of it came an echo of the Lady's voice. *Ah, Guenevere! You are not fated to be like other women. There are things you do not know, and cannot dream. One man alone cannot make all the music of the world. A woman may dance more than once in the course of her days.*

'Yes!' she cried, not knowing what she did. She passed her hand over her eyes. 'Excuse me, sirs,' she said feverishly. 'We were talking of your son – Lancelot, I think you said?'

Ban paused, concealing his surprise. 'Yes, Madame,' he said politely. 'That is his name.'

'He's a fine fighter, Ban, I'll give you that.' Arthur's eyes followed the tall youth approvingly. 'He's young for such a battle, but that's no bad thing these days.'

King Ban laughed ruefully, rolling his eyes. 'Too young, his mother says. She begged me on her knees not to bring him here. She had a mother's presentiment that here – how do you say? – he would meet his fate.'

Guenevere felt words coming from her that she did not know. 'We all have a fate we must fulfil.'

'Nonsense!' Arthur declared, his voice unnaturally shrill. 'Boys must go to war, whatever their mothers' fears! And the son of a king must become a great warrior and a peerless knight.'

'Like you, my lord.'

King Ban's gallantry raised a ragged cheer among the weary group. Guenevere looked around. King Pellinore was leaning on his sword beside King Ursien of Gore, with the faithful Bedivere behind. On Arthur's right stood Sir Lucan and Sir Kay, with Kay's old father Sir Ector beaming like a man possessed. But where was—?

Arthur's face clouded. 'Gawain is with his father,' he said shortly. He paused, and gestured round his little band. 'We must return to the field, before the scavengers descend. Will you go to him, Guenevere, to comfort him?'

Half hidden in the outskirts of the forest was a hermit's cell, its one-time owner now no more than a green mound mouldering in the nearby grass. Seen through the trees, the low stone chamber looked like part of the forest, encrusted with lichen and covered in hanging moss. Inside, a candle burned on a rough stone altar as the light began to fade, and in front of it on a makeshift bier lay the fallen king. Resplendent in his fine armour of red and black and gold, King Lot might have been resting before returning to the fray. Only the enclosed helmet with its visor down told of the bloody havoc of the face within.

Beside the altar Sir Gawain knelt on the cold stone floor, weeping over the bier.

'Gawain?'

He got to his feet. His great face, so like his father's, was blotched with tears, and his hurt eyes were like a child's. Guenevere took his hand. 'This is a cruel blow for you to bear.'

'He died before I knew him.' Gawain gulped, and shook his head. 'And now I never will.' He raised his great hand to cover a fresh burst of tears. 'I was sent away as a page when I was seven, and I've never been back since then.'

'So you haven't seen your family in all that time?'

Gawain shrugged. 'I saw my brothers. My mother used to bring them south to visit me.'

'I never knew you had brothers,' Guenevere said, with a

sick sense of uncertainty. *Gods above, how many more unknown kin were there left to pop up like this out of Arthur's past?*

'Three all told,' Gawain said fondly. 'Agravain, Gaheris and Gareth. I'm the eldest, so they all do what I say. Gareth is the baby, he's only fifteen. He's still not old enough to fight, my mother says, not even as a squire.'

Guenevere's heart burned for the child Gawain had been. 'You weren't old enough to leave home when you were only seven!'

Gawain shook his head. 'Many boys are fostered out much younger, as the King was himself. And the lord who took me in was good to me.'

'So it was he who brought you to London when Merlin called all the lords and kings together to proclaim the King?'

Gawain nodded. 'He did. And he gave me his blessing when I left to follow Arthur, after I saw him draw the sword from the stone.' His sad face lit up. 'Oh, lady, you should have been there!'

'That was the first time you met Arthur?'

'The first time I saw him, or even heard of him. My mother was married before Arthur was born. She . . .' He glanced back at the body of King Lot, lying on the bier. 'Well, lady, you can speak to her yourself. You will meet her and all my kin at the funeral.'

CHAPTER 26

G*oddess, Mother, forgive—*

The air was sick with incense and monkish sweat. The low roof pressed down upon their heads, damp breathed from the very walls, and the flagstones of the floor wept their own tears. The drone of dirges buzzed around their ears. Guenevere threw a glance at Arthur, and the thought came again: *What are we doing in a Christian church?*

She had asked Arthur in tears why this had to be. Before the high altar lay the only reason he could give. In a magnificent gold and bronze coffin, larger than that of any common man, reposed the body of King Lot.

Now as he lay at peace in his last sleep, King Lot's resting place was finer than anything else in the wretched church. A moth-eaten cloth of faded purple covered the altar, and cheap tallow candles guttered and stank in the alcoves in the walls. For the chapel of St Stephen in Caerleon was as rundown and neglected as everything else in this once-great city, which the Roman legions had long ago made their home.

When Guenevere first saw it in daylight, she had been awed by the mighty castle high on its huge bluff, its back to an ancient forest, its moat fed by the Severn Water, the whole site garlanded with green groves and meadows bright with flowers. In the palace itself, four great towers and high white walls rose above countless gilded domes and roofs, the castle itself having grown almost into a town, even without the jumbled dwellings of the townsfolk huddled below.

But on closer inspection, the great town buildings of the Romans lay in ruins, and the rest of the city had been abandoned to its fate. She hated the cracked roadways, the wild dogs howling from abandoned hovels, and the weeds climbing up the columns everywhere. When the Romans came, they had called Caerleon the City of Light. 'We must make a vow,' she had breathed to Arthur, 'that we will bring it back to the beauty it had then.'

Arthur frowned. With a war to settle and a hard peace to enforce, didn't Guenevere know what was important now? 'After the funeral,' he said.

After the funeral.
Goddess, Mother, when would that be?
Already weeks had passed since King Lot was killed. To guard against decay in the summer heat, his body had had to be wrapped in spices, oils and wax, and sealed in a sheet of lead while they debated his resting place.

It had to be a Christian burial, it seemed.

'How else can we mark Lot's passing,' Arthur demanded, as they sat in council the day after the battle, 'and give him the respect any fallen knight deserves?'

Through the door of the tent, a low red sun loomed over the battlefield. Though the bearers were hard at work, the scene was still black with corpses, and the smell of death hung over them like a pall.

Guenevere stifled the anger that rose to her lips. Arthur was right, what else could they do with Lot? They could not bury him by the Mother-rites, for the Mother would never take to Herself a man who ravished girls, and put babes in arms to death. Lot had had his own dark Gods, and worshipped at the altar of their savage will. But she and Arthur could not honour those idols of blood and bone. Only the Christians, it seemed, were prepared to have Lot now.

And he must be buried in Caerleon, Merlin insisted, not on the battlefield where he fell. 'Your people missed your wedding, sire, and a royal spectacle speaks to every soul. A great funeral for King Lot would bring kings and queens to Caerleon, and afterwards we will hold a great banquet for all the people of the land. There all your folk will meet Queen Guenevere, just as when you married, the people of the Summer Country had a chance to meet their new King.'

Arthur looked uneasy. 'But surely Queen Morgause will think us cruel if we bury her husband here in Caerleon, instead of sending him back to his own country to rest in peace?'

'The vanquished do not choose where they will lie,' Merlin said crisply. 'Queen Morgause knows the rules of war. And if King Lot is buried in Caerleon, the Queen of Cornwall can attend the funeral too. Queen Morgause has not seen her mother since she was sent to the Orkneys to be married before your birth. At her age, the Queen of Cornwall could never travel from Tintagel to be with Queen Morgause now.'

Arthur gasped. 'The Queen of Cornwall?'

'The mother of Queen Morgause. Your mother, too, of course,' said Merlin, his eyes glittering.

'I did not know that she was still alive.' Arthur tried to speak lightly, but his eyes gave him away.

Guenevere clasped her hands. *Oh, Merlin, Merlin – see what you do?* But this was not her quarrel. She looked away.

Merlin heaved a dramatic sigh, and ran a withered hand

over his eyes. 'Forgive me, sire, that time has not allowed us to speak of this before. Ever since you drew the sword out of the stone, we have not had a moment without war or the threat of war. The Queen of Cornwall your mother is aged now, but she lives. So does her second daughter, the Lady Morgan. Your half-sister, my lord.'

'My half-sister.' Arthur's face was white. 'The other one I never knew I had. Well, let her come too. It's time I got to know my vanished kin.'

'Then will you send to order her release?'

'*Her release?*' Arthur's face looked dangerously strained. 'Whose?'

Guenevere could bear it no longer. 'Merlin, don't beat about the bush! Tell us what you mean!'

How dared she? Merlin bowed his head, concealing the spurt of anger coursing through his veins. 'Your Majesties know that when King Uther married the Queen of Cornwall she had two grown daughters, of an age to leave their home. The elder, Morgause, was fourteen then and ripe for the marriage bed. But Morgan, the younger, was eleven, and too young to wed. So the King gave her to a convent to be a nun.'

Guenevere gasped. 'Sent to the Christians – to a nunnery, for the rest of her life?'

Merlin glittered at her. 'It is a holy life. And the place had a fine reputation for the rule of its Abbess.'

Arthur closed his eyes. 'Release her at once – whatever it takes. Send her to her mother, and order them a guard of honour to attend Lot's funeral.' He looked at Guenevere and tried to smile. 'Do not weep, sweetheart. Merlin will take care of it all.'

Merlin, always Merlin.

Guenevere forced a smile in answer, and tried to hold back the rage blooming in her heart.

Merlin knew that Arthur's mother was still alive, and had said nothing about her till the death of Lot forced him to show his hand. He knew that the girl Morgan had been buried alive for over twenty years, and kept silent about that too.

What other secrets lay hidden under that wild grey hair? What else was going on without Arthur's knowledge and consent?

And then Merlin had vanished, and not a soul knew where. Guenevere smiled mirthlessly. The old man was away with the Fair Ones, while she and Arthur had had the grim task of bringing King Lot's body all the way south from Gore down to Caerleon for the burial.

For this cursed burial.

Inside the church, the chanting monks droned on. Guenevere stirred resentfully. Why were they waiting? Queen Morgause, she knew, was already here. She had come south with her three sons, pitched her tents outside Caerleon, and sent word that she would attend the ceremony and see her husband buried before she paid her respects to her brother and his queen.

Morgause was here – but not Arthur's mother, the old Queen. She had set out from Cornwall, and Arthur's scouts had escorted her to the borders of the Summer Country. There she had been reunited with her younger daughter Morgan, and there they had rested a good while. Then they made their way to the Severn Water to cross over to the Middle Kingdom. And there the scouts had lost all trace of them.

'Lost them?'

Guenevere shuddered to recall Arthur's fury then. How could a royal party be lost, a queen and princess escorted by a guard of honour from the King, either on the far side of Severn Water, or on this?

The chief scout shook his head in blank despair. 'It is as if they vanished, sire. We can't explain it. We have no excuse.'

'Lost?' Arthur was in torment.

'Arthur, they can't be lost!' Guenevere remonstrated. 'There's no magic about this, there cannot be. It's just that they don't know the country, and they must have wandered out of their way. Your mother is coming to comfort her widowed daughter, and to meet again her long-lost son. She has every reason in the world to be here. What on earth would stop her now?'

What indeed?

But something had.

For King Lot's funeral was about to take place, and she was not here.

'Listen, my love!'

Beside her Arthur sat bolt upright in the pew. From outside the church came a high wailing cry, like that of a spirit in hell. It was the saddest sound in all the world. Guenevere clutched Arthur's hand. 'Dear Gods, what's that?'

On guard behind Arthur, Gawain gave a watery smile. 'It is the sound of the pipes, the music of our land. They are playing the *pibroch*, the lament for the fallen, mourning the death of the King.'

Arthur squeezed Guenevere's hand. 'Then Queen Morgause and her sons are here!'

He leaped to his feet, and handed her into the aisle. The church doors opened to the world outside. Silhouetted against the late September sun was a tall figure dressed in black. Securing her high black headdress and long veil was a crown of gold. Like a pillar of cloud she stood silent and unmoving, staring into the church.

Tall, regal, all in black—

Guenevere's heart shook. Had she known this woman from another world? Was she one of the shapes who had come to her at the start of the Battle of the Kings?

'Your Majesty!' Gawain fell to his knees.

'Gawain, my son!' The Queen moved forward to fold him in her arms. Behind her came three others, all built like Gawain, all with his look.

Gawain leaped up. 'Agravain! Gaheris! Gareth!'

'Brother Gawain!'

The four brothers greeted each other with a mixture of manly restraint and boyish glee. Morgause and Arthur looked at them, then at each other, as if they could never tear their eyes away.

And now Guenevere could see her without fear. Tall and well built, Arthur's new-found sister carried herself with a commanding air. But she had none of the menace Guenevere had felt in the spirit shapes who came in her moment of sickness in the chariot. Morgause was queenly but not divine, a woman nearing forty, whose ample body showed every sign of having borne four great sons. Yet she still had the ripe fullness of a woman in her prime. An undeniable beauty lingered in the full face with its arched eyebrows, strong jaw and red mouth, and her every feature was overcast with the haunting shadow of unsatisfied desire. Her pale eyes searched Guenevere calmly, without threat.

Outside the church the pipes of the highlands were still sounding their lament. Guenevere's sight clouded, and another took its place. *King Uther needed strong allies*, Merlin had said. *Morgause was fourteen and ripe for marriage when he gave her to King Lot.*

She saw a girl's slim white body, and a huge coarse male form covered in black hairs. She saw a scarred brown hand fumbling at a tender breast, twisting a pale rose nipple till it brought a cry of pain, then with a laugh, tweaking and twisting again. She saw long white thighs forced apart, and the weight of a monstrous male body burrowing into soft female flesh. She saw black hairs writhing on its shoulders, down its back, and all over its bulging, rutting loins.

Morgause was a virgin, and she had borne Lot four sons. And it came to Guenevere strongly: *she did not love her lord. How could she, when love to him was the painful use of her body for his passing pleasure, when he was hot for her after the hunt, or lecherous in his cups, or hungry for a woman again, returning from war?*

'Guenevere!'

She came to herself. Arthur was gripping her hand, pale with distress. Gently he urged her forward to meet Morgause, his voice breaking as he spoke. 'Madam, I hardly know how to greet you here. For the death of your husband, I can only grieve. He sought this war, and rebuffed my offer of peace. But if my life could bring him back, it would.'

Morgause inclined her head. 'You are gracious, sire,' she said huskily.

Arthur shook his head. 'You and I are close kin, my lady – indeed the closest, through our mother, who I hope will soon be here. Your sister too – I have sought Morgan's release so that she could be with us now.' Tears were standing in his eyes. 'We have all been strangers for over twenty years. But we are young enough, I pray, to bridge that dark gap of time.'

Morgause, too, was close to weeping now. 'You cannot know – forgive me, my lord, but I never dared to hope – how dearly I wished to know you – and to see my mother and my sister again before we meet at last in the Otherworld.'

'So now your wish is granted!' Arthur cried hoarsely. 'And believe me, madam, you are truly welcome here, you and your fine sons.' Arthur bowed, and took Morgause by the hand. 'Will you permit me to lead you to your place? Gawain, will you escort Queen Guenevere?'

All four moved down the aisle, the three sons of Orkney towering behind. As they took their seats, Arthur gave a signal, and the choir of monks soared into a new chant. A small

man in the gold-embroidered tabard of a priest stepped
forth, attended by two boys swinging incense-burners to
and fro. The smoke of the frankincense and the death-scent
of myrrh breathed from the hissing coals. The voice of the
little priest rose above the moaning of the choir.

'*Domine, domine, miserere* – O Lord our God, have mercy
upon us miserable sinners.'

*Misery and sin, sin and misery, the eternal song of the
Christians,* Guenevere thought bitterly. Truly the burial of
King Lot had begun.

'I am He that liveth and was dead, for behold, I hold the
keys of Heaven and Hell. Believe ye in the Lord Jesus Christ
our God, Who was crucified dead and buried. He descended
into hell. The third day He rose again from the dead . . .'

*Oh, these simple Christians, with their one word, one way,
one truth! Do they think they have the only God Who hung for
three days on a tree, Who passed unharmed through the world
beneath the worlds, Who was born again to save us all? Why do
they insist that their Jesus is the only one Who can rise and live
again, when every single soul rises again, when we are all reborn
from the Great Mother when our time is due?*

Guenevere sat in her place, her soul on fire. She dared
not look at Arthur. Would they be able to smile at this
later on, in their chamber? She did not know. Arthur had
reverence for all true believers, and took them at their word.
He did not seem to think that a faith could be wrong, that
men could be sincerely misguided in their belief.

The priest was beginning his prayers. 'Misery sur-
rounds us, O Lord . . .'

Misery, misery, always misery . . .

A high-pitched wailing howl rent the air. From nowhere
a black cat hurtled down the aisle, and leaped on to Lot's
coffin where it lay in the shadow of the high altar, decked
with sputtering candles and faded velvet cloths. Arching her

back, she crouched, hissing and spitting, above Lot's head.
Then she spread her back legs and voided the contents of
her body on the lid of the coffin, precisely above the dead
man's face below. For a moment she hovered, her black eyes
flashing fire. Then with another bloodcurdling screech, she
leaped away and vanished as she had come.

'*Domine, Domine, salvum me fac* – Lord God, save me,
make me safe! Save us, save us, from the Evil One, from all
the devils and demi-devils, from all the imps of Satan and
the four-footed creatures that do his will!'

Already the little priest was on his knees, bleating out
a terrified prayer against the visitant. Arthur sprang to his
feet. 'Open the doors!' he called. 'Let the beast out, however
it got in.'

Those at the back rushed to obey his command. Outside
the doors stood two women, tall and queenly, dressed from
head to foot in black, with gold crowns round their brows.

The older woman had hair as white as snow, large,
liquid eyes full of joy and grief, and a noble face made
stronger by the passage of time. Yet she was ageless rather
than old, and her beauty was still luminous to all eyes.
Guenevere looked at her in wonder. 'Elf-shining', she knew
this look was called in the olden days. The younger woman
with her had it too.

But the younger had none of the old queen's stillness
and poise. Tall, lean and tense, her black-clad body was
arched towards her mother half in protectiveness, half in
fear and need. Her ivory skin had never seen the sun, and
her deep-set eyes were burning with anger at some grief or
offence. There was something nun-like about her gown and
its severe midnight folds, and her head was covered by a
stiff headdress held in place by a simple crown of gold.

Arthur turned to Guenevere. 'The Queen of Cornwall
and her daughter Morgan!' he breathed ecstatically. 'My

mother and my sister, here at last!' As he moved forward to greet them, Guenevere's senses swam.

For these were the shapes who had brushed past her in the mist. These were the women who had come to the hillside with her, to fight for Arthur at the Battle of the Kings.

CHAPTER 27

'Not sick again, madam?' breathed Ina's voice in her ear.

Guenevere came to herself with a start. The afternoon sun was pouring into the audience chamber, gilding the massive bronze throne where she sat under a royal canopy of red silk and cloth of gold. The walls were bright with tapestries, fresh rushes covered the floor, and a low fire burned on the hearth, scenting the air with juniper and pine. In the body of the hall, the courtiers hummed with excitement as they awaited the three queens. Lords and ladies were blooming like flowers in their colourful array, and all the knights glittering in silver mail. Yes, Guenevere thought, they would welcome the visitors warmly enough.

She had almost no memory of the burial of King Lot. The sight of Queen Igraine and her daughters had wiped her mind clean of all thoughts except one: *These women love Arthur just as I do. They have yearned to know him for over twenty years, and their love has been strong enough to transcend time and place. This is a love stronger than time itself, a bond of love from the time before Time.*

The funeral had taken place, and King Lot was laid to rest. Afterwards they rode out into the sun, through the cheering crowds and up the winding hill back to the palace again. And now the whole court was waiting to welcome Queen Igraine and her daughters with all the ceremony they deserved. Guenevere passed her hand over her forehead. If only she did not feel so sick, so cold . . .

'So, madam?' Ina's low voice broke in on her thoughts. 'You were faint again there in the church, just as you were on the day of the battle. How do you feel now?'

Guenevere smiled up at the small figure hanging over her. 'It was nothing. I don't know what it was.'

There was a pause. Ina's face took on its Otherworldly air. 'When a woman feels sick to her stomach, and pale and faint, it often means a surprise for her husband. And when she's Queen, it spells good news for us all!'

'Ina, for Gods' sake!' Guenevere sat up in a frenzy, her face hot. 'What are you thinking of? Don't say another word!'

Ina dropped her eyes demurely and fell back, leaving Guenevere to a riot of wild thoughts.

Good news for her husband?

What was Ina saying?

Surely not?

No, it was impossible in a few short months!

Guenevere blushed again. Oh, it was true that she and Arthur never tired of the love the Goddess gave. And she knew that wives became mothers by treading the Mother's path. But it was far too soon to think about such things! She was faint from the seeings she had had, that was all.

In the centre of the chamber Arthur was restlessly pacing the floor with old Sir Baudwin, King Uther's loyal knight. His face was pinched and pale.

Sir Baudwin was speaking uneasily, one eye on the door. 'Queen Igraine and her daughters will be here any moment now. All that has passed is old history, sire. Are you sure you want to know?'

Arthur laughed harshly. 'Know what happened to my mother when I was born? Yes, I am sure. What is the mystery?'

Baudwin took a deep breath. 'At the time of your birth, all the world knew that the Queen was with child. So when the child disappeared, all the world wondered why.' He was watching Arthur carefully as he spoke. 'Forgive me, sire. There were rumours that your father had cast you out, or had you put to death.'

Arthur stiffened. 'What for?'

'Because you were not of Pendragon blood.'

'A bastard?' Arthur threw back his head, breathing heavily. 'And do they say that now?'

Sir Baudwin grinned triumphantly. 'Why, sire, they know you are the High King come again. Anyone who knew Uther can see that.'

'Yes, Baudwin,' Arthur said intensely, 'but—'

A royal fanfare sounded in the hall.

'The Queen of Cornwall!' came a cry at the door.

Queen Igraine had changed her black gown for a robe of blue-green silk that ebbed and flowed like the sea round Tintagel rock. A heavy antique crown encircled her tall pointed headdress, and her veil cascaded from beneath it like the foam of breaking waves.

Arthur moved forward like a man in a dream. 'Your Majesty.'

They faced each other, speaking without words, each hungry for the other's lingering gaze. Queen Igraine turned her luminous face up to his. 'My son!' she said. 'My son.'

Her eyes were wells of sorrow and delight. Arthur could not speak. To Guenevere, holding her breath for him, he had never looked more like a great bear in pain.

Queen Igraine fixed her large dark eyes on him. 'They

called you Arthur?' she said wonderingly. She smiled, her eyes bright with tears. 'I never knew your name.'

'*Why?*' The hollow moan finally tore from Arthur's throat. 'Why did they take you from me? Why was I not acknowledged at my birth?'

'Hush, my son,' Igraine said huskily, raising her proud head. 'Do not ask. Let us give thanks to the Mother, Who has given you back to me.'

She held out her arms. The tears were pouring down Arthur's face as he stumbled forward into her embrace.

At the foot of the dais Gawain was weeping openly, and others were furiously blinking away tears. Queen Igraine collected herself, and stretched out a hand, reaching towards the throne. 'Ah, Guenevere!' she said warmly. 'The Mother has blessed my son in his wife!'

Guenevere hastened to clasp the offered hand. 'You are most welcome here, Your Majesty,' she said fervently. 'And your daughters too.'

'My daughters, yes.' The joy faded from Igraine's face. 'Alas, they both have fearful griefs to bear. My poor Morgan finds it hard to be outside the walls that have imprisoned her for so long. She cannot be left alone. Her sister Morgause shares her suffering, and tries to bear her own.' She looked at Arthur with smiles and tears again. 'I lost them both, my lord, when I had you. All my children were taken from me one by one. And, unlike her sister, Morgan could not find within the convent a second family to love. I must go back to them now.'

Goddess, Mother, what these women have suffered in their lives! Guenevere gestured towards the door. 'I will escort you to them, madam. Let us go.'

In the guest apartments, a cherrywood fire glowed on the hearth. Stuffed sheepskin couches offered visitors a plump embrace, and great bowls of Michaelmas daisies made purple splashes on tables of polished wood. The afternoon sun made the panelled room a warm and welcoming place. But the sounds from within were anything but happy now.

'No! No! No!'

Queen Igraine came out of the inner chamber looking pale. Peals of wild sobbing came with her through the door. 'Forgive my daughter Morgan,' she said, with a small distracted wave of her hand. 'I hoped she would be able to see you now. But it is hard for her to get used to being free. From childhood she was forced to live as a nun. She has not been out in the world for over twenty years.'

Twenty years.

Guenevere's stomach turned. She saw a thin child, pale and terrified, surrounded by a flapping horde of nuns, as a flock of crows fall upon a lamb. 'How did it come about? Of course, if you were a widow, perhaps your girls . . .'

'I was not a widow.' Igraine's mellow voice, tinged with the soft sound of the west, was now as bleak as the north wind. 'Let us sit down,' she said. 'There is much that you should know.'

In the courtyard below, men-at-arms, servants, horses and dogs were going about the tasks of daily life. Igraine seated herself in the window, straightened her back, and folded her hands in her lap. 'I was not a widow,' she repeated. 'King Uther made me so.'

'He killed your husband?'

Igraine gave a faint nod. There was a lifetime's sadness in her eyes. 'I was the last sovereign queen in all the south. Uther needed to subdue every kingdom to make himself High King. But, more than that, he lusted after me.' Her voice was iced with pain. 'It meant nothing to him that I already had a king. A lord of my own choosing, my own knight and Chosen One.'

She gazed at Guenevere. 'Like you, our queens make the sacred marriage with the land. Less and less in recent years have we changed our champions every seven years, as our mothers used to do. I made one choice, and I lived by it.' Her eyes grew opaque. 'Duke Gorlois was my champion and my love. Uther made war on us to kill him, and take me.'

Igraine closed her eyes. 'When King Uther made himself High King, he sent for all the rulers of the lesser kingdoms to come to swear allegiance to him. When I came, he approached me in lust to take me to his bed. But I defied him, and hurried back with Gorlois to Cornwall to defend my land.'

She set her mouth in a thin line. 'And not only my land. Gorlois and I had children.'

'Morgause and Morgan?'

A radiant smile broke over Igraine's face. 'Gorlois gave me what every woman wants, a daughter to love. Morgause was born to be the next queen of our land, and she was my heart's delight. And then Morgan came, with her own special joy—' Her eyes glistened with tears, and her voice softened even more. 'Morgan had been blessed by the Goddess in her cradle, as it seemed. Her spirit shadow shone round her as she walked. Even as a child she communed with the Fair Ones, and the people called her Morgan Le Fay. Some thought that her powers would make her the Lady of Avalon in time to come.'

'But then Uther came?'

The Queen's face tightened. 'When I scorned his advances, King Uther swore to take revenge. His council agreed that I had defied the High King. They gave him authority to make war on Cornwall to impose his rule.'

Guenevere shook her head in misery. 'And so he did?'

'He brought his whole army down to crush Cornwall. Gorlois was holding our fort at Terrabil. I was defending

Tintagel, to keep Morgan and Morgause safe. We were well armed and well fortified, and we thought we could withstand Uther's assault. But there was one fighting for Uther we did not know. One you know too.'

Guenevere could hardly breathe. *'Merlin!'*

Queen Igraine nodded, far away. 'When I refused him, Uther took to his bed, sick almost to death with anger and desire. All his lords were in fear that he would die. So his chief knight, Sir Ulfius, sought Merlin out and brought him to the King. Merlin offered Uther a bargain. Merlin would fulfil the King's desire, if in turn King Uther would swear blindly to fulfil Merlin's own.'

'And the King agreed to that?' Guenevere felt sick. 'King Uther swore to give Merlin his desire, when he did not know what it was?'

Igraine inclined her shapely head. 'He swore on the Four Evangelists to do Merlin's will. So Gorlois and I were fighting against malice and magic, not merely a mortal foe. Merlin raised a mist round Terrabil, just as my Gorlois sallied out to attack. Gorlois was killed, and Merlin took the ring I gave him when I made him my Chosen One. Three hours later, Merlin brought Uther disguised as Gorlois through Tintagel's gates.' She gave a weary shrug. 'The guard accepted the ring as a sign to admit their lord, as they had a thousand times before.'

Now the sickness was deep in Guenevere's centre. 'He was planning to come to you, pretending to be your husband?'

'To take me in my bed.' Her eyes flamed again with unquenched fire. 'Thanks to Merlin, his pimp!'

Merlin again!

Guenevere's head was pounding with shock and disbelief. How could Merlin have used his powers so? How could he have schemed to kill an innocent man, to destroy a loving marriage, shatter a family, and force a woman into the bed of her husband's murderer – all for Uther's lust, and his own hunger for power? No wonder he had seen fit to disappear before Lot's burial, and be far away when Igraine arrived!

Igraine was lost now in some long-distant landscape of pain. 'In the morning they brought me the body of my love. He was stabbed through the heart, as Uther had stabbed me through the womb, time and again that night. My Gorlois lay dead in the hall, and Uther called for a priest. The Christian mumbled his dog-Latin, I stood there without a sound, and Uther called us married from that moment on.'

'Ohh.' Guenevere caught herself up. There were no words to say.

Igraine shrugged. 'What difference did it make? The victor always enjoys the spoils of war.'

Guenevere moaned in pain. 'But why did he take your child away from you? How could he bear to part with his own son?'

Igraine shook her head. 'He could not avoid it. He had sworn an oath. The very next morning Merlin came for his reward. Uther had been granted his desire, the old man said, and now he must fulfil Merlin's too. He swore I was with child, and he claimed it for himself.' She laughed, a dry, rustling sound. 'But to part with Arthur served Uther's purpose too. By the time Arthur was born, the world was whispering that this was not Uther's child. They said he was Gorlois' son, and not Pendragon blood at all – a bastard, not true-bred.' She drew a hissing breath. 'Uther thought that he could give this child away, and make more sons as easily as he made the first. He boasted that, with seed as strong as his, he would get a son from me every year. But I saw to it that there would be no more.'

Guenevere shivered. 'How?'

'I took the Mother's way to close up my womb. Arthur

was the last child I ever bore. Then I lost my daughters too
– you know that. Uther let me keep them till the baby came,
because I took the death of Gorlois so hard that he feared
for my mind. But then he wanted all my love for himself.
So he gave them away, and I lost everything. All because
of Uther. Because of his lust.'

From the inner chamber came a low growling moan.
Guenevere's skin crawled. Had Morgan heard all this?
Surely she must hate Uther – and his son?

Her sister Morgause was with her, Igraine said.

Morgause too, a woman nursing her stricken sister,
mourning her dead husband, in the house of the man who
had cost her father's life. The man who had made her a
widow, just as his father had widowed her mother.

Goddess, Mother, save Arthur from this legacy of hate.

Igraine read Guenevere's mind. She took her hand and
searched deep into her eyes. 'Well, Uther is long dead. We
must pray that his evil sleeps with him in his tomb.'

Guenevere's lips moved in silence with Igraine's. *Goddess, Mother, grant the Queen this prayer.*

CHAPTER 28

'More wine, Your Majesty?'

Guenevere shook her head. 'But there, see there?' She waved the attendant on down the long table, where goblet after goblet was being drained in a cheerful toast.

'Queen Guenevere, your health!'

'And a health to the King!'

'Eternal blessings on the King and Queen!'

The hum of revellers rose to the rafters of Caerleon's Great Hall. On the dais where they sat, one long trestle held all the kings and queens and lords, while countless white-covered tables ran off it down the hall. In the gallery above, a consort of minstrels entertained the guests. The vast, flagstoned space was bright with torches and great fires. The feast Arthur had promised his mother and sisters was in full swing.

Struggling and sweating, the busy servants toiled to and fro. Each table had a boar's head and a whole sucking pig, a side of mutton and a crown of lamb. Dishes and bowls of brawn, broth and beans crowded the boards to feed the fighting men, with slabs of coarse black bread and flagons of beer. On the high table, a nest of white swans and peacocks, their feathers tipped in gold, formed a glittering centrepiece. Royal birds for royal guests, the head cook told his underlings, since they were feasting all the King's allies and all the lesser kings who had fought under his banner, as well as Arthur's royal kin.

A feast of kings, with the King and Queen at its head, just as Merlin had decreed. Guenevere smiled. She and Arthur were indeed both at the table, but never more apart. Arthur was at the far end of the narrow trestle gorgeously clad in royal red and gold, but a mile away from her now, and almost invisible behind the gleaming candles, gold goblets, and the mounds of fruit and flowers. She sent a loving message through the air: *Arthur, Arthur, look at me, smile at me now.*

Guenevere – oh, my love . . .

For the rest of his life Arthur never forgot this feast. Shining through the candlelight, radiant in crystal and pearls, floating like thistledown in one of her gossamer gowns, Guenevere smiled at him, and glory filled his eyes. His fingers remembered the satin-smooth feel of her hair, the peach-like bloom of her breasts, the sheen on her silken skin. He thought of the way that she welcomed him to her arms, and marvelled at his good fortune with all the wonder of a humble heart. Oh, my love, my love, my love.

Guenevere caught his eye, and he glimmered back at her with a joy too deep for smiles. His wife ahead and his mother at his side – what more could a man want?

Oh, my love, you look so lovely tonight.

Oh, Arthur, you make me want—
With a conscious blush, Guenevere realised that she was longing for bed, and dreaming of having Arthur in her arms. Shame overwhelmed her. The guests! She must pay attention to the guests.

She looked down the long white expanse of the festive board with an anxious gaze. Tonight Arthur was entertaining both his allies and his new-found kin. But Queen Morgause, they had agreed, could not be expected to face the men who had killed her husband in Arthur's cause. The only solution had been to seat the two groups as far apart as it was possible for guests at the same banquet to be, with Arthur feasting Morgause and her sons at one end, while at the other Guenevere took care of King Pellinore, his son Lamorak and the French kings Ban and Bors.

Behind Arthur stood Gawain and his three brothers, in attendance on Morgause, Morgan and Queen Igraine. For hours now the four sons of Orkney had proved true to their task, showing never a hint of boredom or fatigue. Yet even without four fine young princes standing behind their thrones, Guenevere knew that these women would have been recognised as queens anywhere. Tall as a tree-poppy, Igraine shimmered in a gown like evening falling across the sea. Morgause's large shapely frame caught all eyes in a court gown of draped red velvet, whose sensual folds matched her full peony mouth.

Only Morgan had clung to her plain attire, her nun-like habit and headdress of severe black. Seated beside Arthur, she hung on his every word. The meeting between the two had been as poignant to Guenevere as the reunion between Arthur and Igraine. 'Bring him to Morgan,' Igraine had urged Guenevere, 'when I have calmed her and she has slept a while.' That evening, she and Arthur had returned to the guest apartments to find Morgan standing waiting, supported between her mother and Morgause. Gripping their hands, she was weeping, and shaking convulsively from head to foot.

At the sight of her, Arthur wept too. A long silence had stretched out to fill the chamber with unbearable pain. At last Morgan had thrown back her head and unleashed one endless cat-like wail. Then she threw herself forward into Arthur's arms, sobbing inconsolably while the others looked helplessly on. Arthur had held her till she wrenched herself away and reached up to plant one fervent kiss on the side of his neck. Her small teeth gleamed briefly as she threw him a broken smile, then she suddenly whirled around and was gone. In all this time she had not said a word.

Now as Arthur spoke, Morgan's huge eyes roamed the hall, but she was otherwise composed. There was no sign, Guenevere saw with relief, of the wild distress of before. Indeed, as Arthur tried to put his half-sister at her ease, her clasped hands came again and again to her mouth as if to hide a smile.

Guenevere watched her, trying to understand.

Morgan . . .

She could speak with the Fair Ones, and they called her Morgan Le Fay.

What is it about Morgan? Guenevere asked herself. *Arthur loves her now, and something about her makes me long to embrace her too. But when she came into the hall tonight and I greeted her so warmly, her lean black body arched away as soon as I drew near. When I tried to show her a loving, sisterly regard, she turned aside with a stiffness that was almost like disgust.* Well, so be it. Guenevere stifled a sigh. It would take years before time and love could breed out what the convent had bred in. She would have to learn to be a sister to Morgan without expecting any response, till the poor sufferer was ready to be a sister to her in return.

She caught Arthur's eye again, and he raised his goblet in a silent toast. Her heart jumped with the pain that happiness so often gives. Never had Arthur looked more himself, or more pleasing to her eye. And seated among his mother and his sisters, he had the uncertain joy of a man come home at last, after a long journey full of woe and pain.

A sudden vow sealed itself in her mind. She would never tell Arthur what Igraine had told her, the cruel saga of how he came to be born. He knew only what Merlin had told him, and believed that Uther had sent him away only to save his life. Like every son who never knew his father, Arthur adored his memory and idealised his name. How could she tell him that, judged by the laws of the Mother, the hero he idolised was a rapist and murderer?

Yet when they fell in love, they had promised always to tell each other the truth, to keep no secrets from one another all their lives—

'You have a worry, Majesty?' asked a French voice at her side. Guenevere started. King Bors, quieter than his older brother Ban, was regarding her thoughtfully, his head on one side.

'Not in the least!' Guenevere forced a laugh. She raised her glass gaily to King Bors and King Ban, then to King Pellinore and his son on her other side. 'A toast, gentlemen! A toast to the dear friends who saved my husband's life!'

'Now, madam, no more of that,' King Pellinore said gruffly, turning away. His old ears had gone very pink.

'Yes, indeed!' Guenevere insisted playfully. 'Unless you want me to say that two phantom heroes crossed the plain to save the King, not you and your brave son!'

Now Pellinore's son had changed colour too, but he bowed his head gallantly as he accepted the toast. Raw-boned and golden-haired, young Lamorak looked better than he knew in a tunic of indigo slashed with crimson, and a broad silk sash. Guenevere's imagination took sudden flight. He was a fine young man. He would make a good husband for one of the ladies at court – perhaps even Ina? – and what a catch for her, a king's only son—

A king's only son—

Guenevere turned her head.

His name is Lancelot.

Guenevere's hand flew to her head. Where had she heard these words before? And why did she hear again the shadow of a sigh? She opened her eyes to find the bright brown gaze of King Ban fixed questioningly on her face. 'You have a son, sir, I believe,' she began hurriedly. 'Lancelot, is that his name? Where is he now? And yours, of course, King Bors. King Arthur and I will never forget the noble youths who fought so bravely on our behalf.'

'Ah, Bors' two boys, and my own Lancelot!' said King Ban fondly. The two kings exchanged a smiling glance. 'They would gladly be here if they could, my lady, to kiss Your Majesty's hand.' He laughed merrily. 'But they have gone to a much harder place.'

'It had to be.' King Bors smiled too, but his face was grave. 'Back home in Little Britain, we are always threatened by our overlord the King of France. But we shall fight for Benoic to the last drop of our blood. And our sons must face this war when the time comes.'

Ban nodded. 'So we have sent them to learn the arts of war, which to a true knight must mean *cherchez la femme.*'

'*Cherchez la femme?*' Seated beside King Pellinore, Lamorak's face lit up. 'Father, it's the place I told you about, it has to be!' He leaned forward urgently. 'Excuse me, sirs, have your sons gone to the war college in the north?'

King Pellinore gave a loud snort of disgust. 'Not the school for warriors run by that – that—?'

'That woman?' King Ban burst out laughing. 'Queen Aife is known the world over for her skill in war! And who better than a woman to introduce young men to the cruelties of life?'

King Bors looked steadily at Lamorak, then shifted his gaze to Pellinore. 'Your son is already a fine warrior, sir, as he showed when you saved the King's life. He may have fought this battle as your squire, but the King will knight him for this service, mark my words. His future is set fair. Our sons have promise, Lancelot most of all, but they still need to learn the arts of war. Young knights must take service with those who will bring them on.'

King Ban twinkled at Guenevere. 'And how lucky they are that a queen like Aife will bring them on! Beautiful, clever, bold, and a woman of the world . . .' He rolled his eyes, placed his hand on his heart and gave an extravagant sigh. 'But all young men should be formed by an older woman's touch.'

King Pellinore threw an outraged glance at him, then at his Lamorak. 'You Frenchmen may say so, sir,' he growled, 'but in these islands, we do things differently!'

'Your Majesty!'

The clear, full voice rang boldly round the hall. Unhurriedly Queen Morgause rose from her seat beside Arthur, and dropped to her knees. Her three sons Agravain, Gaheris and Gareth moved from their places to form a line behind her, arms folded across their chests and legs spread wide.

'My lord and brother!' Morgause cried in measured tones. 'I beg a favour, on your honour as a king!'

'Of course!'

Guenevere's stomach tightened in a knot.

Arthur, wait, wait, my soul.

'Name it, my dear sister!' Arthur cried, his eyes very bright. 'If it lies in my power, it's yours!'

Wait, Arthur, think! Guenevere's soul cried to him silently. *This is how King Uther agreed to Merlin's demand, whatever it was. And now you agree to this, whatever it is. Whatever it means – for us – for all of us.*

Morgause clasped her hands together, and raised them
in the air. 'Sire, my eldest son Gawain was your first
companion knight. I beg you, brother, take these three
fatherless sons and be a father to them now.' She did not
look behind. 'Agravain!'

The eldest of the three knelt at his mother's side. King
Lot had been black-haired and red-faced. Morgause was a
darker blonde than Arthur, with shades of red-gold. Her
four sons spanned the spectrum between their parents.
Gawain was fair, his broad red face quick to colour up
at the slightest thing. But Agravain was swarthy, with
heavy brows and a jutting chin. Even kneeling to beg a
favour, Guenevere noticed, he did not smile but stared
straight down the hall. And his burning eyes seemed to
bore into her.

Why was she sweating? Why was the hall so hot? Her gorge
rose, and she felt for her napkin to fan her face. Fever ran
through her veins, and the sickness she had felt before was
clawing at her guts.

Morgause called again, 'Gaheris!'

The next of the brothers knelt by Agravain. Gaheris was
a true red-head, with the milk-blue eyes of the north. As
big as his brothers, he looked quieter and more reserved.
Unlike Agravain, he bowed his head humbly as he fell to
his knees.

'Gareth!'

The youngest of the Orkney princes was as fair as
Agravain was dark. He had the same dusty blond hair
as Arthur, and Arthur's clear grey eyes. His honest face
had never kept a secret, and his smile showed the sunny
disposition of a mother's youngest, best-loved child.

'King Arthur, I give you my sons!' Morgause's deep
voice rang out. 'They are your nephews, and your own blood
kin. Take them, and make them your knights, to serve you

all your life. Keep them always by you, trust them and hold them to your heart, and they will die for you!'

Arthur, wait!

Arthur leaped to his feet. 'Why, sister,' he cried joyfully, 'I grant your wish with all my heart!'

He crossed towards the brothers, embracing them one by one as he raised them to their feet. 'You are mine now, sirs! Follow me, and I will never part with you. And in time I will make you knights like your brother Gawain. I plan to build a fellowship of my own, to follow the example of Queen Guenevere's renowned Knights of the Round Table.'

On the knights' table, Lucan let out a whoop of joy and exchanged gleeful punches and handshakes with Bedivere and Kay. Happiness spread from table to table through the hall. There were rounds of cheerful cries, and the servants rushed to replenish the drinking-glasses all round. With the wine flowing, and the general merriment the room was even hotter now, and the fires on the hearths were leaping up the walls.

King Ban nodded approvingly to Guenevere. 'The King is right to encourage young knights like this,' he said enthusiastically. 'You know how in France we love chivalry. If you and King Arthur would visit us in Benoic, it would be a pleasure to show him how we do these things. And then you could meet Lancelot, and my brothers' sons!'

'Yes indeed!' His brother warmly backed him up.

Only on Guenevere's right was there a chill, as King Pellinore gripped his goblet, and stared into the blood-red wine. Lamorak was looking at his father with foreboding in his eyes. A heavy question hung between them in the air.

'Yes, son,' said Pellinore absently, swirling his wine round his glass. 'I'm sure you're right. But the King has found his kin. What can we to say to that?'

'Say to what?' Guenevere cried, her nerves curling in the heat.

King Pellinore tried to smile. 'Nothing, Your Majesty.'

'Nothing?'

Pellinore frowned again. 'Forgive me, madam, but you are young, royal and beautiful and should not be troubled with such things.'

'Ha!' King Ban shook his head. 'The more beautiful a woman, the more she needs to understand.'

Pellinore's eyes flared for a moment, then he dropped his head. 'You may be right, sir.' He straightened his back, and looked Guenevere in the eye. 'Time for the truth, is it, then? Take all this, madam, as the fears of an old fool. Say I have seen too much blood, and lost too many sons. But tonight the King has taken a nest of vipers to his heart. He has embraced a poison brood born to hate him, and hate all he loves.'

Guenevere leaned forward urgently. 'Gawain is different. He is not one of them.'

King Ban laughed sadly, and shook his head. 'He has not seen his kin for fifteen years.' He looked at her, narrowed his bright brown eyes, and cocked his head to one side. 'You do not understand, my queen.' He nodded to his brother. 'Explain to her.'

Bors leaned forward. 'King Uther forced Queen Morgause to marry a man she did not choose. She lost her father, her mother and her kingdom, and her right to rule. These are insults to their mother, which any son would avenge.'

Why was it so hot in the hall? Guenevere fanned the air.

King Ban nodded sombrely. 'Then Arthur killed King Lot.' He shook his head, and glanced down the table at the Orkney princes clustered around Morgause. 'There is the death of the father, which any son would avenge.'

The insult to the mother, the death of the father, any son would avenge—

Guenevere could feel the heat rising as she spoke. 'But Gawain?'

'Oh, Gawain,' Pellinore waved a hand, 'Arthur can count on Gawain to the death. He is not under the sway of his mother's love, and he does not feel himself Lot's son. He has bound himself to another allegiance now.' He downed the contents of his goblet in one desperate gulp. 'But the other three are princes of the blood. They are the living sons of a dead king. If Gawain will not avenge both his parents and punish Arthur, it falls to Agravain. Agravain is the man.'

'Oh, the heat!'

The heat, the heat!

Flames leaped before Guenevere's eyes. She was in a fire, she could smell burning flesh. She rose from her seat, gagging with terror, her whole being crying out to flee. But she was tied hand and foot, she could not move.

The flames, the heat – spare me, Goddess Mother, spare my life!

Sickness overwhelmed her, and she sank back in her seat. What was this seeing? What did it portend? Women were burned in lands where the Christians held sway, but never in the kingdom of the Goddess, it could never happen to her. And how could she ever deserve to die by fire?

'Well, nephews, on with the revels!' Arthur cried, from the far end of the hall. 'Will you dance now, and gladden our ladies' hearts? We must enjoy you all while you are here, for I shall miss you sadly when you go.'

Queen Igraine smiled her luminous smile. She turned to Morgan and fondly took her hand. 'Morgause has made her request, and the King has answered it. Will you speak now?' she whispered to her daughter. 'Or shall I?'

Morgan blushed violently, shook her wimpled head and covered her face with her hand. Igraine smiled and turned back to Arthur again. 'Morgan craves a favour too. She wants to ask if she may stay here at court. She wants no more than to be quiet here with you.'

Arthur gasped. 'Morgan here with us? Oh, nothing would give us greater joy! Morgan, you must stay with us as long as you like.'

Guenevere looked down the table in anguish, and put her heart into her eyes. *Nothing would give us greater joy? Do you know what you are saying, Arthur, nothing? I beg you, think, ask me, I am your wife!*

He heard her feverish thoughts, and flashed her an anguished look. *Did I do wrong? You wanted a sister, she'll be yours as well as mine.*

Fretfully Guenevere shook her burning head.

Yes—

No—

Oh, do not ask me now—

Then it was darkness and sickness and a roaring in her ears.

And suddenly Ina was at her elbow, pressing a glass to her lips. 'Drink this, my lady.'

Like a child, she did as she was told. It was a heart-warming cordial, and it choked her back to life.

Ina whisked the glass away. 'So, lady, you have a new sister, if the Princess Morgan stays here with us at court,' she whispered, as she fussed with Guenevere's gown. She smiled. 'And unless I am mistaken, the King's sister will have new kin within the year!'

Deftly she eased the weight of the crown on Guenevere's burning head. 'Kin on her brother's side.'

Guenevere gasped. 'Ina . . .' she began warningly, grasping for the remains of her strength.

'When Your Majesty is delivered of your child!' Ina breathed triumphantly. 'So, madam!' Her sturdy fingers caressed Guenevere's temples and gently rubbed her back. 'We must pray for a girl. When will you tell the King?'

CHAPTER 29

S he never knew if Ina was right or not, that first time she was sick. The days passed, and the sickness came and went, and so did her moon-days, as they always had. Every month her body seemed to fill with spirit children, little laughing sprites who leaped into her womb and danced about till she was as sick as any woman breeding for twins or more. Then the moon would swell and grow big in the sky. And every time her pale face lit the earth, Guenevere lost what she was carrying, and her body did not swell.

But she did not tell Arthur – what was there to tell? And she did not grieve. None of these spirits spoke to her as her child. None of them called to her like a young Arthur ready to be born, or cried out to her in her own voice for the chance to live. Then her monthly times became disordered, and she stopped keeping count. When the time came, she told Ina, the Mother would let them know. Till then, they were happy, they would take life as it came.

And they were happy, she was happy with Arthur, happier every day than the day before. Oh, Arthur might fret over Merlin and wonder where he was, for there had been no sign of the old enchanter since Queen Igraine and Morgan came, but she could always tease him out of these thoughts. Day after day, the time slipped sweetly by.

So a sun-drenched autumn ripened into winter, winter roared in like a lion from the Welshlands, and she hugged her love to her heart and marvelled what a year could bring. A year ago she had been waiting for the word, the sign, the man who would fulfil her mother's dying prophecy, *through the fires he comes*. Now he had come, and now when she thought of her mother, it was with soft tears like the mist of the Summer Country that made everything sweet and green again.

And Arthur – at the very thought of him she would slip into the same reverie, the same enchanted state of wonder and desire.

Arthur, Arthur, my love, my only love—

Goddess, Mother, tell me, does he know, will he ever know, the love I have for him?

Hush, I see him now, candle in hand, stepping towards the bed. The light from the fire glances on his bright head, and sets burning the thousand little torches in his eyes. But nothing shines like the smile he has for me, as he mounts the huge bed where I lie under the billowing canopy, and looses the curtain ties one by one, till we are enclosed in the warm womb-like darkness, glowing blood-red.

Carefully he sets the candle in the holder on the bedpost, lighting our little space with its flickering light.

No, do not blow it out, he warns, as I lean up to quench it. You are my wife, I want to see you now.

Arthur, Arthur my love . . .

When he first came to her, she never asked if he had taken his pleasure as a boy with a girl of Sir Ector's household, or when he was soldiering, among the women of the camps. There could have been village girls in Gore for all she cared, even a woman of the world at King Ursien's court who had taken him in hand, to his profit and her delight.

Yet Guenevere did not think so. Even when they had been lovers for a while, Arthur often came to her in tremulous hesitancy, though by now they knew each other well. His blazing purity seemed reserved for her alone. And his high concern for others would never have let him take a girl simply for his pleasure, then cast her aside.

'I have been waiting for you all my life,' he whispered, the first time he came into her, and she never doubted that.

But somewhere, somehow, blessed be the Goddess, he had learned how to love women's bodies, or at least to love hers. He rejoiced in taking her to himself, slowly, slowly, and piece by piece shedding their outer gear. Naked, his great body, scarred and muscular, was like one of the heroes of the Old Ones from the days when they battled dragons and monsters to make the world. He was shy of her touch, but he loved to stroke her skin, to caress her long loins and rounded haunches, and turning her over, to play with her breasts and stroke her belly, till she cried for more.

And cry she did, she cried with a woman's longing when she thinks her moment will not come – and cried even louder with the wonder of it, when at last it did. The first time it came, it swept over her like a wave, a wave of warm darkness that ebbed away leaving her wet and weeping with delight. Then it grew stronger and harsher, gripping her like a great beast, and shaking her in its jaws till she was weak with exhaustion, yet groaning to come again.

All this Arthur viewed with wonder and delight. And so they crept hand in hand to a glade in the woodland, to a cave in a hollow hill, or to the place of enchantment that was their great bed, any time and every time they could. And if she was often drowsy and flushed at noontime, or ready to retire straight after dinner when the night was young, why they were newly married and in love, and all the world smiled on them then.

Those were the dreams of the two of them alone. In between they dreamed a royal dream of the world outside and the changes they would bring. Arthur's country had been like a child without parents since Uther died. It was time to show the Middle Kingdom that their king had come again.

So they called their knights together under Sir Gawain and Sir Kay, Sir Lucan and Sir Bedivere. Sir Griflet and Sir Sagramore, Sir Ladinas and Sir Dinant were in the forefront, together with all the rest of Arthur's small band of companion knights. Arthur surveyed them, in the grip of feelings he could hardly name. Some of these men had marched with him from London when he was proclaimed, others had rallied to join him in Caerleon as the sons of Uther's old lords. But all of them were men of faith and hope, ready to fight for a better world than this.

Now they were all to ride out of Caerleon, each in his full armour, each proudly displaying his chosen colours on his banner, war-coat and shield. White diamond on scarlet ground, blue stars in a silver sky, every knightly device should make any who saw them catch their breath and say, 'There goes a knight of the court of King Arthur, and Sir Wondrous must be his name.'

Each knight was to take a squire, Arthur decreed, a youth he could bring on, who would earn his own knighthood by brave and willing service to his lord. Gawain's younger brothers, Agravain, Gaheris and Gareth, should be made squires now, by their mother's desire and their own. Guenevere looked at the great threesome, saw Arthur's delight in them, and resolved to treat them royally. So the court tailors and armourers were set to work to make each a fine coat of mail, and a smart new surcoat in the colour of his choice. When they rode out, she promised Arthur, his nephews would be as splendid as the knights they served.

Some of Arthur's knights would set out alone, some in pairs, some in threes till each took his own way. At every castle, every manor house, every estate, they were to proclaim Arthur as king, and require a pledge of loyalty in the King's name. All who refused were to be told to bring their grievance to the court at Caerleon, to see Arthur and resolve the dispute.

And now all the knights knelt before Arthur and Guenevere to take their farewell.

'Proclaim the word to all, high or low,' Arthur urged, his eyes ablaze. 'Tell everyone you meet that a new king rules here now. Make them understand that all shall have justice and a fair hearing at our court.'

'And do not fear to do justice as you go,' Guenevere added, 'for you are knights of King Arthur, sworn to defend the weak against the strong. Above all, you must help any woman in distress. Do not forget your oath!'

'Look out for Merlin too,' was Arthur's last word. He swung a leather pouch clinking in the air. 'D'you hear this? There's a thousand crowns in gold for the man who finds my old friend, and sends him back to me!'

The courtyard was loud with the jingling of harness and the clatter of hoofs on cobbles as they rode away. Arthur stood in silence as he waved them off, and Guenevere felt his fear. They all went forth so bravely, but how many of these proud banners and bright swords would come back? They were going to cleanse the kingdom, and who knew what that meant?

For even after King Lot had been overthrown, the country was still burdened by the weight of his misrule. Madmen and beggars, wandering knights and landless men still thronged the roads to threaten travellers, invading lonely manors or seizing undefended estates. Many cruel barons and lesser kings had thrived on the disorder and relished being lords of their own destiny, answerable to none. Those who lived by preying on the poor would not think twice about taking another life or two. And Arthur's knights all knew this as well as he did, as one by one they set forth under their bright banners in that shining dawn.

But one, new to their ranks, was given another task. Lamorak, the son of King Pellinore, had won his spurs, Arthur decreed, and should be knighted now. So Lamorak kept his vigil as a knight novice, his white night of prayer and wakefulness before the great day. Then at dawn he came before Arthur and was made a knight. He trembled all through his raw-boned, well-muscled frame as he felt the gold blade of Excalibur buffet his shoulders with its high singing *one, two, three*. And Guenevere thought again that this man had a deep well of passion in reserve, waiting for the woman of his dream.

'Arise, Sir Lamorak, and hear your command!'

Arthur's orders rolled through the still court. Queen Morgause was returning to her own lands in the furthest north. As she was leaving behind her three sons and protectors, Lamorak was to escort her on the long journey back to the Orkney Islands, and remain as her knight at her court for as long as she desired.

Guenevere listened in silence with a troubled heart.

But Lamorak and his father killed King Lot; he and King Pellinore made a widow of Queen Morgause.

King Pellinore's voice came to her again. *Blood will have blood. This is the vengeance no man can refuse.*

'Think of it, Arthur!' Frantically Guenevere tried to tell him what she had heard from Pellinore on the night of the feast.

But Arthur would not hear a word against his plan.

'No, Guenevere, no!' he said angrily, shaking his head. 'Of course we can't forget that Lamorak and his father killed King Lot. But don't you see that the way to heal it is for the son to make amends? Lamorak is a fine and noble young man. He will serve Morgause devotedly as her knight. He will atone to her for her husband's death.'

'But think of Pellinore! Will he want his only son sent to the Orkneys, so many miles away?'

Arthur held up his hand to bring the discussion to an end. 'Pellinore will be grateful that Lamorak does not have to ride out into danger, as our other knights must, every day they are away. No man ever lost his life at court dancing attendance on a queen. In years to come, he will thank me for protecting his son's life.'

His son's life.

There was a pounding in Guenevere's head, and her sight dimmed. Through a mist she saw Morgause and Lamorak riding out to the Orkneys at the head of a great train. She saw the Queen's rich, full body turning to Lamorak, laughing with him as they rode now into this castle on a crag, now into that palace by the sea.

Then, without warning, the scene was drenched with blood. Waves of black, boiling blood washed over them, and she saw them both go down. Thin wreaths of mist swirled over the sea of blood, and the scene melted like an evil dream.

Goddess, Mother, spare them, spare us all . . .

Guenevere covered her eyes, and tried to clear her sight. How clever Arthur was! There must be some bad blood brewing against Morgause, some threat to her kingdom, that only Arthur knew.

So a blood feud was brewing, but Lamorak would save Morgause. Now her death would be averted through Arthur's foresight and care. Slowly Guenevere's heart revived, and she looked at Arthur with the old wondering love. Already he was taking care of his lost kin. Morgause would live to be grateful that Arthur had sent Lamorak to be her knight!

The farewells were long, and very hard to bear. Morgause said goodbye to her mother with a grief that showed she did not expect to see Queen Igraine again on this side of the grave. The old Queen herself set off on the same day, beginning the long ride south as Morgause and her party took the road north.

Arthur wept heavily as he folded his mother in his arms.

'To lose her, and Merlin too!' he lamented to Guenevere, as Queen Igraine rode away. 'This is the longest time he has stayed away. Where is he, Guenevere? When will he return?' But his real grieving came afterwards, in the hours he shut himself away and would let no one come to him, not even the dogs.

Alone in her chamber, Guenevere struggled with resentfulness and loss. How could he leave her so, just because they had gone? But when she sent messengers asking if she could come to him, he would not admit her, and she had to endure in silence till he emerged again.

And, though Morgause and Igraine had gone, Morgan remained. While Arthur kept to his chamber in the King's apartments, Guenevere tried to get to know her new sister, and make much of her.

But Morgan was a lost soul, cut adrift from all she knew. The clock of life had stopped for her on the day she was sent to the convent, and the world beyond the cloister was too much for her now. Would she like to ride? Guenevere asked, hoping to chase the pallor from her cheeks. But Morgan had not ridden for twenty years and more. Would she come to dinner in the Great Hall, or take a turn about the court? If she had to be near any man except Arthur, even kind old Sir Baudwin or the gentlest of Uther's old knights, she would flare her eyes and flinch like a panicking mare. Then only Arthur could calm her, and she would cling to him like a child.

Arthur could not bear to watch the torment she suffered now. How could his father King Uther have done this cruel thing? And to a little child, he reminded himself in pain. Yet Morgan was not a girl any longer. She was a woman, and a royal woman too.

'I want to give Morgan a true place in the world,' he announced abruptly to Guenevere one day, coming into the Queen's apartments unannounced as she worked on the monthly dispatches from the Summer Country while the couriers stood by. 'She should have her own castle and lands, her own waiting gentlewomen and men-at-arms.'

And her own lords and ladies, her knights and horses, men and dogs and maids? Guenevere looked up from her papers, and blinked in surprise. How long had he been planning this without a word? Long enough, she saw with annoyance, to have decided already what he was going to do. 'You have somewhere in mind?'

'King Ursien has a fine estate in Gore. It lies deep in a valley in the heart of the Wounded Forest, and they call it Le Val Sans Retour. King Ursien has offered it to me as a gift of his allegiance now I have taken my father's place. I mean to give it to Morgan, and install her royally there.'

The morning sun fell on the wall above Arthur's head, fingering the ornate mouldings of white and gold. In a corner of the window a fly buzzed maddeningly against the glass. Guenevere laid down her seal on the surface of scratched oak, and stared at him.

Without discussion, Arthur, without a word?

Why had he not told her any of this before? Why was it so important that Morgan's needs be served? A worm of resentment turned in Guenevere's heart. 'If you're giving out land and estates, Arthur, what about all the others we have to thank? Lucan left the Summer Country and his old allegiance to follow you. King Pellinore saved your life. Others have done you sterling service too. Sooner or later they deserve their reward.'

'And they will have it,' Arthur said shortly. 'But my sister must come first.'

So Morgan was given her estate, her ladies and her knights, her horses and dogs, her waiting gentlewomen and her men-at-arms. Arthur issued orders that she was to be styled 'The Princess Morgan of Cornwall and Gore'. He loaded her with jewels from the royal treasury, and commanded the best of the court dress-makers to clothe her like royalty from head to foot.

'Arthur . . .' Guenevere tried to tell him that she thought he was moving too fast. Morgan asked for nothing. She said nothing when Arthur announced his gift to her in the full court, though the rainbow of emotion that played over her pale face spoke for her in full. Quiet though she was, Morgan's bond with Arthur was plainly the only thing that mattered to her now. Her eyes never left him whenever he was there.

'She follows you everywhere,' Guenevere cried, 'and everyone knows that she wants nothing except to be with you!' *And you watch her, I've seen you,* she longed to say. *I know when you entrust her to the horse-master to take her out for a ride, and then find a reason to ride out that way yourself. I know you have given orders that if she seems distracted or distressed, you must be sent for instantly.*

I know—

Arthur clenched his fists, and an angry colour rose in

his face. 'Guenevere, Morgan has the right to be with me! She has to learn to live like a princess and the sister of a king. She is not a nun any more! And besides—'

He broke off and turned away. Like all their discussions about his family, this was suddenly at an end. But as she watched his clouded eyes and troubled brow, Guenevere knew what he meant.

And besides, his honest heart was saying, *nothing can make up for what my father did when Morgan was a child. But I must try.*

Now Arthur was on fire to make up to Morgan for her lost girlhood as a royal princess. When the summer came, he promised her they would ride to Le Val Sans Retour, deep in the Wounded Forest. There he would make her queen of her own court, and mistress of her domain.

But would she live and rule there quite alone, Guenevere wondered. When she looked at Morgan's long, pale, enclosed face, her great black eyes and full mulberry mouth, she saw the woman in her, not the child. And when the court clothiers had done their work, and her tall, lean body was dressed in the gowns of a queen, she looked everything that Arthur hoped she was, and more. Though she still favoured modest, nun-like styles, the rich silks and clinging velvets Arthur had ordered showed off a woman's small, high breasts and shapely flanks growing more supple by the day as Morgan learned to live.

And Goddess, Mother, no woman should live without love! One night in bed Guenevere nestled into Arthur and said drowsily, 'Morgan deserves to be as happy as we are, sweetheart. We must find her a lover. Any man would be glad to pay court to her.' Arthur would be pleased, she knew, that she cared for his sister's happiness too.

But his whole body tensed, and she felt him draw away from her. When he spoke, his voice was remote. 'If it comes, it comes. Don't think about it, Guenevere. I don't, and neither does she, I know.'

Guenevere felt instantly rebuked. 'Oh, Arthur, I didn't mean . . .'

'Hush, my love.' Gently he laid his hand on her mouth, and they said no more.

But the next day Morgan would not leave her chamber until nightfall, when she appeared in the Great Hall, silent, white and drawn. Her eyes were wild. She sat hunched beside Arthur at dinner, dressed all in black again, and would not eat or speak.

It did not take Arthur's severe look to make Guenevere feel ashamed. *Morgan had great gifts of the spirit, even as a child*, her mother Queen Igraine said. Once before in her girlhood, others had decided her future, and destroyed her world. Could she have sensed that Guenevere had talked about getting her married, planning her life again?

Guenevere tried to shake off the feeling. Unless Morgan had been a mouse in the wainscot or a cat hiding in the hangings, she could not have known what they said in bed last night. But something had aroused that angry, sideways look of hers, something had lit that Otherworldly fire in her black eyes, the glint that hinted of a deeper darkness, a strain wilder and crueller than her nun-like exterior.

Guenevere felt as if she were Uther himself, come back to haunt and hurt a defenceless woman again. Wretchedly she swore a silent oath, 'No more!' Of course Morgan would be happier being courted and in love, as any woman would be. But if this was the way she and Arthur reacted to the very mention of it, then the least said, the better for them all.

CHAPTER 30

The knights rode out in the first autumn of Arthur's reign. By the time the wild hyacinths were scenting the spring air, Arthur and Guenevere were reaping the harvest they had sown.

'Ahead there, against the sun, a mighty force!'

'To arms! To arms!'

'Sound the alarm!'

'What orders from the King?'

Summoned by wild-eyed guards, Guenevere and Arthur looked out from the topmost tower of Caerleon. Banners darkened the distant horizon, above a forest of glittering lances and an army of marching men.

High in the watch-tower, the look-out man called down. 'Black acre on white ground, crowned, the insignia of the Black Lands, and the banner of their King!'

'To your posts, every man!'

Arthur commanded an immediate alert. Flying their own flags in defiance, he and Guenevere met the oncoming host on the plain outside the castle in ceremonial armour and full war array. But the King of the Black Lands had not come to offer war.

'Greetings to King Arthur and Queen Guenevere!' his heralds trumpeted as they drew near. 'The Black Lands served King Uther during his reign. Now we have had word that the rule of Pendragon has returned again. Our King offers fealty to King Arthur as High King. May it please you to accept the service of his sword?'

Before them in the field, a herald knelt at Arthur's stirrup offering a silver ceremonial sword on a pallet of cloth of gold. Arthur reached down for the weapon, and raised it above his head. 'We accept this tribute with a thankful heart!' he called out to the heralds. 'And beg your King to enter Caerleon to receive all the honour we can give!'

The King of the Black Lands was a small sturdy man with bright eyes like a blackbird and a rich, chuckling laugh. They feasted him for three days and nights, and he returned to his kingdom well satisfied, laden with Arthur's gifts. And after him came others, barons and lords and lesser kings, all eager to swear their allegiance and to join Arthur's cause.

'Who sent you here? Who brought you word that Arthur is now King?'

Guenevere asked them all the same question she had asked the King of the Black Lands as he sat at her right hand on the first night of the feast.

'Why, Sir Gawain, the King's knight!' was the King's reply.

Guenevere nodded. Gawain, Arthur's first companion and his most loyal knight. In the months that passed, the names of Sir Kay, Sir Bedivere and Sir Lucan were also heard in the mouths of those who came to pay tribute to Arthur's rule. But every one who went out played his part, above and beyond his calling as a knight.

One by one the tales of knight errantry came in. On a far estate Sir Sagramore had put down a nest of vicious beggars, who preyed on all comers and kept the owner in constant dread. That old lord wept on his knees before them as he told of his suffering, and his joy when Sir Sagramore came to his relief. Sir Griflet had set free a lady who was held a prisoner in her own castle by a knight cruelly set on marrying her against her will. In single combat Sir Griflet had killed the knight who had been such a traitor to his vows, and now the lady begged him, Griflet said, to marry her instead.

'And she is beautiful,' he said lamely, 'and young, and very rich. And yet . . .' His voice tailed off.

'And yet?' Guenevere prompted. 'You do not love her?'

Sir Griflet flushed. 'I think I could,' he said. Frowning uncertainly, he looked very young. 'I have dreamed of loving a lady just like her. But I never thought my mistress would speak first! I thought I should woo her a long time before she would yield.' He sighed as if his heart would break.

Guenevere tried not to smile. 'Upon my word, Sir Griflet,' she said gravely, 'this is a true conundrum for your honour as a knight!'

But where was Merlin? One by one the knights rode back to court, and each was feasted as the hero of the hour. None had seen Merlin, and as Arthur listened to their tales, he felt a shadow even on the keenest joy. But for Guenevere, to see them all return alive was the best reward she could have.

Lucan came in first, laughing in triumph as he galloped into the courtyard, his red banner fluttering as boldly as the day he rode away. Then Sir Kay limped back, nursing a bad wound in his leg, taken as he fought a dwarf who had turned against his knight.

'I found him leading his lord bound to his horse, beaten unconscious and tied face down across the saddle, half dead already from the handling he had had,' Kay said grimly. 'The dwarf claimed that another knight had done this deed. But when I went to release his master from his bonds, the treacherous creature stabbed me from behind, half severing my leg!'

He laughed sardonically, relishing the jest. 'I'll never run or wrestle now with Your Majesty as we did when we were boys, or sit a horse again with the best of your knights. But that villain did not live to raise his hand a second time. It was his habit to take employment with wandering knights, then kill them for their armour and their gold. Well, he won't prey on any more innocent men.'

'If King Arthur and his knights can cleanse this land, Your Majesty,' the King of the Black Lands muttered to Guenevere at the feast, 'all men will be begging to serve under his banner as High King. None will deny him!' He raised his goblet and the candlelight flashed through the green glass into the heart of the red wine. 'None will dare!'

Now, night after night, the Great Hall at Caerleon rang with the sounds of revelry it had forgotten for so many years. From their seats at the high table, King, Queen and court looked down on a sea of glittering chain-mail, glowing velvet, and bright, fluttering silks.

'What shall I feast you with tonight, my love?' Guenevere murmured to Arthur as they lay in bed. 'Roast sucking pig and rabbits in a crust?' And she got no further, as he stopped her mouth with a kiss.

Laughing, she pushed him off. 'Arthur, help me, I have to give commands to the cooks, they'll be here for their orders any time now!'

'Tell them – whatever you want.' Sleepily he nuzzled her ear and his hand wandered to her breast. Her resolve wavering, she yielded to the moment as his fingers teased her nipple this way and that. Then her conscience pricked her as she remembered all that had to be done. *The food for the feast, the order of seating at the high table, more cooks for the kitchens, more provisions for the stores—*

She grimaced and abruptly sat up in bed. 'What do you want the minstrels to play tonight?' she demanded, swinging her feet to the floor.

Arthur laughed, and rolled over on to his back. With his arms behind his head he watched her contentedly as she made for the door, calling to Ina as she went. 'You know I have the rough tastes of a soldier, Guenevere. Command the minstrels yourself if you want anything more than the old songs of love and war!'

On high days they would clear the hall for dancing, and each knight would take his lady on the floor. Three thrones now stood on the dais since Arthur had persuaded Morgan to take her place with them. Kay would sit out at her side, making sharp jibes against the dancers, bringing brief smiles to Morgan's plum-coloured lips. Would he win her heart as well, with his dark face and wicked tongue, Guenevere wondered idly, or would she cast her eyes on Sir Lucan, the golden lord? But she kept these thoughts to herself, and was simply happy to see Morgan smile.

And one night when the sun had left the sky, a bard came and begged admittance to the hall. He was a man of might, the servants said. His last king had rewarded him with a dozen white ponies, twenty purple cloaks and a hundred gold crowns. Once heard his voice would never be forgotten, and his songs passed through his hearers' hearts, changing the colour of their dreams.

'Can any man be so good?' Arthur asked good-humouredly. 'Well, let him in. There is always much to be learned from men of prowess.'

Proudly the bard stalked up to the royal dais. A short man of middle age, he had the pale eyes of a prophet and the solemnity of a child. Whatever had happened to the purple and gold, he wore none of it. He stood before them in a simple green-stained robe like a woodland sprite.

'Hear me!' his plangent harp rang out. 'Never more, by forest pathway or the deep lake's shore . . .'

He sang a lament of loss, weaving a haunting beauty out of the melodies of pain. Guenevere thought of her mother, and was stabbed again by grief. The whole hall was hushed with the sorrow of his song. A slight sound beside her made Guenevere turn. Arthur was weeping openly, his hand over his eyes.

'Oh, Guenevere,' he murmured, 'I know it now, this music tells me so. Merlin is gone. I shall never see him again.'

The song broke off on a high discordant note. The bard came to an end with a plaintive lingering cry. He gave one last sweep of his harp, the air quivered, and the whole hall was still. 'My Gods are not with me, I may sing no more tonight,' he announced harshly, bowing before the throne with an unblinking glare. 'But a brother bard has travelled with me to this place. He will sing for you in my stead.'

Arthur raised his head. 'No, no,' he said wretchedly. 'We will hear no more tonight.'

Something made Guenevere lay her hand on Arthur's arm. She leaned forward. 'Bring in your fellow singer,' she told the bard.

Beside her she felt Morgan stiffen, hunch her back, and catch her breath in a sharp hiss. But moments later she had her reward in Arthur's gasp of delight, and the tears filling his eyes.

A familiar figure stepped in, hooting and cackling, waving his arms in the air. His eyes were very bright, and he walked with a new, proud, prancing gait.

'Merlin!' Arthur wept. 'Oh, Merlin!'

'The Lord Merlin!' chanted the chamberlain.

Almost unnoticed, a slight figure walked by his side, with her Maidens following behind.

'And the Lady Nemue!' the chamberlain called again.

Guenevere sat bolt upright.

Nemue!

What was the priestess of the Lady doing here? They had not seen her since their wedding day, when she had come to the feast with all the Lady's gifts. Surely she had gone straight back to Avalon to serve the Lady there?

And yet—

'Who is that woman?' Merlin had said, his eyes on fire as he raked her from head to foot.

And now here he was, and here she was too—

'So! So! So!'

Merlin was nodding and grinning like a madman, urging Nemue forward like a proud husband with a new young wife.

But Nemue was as cold as spring water over stones. 'My greetings to Your Majesties, and the fond wishes of the Lady of the Lake,' she said evenly. 'Lord Merlin has been gracious enough to stay with us in Avalon. And it seemed a good time to return the visit here.'

'You are welcome both!' Guenevere cried, her mind racing. Tomorrow, she promised herself, she would have the chance to speak to Nemue on her own. Tomorrow, she knew, she would have the full tale of this.

But Nemue said nothing. Merlin betrayed himself. He was the gossip of the palace by the break of day.

'The maids found him lurking outside the priestess's chamber before dawn,' Ina began impressively, as soon as she entered to wake Guenevere for the day. 'Some of them thought that he'd been there all night. He was grinning and full of himself, groomed and dressed up like a young knight. As soon as Nemue came out, he glued himself to her side. Her Maidens say he is besotted with her, and he won't leave her alone.'

'Besotted? *Merlin?*' Arthur said angrily, when Guenevere took the news to him. 'With Nemue? I don't believe it! Merlin has no such weakness, he is above such things. He has not cared for women since his wife died, or thought of fleshly things since the cruel battle that took all his other kin. He told me so himself.'

'But that was long before he met Nemue. She is young and lovely, and gifted with the power. And surely anyone can fall in love?'

'Not Merlin!' Arthur cried in distress. 'Not with a holy Maiden, a priestess sworn to the Goddess.'

'People do not choose where they fall in love,' Guenevere tried to say. 'The heart is a hunter, it strikes where it will.'

'Guenevere, listen to me!' Arthur was in agony now. 'Not Merlin, *no!*'

How could she make him see it with her eyes? And what would Morgan feel, now that Merlin was here? Morgan must know from Igraine whose hand had brought Uther to her mother, whose magic had driven her father to his death. How would Morgan react to Merlin, whose enchantments had ruined her life?

But Arthur would have none of it. 'You forget that Morgan was only a child then, Guenevere!' he said impatiently. 'If she knew any of this at the time, it will all be forgotten now. I shall make the two of them the best of friends, you'll see!'

So at dinner that night in the hall, he insisted that Morgan sit on his right hand, and Merlin on his left. While Guenevere watched from the far end of the table, she could see him struggling to make his claim come true.

At first Morgan would say nothing, not a sound. But slowly Arthur drew from her a word or two, then her shy sideways glance, and finally a smile. As for Merlin, his eyes flashed and his cackling laugh rang to the roof. Energy pulsed from him, and he threw back glass after glass of wine. Guenevere did not know what to make of it. Never had she seen the old man in such high spirits, and never at such ease in female company, relishing the feast.

Seated at her right hand, Nemue watched Merlin and Morgan too, with the ghost of a smile. 'I can hardly wish on the Lady Morgan the burden I have borne,' she said softly, in her strange, rusty voice. 'But the love of Lord Merlin is a weight I dearly long to pass on. I shall stay only a short while to recover from the journey here. Then I shall hurry back gladly to the Sacred Isle.'

'He fell in love with you at our wedding?' Guenevere knew it was true before she spoke. 'And he followed you to Avalon?'

Nemue nodded. 'He will give me no rest,' she said simply. 'He is with me all the time. That is why I had to bring him back here to you. On the Sacred Isle, he dogs my every move. My life has been intolerable since he came.'

'What does he hope to gain by hounding you?'

'He wants to possess me, body and soul. He is after me every day to yield to him.'

Guenevere was astounded. 'But he knows you are sworn to the Goddess! Would he violate your sacred oath?'

She shook her head. 'He does not care. I am his fate, he says, and he is mine.' She gave a weary smile. 'And he tells me I was born to lie with him. When I do, he says, he will give me knowledge of all the secrets of the world. His power will flow into me, and I will know all he knows. He will make magic if I lie with him.'

Merlin's magic? How could that impress a Maiden of the Lady, a priestess of the Great One herself? It was so absurd that Guenevere wanted to laugh. Then she thought of his old man's wizened hands, his crusted eyes and yellow teeth, his bent and ancient body, his sour, musty smell, and shuddered from head to foot. *Oh, these men! These lecherous old men!*

She tried to keep the disgust out of her voice. 'He loves you, then?'

'So he says.' Nemue sighed. 'Yet at other times he curses me for a witch, and calls me all the devils in the world. He moans and weeps and says I have numbered his days. I am the demon of his downfall, he says, and I will bring him to his grave.'

'His grave?' A wave of the old sickness gripped Guenevere again. 'He thinks that you will be the death of him?'

'Worse.' She was pale, but very calm. 'I will bury him alive, he prophesies. He will be put in the earth, and a stone rolled over him to seal him in his tomb.'

A cold wind blew by them like a breath from the Underworld. Guenevere forced herself to laugh. 'What nonsense, he must be mad! Tombs and moving stones? Surely he borrowed this from the Christians, who claim that happened to their God. As if you would ever do such a thing!'

Nemue closed her eyes. 'I hear the truth in what he says. But my sight does not show me how.'

Guenevere stared at her. Nemue? Bury a man alive? Never – never in the world. Nemue was all goodness, like the Lady herself.

A glance down the far end of table was enough to set such thoughts to rest. Merlin was grinning now in his happiest fashion, and Morgan looked easy too. And Arthur was basking in the joy among them all. He looked up at her, and raised his glass in the familiar toast. Guenevere returned his pledge with a silent vow. *To you, my love! And the blessings of the Great One on all those you love!*

Afterwards she thought she was never happier than when they left the hall that night. Walking with Arthur to their apartments she was brimming with contentment,

rosy with joy. How wise Nemue was to bring Merlin here!
Now she could ease her burden, and even Morgan seemed
charmed by the old man tonight. And Arthur would be
happy, the one thing that mattered above all.

'Admit it, Guenevere!' Arthur teased, as they dismissed
the servants and tumbled into bed. 'I know you love Morgan
and want to protect her, but you have to confess that you
were wrong about her hating Merlin, and bearing him a
grudge. You saw the way they talked. They took to each
other like ducks on a pond!'

'I admit nothing!' Guenevere retorted, poking him in
the ribs. 'Morgan wants to please you, and her good nature
made her behave as well as she could. And I don't think
that Nemue has seen the last of Merlin yet.'

'Well, well, little pessimist,' Arthur yawned, drawing
her to him and tucking her head under his chin, 'you'll see
I'm right. Wait till tomorrow and I'll show you how well
things are going for us all.'

'I can't wait!'

And, drowsily wrangling, they fell asleep.

That night she slept sweetly, without care or the thought of
care. She lay on the downy pillows in the shelter of Arthur's
arms, sleeping like a child. And, like a child, she would have
given anything not to awake the way she did.

'My lady! Oh, my lady! Wake the King!'

Guenevere came to with a sick, lurching start. Gaunt
and stark-eyed in the light of one quavering candle, Ina
stood at the side of the bed, clutching a shawl around
her nightgown, crying and trembling with fear. 'In the
royal guest apartments,' she wept, 'no one knows what's
happened – but the Princess Morgan – oh, madam, I can't
tell you what they say!'

At the end of the corridor, a handful of frightened

servants and a few of the guard clustered around the open door. The room within gaped black as a burial barrow, with the same brooding sense of earth and death. The only light came from the fire on the hearth as it struggled to stay alive, the dull coals throwing sudden spurts of blue and yellow flame high in the air, only to fall back with a sick hiss. An unclean smell – bats, rats? – seeped out to meet them as they ventured in.

They found Morgan crouched white and speechless at the head of the bed, her knees drawn up to her chin, one thin bare shoulder shivering through her torn nightgown in the cold of the night. Her mouth gaped, and scenes of fresh terror were vivid in her eyes. At the end of the bed stood a figure scarcely visible in the firelight, crying out and shouting in the dark. It was Merlin, half naked and raving, one arm clutching a blanket round his sunken loins, the other thrashing the air.

As they came in, the fire sank down, hissing on the hearth. 'She has bewitched me!' Merlin ranted madly, tossing his long grey hair. 'She follows the Old Ones, and knows the blackness of the Gods. Her dark magic has done for me, she will bury me alive!'

Dimly he focused on Arthur at Guenevere's side. 'She will betray you too!' he screeched. 'All women betray. They are the work of the devil, and this one is worst of all! Keep well your sword and scabbard, for they will be stolen from you by the woman you most trust!' His eyes rolled towards Arthur and flared with alarm. 'She is child of Satan, and she will bear Satan's seed. In incest will she spawn, and her offspring will be Death!'

He screamed, and his eyes widened in pure terror. 'She will put me in the earth alive, she will roll the stone on me!' He pointed a quivering finger at Morgan. 'She will shit on my head, she will dance on my grave!'

CHAPTER 31

'Look to your sword! Look to your scabbard too! You will be betrayed by the woman you most trust!'
Merlin's high wailing cry rang round the room. Then he began to sing to himself and smile at his fingernails, flicking them up and down.

A strange sick smell hung heavy in the air. Arthur's eyes were wild with question and reproach. 'The woman I most trust? What is he saying, Guenevere?' he whispered. 'What does he mean?'

Morgan still huddled, rigid with terror, against the wall at the head of the bed, hugging her knees, her chin on her chest. Merlin's eyes rolled over her, then turned upwards till only the whites could be seen. The blanket he was clutching slipped to the floor. Slowly he raised his arms above his head, waving them like snakes.

Naked as a radish in the firelight he began a stately dance, crooning to himself. Lost in his footwork, he trod carefully to and fro, pacing around the bed. Morgan hurled her thin body away from him, cowering against the hangings at the back. Shuddering violently, she opened her mouth in a silent scream.

'Help her! We must help her!' Guenevere caught at Arthur's arm. But he was staring at Merlin like a man possessed.

Clustering round the doorway now and blocking the corridor beyond was a clutch of terrified servants and men of the guard. Guenevere beckoned the nearest. 'Who is the captain here?'

A large plain-faced man stepped forward. 'I am, Your Majesty.'

'Get all these people out of here at once. Put two men on the door, none to be admitted except by my word. Send a picked guard of your six best men here this instant, do you hear me?'

'Yes, madam.'

She hesitated. 'And have the captain of the guard-tower – or wherever prisoners are held here in Caerleon – come to me at once.'

He bowed his head. 'It shall be done, Your Majesty.'

Trembling, she summoned Ina to her side. 'Call the King's doctors, send them all here now. And ask the Lady Nemue to come.' Ina nodded and vanished, stifling her tears.

'She is the Bride of Death,' sang Merlin, in the thin high voice of a bat or an owl, 'the Black Mother comes to take her children home . . .'

Delicately he continued his small crazy dance, naked and unashamed, revolving before their eyes. The firelight fell on his emaciated chest, his pouched and hollow belly, his withered flanks and ancient, shrivelled sex. Guenevere's skin crawled. Gods above! He was as mad as a storm at sea, as wild as the wind in the trees. Would Arthur do nothing to spare his old friend's shame?

At last Arthur seemed to hear her angry thoughts. He moved forward and picked up the wrap from the floor.

'Come, Merlin,' he said, in a voice of muffled pain. Towering over the old man, he bundled him into the blanket and lifted him off his feet, carrying him like a child. He threw a look of agony at Guenevere. 'He did not force her! I can't believe that of him!'

'Well,' she muttered grimly, 'we shall see!'

'Ask Morgan! She will tell the truth!'

'Leave her to me, get Merlin away from her now!' Guenevere said urgently. 'Take him to his quarters, and stay with him there. Don't leave him alone. As soon as they come, I will send over the doctors, and—'

Ye Gods, how could she say this?

'—and the captain who takes charge of the prisoners.'

'He must have mistaken Morgan for you,' she said sombrely to Nemue. 'His lust burst its bounds, and he tried to possess her, thinking it was you. When we came in, he did not know who she was.'

Nemue lifted her head. 'Perhaps,' she said oddly. Her eyes were as green as glass. 'How is he now? And Morgan? How is she?'

Guenevere looked around. They were in the anteroom of Morgan's apartments, cut off by a stout oak door from where she lay asleep with the doctors at her bedside. But who knows what the troubled can hear, even in their dreams? She lowered her voice. 'Arthur stayed with Merlin till the doctors had given him something to make him sleep. Then he was taken to the guard-tower, and placed under lock and key.'

She winced, remembering Arthur's grief and distress. 'The cell where he lodges is rough housing for any guest, let alone an old man, and one of Arthur's royal kin. But we dare not risk this happening again.'

Nemue shook her head. 'There will be no repeat of last night's scene.' She gave an angry laugh. 'I blame myself. The Lady will be very much displeased. She will say I was wrong to bring Merlin here. In truth, I saw an end to my burden in this place, but I did not see far enough.

Now I know Merlin was right. He is my fate, as I proved to be his.'

'What do you mean?'

Nemue raked Guenevere's face with her long, searching look. 'No matter,' she said coolly. 'Give me an enclosed litter and six good strong men, and I will take charge of Merlin.' She paused. Once again a veil passed over her eyes. 'Just as he knew I would.'

'You shall have whatever you need.'

'I will carry him back to Avalon, to our healing chamber inside the hollow hill. Merlin can rest there until he has recovered his wits.' Nemue paused. 'Or live for ever in seclusion, if he is fated never to be whole again.'

And suddenly Guenevere saw it, Merlin's last retreat, a cool, quiet space cut into the hillside, hollowed out of the living rock. A flight of stone steps led down into it, and the white hawthorn of the Goddess blew on the hill above. Inside, all the walls, the floor, and the round dome of the roof glittered with brilliant white fragments of natural quartz. It was a crystal chamber, a cave of broken reflections for a broken mind. And the only way back to the world above was past a great disc of white stone that rolled into place for a door.

All this Guenevere saw, shuddering at the sight. Dimly she tried to make sense of it all. 'But Merlin—'

Nemue read her thought. 'Merlin foretold his fate. He had the power to shape another for himself, if he so chose.' She lifted her head, scenting the air like a doe at the running of the herd. 'I must go. The Lady calls.'

Don't go, don't leave me, Guenevere wanted to cry, *I am calling too!* But she could not. 'What about Morgan?'

'Never fear, Guenevere.' Nemue's eyes glinted. 'Morgan will always tell you what she wants.'

*   *   *

But Morgan did not, for she could not speak. Guenevere sat by her bed as the doctors vainly clucked and fussed. In the guard-tower, she knew, Arthur was nursing Merlin, weeping over the frail madman in his arms. As Ina softly moved around the room, tending the fire and making all neat and sweet, Guenevere held Morgan's hand and tried to talk to her.

'Morgan, don't be afraid. There is a guard of arms outside your door. He cannot hurt you now. And he will never threaten you again.'

Whimpering in her throat, Morgan clung to Guenevere like a child.

'He is gone,' Guenevere said firmly, raising her voice, 'gone for ever. No man will ever force you again.'

The bruised damson mouth opened in a tight cry of woe.

'Tell me, Morgan!' Guenevere pressed her hand. 'Did Merlin ravish you? Did he try?'

'Aah!'

A tide of grief and fear gushed from her lips. Guenevere could not understand a word she said. Clasping her in her arms, she tried to calm her down. At last Morgan grew quieter, and there was no mistaking what she wanted now. 'Arthur!' she wept piteously. 'Arthur, Arthur!'

Arthur, Arthur, always Arthur. Did Morgan have no other thought in her head?

Yet how could she be jealous? Guenevere was suddenly, sharply ashamed. Arthur was the one good man Morgan had known. Her need of him was greater than Guenevere's, or even Merlin's now. With an inward sigh, Guenevere sent for Arthur, and set herself to wait.

And it was a long sore wait all through that endless summer, that golden autumn, that long wintertime. Arthur rode with Nemue to take Merlin to Avalon, guiding the enclosed litter with its sleeping burden every step of the way. Only as they led him into the underground chamber did Merlin seem to collect his wandering wits. 'So, the old hawk goes to his moulting house!' he cried. 'Old Merlin goes to his long, last home!'

'Only till you are well again,' Nemue gently replied.

Merlin looked straight at them, Arthur said, and for the first time seemed to know who they were. Gravely he shook his head. 'Till the King comes again,' he said, 'I shall be here. For the King that is and shall be, he will return. And when he comes again, I will be here!'

Now the summer held no hope that Morgan might go to her new home at Le Val Sans Retour. The great estate that Arthur had gifted to her had to be managed by stewards, for Morgan could not travel, she could not sit a horse. She was worse now than when she had first left the convent, and the doctors had no idea when she would be herself again.

Other woes crowded in to torment them too.

'We were happy to think that all the world loved us, because we only wanted to love them,' Arthur commented grimly, as they sat in the audience chamber, hearing reports of the land. 'When our knights rode out in glory, they won many hearts to our cause. But the country as a whole has not yet been won.'

Guenevere nodded soberly. After the first response to Arthur's call, many petty kings and lords were sitting on their hands now, waiting to see which way fate would fall. They fobbed off his overtures with empty words, and could not be trusted or counted on as friends.

And other rogue knights and evil lords, whether lurking in hidden hideouts or flaunting themselves in great castles, had grown so strong that one or two knights riding alone could not challenge them. The wisest course, confessed Sir Ladinas and Sir Dinant, who had seen such men, had been to turn their backs on these dark places, and ride on. It would take Arthur himself with a whole band of knights and a troop of good men to deal with them.

And when they all rode out next time, there would be a far worse enemy to face. Sir Tor had ridden due east from Caerleon, passing through London to the flat-lands beyond. Now he stood before them, clutching his helmet, still covered with the grime of the roads. His young face was worn with hard riding, and there was something about him Guenevere had not seen before.

'News from the Eastlands, Your Majesties,' he said bleakly. His eyes were very dark. 'The Saxons are raiding the coast again, and their bands of warriors are settling the eastern shore. All the invaders have rallied under one flag, hungry and desperate men fleeing famine in their own lands.'

'What of the local people?' Arthur leaned forward, gripping the arm of his throne. 'How goes the resistance there?'

Sir Tor's young eyes showed what he had seen. 'The Saxons impale the women and crucify the men. Only a handful of old ones and children flee into the woods.' Tears stood in his eyes. 'There is no resistance, sire!'

Arthur turned colour and bunched his massive fists. 'There will be!' he cried. 'As soon as they feel our swords!'

CHAPTER 32

B ut it was long before Arthur could make his boast come true. In vain did Guenevere urge that either he or she should set forth. A sudden attack, she argued, could burn the invaders from their camps, and Arthur listened so far as to order Sir Tor back to the Eastlands to prepare the way. Yet winter came down on the eastern shore, and Arthur had not stirred himself to act. Day and night he brooded alone in his chamber, and Guenevere hated his sorrowing, because he turned away from her.

Now she saw what it had meant to him to be 'Merlin's boy'. Growing up without a father, in Merlin he had found father, friend and mentor all in one. With the old man gone, he had lost his sense of his destiny as High King.

So he turned to Guenevere. Now every day it was 'What do you think, Guenevere?', and to the servants, 'Do not ask me, the Queen will deal with this.' Kings and lords came and went, as did those seeking justice, and the poor and needy too, and Arthur sat by Guenevere's side to receive them, a noble husk.

The worst of all came now when they were alone. Then he would clasp Guenevere in their bed, not with the boyish sweetness he used to show, but with a fearful hunger, like a starving beast. He would sometimes hurt her in this harsh love-making as he tried to lose himself in her. Yet when she tried to tell him, suddenly she became the one hurting him. His eyes turned dark with horror and he had to restrain his tears.

Often he spent hours alone with Morgan in her chamber, sending word that Guenevere was to dine by herself that night. She never knew if they talked about Merlin while she kept the high table alone in the Great Hall, or even if they talked at all. Perhaps they sat in silence, each locked in terrible pain. But afterwards he came to her in her bed and took her fast and brutally, without speaking, and it seemed to her, without love.

Afterwards he wept like a beaten child. Then she would find herself weeping too as she tried to comfort him. 'Oh, my love, take heart – Merlin is not lost, he will come back to you, he will recover his mind.'

In the dark she felt his hard hand on her mouth. 'It will not happen, Guenevere. Merlin will not return. I have seen the future, and it cannot be. And I must learn to live with what the Great Ones have decreed.'

This sickness gripped his heart all winter long. And it came to her what would make Arthur whole. A man who loses his father lives again in making a new life. She must give him a child.

Yet for no reason, her monthly times were becoming weaker and further apart. Now all the tears she shed over Arthur seemed to have dried up the well-springs of life itself in her. She was a husk of the woman she had been before. She had nothing left to flow.

She was in agony, weeping to Ina, *Why can I not conceive?*

Ina brooded for a while. Then she sent in secret to

her kinswoman in Camelot who had woven Guenevere's wedding gown, because she knew about such things.

'Take your grief to the Goddess,' the word came back. 'She will give you the daughter you desire.' So Guenevere prayed to the Goddess morning and night. But all the prayers in the world were of no avail without a man. Now Guenevere sought Arthur's love to get what only he could put into her womb. Yet, try as she might, there was no sign of motherhood for her.

And now Arthur was to go away from her, and leave her nursing her hunger in a cold, empty bed. For when the rivers thawed and the spring rains covered the land, Sir Tor stood before them again, back from the Eastlands once more. In his hand he held a hank of pale gold hair, and he stared as though he had seen into hell.

'They have returned!' he ground out. 'And they are killing the children, the length and breadth of what they dare to call "the Saxon shore".' He brandished the hank of hair, and wept aloud. 'She was seven years old. They cut off her hair, and speared her to a tree.'

Arthur sat like a figure carved in stone. 'She will be avenged,' he said quietly.

And a week later he was gone.

That was the first time Arthur went to war, and the first time she was alone.

Alone but for Morgan, and Morgan was different now. When spring began she could still be found lying on her bed and staring at the wall. At other times she would throw herself into feverish activity, walking for hours with a strange jerky gait. But when Arthur gave the call to war and the trysting-horn sounded far and wide, Morgan was spurred into sudden action. Now she was up with the dawn every day, riding tirelessly at Arthur's side as he called in

his troops and selected the best of them to make up the war
band he had in mind.

Guenevere could not bear the thought that he would
go. It made her moody, shivery, often in tears.

'Take heart, my lady,' urged Gawain in bluff embarrassment. 'We will make mincemeat of the Saxons, and any
who dare to withstand our King!' He shifted his great feet.
'And never fear, the King's knights will see that he comes
safe home. Don't think you'll lose him – they'd have to kill
every one of us first!'

Gawain meant well, Guenevere knew, but he did not
understand. Arthur would go into battle armed with the
scabbard of her mother, her wedding gift which would
protect him at all times. While he wore this, Arthur could
shed no blood. No, that was not her fear.

And she had weeks to endure it, weeks when her
only lifeline was the thought of Arthur and the memory
of his love. It was Morgan who drew it from her, the
morning they heard that Arthur's work was done, and he
would soon return. The only sound was the soft hissing
of the fire they had burning in the chamber, for the old
castle was still cold in March. Morgan sat in silence beside
the fire, plying her needle industriously at her embroidery frame, a habit of the convent she never seemed to
break.

Guenevere was striding up and down, a habit of her
own when in distress. She did not know she had her arms
clasped tight across her stomach till Morgan spoke.

Her voice was as husky and dry as a snake shedding
its skin. 'You are grieving that nothing grew in there while
Arthur was away.'

To Guenevere's surprise, hot tears welled up and threatened to flood her eyes. 'Oh, Morgan, I fear nothing will grow
there at all!'

Morgan could ask a question without words. 'Why?' said her long pale face.

'My mother had only one child in all her life. Yet she changed her Chosen One every seven years, and made much good earth magic. I think I come from poor breeding stock.'

Morgan's back hunched, and she spat like a cat. 'Women are not breeding stock!'

'I know, I know,' Guenevere said weakly. 'But, Morgan, pity me! I want a daughter, and I want to give Arthur a son. Yet I am barren! I cannot conceive!' She could not stop the tears.

Morgan pushed aside her embroidery and sat deep in thought, her dark, enclosed face marked with a bitter frown. 'You need a seeing, to give you a sight of what is to come,' she said at last. 'Or a casting. The runes do not lie.' She stared into the fire. 'Choose.'

'Not a seeing!' Guenevere cried with a shudder. 'When it possessed me, it would make me sad afterwards, and sick as a dog again. But, Morgan, what do you know about these old ways? In the convent, surely you never had the sight, or learned to cast the runes.'

'Ina knows.'

'Ina?'

Morgan cocked her head, and listened with her inner ear. 'Ina,' she said. 'Listen.'

A moment later Ina slipped in, her eyes glowing like a mermaid's, bright with sea-fire. Guenevere stared.

How did Morgan . . . ?

Come to that, how did Ina . . . ?

Do not ask, said an inner voice. *Let things take their course.*

Ina had a pouch of velvet on a cord round her neck. 'From my kinswoman in Camelot, madam, who made your wedding dress,' she whispered as she lifted it over her head.

Without a word all three drew together in a circle round the fire.

Guenevere was torn between fear and desire. The flickering flames lit the two faces beside her with an Otherworldly light. 'Cast your runes!' She nodded to Ina. 'Begin!'

Ina knelt before the fire, closed her eyes tightly, and began to hum. A high, throbbing rhythm filled the air. Blindly she groped in the pouch, and cast what she drew out on to the fire.

There was a low rushing sound, and a mist arose from the glowing logs. The air grew dark, with odd flashes of pale light. A rich smell filled the room. It seemed to feed the hunger of Guenevere's very soul, and she found herself gulping it down. She did not care that her head was reeling and her wits beginning to swim. 'The runes!' she cried to Ina. 'Cast your runes!'

Was it still Ina humming, or had Morgan joined in the low, pulsing chant? Guenevere's ears caught odd words of strong magic, the forbidden words only the most powerful dared say. But who had said them? Had she said them herself?

'The runes—'

'The runes—'

A great whispering filled the room. Ina opened the neck of the velvet bag, and deftly tossed the remaining contents into the air.

Out of the pouch flew a handful of downy feathers, a rain of bright shining stones, and a clutch of little bones. Stark white and fragile, they could have come from the body of a weasel, a young rabbit, or an elver from some silent, hidden pool. But this ancient magic could only work with the bones of babies that never were, everyone knew. Only an unborn could call to another across the world between the worlds and the dark chasm of time.

The loud whispering was now humming inside Guenevere's head. The sound of the spell seemed to hold the runes suspended, keep them floating in the air.

'Why?' she cried weeping as they drifted to the floor. She grabbed Ina's hand. 'Why can I bear no child to the man I love? Where is the daughter I dreamed I would have?'

Ina spoke to the runes in a song without words. Delicately they settled to their places on the floor. Guenevere covered her eyes with her hand. 'Tell me!' she whispered. *'Tell me!* What do they say?'

From her left there came a sharp, hissing breath. She thought she heard Morgan give a sharp cry of pain, but Ina's voice drowned her out. 'Look, madam – *look!'*

Guenevere opened her eyes. Ina was twisting the empty bag in her hands, staring wide-eyed at the shape on the floor. Morgan was hunched forward, coiled like a snake about to strike.

'See, my lady, see!' Ina cried ecstatically. 'Now we have something to tell the King when he comes back! Oh, madam, at last!' She burst into tears.

Outlined on the rug before the fire, the stones had settled in a circle, making a full round shape like the body of a woman with child. Inside the ring of stones, one bone lay like a spine, and the others had fallen at angles outside, like half-formed arms and legs. At the top where the head should be, the feathers lay clustered in a downy heap.

'The Goddess be thanked!' Guenevere wept, afraid to believe her eyes. 'The sign of a baby! I will have a child!'

'Yes, madam!' Ina laughed and wept at the same time. 'And just think how delighted the King and we all will be!'

'Ina, with the King away, when will I start this baby? When do you think it will come?'

'Fools!'

Morgan's face was twisted with an anger Guenevere could not comprehend. 'This is not a child to come!' she muttered madly. 'Do you not see? You are carrying this baby now!'

CHAPTER 33

'By all the blessed Gods!'

Arthur listened speechless to Guenevere's trembling disclosure, then terrified her with a wild joyous roar. Afterwards he held her in his arms, and wept aloud. 'I knew it, Guenevere,' he said, laughing and crying with joy. 'I dreamed this would be.'

Guenevere did not know whether to be pleased or put out. 'And did you also dream what sex our child will be?'

He nodded in all seriousness. '"A girl for Guenevere," I dreamed, not a boy for me this time.'

He seized her hands excitedly, and pressed them to his lips. 'We'll call her after your mother – Maire Macha, wasn't it?'

'Yes.' Guenevere was near to tears. 'It means "Battle Raven" in the old tongue.'

Arthur's face glowed. 'That's wonderful! I'll teach her to ride as soon as she can walk, and we'll take her through all the skills of war and make another "Battle Raven" out of her!'

They spent hour after happy hour in talk like this. Next time, he promised joyfully, he would try to dream a son. For the Middle Kingdom would want a king when they were gone, just as the Summer Country would need a queen. And they would have many children, he swore, hugging her in his arms, lovely boys and gorgeous girls, all as beautiful as their mother, as she was now.

And meanwhile he had great news of his own. He and his knights had swept down on the Saxon shore without mercy, raging like a storm from the sea, to punish the invaders and put them to flight. One by one he had destroyed their camps, burned their ships, and avenged their cruel deeds. Those lucky enough to escape with their lives would be in no hurry to return.

Afterwards he had seized what they had plundered from churches and castles far and wide. Chests of gold and silver, sacks of jewels and plate, great gilded crosses and altar ornaments had all been returned to their rightful owners when they could be found. But many had been killed, and some had died of grief. So the remainder would be given out among his followers to reward their loyalty.

But the lion's share, Arthur vowed, must go to the daughter who was to come. For there was nothing more important in the world.

'We must go to Camelot for the birth,' Guenevere breathed to Arthur, lying in his arms on the first morning of his return. 'A Queen of the Summer Country must be born in her own land.'

Arthur tensed imperceptibly, and did not speak. 'Morgan will not like it,' he said at last. 'I don't know if we can move her now, the way she is.'

Guenevere did not hesitate. 'Morgan must do as she and you think fit. But my daughter must be born in Camelot, and her father should be there.'

Arthur gripped her to him like a precious thing. 'Oh, my love,' he groaned, 'forgive me, of course the baby must come first!'

He kissed her, then jumped out of bed. 'We'll go to

Camelot now!' he cried. 'That way we'll travel while you can still sit a horse, and won't have to go at a litter's plodding pace. And we'll hold jousts and tournaments there to pass the time, while your people are waiting to meet their new princess!'

He strode round the chamber glowing with the brilliance of his idea. 'A royal tournament at Camelot – oh, Guenevere, what a thing that will be!'

There was a soft knock on the outer door. 'A visitor from London, my lord,' came an attendant's voice. 'The—'

'Enough!' groaned Guenevere. *Goddess, Mother, can't I enjoy my love for a second? Why must they press in on us like this?*

'Sweetheart, don't upset yourself!' Arthur ordered, with a look of alarm. 'For the baby's sake, you must be careful now. Leave this to me, whatever it may be.'

I should get away more often, the Abbot thought, pacing Caerleon's Great Hall as he waited before the throne. A journey like this is a renewal of faith. To see these old strongholds, how fine they are!

He stopped to survey the towering walls, the long, mullioned windows, the massive hammer-beams supporting a ceiling that was almost out of sight. If ignorant pagans could raise these mighty piles, dragged down as they were by sin and wickedness, what glorious monuments could the faithful raise in time to the One True God? What soaring columns and elevated traceries, what lofty roofs and monitory spires could be built by Christians to honour Him and His Son?

Yes, he had been right to come. The journey from London had been a joy in itself. Wandering westward on a patient mule, he had doubted at first the wisdom of coming here. The event that he thought had played into his hand seemed a slender basis to call upon a king. But as day succeeded blessed golden day, he had felt more and more sure of the hand of God.

For God was all around, in the tender green of the leaves of the unfolding beech, in the song of the cuckoo high up in the sky. Hating their winters here so much, he scolded himself mildly, I forget their sweet summer days, their white and blue heavens, their lady-faced flowers by the wayside, the softness of their grass.

His soul lifted. For all these things, praised be Thy name, O Lord.

And not only for Thy bounty may Thy holy Name be praised, the Abbot prayed devoutly. Through days of hope and nights of earnest prayer, the long slow journey had restored his faith in God's purpose, and his own part in it. God's meaning had been plain. The Lord had cast down the mighty, He had punished the unbeliever with hellfire and suffering. Now all that remained was to make a Christian use of it.

'The King! Prepare to meet the King!' came the cry at the door. Arthur strode in. 'Father Abbot!' he cried. 'I am glad to see you here! It is many months since I stood with you and Merlin in the churchyard of your great church. But I shall never forget the good will you showed me then, when I was very far from all of this!' He threw out both his arms.

The Abbot bowed and smiled. 'We had faith in you, sire,' he said smoothly. 'It was plain that God had called you to a high destiny. But He has also sent you a hard cross to bear. We were sorry to hear of Lord Merlin's sad collapse. Madness is a torment like no other. I have come in person to condole with you.'

And to replace that old villain with a Christian father in your heart, he could have said. To stop the flow of superstitious ignorance, and bring you to the knowledge and love of God.

Arthur's face clouded. 'It was a grievous loss. He was a man of such prodigious gifts – so wise, so loving, and so good to me.' His eyes filled with tears. 'Truly I have lost a father in his love!'

A father of all darkness, the Abbot thought, folding his hands in his sleeves. 'A father indeed,' he agreed.

'And he may recover his mind,' Arthur said urgently. 'Will you pray for him?'

'We shall, my son, we shall,' said the Abbot, making a mental note to ask God to keep Merlin's wits in their finest disarray. 'And in the meantime, we hope to be of service to you. No man can emulate the father and friend you have lost. There can be only one Lord Merlin on this earth. But among our ranks we have men of vision and power. The spirit which led us to embrace your cause is at your disposal now.'

'Why, I thank you, sir, with all my heart,' cried Arthur, with open gratitude.

How young he is, how young, the Abbot thought. Well, all the more apt to be an instrument of God. 'One scheme of yours, sire, where I thought we might be of use,' he went on seamlessly, 'is the question of your knights. All men know that you want to create an order of men dedicated to the highest ideals, who will flee temptation and advance the good. We too have young men who undertake such vows. They agree to renounce the vanity of worldly goods, and give up the life of self-pleasure and joy. They swear to live chastely and defend the right. I would like to offer you all our assistance, sire, in shaping the rules of the Order of the King's Knights.' He paused, weighing Arthur up. 'Like your dear Queen, we all love this land, and wish to see it flourish. Like her and yourself, we all worship the good,' he concluded piously.

Arthur stared at him, wide-eyed. 'How fine of you to think of this, Father!' he exclaimed. 'And, of course, you're right, there is much in common between your cause and mine.' He clenched his fist and happily punched the palm of his other hand. 'Advise me on my Order? You shall indeed!'

The Abbot bowed. 'You are most generous, sire.'

'As any man would be. I have had great news today, Father Abbot, the word that any man, any husband is longing to hear!'

Perdition seize her, the concubine is with child, was the Abbot's bleak thought. 'God's blessings, sire!' he said.

'The Queen is bearing the next of her line of queens!' Arthur announced, glowing with pride. 'I have been given a sign in a dream. The child will be a girl.'

The Abbot nodded. A pagan sign, very well – dimwit tomfoolery, nothing more. In time God will show us His will with this child. 'God is with us, sire. He sent me to you at the best of times.'

Arthur took his arm confidingly. 'We have not yet told our council the good news. You are the first to know, and I must rely on your discretion till our lords are informed.'

'Indeed, sire,' the Abbot purred. 'My lips are sealed by my own vows to God. But in time, I trust, we may honour the event.'

He drew a breath and sent a prayer winging heavenward. Lord God, hear me, let this shaft find its home. Slowly he eased himself down on to one knee. 'I have a boon to beg, in the name of the faith we showed you in your hour of need. How soon, sire, will you bring us the infant to invoke God's blessing and glory on its head? And in memory of your beloved Lord Merlin too, when may we baptise the next holder of the Pendragon name?'

Camelot, city of her childhood, home of her heart – the white palace on its sweet green hill, the gold-roofed towers bright with banners in the breeze, lay below her in the long-lost valley again. As they drew near, the streets were lined with townspeople cheering themselves hoarse, throwing flowers, reaching out to touch their stirrups as they passed.

'The Queen, greet your Queen!' Lucan cried, as he spurred ahead of the procession. 'Welcome the Queen, the King and the Princess!'

'The Queen, the King and the Princess!' Gawain, Kay and Bedivere echoed as they galloped on down the hill. 'Make ready to greet them now!'

For Morgan had come with them, after all. She had had to travel in a litter, but when she had no fear of being stared at, she would have the curtains of her travelling bed drawn back. Then Arthur and his knights would take turns to walk their horses alongside, and entertain her as the royal train plodded along.

To everyone's surprise, Sir Lucan the ladies' man was the most dutiful of all. It was odd to see his red-gold head leaning in to Morgan's dark one, and to think of a man so loved by women dancing attendance on a woman who had never known men at all. Indeed, with her plain black robes and fierce shyness, Morgan still seemed very much the nun – hardly what Lucan was used to in a woman, Guenevere smiled to herself.

But now, arriving in Camelot, Lucan was determined that Morgan would not be overlooked.

'The Princess Morgan of Cornwall and Gore!' he announced to the crowd of onlookers, whooping loudly as he drove his horse across the causeway with Gawain, Kay and Bedivere on his heels.

'And the King!' bellowed Gawain.

'And the Queen!' cried Kay sharply, not to be outdone.

The quiet Bedivere had the last word. 'The Queen, the

King and the Princess, give them your welcome here in
Camelot!'

'The King, the Queen and the Princess!'

Now all the people lining the road took up the cry,
roaring and cheering as they rode in. And Arthur's four
companion knights reined in and stood by to form a guard of
honour, grinning like idiots as they were welcomed home.

CHAPTER 34

'You will find all in order, Guenevere,' said King Leogrance with gruff satisfaction as they sat at the feast that night. Guenevere breathed in the rich scent of pork and herbs, boiled bacon, savory and winter greens, and could only nod contentedly in reply.

Yes, her father the King had a few more lines on his face, and more than a few white strands in his iron grey hair. But he still seemed happier now than she ever remembered him. On her other side, Arthur was listening to Taliesin with a passionate attention, and she could see that he was ready to venerate the Summer Country's Chief Druid just as she did. Only one face from the days before she married Arthur was nowhere to be seen among the crowd in the Great Hall. She leaned across to Taliesin. 'What news of Cormac? How is he these days?'

She knew that she could trust Taliesin to know without words that she had never told Arthur of her earlier love. Told him? What was there to tell? And love? Not as she had ever known love with him.

Taliesin favoured her with his sweetest smile. 'He has fulfilled his heart's deepest dream. He has gone to the Island of the West to join the Druids who worship the Mother there. It is green and fertile, he says, and the soft rain wraps the isle in mists for months of the year. There they can keep the worship of the Great One undisturbed. I do not doubt he will be a great bard, even a High Druid in his time.'

'Blessings on him, then!' Guenevere said fervently. 'And on the Mother too. She has called a good man to Herself, and he has won what he sought all along.'

Now the rafters were ringing with cheers and laughter, loud good-natured fooling, and a thousand loyal toasts. Again and again Guenevere raised her glass to acknowledge a tribute from the crowded hall. There was only one faint shadow on her joy. 'How is my kinsman Malgaunt? What's the news of him?'

King Leogrance reached for a dish of quails, and laughed. 'Malgaunt? He lives peacefully at Dolorous Garde, running his estate and doing what he does best. He spends his days in war-games, training the young men who come to him to be knights.' He cocked his head and wagged a finger at her. 'Hear me, daughter. The time has come to forgive your kinsman for his deeds of long ago. They say Malgaunt's knights are now the best in the land. I know he has vowed them to the service of the Queen.'

'Make peace with Malgaunt? Invite him back to court?'

He was eyeing her shrewdly now. 'Well, that's for you to decide. The rest of the country also sleeps in peace,' he raised his glass, 'thanks to Lord Taliesin here!'

Taliesin bowed and smiled, shaking his white head.

'King Leogrance fails to mention his own vigilance,' he murmured, 'and the care he gives to our country's welfare. Our army is still the finest in the land, and our knights the bravest in all the world.'

He waved a hand down the room. Below the dais where they sat, the Round Table stood in the centre of the Great Hall. It was covered in white damask now for the feast, gleaming in the candlelight like the face of the full moon.

As the Queen's champion in Camelot Lucan sat in pride of place, with Gawain to his right, and Kay and Bedivere on his left. Beside Gawain, wide-eyed and silent, sat his three brothers, the dark-faced Agravain, the quiet Gaheris and lastly Gareth, the baby of them all.

All round the table the knights of Camelot were greeting Arthur's knights like long-lost brothers. Sir Griflet, Sir Sagramore, Sir Tor, Sir Ladinas and Sir Dinant were carousing as if they were at home in Caerleon, to judge by the raucous laughter and the red wine flowing like blood. Yet there was wonder, too, on the faces of Arthur's knights, as they saw how their fellows lived in Camelot. Only Lucan, born and blooded here, was unselfconsciously at home.

Guenevere looked around the hall. Everywhere her eye fell, a fine lord in gold and velvet raised his glass, a reveller rosy with contentment stood to honour her with a toast, a stout, beaming matron or blushing maid popped from her seat with a curtsey, and a joyful smile. From the table of the Queen's former champions, old Sir Niamh surged to his feet, his glass in the air.

'A health to Your Majesty!'

'Here's to our Queen!'

'And the King! A health to King Arthur our lord!'

Above the merriment, the sweet voices of the minstrels wove in and out. The smell of good food filled the air, the fires roared up the chimneys, and loving glances met them on all sides. In Guenevere's rounding belly, her daughter kicked sweetly, like the pulsing of her heart. Yes, Camelot was the place Maire should be born.

And in Camelot, as Guenevere hoped, it was as if Merlin and all the poison of his madness had never been.

'A tournament, Guenevere!' Arthur cried. 'We must have the tournament I promised you!' He caught both her hands, and kissed them fervently. 'I will wear your favour in the lists, and vaunt the beauty of my lady over all who come!'

'A tournament, a royal tournament!'

The heralds' silver trumpets sounded far and wide. Messengers were sent to Arthur's old friends King Ursien away in Gore, King Pellinore, and the French kings of Little Britain Ban and Bors, as well as a host of others. The roll-call of those who took up Arthur's challenge was enough to make any heart beat faster – King Marhaus of Ireland, King Phelot of the Lakes, the King of Sorluse and King Faramon of the Green, and many more, fearless jousters all.

And how could they leave out Malgaunt? He had always been one of the best swords in the Summer Country, King Leogrance said, and Guenevere knew it was true. So Malgaunt was invited, and Guenevere did not know whether to be pleased or perturbed when he sent word he would accept.

All Arthur's knights were summoned from Caerleon to try their skill. Only Sir Lamorak was too far away at the court of Queen Morgause. King Pellinore did his best to hide his grief that he would not see his son. 'The French kings can be with us from across the sea faster than a rider from the north,' he said sombrely. 'It must be eight hundred miles to the Orkneys, and more.' It was cold comfort to him, Guenevere knew, that Queen Morgause never failed to praise Lamorak to King Arthur, how much his service pleased her, how devoted he was.

Arthur threw himself into the preparations for the tournament as if it were another war campaign. There would be jousting and single combat between knights on foot, he said, but the centrepiece must be the mock-battle between the two armies of the day, when he led his knights to champion his lady against all challengers.

'I will lead the Queen's knights,' he said gravely, pacing to and fro as Guenevere rested on a day-bed in the solar, basking in the sun, 'and Gawain must lead the opposing party.'

'Why Gawain?' Guenevere laughed. 'Surely you want the best opponent for the best sport? Lucan is a far better jouster than Gawain. And besides . . .'

She looked at the court ladies clustered in brightly coloured groups, standing round the long chamber like banks of summer flowers. The ladies of Camelot had been taking a keen interest in Lucan from the moment he returned. Already, Ina said, there was a rumour that he favoured one here above all, but so many were claiming the honour that no one knew who it was.

Guenevere laughed again. 'Besides, Gawain has no lady of his own to fight for, as you will champion me. In Camelot, Lucan can flaunt the favour of a hundred women, they all love him so. And the knight who opposes you should have a lady, by the rules of chivalry, to champion in the lists.'

Arthur's eyes lit up. 'Of course!' He turned his head. 'Lucan!' he called to the knot of knights standing by.

Gawain hurried up. 'My lord, Sir Lucan is not here.'

'Where is he?'

Gawain seemed reluctant to answer. 'I do not know, my lord. He was here a while ago. I will search him out myself.'

A little later, Lucan strode swiftly in. 'I was sent for, my lord, by a lady – I could not refuse. I beg your forgiveness.'

Arthur roared with laughter, and slapped his shoulder. 'No apologies, man! That's why I sent for you. Whoever your lady is, you must defend her at our tournament. You are to command the opposing band of knights to do battle with mine.'

Lucan's eyes flashed. He nodded slowly to himself.

Then he turned and looked Arthur in the eye. 'Your lady is the fairest in the world,' he said simply, with a bow to Guenevere, 'but when the day ends, the world will also know the fame of mine.'

But who she was, it seemed, they were not to know. For when the day came and the combatants turned out, there was no doubt whose favour Arthur wore. Clad in gold armour, he wore high on his sleeve a rosette in blue and gold, the colours of Guenevere's gown. As he galloped up beneath the viewing gallery where she sat among the ladies, all the world could see whose knight he was.

But when Lucan came into the arena armed all in black, there was no sign of a lady's favour anywhere. Who had Lucan chosen to defend? The sun beat down, heightening the feverish expectation of the crowd and every female head in the gallery craned to see.

'There it is, madam!' Ina cried at last. 'There, look, next to his heart!'

Almost invisible against Lucan's black armour, there it was, a small black glove pinned to the sash across his breast. A glove, then – but whose? From the disappointed faces in the gallery, it was easy to see whose it was not. But none of the others was wearing the secret smile of the mistress whose knight is sporting her favour and hers alone.

Guenevere turned to Morgan sitting silently at her side, a dark shape amid the flower-like finery all around. However many gowns Arthur lavished on her, sooner or later she would appear again in black. Guenevere laughed. 'Every woman in the Summer Country would be happy to call Lucan her lord. Why doesn't the lucky lady want to be known?'

But Morgan did not hear. The noise of the crowd was deafening, and even in the shade of the gallery there was no respite from the heat. Turning her head this way and that, Morgan was fanning herself frenziedly, and her gaze roamed round the viewing gallery like a caged thing. This was Morgan's first tournament in twenty-odd years, Guenevere thought with a pang. It must be ordeal enough in itself for a woman so awkward and shy, without having to listen to idle court gossip as well. Enough! She stole another look at Morgan's blank eyes and pallid face, and vowed to say no more.

'To the lists!' cried the heralds. 'All the combatants to the lists!'

On the edge of the field, all the kings and knights were massing for the parade, with the lords of the blood royal leading the way.

'Prince Malgaunt!' bellowed the heralds. 'The Queen's kin and lord of the Summer Country, the Prince Malgaunt!'

Guenevere looked down. A tense figure in green and gold was galloping down the lists. The rider reined up below the gallery, lifted his visor and called, 'Thanks, gracious Majesty, for your summons here! Your servant Malgaunt offers his devotion to the Queen and King. He wishes only to polish his rusty war skills today.'

Guenevere could not help but smile. For all the fine words, Malgaunt's face still wore the same dark sardonic grin, and his arrogant carriage had not changed at all. But he bowed to her like the flower of chivalry, and doffed his helmet like a perfect knight.

She shook her head. Why had she ever been afraid of this man? 'You are dearly welcome, Prince Malgaunt!' she called down. 'May the Goddess bless your sword!'

'And Her blessings on you too, my queen!'

He galloped off down the field. Guenevere nodded, and smiled again to herself. The leopard could never truly change his spots. She only wanted Malgaunt to obey her rule.

And simply by being here, he had shown he was ready to do that.

She sat back with a sigh, and stole a look at Morgan, still sitting beside her grim and white-faced. She was staring down at Lucan, lost in thought. A pang of raw pity struck Guenevere to the heart. How Morgan must long for a knight to love her as Lucan loved his beloved unknown! But as for that, only time would tell.

CHAPTER 35

'Clear the field for the fray, all non-combatants leave the field!'

'Sir Griflet, Sir Griflet, *à l'attaque!*'

Below them, young Sir Griflet was opening the first joust. Dressed all in red, he charged down the lists to unhorse Sir Sagramore, clad unluckily in green, but Sir Sagramore turned the tables one more time before Sir Griflet won the best of three.

Guenevere looked down on the hot jousting field, watching the fierce flow of action on all sides. Sir Bedivere unhorsed Sir Kay, then Sir Gawain knocked them both down, one after the other. King Pellinore trounced King Phelot, King Bors dismissed him, and King Marhaus forced a submission from King Faramor of the Isles. King Ban and King Ursien battled till both could hardly stand, and the stewards declared a joint victory.

Then came the first tourney, when Malgaunt and his knights took on a team of more than twice their number, and beat them to the ground. But for Guenevere and Maire too, Guenevere fancied as the baby squirmed with excitement and kicked her ribs, the greatest moment came when all the jousts and combats were done, and her own knight all in gold rode out at the head of his men to do mock-battle with Sir Lucan, the black knight.

'For Arthur!' Guenevere cried. 'King Arthur!'

Waving and cheering, she tossed her handkerchief into the ring. A thousand voices took up the cry, cheering Arthur on.

But to many there Sir Lucan was still the Queen's champion, and in the Summer Country, he could do no wrong.

'Lucan!' howled his admirers. 'Sir Lucan for the prize!'

And Lucan flashed his white smile, shook back his red-gold hair, and bowed to the ladies in the viewing stand just as he had the last time Guenevere sat there, when her mother was the lady of his heart. A moment later, Lucan had covered his bright hair with his black helmet, and the mock-armies of the two leaders were massing for the attack. The two forces drew up at either end of the arena, and made ready for the charge.

Guenevere found herself trembling with a sudden fear. Her hands were clammy, and the baby leaped in her belly like a frightened colt. She turned to Morgan and clutched at her for support. 'What is it?' she wept. 'Something's happening, what can it be?'

Morgan turned her white face and lost gaze on Guenevere. 'Why, Guenevere,' she demanded in her harsh dry voice, 'what are you afraid of? There is nothing to fear.'

As she spoke, the trumpets sounded and the stewards signalled for the contest to begin. Arthur streaked forward at the head of his men like a bolt of lightning, a golden avenger. And bearing down on him with all his knights on his heels was Lucan, the knight in black.

A great wave of sickness clouded Guenevere's eyes. She saw Arthur prostrate on the ground while Lucan stood beside him, drenched in blood. She saw again the sight she had had when Arthur and Lucan did battle in the Great Hall, when Lucan challenged Arthur for her hand. Arthur lay unmoving, surrounded by queens all in black, and Lucan's wounds showed that they had battled to the death.

Help Arthur! And help me, help me now!

She turned to Morgan, choking back a scream. Beside her Morgan's eyes were closed, and her lean body was rocking rhythmically to and fro. She was hissing and muttering to herself and plaiting her long white fingers in and out, weaving some strange cats' cradle of the mind. *Bless her, bless her!* Guenevere cried in her heart. Morgan was praying for Arthur's safety, raising some goodness to cast around him now.

Guenevere breathed hard, and forced herself to be calm. A pregnant woman was always prey to morbid fancies – there was no reason to fear for Arthur's life. A tournament was a game, nothing more. All this was in sport. The old enemies were friends now, drawn into the circle of Arthur's peaceful rule. Not a soul here would want to harm the King.

On the field below the teams were spurring forward, furious to engage. The leaders met, and the clash of their swords rang out. A moment later, the two sides met head on. The wild whoops of joy and cries of glee left no doubt that to the combatants, this was not war or death. But nothing could lift the weight of terror pressing on Guenevere till she could hardly breathe.

Yet Morgan must be right – what was there to fear? Here and there a knight pulled out of the mêlée, and limped off ruefully as he unlaced his helmet and retired from the fray. The worst any man suffered was a tumble from his horse, a bruised fighting arm or broken sword. Guenevere tried desperately to subdue her fears. What was the matter with her, why was she so full of dark imaginings and black dread?

'Domine, veni, proh, superi!'

Beside her Morgan kept up her incantations, a dew standing out on her forehead as she prayed to keep Arthur safe. Strange words of power mingled with her Latin from the convent, and Guenevere knew she would protect Arthur if she could.

If she could—

Guenevere moaned aloud. There was danger here, she knew it. But what? And where?

And then she saw it, flashing through the air.

In the press behind Arthur, Sir Griflet was struggling to push back one of Lucan's band who had driven deep into Arthur's flank. But Sir Griflet had fought many jousts today, and the great broadsword he was wielding was too heavy for him now. As he swung wildly at his opponent, he lost his grip. His weapon flew from his grasp. Powered by its own force, it described a glittering arc, falling point down towards Arthur's undefended back.

'Alla baal princips noctis, domines tenebrae sint mihi propitii! Venite iam Demogorgon, Gehenna, venite instanter ut moriat!'

Morgan's mutter rose to a screaming drone. Guenevere felt her head splitting and the darkness coming down.

Then came a low sweet sound on her other side. And there was her mother, smiling through the dark. Her force swept through Guenevere, and she surged to her feet. 'Lucan!' she cried at the top of her lungs. *'Lucan!'*

Lucan did not fail. His sharp ears picked up her cry, and his quick glance saw the danger Arthur was in. As the sword was falling, about to slice through Arthur's neck, Lucan lunged past him to block its flight and send it spinning to the ground.

Morgan's frail form slumped in her chair, and she let out a long hissing breath. Ina was at Guenevere's side, hysterical with fear. 'The King! He nearly died! Oh, madam, they must stop the fighting now! Tell them it's over, order them to call a halt!'

Guenevere shook her head. 'No,' she said weakly, 'the danger has passed. And the King will be angry if we cheat him of victory now.'

But when the heralds blew their trumpets, and the stewards went into a huddle to decide which side had won, Arthur laughed with delight, and gave the victory to Sir Lucan and his men. So Lucan stepped forward, laughing too, to collect the gold, armour and weapons lavished on the winning band.

There was only one shadow on that happy day. Poor Morgan was ill again, and had to be helped to her bed, reproaching herself, Guenevere knew, because she could not save Arthur from the falling sword.

Yet the evil came and it had been thwarted, and there was nothing more to say. And though they both had seen Arthur's death, they did not speak of it, and Guenevere knew they never would.

So the summer passed. As autumn came, Guenevere dreamed that she saw her daughter walking in a sunlit garden, holding her dead mother by the hand. Was this a bad omen, she moaned to Ina, threatening the baby's life? Or would the small, smiling spirit be her mother come again, with her laughing ways, her loving heart, her love of life?

September and October came and went, and Guenevere grew sadder every day. Then another dream of fear came in the night. Chains of iron were binding her belly, closing the gates of life to stop the child from entering the world.

'She will not live!' Guenevere wept in Arthur's arms. 'She has been too long in the womb. She has gone already to the Mother as one of Her spirit children, too good for this world!'

'Hush now,' Arthur soothed. But he held her tensely, and she knew that the waiting was hard on him too.

'Or she will be like one of those half-formed creatures born to the inland folk who breed among themselves, a child with a pig's face and eyes like slits, a lolling tongue and an ever-open mouth!'

'Hush, hush, my love!' Arthur said angrily. He could not bear these moods. 'Don't say such things! This talk could harm the child more than anything else. I will ask Morgan to come and comfort you.'

But Morgan spent all her time in her chamber, and what she did there, no one seemed to know.

'As long as she is happy with us here in Camelot,' Arthur said.

And, not for the first time, Guenevere had to be content.

Every morning now Arthur rode out before dawn for the last of the hunting before winter closed in. All round Camelot soft glinting mists arose from the morning meadows, and ripe fruit rotted on mossy apple trees. A golden October dragged to an end with Samhain, the feast of the undead that the Christians call Hallowe'en. In Caerleon their churches would be full of dirges as they chanted for their saints.

'As if only Christians lived to be born again,' Ina said, with a laugh that morning as she drew back the curtains to let the dawn in.

Guenevere lay back in bed and laughed too, and a pain shot through her womb. 'Ina!' she gasped. Ina ran for the midwives as Morgan flew through the door.

'Take heart!' she rasped. 'I am here to help you now.'

She gripped Guenevere's hand. As she did so, a pain like nothing else seized Guenevere's body, and swept her away.

The hours passed in a haze of mounting torment. Day

faded into night, and she laboured on. As Morgan held her hand, the sharp agony grew stronger, till she was screaming for relief. Hour after hour, Morgan never left her side. No sister could have been more selfless in her love. And all the time the pain was getting worse.

Through the window now they could see the first pale streaks of dawn. Outside the chamber Arthur paced up and down, banished by the midwives from the scene of birth. 'As long as Morgan is with her,' he told Ina, 'part of me is there too, and Guenevere is not alone.'

But in labour, every woman is alone. And never more so than when she can feel the baby growing weaker as her own strength fades.

'Courage, lady, courage!' Ina moaned, hiding her face in fear.

But Guenevere could see the midwives frowning and shaking their heads. 'I never saw the like,' muttered one of them anxiously. 'The pains shake her as a terrier shakes a rat.'

The other mumbled a prayer before she spoke. 'Her hard travail came on too fast. And a ragged labour is the worst of all.'

'Why ragged? What do you mean?' Guenevere croaked. They gave her water, but they would not answer her. And still the pains were sweeping her away.

As the hours passed, she sweated to be delivered, wept and prayed. 'Goddess, Mother, spare my child!' she moaned. 'Let her be born, let her come to life!'

She could feel the pressure of Morgan's hand urging her on. But the child seemed rooted in her, like a rock or a tree. Was there a power here, against her baby's life? Realisation dawned, and the hopeless tears rained down.

Merlin! Oh, Merlin! Even in his crystal cave, it seemed, the malice of Merlin would not sleep.

'Mother!' she screamed. 'Help me, Mother! Save me from my enemy, save me now!' But all she could see were Morgan's great eyes by the bedside, black pools of grief to drown her and the child—

Drown—

Drown the grief, die, and sleep for ever, free of this pain—

Now the baby was suddenly still in her womb, and she felt her pains fade. She was drifting away, dropping slowly into the welcoming black pool, slipping into sleep, free at last . . .

There was a sudden loud commotion at the door. 'Oh, sire, you should not be here!'

Arthur's voice cut across the protests of the midwives. 'I am the King. And I will see the Queen!'

Suddenly he was at her side, his face registering the horror of what he saw. 'Oh my love, my love!' he murmured brokenly. He turned to Morgan. 'You too – you're exhausted. When did you last eat?'

Morgan hunched her back and shoulders like a cat. 'You must go,' she said rustily. 'This is a place of birth. Men have no place here.'

Arthur shook his head. 'No, Morgan. I have come to relieve you, to send you to your bed.'

Morgan leaped to her feet like a cat about to spring. 'No!' she hissed. 'It is almost over, I will not leave her now!'

Arthur took her by the arms. 'I have given orders, Morgan. If one of you has to suffer, the other need not too. Your waiting women are outside to take you to your chamber. And I will take your place here with Guenevere.'

'No!'

'Morgan, yes!'

Morgan glared at Arthur, then rushed from the room. Guenevere felt her heart dissolve in fear. As Arthur leaned over her and stroked her clammy head, she could see her own pain mirrored in his eyes. *The midwives have told him,* she thought dully, *that Maire will not live.*

The door of the chamber banged shut behind Morgan. A breath of fresh air rushed in, and Guenevere took in a deep, hungry breath. Her lungs expanded, and she felt as if a weight had gone from her chest. Then her pains began again, angry and strong. She cried out, and the midwives all cried too.

'Help, here!'

'Help the Queen!'

Now it was one mad flurry and a whirl of sudden action where all had seemed dead before. The pangs gripped her and forced her forward and now she was bearing down, bent double like a hag.

'Sire, give us room! You must leave now!'

The midwives hustled Arthur from the chamber.

'She's coming!' Guenevere cried. 'Maire comes!'

With a tearing, screaming roar something burst out of her womb and tore out through her legs. Her body arched in the one last desperate heave. Then there was nothing but a warm rush of blood and no pain, no pain, no pain.

'Come, little one, come to us! Come to your life in our world! Come!'

The midwives were calling the baby into life. Guenevere lay back on her pillows and sobbed out her heartfelt prayers. *Goddess, Mother, praise and thanks, give Your blessing on my daughter, make her long to live, long to reign.*

But why the silence at the end of the bed? Where were the midwives' cries of delight, the joy to welcome a new princess to the world?

Panic seized Guenevere. The baby was not dead, she knew it, she could not be. She reared up on her elbow, and the blood ran out between her legs. 'Where is my daughter?' she cried in frenzy. 'Bring her to me now!'

At the foot of the bed, Ina stood with the midwives clustered around a small grey lifeless form. One deftly thrust her fingers down the child's throat, and another fiercely pinched the tiny heels and feet. Guenevere whimpered in distress. Ina threw her a glance: Do not fear, madam, this has to be, so that she might live.

And there it was, a strong lusty cry. Wail upon wail of anger filled the air, as Maire protested at this rough handling of her royal person. It was the sound of life itself, taking its first breath. A wave of laughter and delight swept the room.

The baby was whisked into a clean white wrap, and Guenevere could see her tiny face being swabbed with a soft cloth. 'Clean her up later,' she called weakly but in triumph. 'Let me see her now!'

The three midwives paused in their ministrations and brought them swiftly to an end. Then the leader handed the baby to Ina to bring to Guenevere. If they glanced oddly at Ina, Guenevere did not notice, any more than she noticed the look on Ina's face as she drew near.

'Your Majesty,' she began stiffly, 'the baby – you should know—'

What was she saying? Fear fell on Guenevere, blotting out the light. She reared up like a madwoman. 'Give me my daughter!' she screamed wildly. 'Give her to me!'

Without a word Ina leaned forward and laid the swaddled bundle in her arms. Guenevere tore aside the wrappings to greet Arthur's child.

And found herself looking into the face of Arthur himself – crumpled, newborn, but Arthur to the life. From the cool grey eyes to the strong fists and soft wisp of shining hair, this was no daughter, it was Arthur's son.

CHAPTER 36

I t was a boy.
The baby was a boy.
The tiny body was as heavy as lead on her arm.
Guenevere turned her face to the wall and the tears fell like rain. *Maire, my daughter, where are you, where did you go? Mother, Mother, help me now. I can't love him, I don't want this child.*

There was a strange noise at her side, half-way between the cry of a curlew, and an old man's cough. The child was looking at her with a gaze of wondering love. His eyes were as blue as the bloom on a mallard's wing, and as bright as the sun on a silver inland sea. Something surged within her that she never knew before. And then she knew what she must call this child.

'Amir?' said Arthur, in a doubtful voice, cradling the white bundle uneasily on his great forearm. He was still recovering from the shock of having a boy, and holding the child made him nervous, clumsy and strange.

'Amir,' she said drowsily. 'It means "Beloved" in the old tongue.' The midwives had given her a thick sweet drink to make her sleep until her milk came in. 'Amir. Because we love him so.'

Amir stirred, and nodded his downy head.

'See?' Guenevere crowed. 'He already knows his name!'

'Amir.' Arthur tried again, rolling it round his mouth. 'What about Uther, after my father? Or Leogrance, after yours?'

Amir's tiny face puckered, and he looked as if he was going to cry. Guenevere shook her head. 'Amir,' she repeated. 'Beloved. That is his name.'

'Such a big boy!' exulted the midwives. 'Such a fine healthy lad!'

He was the perfect baby, gifted with Arthur's well-boned sturdy body, bright open face and loving, tender ways. But from the moment he was born, his blue-grey eyes had an Otherworldly look.

Morgan saw this as soon as Arthur brought her in. She pounced on the cradle with a frown, and hung over it for a long time, staring deep into Amir's eyes.

'You are reading his future,' Arthur said, with sudden anxiety. 'What do you see?'

'I see him as one of the spirit children, one of the stars in heaven,' Morgan said at last, with an odd laugh. 'He was born to serve the Great One.' She let out her breath in a long hiss of relief. 'She will take him to Her.'

'Of course,' Guenevere agreed smugly, brimming with pride. Already she had decided when Amir should go to Avalon to serve the Goddess, and learn the old ways. And of course the Mother would take him to Her. Everyone would – for who could help loving this child?

'Come to your aunt, then, little prince.' Morgan reached her long thin arms into the cradle and picked the baby up, muttering under her breath. Amir stared at her wide-eyed, then broke into a piercing scream.

'Amir!' Arthur frowned angrily.

'Oh, Amir!' Guenevere could have wept. Morgan had to love this baby, for Arthur's sake.

Ina ran to take the baby and soothe his cries. 'Take no notice, madam,' she cried. 'All newborns are like this, they have to stretch their lungs!'

Morgan smiled, and slowly nodded her dark head. 'It is well.' She turned to Arthur with her rusty laugh. 'He has his father's strength. Before we know it, he'll be off with you to war.' Her black eyes gleamed.

'The sooner the better,' Arthur cried. 'For a son of mine!'

What were they talking about? Guenevere felt a sudden thrill of fear. She sank back into the pillows, and held out her arms. 'Let me have my son.'

Ina hastened over and Guenevere clasped him to her heart. His high wail stopped instantly, and he nuzzled his small head into her, as warm and sweet as hay.

'Amir!' She kissed the soft spot on the top of his head.

At the end of the bed, Arthur stood watching, half frowns, half smiles, with great tears in his eyes. And once again Guenevere thought that she had never been so happy in her life.

Three days later, Morgan told Arthur that it was time for her to leave. She was strong enough now to travel to her own estate. Arthur was distraught. 'Don't go now, Morgan,' he begged, 'just when we need you most! Think of Amir. You are his aunt, and he has few enough kin. Stay a while – at least till he can talk, and say your name!'

But Morgan's mind was set, and Arthur always feared to stand against her will. Guenevere saw her off with sadness, and waved her away in tears. But when she was gone, she missed her much less than she thought she would.

Spring came in with green buds misting the mountains, and lambs calling from every hilly bourne. Amir was bigger now and growing so fast, his nurses said, that it would not be long before he could ride and walk. When the Lady's messenger came from Avalon, Guenevere thought that he brought no more than Nemue's regular greetings from the Sacred Isle. The little priestess had fallen into the habit of sending news of Merlin to soothe Arthur's grief. The old man was healing well, Nemue would write, and was surely in the best place with them there. As she read, Guenevere would feel again the call of Avalon, and gently revisit the happiness of her past.

But now her face grew dark and her eyes flared with anger and shock. She turned on the messenger. *'Christians on Avalon?'*

The messenger was one of the Lake villagers, small and squinting through a birds' nest of black hair. He nodded. 'Monkish men.'

Guenevere turned again to the letter in her hand. 'They asked the Lady for a cell on the Sacred Isle,' Nemue had written in her runish hand, 'to join their prayers to the worship of the Goddess for the peace of the world. Very holy men, it seemed, and so mild and sweet-souled that the Lady was inclined to grant their request.'

Guenevere covered her mouth with her hand. She wanted to be sick. Whatever did it mean?

The Lady mistrusted the Christians, and with good reason, given what they believed. She even feared that they had designs on the Hallows themselves, hoping to use the regalia of the Goddess for their own ends.

Yet, as one sworn to the Mother, the Lady also lived by the sacred words, *religion should be kindness, all faith should be love*. She would never forbid the worship of others, Guenevere knew. She truly believed that all souls were one in the Mother's love.

Perhaps she thought now that sharing and growing together was the way of love. And perhaps she was right. Yet still Guenevere wondered with a lingering dread – *Christians on Avalon?*

The next day Arthur came into the nursery as Guenevere was lulling the baby to sleep, and said abruptly, 'Guenevere, Amir must be christened before long.'

The little room was sweet with Amir's scent, and drowsy with the murmur of his gathering dreams. A milky twilight played over the walls, and her hand continued its rhythmic, soothing circles on his tiny back as she forced herself to hear what Arthur said.

'*Christened?*' She could not believe it. 'Baptised by the rites of the Christians?'

Arthur nodded. 'He'll rule a Christian country when he's King – you know the Middle Kingdom gave up the worship of the Old Ones long ago. And there are Christians everywhere now, even in the Summer Country, even here.'

He could not have said anything to distress her more.

'Yes, indeed!' Her anger boiled up till it could not be contained. 'And they're on Avalon too, Nemue says! Cells of monks already – they'll be wanting a church there next!'

But Arthur was not listening. 'It would have to be in Caerleon, of course, not here in Camelot. Amir could be shown to my people there at the same time. Or else I could take him to London, and have him baptised in the great church there.'

I, he said, not *we*. A chill crept round Guenevere's heart. *This was something that Arthur planned to do alone – to bring her child to an alien faith.*

She struggled with the darkness in her soul. 'Baptised by the Christians?'

'As I was myself, according to Merlin,' Arthur said carefully. 'The King my father ordered him to bring me to the Father God, as well as to the Mother, if I was to be High King.'

The Father God—
The enemy of the Mother, foe of foes.

Could she do this? Did Amir have to suffer it?

Guenevere paced around the chamber, wrestling with her pain.

Amir would have to rule Christians when he was King, that much was true. And a good ruler should be king to all his people, not just a few. And Arthur was Amir's father – he had a right to be heard.

What was she worried about? Whatever Arthur did, Amir would always be hers. As long as she was alive, her son would know the Goddess and learn to keep Her ways. A dash of Christian water on his head could make no difference to that.

Arthur was watching her closely, anxious that they should agree. 'He will need godparents,' he said slowly. 'Men and women who will care for him as we do. Who would you choose?' He smiled into her eyes. 'Who will you have to stand up for Amir at his baptism? Name them, and they are yours.'

Guenevere stared at him.

Mine.

A Christian baptism, but godparents of my choice?

Of course!

Guenevere laughed aloud. She caught Arthur's eye, and gave a slow comprehending nod.

Oh, my love, my love—

How could she have doubted him? As always, he had a plan. A formal baptism to ensure that the Christians would accept Amir. A public declaration to content those who cared about such things. But her choice of godparents, to surround Amir with those who would defend the old faith with their lives, and hold fast to the old ways.

'Oh, Arthur! Oh, my love!' She grinned at him.

Arthur beamed with delight. 'Who, then?'

'Godparents? My father for one,' she said, without hesitation, 'and Lucan for another.'

'Good choices, both,' Arthur said, still twinkling away. 'And Malgaunt!'

Where Malgaunt's name came from, Guenevere did not know. But her angry kinsman was a man redeemed, her father said. Her former enemy was now devoted to her cause. And Amir was Malgaunt's own kith and kin. He was a son of the Summer Country, born to rule. Malgaunt would defend that to the last drop of his blood.

'Malgaunt! Yes, indeed, he shall be one,' Arthur agreed. 'And for godmothers? I thought I should ask my mother and Morgause.'

And there's another, Guenevere thought, *who has no cause to love the Christians, and every good reason to adore Amir.* 'And your sister Morgan. She must be Amir's godmother, she loves you so.'

But when the day came, it was Morgan who stood alone at the font with Amir in her arms. Queen Igraine sent a tiny jewelled dagger made of gold, and a boy-sized silver sword. And Queen Morgause sent a heavy silver christening spoon engraved with runes, and a gold bowl bearing the letter 'A'. But Queen Igraine could not travel so far from Cornwall, and Queen Morgause had to stay in the far Orkneys.

'Since you have all my four sons with you there, my lord king and brother,' she wrote fondly to Arthur, 'there is no one here I can entrust with the running of my kingdom – not even my faithful Sir Lamorak, the knight you gave me who is now my right hand.'

In the end they had fixed on London for the christening, as a way of telling the world that King Arthur had a son.

'Amir has the rest of his life to get to know the people

of the Middle Kingdom, and they him,' Guenevere pointed out. 'But if he is christened in London, all the country will hear of him then.'

'And the Father Abbot is wise, Merlin told me that when I was proclaimed,' Arthur said eagerly. 'He is a man of love and peace, not given to the sword.'

Guenevere laughed. 'Why, he sounds almost like one of us! If my son must be christened, I think that London and the Abbot will do very well.'

Arthur laughed too, and hugged her in his arms. 'My love, my queen, let it be London, as you say!'

London.

Without warning, a great darkness filled her eyes. She saw London town by night, and the proud walls and tall towers falling under a rain of Saxon spears. Below the ramparts, dark shapes were raging through the shadows, huge horned men hacking about them, dealing pain and death.

She could hear the grunting cries of their ugly tongue, the screams of children spitted on their swords. Blood drowned her sight. She shouted out, and clutched Arthur's arm. 'The Saxons!' she cried. 'They are coming again, they will take London when you and Amir are there!'

'The *Saxons*?'

Arthur was aghast. 'How did you know?' He paused and checked himself.

'Know what?'

'I was going to tell you.'

A cold hand gripped her gut. Slowly she released her hold on his arm. 'Tell me what?'

'Word has come from Sir Tor,' Arthur said shortly. 'I would have told you—'

'You always told me everything before.' She was shivering now from head to foot.

Arthur ignored her, and pressed on. 'The Saxons are

raiding again on the east coast. Only a handful, but Sir Tor thinks we should crush them now. I'll have to raise a war party, and drive them back over the sea.' He nodded to himself. 'After I've taken Amir to London to be christened.'

'You'll take him to London?' A violent juddering seized her, and she burst into tears. 'The Saxons will be there in London now! They'll kill Amir!'

Arthur gripped her by the shoulders and shook her forcefully. 'For God's sake, Guenevere, hear me if you can!' he said, with furious emphasis. 'The Northmen are sea-raiders, pirates, water-rats! They never venture so far inland for their prey! And they'd never attack a great walled city like London, defended from every tower!'

She could hardly hear him. *Amir, the Saxons, Saxon spears, death* swam before her eyes. Then Arthur was roughly shaking her awake. 'Guenevere, it can't happen!' he said sharply. 'Listen to me! I won't hear another word!'

He pushed her away. His eyes were as cold and grey as the North Sea. 'One day Amir will meet the Saxons in the field, warrior to warrior, man to man. But not till he is trained to face their swords. Until then, you have nothing to fear.'

She could not argue. But, oh, it was cruel to let Amir go! They rode out in glory, Arthur at the head of all his knights, Amir behind him in his nurse's arms. Behind them rode Gawain, Kay, Lucan and Bedivere, denoted by Arthur the four knights of the Prince's guard, each showing in his face the pride of this special task.

It was a mighty train, worthy of a great king and his son. A cloud of dust followed the tramping feet, and the rising sun burnished their helmets with fire. But when they had gone, the world was an empty place.

The days that followed were worse than she had dreamed. Life without Amir was no life at all. Each dawn she woke with a hollow in her heart that turned to black emptiness as the day wore on. Fear for her child dogged her by night and day, though she knew the journey to London was as safe as any in the land.

But she had to trust her husband. And young as Amir was, she must not smother him.

'He will be a fine king one day, won't he?' she pleaded with Ina. 'And a great warrior, say he will!'

'Who, Prince Amir?' Ina responded stoutly. 'With or without my say-so, he will be the most famous king of all these islands after King Arthur, bless his little heart!'

Now she spent all her days and half her nights in the tower of Camelot, where a lifetime ago she had watched for Malgaunt until dawn drove her weeping with cold to bed. And from her high eyrie she saw at last the sight her heart was hungering for, the glint of the sun on a thousand glittering spears.

Arthur's great train was surging over the hill.

'Ina, Ina,' she cried, straining to see through a mist of joyful tears, 'they are back from London. Can you see Amir?'

Ina craned out through the window, and caught her breath. 'There, madam, in the front, riding with the King!'

And there he was, just as Ina said. Perched on the pommel of Arthur's saddle, supported by his father's great body and secured by his strong arm, Amir was riding too, his eyes like saucers, crowing with delight. Guenevere looked at Amir at the head of the band of knights, back from his first great adventure, and knew what she had to do.

CHAPTER 37

*H*ow long had she been dreaming of this?
Since the wedding-day?
Before.

But the last dream came when Arthur was away. She passed in sleep to Avalon, and came to Merlin, at peace in his crystal cell. The old man seemed to be dreaming too, lying full length on a couch with a ring of candles like stars around his head, and all his ancient books of magic by his side.

Why did you raise your powers against Amir? she wanted to say. *Why did you bind my womb, and keep him imprisoned there till he nearly died?* But he opened his eyes and looked straight at her. And it came to her, *All that is past now.*

Merlin's eyes were calm and golden, not the feverish yellow that they had been before. 'You have dreamed of giving the Round Table to Arthur, for the love you have of him,' he murmured, in a voice like the wind in the trees. 'Do so, for it is right. He has proved worthy, and his knights are the finest to be seen. But remember to make a seat for the boy who is to come. He will be the son of the most peerless knight in the world, and he is destined for the highest adventure of all. Call his seat the Siege Perilous, for he will face many dangers and defy them all. In his time he, too, will be the best knight in the world, and when he comes, the Table will be complete.'

Guenevere awoke sobbing, her heart breaking with joy.

At last! *Goddess, Mother, praise and thanks to You—*

After all this time, Merlin's enmity was appeased. Even from his retreat in his crystal cave, Merlin had foreseen Amir's destiny. He knew that Amir was a marvellous boy, and he loved him already as Arthur's son. So he had given his blessing on her gift to Arthur, and that would mean as much to Arthur as the thing itself. She could not wait to share her dream with him.

The Round Table hung in its place on the wall of the Great Hall. Beneath it stood the knights' sieges, each with a name in gold.

Guenevere turned to Arthur, and took both his hands. 'The Round Table is yours. This is my gift to you for your love to me. From now on, your knights and mine will be joined in brotherhood as well as in name. Now they will no longer be the King's knights or the Queen's, but all Knights of the Round Table, going forth in both our names.' She gestured to the sieges along the wall. 'Some of these have been empty for a good while. Let us hold a solemn ceremony to create a new fellowship of knights, rededicate their sieges, and bless each one as they take their seats. How do you like this?'

Arthur shook his head in loving disbelief, and gazed at the bright, hopeful face before him, the tremulous smile. Whatever had he done to deserve this? His heart swelled with love. What a woman! Would she ever know what she meant to him?

Overcome by emotion, he turned his head away. At the end of the line, one seat stood apart, the cover over its wooden canopy already in place. 'Why, sweetheart,' he said wonderingly, 'whose place is that?'

To his surprise, he saw Guenevere's eyes fill with tears. 'The best of all,' she whispered, drawing him down the room. 'Come, my love, and see!'

With a trembling hand, she lifted the red velvet and held it aside. Beneath the cover the gold letters pulsed and glowed. Arthur stood in silence as he made them out.

> *Here is the Siege Perilous, for the Knight who is to come. He will be the most Peerless Knight in all the World, and when he comes, the Prophecy of Merlin will be fulfilled.*

He was shivering. 'What knight will sit here?'

Guenevere was shining like the moon. She took his hands. 'The son of the best knight in the world.' She was transcendent now with joy. 'Your son. Amir.'

Arthur felt colder still. 'Amir?'

Guenevere laughed, a deep triumphant sound. 'Oh, it is destined to remain empty for a decade and more, of course. But hear me, Arthur! His name will be the brightest of them all. Merlin has told me so!'

'Merlin?'

Arthur was suddenly terribly afraid. In the distance he heard Guenevere's voice recounting her dream and Merlin's prophecy, and his heart quailed. How could it be true? His son could not fulfil this destiny. For he was not the best knight in the world. He knew that, whatever others thought.

But when Guenevere gave him Merlin's blessing on Amir, he wept aloud. And at high summer, when the roses were breathing out the joy of June all around Camelot's walls, the knights were assigned to their new places with all the ceremony that could be devised. When all had been seated, Arthur and Guenevere gazed upon Amir's chair, clasping each other and hardly daring to believe. Then Guenevere gave the signal for the cover to be lowered over the Siege Perilous, with its blazon of future fame. If Amir was as big and forward as his father, it would not be long before he was taking his place here.

So began the wonder years, Guenevere was to say, *the years the world remembers, when all our knights were bold and all their ladies fair—*

Arthur's knights were enrolled in the noblest band of chivalry the world had ever known. Each day now Gawain, Kay, Lucan, Bedivere and the others practised their knighthood in the lists, or rode out adventuring with Arthur to see justice done. In the Middle Kingdom too, Arthur's knights under King Pellinore were slowly purging the land of the evil King Lot had done. The menace of the invaders from the north meant no more now than an annual war-party to patrol the eastern shore and throw the raiders back to sea again before they could get a foothold on land.

Now those who had held out against Arthur saw the error of their ways, and yielded to him as High King. One by one all his old enemies, the hostile kings Rience, Vause, Nentres, and Brangoris, even King Carados of Northgales and the dreaded Agrisance of the Isles lowered their swords to him.

And each time Arthur and Guenevere rejoiced again. Each bloodless victory added to the glory of their court. Love and acclaim greeted them on all sides. From the white towers of Camelot to a golden Caerleon, restored to its former glory, there seemed no limit to what they could do.

For their tournaments now, kings and knights came from far and wide. The French kings from Little Britain were often outdistanced by those from Italy, Spain and Gaul, and even from the old Roman Empire, Constantinople and Alexandria. Each was a more glittering occasion than the last, the knights hardier, the kings more noble, the lances sharper and brighter, and the swords and chain-mail more silver than the gleam of the salmon as it slips down to the sea.

And at each tournament now, Arthur would allow no one to open the proceedings but Amir. Escorted by King Leogrance and Malgaunt, with the four cherished knight companions riding behind, he would ride the jousting field from end to end, carrying Amir in pride of place before him on his horse.

Then Morgause sent a present for Amir. They stood in the courtyard as the gift was unloaded from the wagon in which it had travelled down from the Orkneys in royal state, like a king itself.

Guenevere gasped. 'What is it?' she laughed.

Rearing and snorting, the fiery creature was standing up on its short back legs to punch and fight the air. It was one of the tiny barrel-bellied ponies of the Shetlands, legendary for their spirit and tirelessness. 'You will find him,' Morgause had written, 'bold enough for a prince.'

'Excellent!' Arthur roared. He turned to the wide-eyed Amir at his side. 'Now you can ride your own mount, sir, like the Emperor of Rome.'

Amir looked up, his clear eyes wide with awe. 'Can I, Father?'

'Yes!'

'At the next tournament?'

'The very next, my son.'

Guenevere stared at Arthur in disbelief. 'Arthur, he's only—'

What was she saying? Arthur knew how old he was.

Gods above, the pride and pain of having a son! Guenevere looked at Amir, grieving for the safety of the small, sturdy frame and well-formed limbs. Was he really old enough to ride with Arthur and take the reins alone?

But Amir was fearless, she knew. And when the tournament came, he would not be denied. So Guenevere had to watch as the boy rode with Arthur at the head of the procession, leading the combatants down the field to open the tournament, a little figure almost lost between the great legs of the chargers and stallions.

He's so small, so near the dreadful hoofs.

She must not think of her mother going down under Lucan's horse. *Think of Amir if you love him*, she commanded herself through the pain of unshed tears. *Think what this means to him*. Gripping the rail, she leaned out of the viewing gallery to watch his progress round the field.

The knights were all parading round the arena now, and out to the field beyond. As the blue flag of France passed below the gallery, Arthur's old friend King Ban caught Guenevere's eye. Riding beside his brother King Bors, he was resplendent in silver, blue and white. 'Greetings, Majesty!' he called merrily, raising his sword to the gallery, and kissing the blade. 'And greetings from our sons, who are here for the first time to honour your tournament!'

King Bors bowed and turned to the three armoured figures behind. 'Lionel!' he called. 'Bors! Lancelot!' At his command all three riders raised their swords and greeted her as King Ban had done.

'King Ban!' she cried abstractedly. 'And King Bors! You are welcome all, and your noble sons!' But her eyes were on Amir, and she hardly saw anything else.

Afterwards she could remember glancing down at the three riders and knowing who they were, the two sons of King Bors and King Ban's only son, the boy hero of the Battle of the Kings, young Lancelot. Later she tried to recall their faces, their weapons, or anything about them at all. But all she could call back through the mist of time was a clutch of tall young men riding behind Ban and Bors.

That, and the white horse of the leader as the three of them followed their fathers into the field. A boyish form clad in shining silver armour, buffed and polished like no other on the field. And, above it all, a pair of burning brown eyes raised in wonderment to the gallery as she sat on her golden throne all in white and gold, her gaze following Amir with a mother's adoring love.

CHAPTER 38

Gold was the colour of those years, she would always say, *it was a life of gold*. Joy filled the air like wine, they breathed it night and day. And this golden life they lived for seven years, while young Amir throve, and grew tall.

Yet what did they know of the evil brewing far away? They knew that across the northern sea lay lands where grey plains stretched out to a cold horizon, whipped by an endless wind. They knew that gales from the ocean choked all the air there with salt, and rotted the crops on their stalks. And they knew that when famine gripped their wives and babes, the men of these lands would take to the boats and begin raiding again along their eastern shore.

But in the warmth of the Summer Country, they did not know when the Saxon lands survived a hard winter famine only to meet a spring pestilence crueller than any before. The dry-burned crops would not thrive, and disease withered even the best of the tribe.

Soon cattle were casting their calves, and babes-in-arms were dying at the breast. The old King watched his people dwindle, and dreamed of the new homeland where the sun always shone. There cattle and children grew fat, horses fed in lush pastures, and rosy-faced women smiled at their sun-browned men. He remembered the place from voyages long gone by, when he led the men in raids on its eastern shore.

His men waited it out while their slaves and elders died. They bore with patience, too, their children's deaths, for a man can always sow his seed again. But then a woman died that the old man's nephew had brought back as a captive from that eastern coast, and he loved her more than life.

She had never once smiled since he took her from her land. She had never borne him a child, though he took her every way he knew. His brothers warned him that she must have found the old way to close up her womb, and he should drown her as barren, or burn her as a witch. But he loved her haunted eyes and downcast mouth, his flesh craved her thin body with its awkward bones, and his soul yearned to make her smile again. One day she would be his, body and soul, he knew. And when she died, he knew that day would never come.

Then his heart burst with hate for the old man. 'He has the dream-sickness,' he announced to the younger men. 'We must take to the boats, and cross the sea again. He can stay.'

But his uncle would have to go with them, he knew. Then as soon as the war-ships were out of sight of the land, the old man would be told it was time to greet his Gods. He would be given to the sea, and the tides would wash his bones. His death would bless their expedition, and they would prosper in their raid. Then the tribe would have a new leader, for his nephew would take his place. And the old man knew that too.

Enough!

No more dream-weaving, spinning out the frayed hopes of tired, sick old men. It was the hour of the trysting-horn, time to raise the boats and sharpen the swords and spears.

He lifted his head, scenting like a wolf this way and that. 'Ulf?' he called.

None of this Guenevere could have known or guessed. But afterwards she would torment herself with the same endless refrain, picking at the scab of suffering till it ran.

Was that the still point of the turning circle, the moment before we plunged into the dark? Had we risen so high on the wheel of fortune that the Dark Goddess Herself was moved to throw us off?

Or did I love too much? the endless lament went on. *That is the most common crime against the heart. Amir's body was so small and firm, his straight, smooth limbs without seam or scar, his hair as soft as thistledown and as sweet as summer hay. His golden skin and shining eyes made him so precious to me that, after the christening, I vowed that he would never leave my side again.*

When a man and woman in love create a child, that changes their love in ways they do not know. One love drives out another, as fire drives out fire, and pain will kill pain. In the darkness of my heart now I loved Amir more than Arthur, more than I could ever love a man. That is the secret crime of motherhood, the truth so stark that women will not own it, even to themselves. That is the choice every mother has to make, if her child is to thrive. And that choice is the cruelty at the heart of life itself.

When I had Amir, I was given another soul to love. I had another Arthur, and my love grew to take in both of them; it would have spread to include all the world.

But for Arthur, the hard knowledge came to him as it comes to all men, that he would never be loved in that way again. Never again would he have first place in my heart. And proud though he was to have a son, his world shook on its axis when he saw that he could no longer call himself the centre of mine.

And he had his own feelings about Amir, and they changed

things too. Arthur never knew his own father, and then he lost in Merlin the only father he ever had. Now with Amir, Arthur could be the missing father, become the man he had lost and never ceased to desire. He saw a line descending after him, all stretching down from Uther as High King. And as Amir grew, as Arthur's own fame increased, and his knights won glory for him high and low, so little by little Arthur's hopes were drawn away from me and more and more to his dream of the rule of kings – where I could not follow, where the Christians led, and where others, too, would have him go.

Did I see this at the time? Only with hindsight, when I looked back. But I have to hurry to set it down now, quickly now, for the darkness is coming as I tell you this.

We had our dream of gold. And afterwards came the night.

The shadowy shapes stood frozen among the trees. In the fitful moonlight, they could have been trees themselves. But their horned headgear proclaimed them for what they were. They were blood-predators, rank with the smell of death, and the wild creatures of the woodland shrank down in their holes in fear.

The leader stood at a distance ahead of his men. 'Ulf?' he hallooed softly like an owl.

Ulf heard his name in the owl-cry, and could have snarled back in rage. What now, Curnic? What further madness are you leading us into tonight?

He clenched his brawny fists. Since the start of this raid, his brother had turned to him again and again, and never once taken the advice he freely gave. Ulf had been forced to watch as everything went wrong, had been dragged into actions he knew were doomed from the start.

What had come over Cunric? Ulf fretted, as he moved forward, his long legs covering the ground with smooth silent strides. When the old man failed, there was no doubt who should follow him. They had all looked to Cunric to renew the life of the tribe.

Was it the death of that sallow-faced slave-girl of his? Or was it the word of his uncle as he met his death? The old man had stepped out into the cold grey waves calmly enough. But as he went he smiled and said, 'Nephew, my sister calls from the other side. I shall tell her you will soon be there.'

Ulf shuddered as he came up to Cunric's side. A sister's son was the dearest of any kin. So the curse of a uterine uncle was hardest to bear. That would be enough to rob any man of his power, and something had happened to weaken Cunric's grip. From the first raid to tonight's hurried flight, they had spent too many lives for too little gain – for none at all, in fact.

'Ulf?' Cunric hissed. His eyes were fixed straight ahead.

Ulf signified his presence with a soft grunt.

Cunric inclined his head. His horns moved in the moonlight like living things. 'There,' he murmured. 'See there!'

Ulf's face twisted with unexpected relief. A small village, undefended, hidden in the heart of the wood. No monastery, no church with the lure of gold crosses and jewelled reliquaries, but a simple hamlet trusting to its distance from the shore to give it protection from their lightning raids.

Ulf gave an ugly grin. These people were not to know that this was no random strike – that they needed a place to lie up and recover till their Gods smiled again. His eyes roved over the snug dwellings, with their tidy cattle byres by their back doors. There would be pigs to roast, and chickens to kill. Bread too, and beans, and mead and beer for sure. The men would feast tonight as well as kings feasted in the lands they had left. And afterwards there would be plump fowl of another kind, fat, squealing village daughters and their mothers too, wide-eyed and panting just as he liked them best.

For a moment he was distracted by the thought of the pleasures to come. The whole troop of them taking turns with a weeping dame, slicing off her clothing strip by strip, while she tried in vain to cover her nakedness. Then mounting her turn about too, and forcing her husband to watch. Getting the boldest girl drunk, and making her dance while they threw knives at her heels and ears. Spreading the fattest one out on the table amid the ruins of the feast, and teasing her pink nipples with his dagger-point till the red blood flowed and he could suck it off—

'And there—'

Cunric's hissing voice recalled him to himself. As they watched, the door of the nearest house opened on to the night and the owner strolled out, leaving the door ajar. Moving off into the wood, he turned in to a tree and began to relieve himself.

Within the house a candle lighted their way. The door stood open as if to invite them in. Ulf's eyes met Cunric's and the leader nodded once. Then he began to lope across the midnight grass. On his heels ran a band of desperate men. The sleeping village would sleep no more that night.

Guenevere sat in the solar watching the sunbeams playing hide and seek in Amir's hair. It had been a golden November and she basked in the winter sun, curled upon a couch with her son like a mother cat. Her contentment was complete.

'Guenevere!' She looked up to see Arthur approaching with a frown on his face, and a letter in his hand.

She looked up with a pang of guilt. She knew that she left more and more of the business of state to Arthur, because she only wanted to be with Amir. There was nothing she loved as much as watching him at his lessons or reading to him with his small body close to hers, as she was now.

'Father!' Amir lifted his dusty fair head in delight. But with the sure instinct of an only child, he knew at once that he was not wanted now. Without a word he slid from Guenevere's knee, and went across to his nurse before Arthur could send him away.

Arthur scarcely seemed to see him go. 'Bad news from the east coast, Guenevere,' he said abruptly. 'A raiding party of Saxons has made land. They've taken one of the inland villages, and the word is they are digging in.'

'Digging in? What, now, with winter almost here?' She was horrified. 'Gods above! If they're making camp—'

Arthur nodded grimly, and finished the thought. 'They mean to stay.'

Fingers of fear made their way round her heart. 'That means there's a terrible famine in their homeland, and only death awaits them if they return.'

'But if they stay, they become settlers, not summer raiders any more,' Arthur said heavily. 'Then more and more will come, and the coast will once again become "the Saxon shore".'

He sighed, and his eyes wandered to Amir in the corner with his nurse. 'Ha! Soon they'll be taking our women to warm their beds and comfort their long, cold nights. Then they'll have children by them, and every son born here will be reason to stay.'

He slapped the letter hard against his thigh. 'We must root them out, like the vermin they are.' He lifted his head, and snuffed the air like a hunting dog. 'Well, so be it! The knights will welcome some action before winter sets in.'

A raw foreboding struck Guenevere's heart. 'Arthur, is this wise?'

'What do you mean?'

'The Saxons are desperate men, they won't go easily.'
She was shivering now, and fear made it hard to speak.
'Winters are cruel on that eastern coast. They'll find no
sustenance, and they'll get no help from the people there,
indeed the locals will pick them off as best they can. Why
not let nature fight for us, and see how many are still alive
next spring? If you go now—'

'Guenevere, Guenevere.' Arthur was shaking his head
impatiently. 'Leave this to me, will you? You are no soldier – I know what to do. We go now, and strike fast
and hard, so they won't have time to put up any resistance at all.'

'But, Arthur—'

'No, Guenevere!' He frowned at her troubled face. 'I've
made the decision, and I've never taken an easier one in my
life. It's the right time. A child could do it, if we go now!'
His face lit up with a strange and different light. 'I'll take
Amir! It'll be his first campaign!'

She could not believe it. *'Arthur, I beg you, no!'*

'Why not? I was around his age when I went to war for
the first time,' Arthur retorted. 'It was only a skirmish on
the borders of Gore, but it was war enough for a lad. Kay
and I went as pages to a couple of Sir Ector's knights. We
got nowhere near the fighting, but we came back as heroes
in our own eyes just the same!'

Heroes.

Every boy longs to be a hero, and Amir will be the same.

She knew that the boy would be hearing every word.
She lowered her voice and tried to speak calmly. 'Arthur,
this is not just a skirmish. The Saxons are only here because
there is nothing for them at home. Men fighting for their
lives will fight to the death.' *Listen to me, Arthur!* her eyes
said to him. *Can we discuss this alone?*

But Arthur was not looking. He waved an impatient hand. 'Amir won't be fighting, don't you see that, Guenevere?'

'He shouldn't be there at all!' She could have killed him. 'He's too young!'

'Nonsense!' cried Arthur breezily. 'It's time he left the house of women and learned to live with men.' He raised his hand. Amir was watching him steadily, his great eyes fixed on Arthur like the hope of things to come. 'Amir, come to me. Tell me, would you like to go to war?'

Amir lifted his bright head like a flower, and his eyes spoke for him. He was glowing with his Otherworldly light.

'You see?' Arthur crowed. 'It's all settled, then. We'll leave at first light, in two days' time.'

CHAPTER 39

Nothing she said could move Arthur now. Patiently he repeated that Amir would be nowhere near the action, not by several miles, that a whole troop of men would guard him day and night, that it would be no more than a fracas, and over in a day.

'If all this is true,' Guenevere forced out through clenched lips, 'what's the point of taking him at all?'

Arthur's eyes were alight with memories of old camp-fires and escapades of long ago. 'To make a man of him!' He sighed in exasperation. 'Oh, Guenevere, it would have had to come in time. How old would Amir be before you agreed he could go to war? Ten? Fifteen? Twenty?'

'Never!' she burst out.

Arthur gave a short laugh. 'You'd never say that if he'd been born a girl! If Maire had come instead of Amir here, you'd have told her all the stories of "Battle Raven" to make her brave. You'd have taught her yourself all that your mother taught you. Maire would be practising her sword-play now, not hanging round her nurse's knee reading books like Amir.'

Now it was her turn to be caught on the raw. *'If Maire had come.'* Oh, this was cruel! He must be angry, to throw that in her teeth. He knew how it grieved her that Maire had never come.

And there was no reason for it, all the midwives said. In Camelot, Taliesin and the Druids prayed every day for the increase of the Queen and the royal family. On Avalon, Nemue and the Lady had asked the Goddess to bless her moon-times and help her conceive.

Yet still Maire did not come.

And it was true, she would not hold back a girl from her destiny in war.

She bowed her head and tried to stem the tears. 'Let me see to Amir's things, then. When do you leave?'

All the time they were away, Guenevere felt the darkness coming, she felt it all around. Yet she had no seeings, only racked and jumbled dreams that fled away as soon as she awoke.

And the messages Arthur sent faithfully every day brought nothing but good news. Every day, too, came Ina's reminder that she should trust the King. 'Would King Arthur put his own son in danger?' she demanded with a laugh. 'Would Sir Gawain, or any of them, risk the life of their prince? They'd cut their arms off first!'

One last death – one last blow for the Gods – then the Dark Ones could take his spirit home—

Rocking in the saddle, Ulf knew he was losing blood. They had been glad to find good horses in the village, but that would not help him now. His soul was singing through the hollows of his veins, and his eyes were growing dim. And above the din of battle, the old refrain still hammered through his head, wrong, wrong, all wrong.

Every step his brother took had given Ulf cause to doubt. 'Why this village, Cunric?' he had demanded. 'They never defended it and neither can we.' Every answer Cunric had given him had been proved false. 'Pendragon will not set forth in winter to drive us out,' he'd bragged. 'We have until the ice breaks to fatten ourselves here.' So when Arthur came, they were all unprepared.

But before that, Cunric had started muttering to himself, and communing with spirits in the wood. One had come to him, and offered him a pact, he said. In return for a death service, she would bring them all safe home.

'Only one death, Ulf!' Cunric had urged. He laughed oddly. 'And only a little one!'

Ulf laughed now to remember sharing that joke. The death of a child was nothing, he had killed hundreds for sport. And he had believed Cunric that if they killed this child, then his dark spirit would bring them home.

But he had never known men who would fight for a child the way these knights had done. And the Gods alone knew how Cunric was faring against the main force. His brother had underestimated Arthur Pendragon once before, when he said he would not come. Ulf knew in his soul that no man lived to do that twice.

He laughed again, feeling his wits grow light. How long he could stay in the saddle, he did not know. His war-hardened body had continued to grip and hold, to thrust and meet the resistance of screaming flesh, to know the triumph as a blow struck home. But still he could not get anywhere near the boy.

The boy.

There could never have been a child like this before, calm and unafraid in the midst of a battle, with men dying all around. What was he, Ulf wondered, a halfling, a changeling child? For truly he had a more than human air.

Ulf could see him now through the defending wall of knights, all frenziedly hacking to right and left as the boy remained pale but composed. What other child could sit his pony so, the still centre at the eye of the raging storm?

Gods above, he was a boy to fight for, Ulf grudgingly conceded to himself. A well-shaped head set on a slender frame, tall for his age, and beautiful as a girl. His mouth, his skin, his eyes, his thick mop of hair picking up every glint of gold in the moonlight would all flatter any girl's face too. But the set of his back, the thrust of his jaw and the fearless, unruffled stare were all male, and all royal prince. A noble child, Ulf nodded to himself. Pity he had to die.

But die he must, by Cunric's orders and the Dark One's besides. For in his last moments, Ulf had seen her too. She was lean and white with great eyes as big as plates and a purple mouth. She rode naked through the air on a black chariot, with black knives on her wheels. And she came straight to him, brandishing her whip to drive his horse back one more time into the seething fray.

'The Prince!' the dark spirit whispered, rolling her red-black eyes. He could see her angry nipples with their piercing glare, the lips of her furious sex speaking to him as she lashed him with words. 'The Prince,' she commanded, leaning out of her chariot with one white breast dangling as long as her arm, and a red pointing finger as long as his own leg. And suddenly he knew what she had come to say.

Home.

'Kill the boy, and I will bring you all safe home,' she had promised Cunric, and Cunric had swallowed it. Ulf laughed long and hard for the last time.

Home.

She never meant the land that they had left.

But home to the world beneath the worlds, to the last, lost land of their Gods of blood and bone. Home to the long hollow in the hill, to the burning ship, to the grave in the depths of the sea.

Home.

He was almost home now, almost there. Just one more

blow, one death, a little death. The child's life as the price of his right to walk the Otherworld in power until he came again.

So be it.

As the Dark Ones willed.

Ulf looked steadily at the boy with the last of his fading sight. His bloodless lips moved as he begged the Great Dark One to ride on the point of his spear. It seemed to him that her snaky head nodded *yes*. Gripping the long shaft with both hands, he fixed the boy in his final pinpoint of vision, and thrust with all his force. He saw the glinting metal travel through the ring of knights, he saw the defender's sword making straight for his heart, and he saw no more.

'Of course the King will bring the Prince safely home!' Ina whispered in Guenevere's ear every day. And soon Guenevere knew how foolish she had been. She was in the solar with a few of the lords and ladies making the most of the winter sun, when there was a flurry of arrival at the door.

A soldier stood before her covered in mud, but grinning from ear to ear. 'Word from the King, Your Majesty,' he beamed. 'The danger is over, and he is bringing the war-force home. The attack on the Saxons went just as he planned. There was a small group, no more, who had invaded a village, and put the people to death. Now they have met the fate that they deserved, and there are none left to trouble the eastern shore.'

'Goddess, Mother, thanks!' Guenevere sobbed, beside herself with relief. 'And Prince Amir?'

'Safe and sound far from the action, in the care of the King's four knights and a picked troop of men. The King sends to say he will join forces with them, and they'll all make their way gently home.' He laughed exultantly. 'The

Prince's first expedition! And I served with him. Our Prince
Amir!' His ruddy face creased with delight.

Guenevere nodded, giddy with relief.

Amir safe and sound.

Goddess, Mother, thanks and praises for saving my son.

And suddenly there was Arthur himself in the doorway,
pale as the dead, grey as a living ghost. In the passageway
beyond lurked Gawain, Kay, Lucan and Bedivere, all white
and staring too, like watchers at a death.

'He's dead, Guenevere,' Arthur cried, in a voice not his
own. 'Amir's dead. They killed him, after all.'

CHAPTER 40

'Where is he? Bring me to him, let me see my son!'

'He's dead, Guenevere, gone. We had to bury him.'

'Take me there! I want to see him – bury him myself.'

Arthur closed his eyes and turned his head away. 'No man on earth would know the place again. We had to hide him from the Saxons before they could gather for another attack. So we buried him on the seashore, where his grave could never be found. Sometimes the sea covers it, then when the tide ebbs, his bed grows small again.'

'No!' Guenevere screamed. She ran at the knight companions, clawing at Gawain's chest. 'Gawain, say this isn't true. Bedivere, Kay, I beg of you – Lucan, you wouldn't lie to me!'

Gawain and Lucan exchanged looks of anguish, and Bedivere wept softly to himself. No one moved or breathed. There was no sound but the silence of the dead.

'Guenevere—'

Arthur came to her, and tried to take her in his arms. But she fought off his grasp, and struck him in the face, and walked away without a backward glance.

She was calm then. All around her there were screams

and sighs and tears, but she was quiet and she knew what to do.

And what to say to the voices in her mind.

Why? screamed a voice within. *Why him, why Amir?* But she knew why. It came to her in odd snatches above all the other sounds, the piteous howls and screams inside her head, as she went to the stables, took a horse and an old cloak hanging there, and rode away.

It was the tainted legacy, she knew that now. Slowly she puzzled it out, piece by piece. It was the blood of Arthur on his only son.

For Arthur was born of the evil of two men, when Merlin and Uther plotted to take Igraine. He came into being through a forbidden sin, a sin against the Mother, a man's lust that wronged a woman and destroyed four blameless lives. Yet, for all their schemes, Uther and Merlin had made Arthur an unknown bastard, and left him with a twisted claim to the throne.

And Merlin was a bastard too, sang the voices in her head, *did you know that? He was a by-blow of the Pendragons in the female line.*

Of course.

It all came back to her now, all the old rumours she had heard about Merlin when she was a child. His mother was a princess betrayed by the man she loved, who proved to be a devil in disguise. So Merlin was the son of a fiend, and his life was twisted too.

Guenevere laughed, rocking and smiling to herself.

Of course.

That was why Merlin did not think it was evil to bring King Uther to Queen Igraine's bed. Or to kill her husband Duke Gorlois, so that Uther could have Igraine. But it was cruel, it was wicked beyond belief. Igraine had been hoodwinked, blinded, betrayed, to lie with Uther while her husband was still alive. Then Uther gave

*her only thirteen suffering hours between the time he killed her
husband, and the day he married her.*

Arthur was born of this, the voices sang. *No wonder Amir
died.* She pondered hard, her slow thoughts struggling to
keep pace with the steady onward trudging of the horse's
hoofs. *Could a man like Arthur, ill-starred from birth with
adultery, rape and death, hope to make a good marriage, or keep
safe a child of sin?*

*A child of sin, yes, his father's sin that he could not escape.
But how was Amir sinful in himself?*

Why did he die?

Why?

Why?

'I didn't hear you, madam. What did you say?'

It was Ina, her face swollen and tearstained, riding
beside Guenevere huddled in a cloak. Guenevere stared at
her. What was Ina doing here, with this guard of men? And
why was she looking at her like that? 'I didn't say anything,
Ina. Did you hear a voice? What did it say?'

Ina bit her lip. 'I thought you were speaking to me,
madam. You were crying and singing a little while ago. I
must have been mistaken, forgive me.'

'Forgive him? No, tell the King, I never will forgive.
I will not look upon his face again. Your face is wet, is it
raining? You're shivering, why has it gone so cold? Do you
know where we are? Are we far from home?'

It was cold on the boat, and the night was very dark. But
she knew the call of the marshfowl on the Lake, and the
silver glow of the sky. Now she could smell the apple
blossom as it breathed from the orchards above the lake,
she could see the stone jetty beckoning, and the small
figure holding aloft the lantern as it shone through the
night.

'Can you manage, lady?' Ina breathed, as she took Guenevere's arm.

Guenevere laughed like a simpleton. 'Manage? Of course I can manage! D'you think I don't know my own way home?'

Avalon, Avalon, home . . .

She was in a narrow bed in a white cell, just as she had been as a girl so long ago. They all came to her there as she lay in her waking sleep, King Leogrance her father, Taliesin, even Malgaunt, standing by her bed with eyes of burning hate. She knew she should tell Malgaunt not to hate Arthur, but she did not think she would.

She laughed instead. 'Kill him,' she said. 'Why don't you kill him for me, Malgaunt? He killed Amir.'

Then there were hushing sounds and shocked apologies, but not from her mouth.

One day she travelled to Merlin in his cell. He lay on his dragon couch in the healing hollow of his crystal cave, and a million shafts of light lit his amber eyes. He raised his hand to welcome her spirit shape, and conversed with a gentleness she never knew before.

'So your body recovers, does it, Guenevere?' he said. 'Give your heart time, it will take longer to make that well.'

Through his eyes she could see herself sleeping in her bed in her own cell, stretched out like an effigy on a tomb. She could look into her body and see her suffering heart oozing with pain, weeping the tears that her eyes would never shed. Merlin looked with her, and sighed. 'Well, well,' he said. 'Well, well.'

'It is not well.'

She did not know the broken voice that issued from her mouth. She only knew that she had to challenge him, force

him to see the vast evil he had done, before she killed him
to revenge Amir's death.

'You killed Amir.'

Merlin smiled sadly. 'I did not, Guenevere.'

She snorted with disgust. *'Liar! And murderer!'*

'So!' Merlin heaved a half-sigh. 'I killed Amir?'

'You practised against him with your evil art.'

Merlin nodded. 'So!'

'You told the Saxons Arthur would bring his son.'

He nodded again. 'It is true that they knew to lie in wait
for him.'

'And they killed him. But you aimed their spears.'

Was it her madness, or the singing in her ears? But
Merlin's voice rang out low and true. 'That is one story,
Guenevere. But hear another before you depart.'

She could feel her will failing as his words rolled round
her ears. Her body was feeling its emptiness, the white form
on the bed was drawing her spirit back. *Hold on!* she told
herself in desperation as Merlin spoke. *You have challenged
the old villain, he must not escape now!*

And still Merlin's voice tolled darkly like a passing
bell.

'Think what you have known about me since you first
knew Arthur's name.' Inside the still chamber, dazzling
fragments of light played around Merlin's head. 'One thing,
above all, I think men would say of me.' He paused, and a
touch of the old Merlin flashed out in a crooked grin. 'You
never loved me, Guenevere. With good reason, since we
fought for Arthur's soul. And I fought without scruple,
without mercy, I will confess. But one thing in my life has
given it truth and dignity. I have loved Arthur, more than
life itself.'

He loved Arthur, yes, her fading spirit unwillingly acknowledged it. *But hold on, hold on, there is more to come.*

'And I love him still,' the singing hum went on. 'I would never have schemed against the son he loved. I would have given my own life to spare him pain. I did not kill Amir.'

'*You did! You did!*'

'No, Guenevere. And I suffer too. My poor Arthur is now at the worst time of his young life. But no grief lasts for ever. He has lands to conquer, hearts to win, and years to reign. I have seen his destiny, and he will be High King. He will recover, through me and my love.'

A whispering sigh filled the cave and echoed through the earth. 'And when he does, I shall recover too. He will rise and come again, and so shall I. When the sleepers awake, Merlin will rise with them.'

She could feel his power soaring to the climax of his song.

'Ask yourself then why I should kill Amir. The beloved son of the man I most love was a son again to me.'

She was fading now from his sight and her own, losing her senses as the world grew dim. But Merlin's voice strengthened till it thundered through the cell. 'Because you were sick with self-love, Guenevere, you thought that Amir was yours alone. And because I hated you, you thought I must hate him. But I love Arthur, and he was Arthur's son.' His voice was hissing now. 'Ask yourself then, why would I kill Amir?'

One fragile howl escaped her tortured lungs. '*Then who did?*'

'Ah!' Merlin's golden eyes had shrunk to pinpoints of black. 'Who indeed?'

When she awoke, she was lying in her bed. There was no sign that she had ever left it to visit Merlin in his crystal cave.

For a long time then she did not know if it was night or day. Around her, Maidens came and went on silent feet. They gave her potions in a silver cup, and fed her on sweet fumes when she could not eat. They gave her blessed oblivion from strange flasks, and then the voices in her head would sleep a little too. Yet all the time she knew that he was dead.

'*Amir!*'

They said she howled like a dog and knocked her head against the white stones of the wall. One day she awoke and her mouth was full of blood. Another time she found scratches on her face and breasts, and they told her she was wailing in the night. But she had dreamed a black cat squatted on her chest, hissing and spitting, and its claws slashed her flesh. And still the pain went on.

Then she dreamed of Amir; he came to her every night. He stood by her bed in the cool pale cell with his clear gaze and Otherworldly air. She could see his warm, sturdy little body, the sideways tilt of his head, his bright hair and loving smile. He would come to her, it would be as it was before, but as soon as she reached out to hold him in her arms, he would fade away.

And always there were the messengers at the door speaking in the voices of Gawain, Kay, Lucan or Bedivere, and Ina answering them.

'No, no, she will not see you, she is not well enough to see anyone.'

'The King says—'

'The Queen has forbidden us to hear what he says.'

'He has sent a hundred messengers, how many more must he send?'

'The Queen says she will never hear from him again.'

'Would she want him to turn to the Christians? They are all around him now like flies around a corpse.'

'The Queen will not care.'

'But she has no idea how he suffers, without his wife, without his son. Gods above, he's going mad!'

'Sir—'

She could hear Ina choosing her words with care. 'The Queen my lady is already mad – as any woman would be, whose husband killed her son.'

One day she awoke to a scent she thought she knew. One of the Maidens of the Lady was setting a posy of pale mauve sweet-faced flowers beside her bed. She touched them wonderingly. 'Violets? In December?'

The Maiden shook her head. 'Oh, my lady, it's not December any more. You have been here longer than you think. The snowdrops have come and gone, and the violets are in bloom.'

Nemue entered as she spoke. 'Spring is here, Guenevere. The Lady will see you now.'

CHAPTER 41

They carried her in a chair down the steps of the little white guest-house, over the greening grass. Daisies and buttercups nodded along the way, and silver-pink apple blossom arched above her head. She could hear the drowsy coo of doves, and see their white wings fluttering in every tree. Had Amir gone with them? Had his white soul taken wing and fled to the sky?

The Lady's house was warm, and her dragon-lamps were glowing with golden fire. As the attendants brought Guenevere in, the dogs howled mournfully, and the leader padded forward to lay his heavy red head on her lap. As soon as they were alone the Lady put back her veil and spoke, leaning forward on her throne. 'There are no words for your sorrow, Guenevere. But try to accept our love.'

Guenevere bowed her head.

'And first you must know how Amir died.'

'No! I—'

The Lady's voice was like the storm on the mountain-top. 'You must know. The first troop of Saxons was only a decoy. While Arthur attacked them, a whole war-band fell on the group he left to guard Amir.' She paused, and seemed to be choosing her words with care. 'It was as if they knew that the King's son would be there.'

Guenevere moaned with pain. 'But still he should have lived! Gawain and the others were there to defend him to the death.'

The Lady sighed. 'Oh, they tried. You did not see their wounds. But they did not see the Saxon spear that took Amir's life.' She drew a harsh breath. 'The dog who killed him died the next second, transfixed by all their spears. Then their greatest fight was to save Amir's body and bring him safe away for burial.'

Guenevere nodded, wild with pain. She knew how the horned men loved to spreadeagle the bodies of monks on their own church roofs, play football with babies cut from their mothers' wombs, and make cups out of captives' heads. And her child lay in the cold sand where she could never hold him, never make him warm again. 'But Amir . . .'

'. . . rests in the arms of the Mother, washed by the sea, just as he slept in the waters of life when he grew inside your womb.'

There was a long pause. Somewhere in the silence Guenevere heard herself weeping, and could not stop.

She tried to draw a breath. 'Lady, can I stay here on Avalon with you? My other life is over.' A fleeting vision blinded her eyes, Amir's tower room in the palace, with his painted wooden horse, his scattered toys and truckle bed. 'I can never go back to Camelot again.'

The Lady nodded. 'You have had this dream since your girlhood I think. To live the life of joy and prayer and peace here on Avalon, attended only by Maidens and by the men we choose?'

'Yes!' Guenevere cried. 'And to serve the Goddess!' She was sobbing hopelessly now. 'And who better to serve the Mother than a woman who will never be a mother again?'

'Never is too long a word to say.'

'Never!' She wept. 'My life with Arthur is over. Let me join you here!'

The Lady paused. 'Is that your only question? You have something else to ask of me, I think.'

Guenevere could hardly speak. 'I must see Amir – one last time, if no more. When my mother died, I heard her and saw her, walking between the worlds. But Amir . . .'

The Lady raised her hand. The inner door opened, and four Maidens appeared carrying a great bowl made of oak. Gnarled and black with age, it was filled with water that seemed to tremble with a life of its own. Guenevere rose from her chair, took a few weak paces forward, and fell to her knees.

As the maidens set it down, the black water became as still as a mirror. The oak bowl whispered to itself in its shining depths. The Lady stood across from Guenevere, staring intently into the shimmering water, touching her clasped hands to her forehead, then to her lips, and last to her breast.

'Come!' she called softly. 'Amir, hear us, come!'

Half singing, half chanting, she began the words of power. The light in the dragon-lamps flickered and grew dim, and the fire sank down on the hearth. Even the dogs stretched out and did not stir, cast into a twilight sleep. Guenevere watched the oak bowl with her heart in her eyes, reaching out, craving for a sign. The water was clear now, and as black as the heart of the marsh, where the bog waits to drag down the unwary to their deaths.

Blackness and silence, still water, emptiness. She could not bear it. 'There is nothing there!'

'Patience!'

The Lady raised her hand and cast something into the bowl. The water hissed and gurgled, and began to seethe in shades of black and green. When it settled again, there was a film on the surface, and shapes moving across it as if on the landscape of the moon.

'Amir, come!' the Lady crooned again. She leaned towards Guenevere. 'What do you see?'

Guenevere strained till she felt that her eyeballs would burst. 'Nothing!' she wept.

'Look again.'

This time, as she looked, she saw the mists swirling through the world between the worlds. A host of white stars shone brightly in the skies, all the children of the Goddess taken home before their time. But which was Amir?

'*Amir!*'

She called his name again and again. The stars twinkled on.

'Amir, Amir!' she cried. He was not there.

Now dark clouds were boiling up through the pale wraiths of mist, great swollen billows, yellow and purple and black.

'It is coming,' the Lady murmured, watching the bowl intently as the storm gathered, and darkness filled the sky. Now a high wind was bending the tops of the trees, and lightning split the night. Then the skies opened, and rain fell in torrents from the threatening sky. And through the dark came a small figure, weeping and alone.

He was far away, and she could not see his face. His head was bent into the wind and rain, and his shoulders shook with sobs. But he was worlds away, and she could not comfort him.

'*Amir!*'

The Lady held up her hand: 'Watch, and see!'

The surface of the water shivered, and he was gone. Now four other figures galloped into view through the storm-tossed clouds, all muffled against the weather but riding for their lives.

Guenevere stared in disbelief. 'It's Arthur's knights!' she cried. 'Gawain, Kay, Lucan and Bedivere! But where are they going? And why are they so small?'

'Watch!' The Lady laid her finger on her lips.

The four horsemen galloped on through the dark. She watched them pass through petrified forests, and over dead mountains where undead things escaped from their graves, and lived. They crossed the old Roman roads still carved into the landscape centuries after those who made them marched away and died. From there they took to the lanes, then to the greenways, and then to the single tracks. And at last they came to a valley where the road ended in a place of no return.

A dark castle stood there, deep in the valley's end. As they raced towards it, one lone horseman, a solitary figure as heavily muffled as they were, rode out of the castle to meet them, one upraised arm pointing back the way they had come. All four pulled their horses round at once, and fell into place behind the solitary rider. And now all five were galloping back, riding furiously into the mist until the darkness swallowed them up.

Then came a crying without words, and the first small figure was there again, walking and weeping and hiding his eyes. Now he was wandering in a living forest, and the rain beat down through its leafless branches as he moved sobbing through the trees. As he passed by, some of them tried to catch him, leaning down to enfold him in their grasp. One in particular wound its slender long black limbs around the small helpless form, and Guenevere thought it smiled to itself with a woman's secret smile.

She opened her mouth in dread. The Lady shook her head.

'For the third time, watch!' she warned.

The dark forest and the small figure dissolved. The

water in the oak bowl rolled over sluggishly, and settled back to an oily, sullen sheen. Guenevere's soul seethed with anger in her breast. It was all over, and she had seen nothing. It was a fraud. She had been deceived.

But the water quivered again, and seemed to sculpt itself now into more powerful shapes. She saw Arthur's city on the hill-top, then the castle of Caerleon itself. She saw the five riders gallop into the courtyard, and a moment later, all five tiny figures were racing into the palace, hot on some quest.

Four of them ran to the King's private quarters, where Arthur would surely be. But the fifth, the muffled rider from the hidden valley, turned another way and made for the chapel where the kings of Caerleon had kept their devotions since turning to Christ.

Now Guenevere was inside the chapel, looking down on an altar lit by two great candles in tall stands of brass. The choir stalls were filled with black-robed monks, their heads bent in prayer, and a solitary priest knelt at the altar praying too. Below the altar, the small figure she looked so hard for lay face down on the floor, arms and legs stretched out in the shape of a cross.

'Amir!' she screamed.

What was he doing there? He had died in the east, he had been buried on the Saxon shore.

Inside the chapel the candle flames leaped up shivering. The newcomer approached Amir as he lay on the ground, but as in a dream, both figures were the same size now. The stranger leaned down and placed a hand on Amir's shoulder as if to comfort him, less like a knight now than a monkish figure muffled up in black. And the prostrate figure started and came to life, and it was not Amir but Arthur after all.

Arthur, oh, my love . . .

Arthur but not Arthur, a grey-faced stranger, gaunt and raving-wild.

'You!' he cried to the stranger with a mad laugh. 'What are you doing here?'

Against Arthur, the knight was short, and slightly built. But the voice was harsh and strong, and Guenevere knew it as in a dream.

'What am I doing here? I am here for you.'

'God bless you!'

Arthur folded the newcomer in his arms, and crushed him to his chest. Then he burst out weeping, and pushed him away. 'You know—' a fit of passion shook him '—you know what I have done?'

'Oh, my good brother, hear the word of God. In the midst of life, you know we are in death.'

'*Goddess, Mother, no!*' Guenevere clutched at the Lady's hand. 'Is Arthur to be tormented by Christians at a time like this?'

The Lady's voice chimed like a death-knell. 'Watch and see!'

'Is this their Christian consolation,' Guenevere raged, 'this ranting talk of death? I know my child is born to live again! The crown of life is life again, not death! Why do they say that?'

She heard the stranger speak to Arthur as if in answer to her words. 'The Lord gives, and the Lord takes away.'

Arthur reached out and tenderly put back the newcomer's hood. 'Bless you, Morgan. Oh, thank God you've come!'

CHAPTER 42

There was a silence in the Lady's house. The water hissed sullenly as a green flame flickered round the bowl and died. Even the walls seemed to be holding their breath. Guenevere was dumb.

'So, Guenevere.' The Lady rose to her commanding height. 'Both of your questions are answered now. You are not to see Amir. The Mother has made him one of the star children in the sky, and which he is, you will never know. To love them all will be your duty now.'

'But I saw him – in the rain, in the woods—'

The Lady shook her head. 'The figure you saw was your husband, not your son,' she said gently. 'You were watching Arthur all along. You did not see Amir. And that answers your second request. It is a sign that you cannot be one of us here on Avalon. You have not been granted the power to see into the Beyond, not even to reach the one you love most.'

Grief overwhelmed her now. *Why not?*

'Oh, Guenevere,' the Lady smiled her oldest, saddest smile, 'it shows that you are wedded to the here and now. Your mind is chained to the man you thought you had cast off. Each time you thought you saw Amir in the oak water, it was Arthur whom you saw.'

'Tell me why!'

'Because he is still your husband. He is the man written on your heart, till your heart writes him out.'

'But I hate him! He killed Amir! Arthur is dead to me!'

The Lady paused. 'He is dead indeed, if you choose to punish him with your hate. It is death for a king to lose his closeness with the queen he has married, for she is the sovereignty of the land. And the end comes for Arthur when he loses you.'

Oh, Arthur, Arthur—

'But why is he mourning Amir among the Christians?' Guenevere cried wildly. 'And Morgan? What is she doing there?'

'What you saw happened a good while ago,' the Lady said very quietly. 'Arthur turned to the Christians when you left him alone. He fell into a sickness of the soul, and Gawain and the others were beside themselves with despair. So they rode to beg Morgan to come and care for him. She was ready for them, as you saw, and she went back with them.' She paused. 'You have been absent here for many months, Guenevere. And Morgan has been with him all the time.'

Guenevere was not listening. 'But why should she offer Christian consolation in Arthur's hour of need? She has no reason to love the Christians, after what they did to her!'

The Lady spread her hands. 'The Christians' is the only faith she knows.' She paused. 'And she loves Arthur. She is offering him the only solace that he has.'

Oh, Arthur, Arthur.

No one to comfort him, lying on the cold stone floor.

No one to love him, nowhere for him to turn.

'Oh, Arthur, oh, my love,' she wept. 'What are you going through all on your own?' A great sob crept up and racked her unawares.

The Lady's face was a mask of sorrow now. 'All suffer, all alike,' she said heavily. 'And all alone. Nemue has told you that the Christians are here with us too. We have a cell of them now on Avalon, holy men I thought, who would join their prayers to ours.'

She took a breath, and paced about the room. 'Well, our brothers in love have grown strong, even impudent. The first two were gentle, trusting souls. But then others came to join them, a different kind. Not content with their own simple cell, they wish to worship in our holy places now. They have even asked to use the sacred Hallows in their rituals.'

'The Hallows of the Goddess?' Guenevere gaped in disbelief.

'I have refused, of course,' the Lady said, her musical voice hitting its strongest note. 'But who knows how long it will be before they ask again – and how long before asking gives way to demanding, and demanding to taking by force?' She passed her hand over her eyes. 'The thought of it clouds my sight. Since they have been on Avalon, I do not see as well as I did before.' She made a moody gesture towards the bowl. 'This vision of Arthur is the last thing I saw, a good while ago now.'

Guenevere shook her head. The Lady sat brooding, then stirred and drew herself up. 'But that is no concern of yours, dear Guenevere. You have seen Arthur wandering in the darkness of his soul. Can you find it in yours to return to him again?'

'Oh, Lady, need you ask?' Guenevere struggled to her feet, cursing her weakness through her flowing tears. 'We shall be gone as soon as horses can be prepared. And, with luck, we'll reach Caerleon before the dawn of another day!'

Hour after hour as they rode, the same thoughts ran like

mice between her tormented mind and her over-burdened heart.

Arthur, Arthur, oh, my love—

How wrong it was, how cruel of me to leave you so!

I blamed you for Amir's death, and wanted you to suffer too. I wanted to cut you out of my life, never to see or hear of you again. If I had loved you truly, I would have thought of your grief, your pain, and tried to reach out to you. Well, it is not too late. I will be a true wife to you again, and we will comfort each other for the loss we have had.

I thought there would never be another child, never another Amir. But maybe we can still have the daughter we both dreamed, and even sons too. The Lady told me, 'Never' is the word I must not say.

Oh, my love, my love, let us see.

Let us try.

I will try.

Let us try.

They rode through the night at full pelt, Ina and Guenevere and their troop of men. Her riding legs had gone after so many weeks in bed and in the end she had to be tied to the saddle, but her horse was sure-footed, and she knew she would not fall.

A blazing fire of love warmed her all through the night.

Home.

They were going home.

Goddess, Mother, thanks—

Ina could have wept with joy. Blessed be the Goddess, the Queen had come to herself again. All her prayers, all her tears, all her care through these long weary months were rewarded now that the Queen had forgiven the King.

In between her prayers, she wanted to sing and dance.

'Think of it, madam, what a surprise for them to see us back!' she called out exultantly to Guenevere, pale and incandescent at her side. 'But above all for the King! How happy he will be!'

At the ferry they crossed the Severn Water with all the swiftness of a dream. Guenevere felt herself borne up by enchanted hands as they pressed on, never stopping all through the night.

They came to Caerleon at last, at the darkest hour, when even the gate-keepers were asleep. There was no sound in the sleeping castle as they slipped through the gatehouse past the astonished guard, and hurried indoors.

'It's almost dawn, my lady, it won't be long till you can wake the King,' Ina said excitedly, as they hastened up the stairs. 'Will you rest in the Queen's apartments till then? Shall I command hot water for a bath?'

'Neither!' Guenevere cried. She was weak and trembling, but she felt like a girl again creeping up on her lover in a game of blind man's buff. Gods above, she was only just beginning to realise how much she had missed Arthur all these cruel months!

She sped along the sleeping corridors in a frenzy of love.

Oh, Arthur, Arthur—

Both of them had forgotten kissing, she thought. Now she would surprise him as he slept, and wake him with both her hands over his eyes and a sweet kiss on his mouth. *We have been so long without kisses, without love for months, ever since I left.*

They turned into the corridor to the royal apartments. Guenevere laughed with joy to see the faces of the guards outside Arthur's door. Shock seemed to hold them rooted to the ground, then one began to gibber as if he had lost his mind. The other stumbled forward, and made a wild attempt to bar her approach.

'Don't you know me, guardsman?' she cried. 'Do you forbid the Queen access to the King?'

'No, Majesty, no!' the wretch stuttered, turning an ugly red. 'But I beg of you, let me go first, let me wake the King—'

His face was bulging, and tears stood in his eyes. What was wrong with the man? Behind her his fellow was muttering madly in Ina's ear. What had come over them all?

She took a step forward. 'Let me pass.'

Suddenly she felt Ina's hand pulling her back. 'Don't go in, lady!' she cried. 'The guard says – the King is – he's sick, did you say, soldier? There may be infection here.'

'Aye, madam, the plague, yes! Who knows?' gabbled the other, staring at the ground. And why was he too sweating like a pig?

Guenevere brushed them aside. 'The King will receive the Queen,' she said firmly, 'at any hour of the day or night.' She laughed in pure delight. She could feel love stirring in her heart for the first time since Amir died. 'He will rejoice that his wife has come safely home.'

She reached for the heavy double doors, and hurried through into the outer chamber where they had so often sat. And then she heard a sound, a low groaning from the bedchamber beyond, and Arthur calling, calling someone's name.

Oh, my love, my love!

Poor darling love, are you having nightmares, crying out in your sleep for me?

They were outside the bedroom and the sounds were louder now, and shorter and sharper too, rhythmic groans and cries. Now she could hear the accelerating pulse of grunts, and the sharp intake of breath.

What?

She raced forward and threw open the door.

Ahead of her stood the King's eight-poster bed of state, its huge canopy glowing with red and white, its gold swags and tassels gleaming in the light of the candle at the head. On the bed with his back towards them, surrounded by tumbled bedding, knelt Arthur, as naked as the day. As she watched he dropped forward, and sank and rose, and plunged again, his back and flanks straining in the act of love.

She could not look away. Her eyes were scalded by the sight of him, by his manly beauty, the wide shoulders and narrow waist, the well-made hips and tight buttocks clenching and relaxing with every groan and thrust. And beneath him on the bed she could see the body of a woman, and two long white female arms thrown back as Arthur's hard brown hands pinioned her and held her spreadeagled in the time-honoured posture of submission to a man. She could hear her too, hissing, *'Arthur, yes, yesss, Arthur! Arthur, yesss!'* like a cat on heat.

'ARTHUR!'

Her scream came from the bottom of her lungs. Arthur's head snapped back. His eyes froze in shock as his mouth opened in an answering scream.

But Guenevere's scream went on. For as he pulled back, she saw his partner in the bed. She lay there naked too, as naked as a needle, her breasts exposed, her mulberry nipples staring at Guenevere like savage eyes. Slowly her lips parted in a knowing grin. 'Well, Guenevere?' she seemed to be saying with her taunting gaze. 'What now?'

And Guenevere could not stop screaming her name.

CHAPTER 43

'*M*organ!'

She uncoiled her long lithe body like a snake. Stretching her arms, she arched her hips and writhed from side to side. Her black hair spilled across the pillow and down over her white shoulders, and she glared and glittered with evil beyond compare.

Arthur's whole body sagged, and he stumbled like a drunk from the bed. She rolled luxuriously in the space he left, spreading her knees and flashing her gaping sex. Her black eyes and red mouth, her purple nipples and the livid lips between her legs all stared at Guenevere. And still she was screaming, screaming out her name.

'*Morgan! Morgan! Morgan!*'

'My lady, don't – don't take on so! You'll make yourself ill again.'

Ina tried to take Guenevere by the arm, weeping with fear. Morgan's gaze flickered over both of them, then returned to Guenevere. She lay back on the pillow, and calmly tortured her with her gaze. Ina was right, Guenevere told herself madly, she must be calm. She had to be as cool as Morgan, or she would go mad.

Arthur was still standing by the bed. His face was flushed, and there was no spark of recognition in his eyes.

His hands were twitching at the blanket he had fumbled up round his loins.

Goddess, Mother, what has she done to him?

A shaft of memory stabbed Guenevere like a knife. She saw another man standing like this by a bed, raw and exposed. She saw Merlin caught in the same attitude of shame, beside this same woman, with the same look of terror on his face.

'Arthur!' she cried to him from her soul. 'Arthur, speak to her, tell her to go!'

'Go where?' said Arthur oddly, cocking his head on one side. 'She lives here now. Guenevere went away.'

Ye Gods, was he mad too?

She ran to him and struck him in the face. 'Arthur, I am Guenevere! I am your wife, and this whore of yours must go!'

'Morgan?' He gave a small wild laugh. 'You can't mean Morgan, she's my sister, she's not a whore. She told me that in all the old faiths, as far back as the land of Egypt, brothers and sisters ruled together for the good of the land. They became Gods, and shared the finest love.'

'Love?' Guenevere screamed. 'Arthur, she doesn't love you, she hates you, can't you see? She is punishing you for what your father did to her mother, and to her. This is her revenge – and Merlin was the first!'

'Merlin, yesss!'

There was an animal hissing from the bed. Guenevere shook her head and tried to blot it out. 'She trapped Merlin, and destroyed his life just as he ruined hers. And with Merlin out of the way, you were next!'

Try as she could, she could not stop herself from glancing at Morgan now. Morgan smiled an ancient, evil smile. Her midnight eyes were saying, *Yes, and you were next.*

She lay there taunting Guenevere, laughing at her

humiliation and her shame. Guenevere raised her fists and bore down on the bed. 'Get out!' she screamed. 'Get out!'

'Arthur, help me!' Morgan wailed, cowering down in the bed.

He came from behind, gripped Guenevere by the arms, and dragged her away. She called frantically to Ina at the door. 'Run, Ina, run for Gawain and the others! Say the Queen's life is in danger!'

Morgan leaned forward and fixed Ina with a glare. *'Don't move!'* she hissed. She raised a finger and pointed, muttering under her breath.

Ina's eyes bulged with fear, but she turned and ran.

'So, Morgan!' Guenevere cried viciously. 'Now we shall see who is Queen here!'

Morgan sat up swiftly, and reached for a robe. *Blue silk, with sleeves like harebells,* Guenevere noted dully, *fit for a queen.* Arthur had given it to her after Amir was born. Was there anything of hers Morgan had not had?

Like a man in a dream, Arthur took a robe and covered himself too. He moved as if he did not know where he was. Had she drugged him, had she enchanted him, what?

Guenevere reached out to him. 'Arthur, listen to me!'

Arthur shook his head. 'Are you really Guenevere?' He sounded like a child.

'Of course I am!'

Morgan snickered softly in the bed.

'You came back once before,' he said wonderingly, trying to touch her hair. 'You came in the night, and told me you would never come back to me again.'

What was he saying? Guenevere beat his hand away, and clutched at her head. Had her spirit left her body on Avalon; and come here to curse Arthur with the hatred she felt then? Or was it an apparition he had seen, some magic made by Morgan to bring Arthur into her power?

She grabbed Arthur by the arm. 'Arthur, I never came to you at night! She must have told you that. And you believed her – because you wanted her!'

She could hardly speak for the stabbing in her heart. The tears were streaming down. 'Arthur, *why*? Why did you do this? You killed Amir, did you have to kill me too?'

Arthur started violently. 'Don't say that!' he howled. He pointed to the figure in the bed. 'She never talked about him! She helped me to forget!'

She helped him to forget.

Guenevere looked at the figure on the bed. Her skin was white against the deep blue of the robe, and her huge black eyes were fixed on Arthur, drinking him in. With her raven hair tumbled down around her shoulders, her slender body still carelessly displayed and her long bare legs, she was a prize for any man alive.

Guenevere laughed savagely. And she had wondered how Morgan enchanted him? With no more than the oldest power of all, she thought with bitter grief, the trick of leading a man by what lies between his legs.

And she had been forced to see it, watch her own husband stripped and degraded in the act of lust! Loathing for Morgan rose like vomit in her throat. She clutched her stomach and tried to hold it down. 'For the last time, Arthur,' she wept to him, '*tell her to go!*'

But he stood there wavering, torn between them both. He could not choose. Something died in the depths of Guenevere's heart. And she knew that, like Amir, it would never come again.

'My lord!'

'Save the Queen!'

From far off came the sound of pounding feet. Gawain, Kay, Lucan and Bedivere burst through the door with their swords drawn, their faces half-way between sleep and wild alarm, their clothes thrown on in the heat of flight.

'What's happening, my lady?' Gawain cried. In the next moment, all four of them caught sight of Morgan in the bed.

Dear Gods! thought Kay in blind horror. He looked at Arthur in wild disbelief. Then the next thought came with a dull recognition of something seen and not observed, observed and only partly understood: Why am I not surprised?

The King's sister! shot through three other heads at once. Morgan was hastily swinging her long legs to the floor and dragging her robe around her nakedness, but there could be no mistaking what she was doing there. Gawain flushed crimson, and recoiled. Bedivere covered his face, and turned away. And Lucan was staring at Morgan as if the sight of her scalded his eyes.

'*Get her out!* She has no right to be here, get her out of my sight!' Weeping, Guenevere pointed to Morgan.

Why did they all stand there like men of stone? Why did they look at Arthur, and not at her?

'What are you waiting for?' she screamed. 'I ordered you to get this woman out! Now – at once!'

Kay turned to Arthur. 'Sir!' he begged furiously. 'Tell us what to do!'

'Lucan!' Guenevere moaned. 'You are the Queen's knight, do my bidding now!'

Lucan did not move.

'*Lucan!*'

Why was Kay looking at her as if she was mad? His hand was twitching as if he wanted to slap her face. 'You forget, madam,' he cut in harshly, 'he serves the King now too.'

Guenevere flinched under Kay's jaundiced glare. Her will collapsed. 'Gods above, is there no man I can trust?'

The silence was the silence of a tomb. Morgan straightened herself up, drew her robe together, and slid towards the door.

'I am sorry you were troubled, gentlemen,' she said huskily, lowering her eyes. 'I am here only for the King, you all know that. I would not have had this happen for the world.'

And suddenly she was leaving with soft words and false apologies, flaunting her injured innocence to the world, as if the whole thing were no fault of hers at all. Guenevere stared. *Here with my husband, rutting in my bed?* It was all too much to bear.

'Morgan!' she howled. 'I know you, Morgan, I know all you have done!'

'Oh, not all, Lady Guenevere, not all.'

Lucan was pacing towards Morgan, gripping his sword. 'In the King's bed, traitress?' he shouted, in a voice thick with pain. 'You were my lady, and I honoured you! I wore your favour in the tournament, and loved you only, all these weary months. And all the time—'

Morgan bit her lip, and tried to hold him in her gaze. 'Lucan—'

But he was blind and deaf to her now. 'You told me the King would be angry that I dared to love his sister! You lay in my arms and swore our time would come—'

Morgan's white face gleamed in the darkness like one of the undead. 'Hold your tongue, fool!'

Lucan was in agony. 'I thought you were mine! I gave you all I had, body and soul!'

'What?' Arthur stirred like a man awakening from a dream. He looked at Morgan in wild disbelief. 'You told me I was the only one you ever loved. You said I was the first man in your bed. You said our love was more than life itself.'

'"Fairer than the morning and the evening star"?'
Lucan's eyes glittered with unshed tears

Arthur gaped. 'She said that to you?'

Morgan passed her tongue over her lips, casting around
like a wildcat in a trap.

Guenevere grabbed at Arthur again. 'Remember Merlin!' she cried out to him. 'She made us think he raped her!
Do you still think that now?'

Arthur looked at her in horror. 'What?'

'Ask her!'

'It's a lie!' Morgan rasped, huddled by the door.
'Guenevere hates me – she made it up!'

Lucan gave a savage laugh in Arthur's face. 'Do you
believe that?'

Arthur clutched his head, and howled like a dog. 'She
destroyed Merlin! What else has she done?'

'More than you know, my lord.'

Lucan was sweating, his face covered in a thin sheen
like rain. 'Remember the tournament? The sword of Sir
Griflet flying through the air, that almost killed you, till
I turned it away?' He raised his own sword and pointed
it at Morgan's throat. 'My guess is that your power, lady,
sent it on its way – unless I am mad too?'

Morgan gave a scornful laugh, her eyes glittering with
black fire. Guenevere watched the pinpoints round Morgan's
pupils flashing to and fro. Then she seemed to be watching
one point above all, deadlier than all the rest.

It was the tip of a blade sliding through the dark, the
point of a spear. And now she saw it slipping unnoticed
through a ring of swords all clustered round her son. She
saw it pierce his chest, and find his heart. She heard him
scream, and then she watched him die. She saw the blow
that killed Amir in Morgan's eyes.

'Amir!'

Guenevere ran to Arthur and clutched him by the arm. 'Arthur, she killed Amir!' she babbled. 'You said it was as if the Saxons knew you would be there!'

Arthur looked at her, and she saw his eyes take fire. Madly she ran on. 'She foresaw Amir's death!'

Her mind whirled back to the scene in the nursery when Amir was born. What was it Morgan said then? The husky voice wove back to her through the mists of time. *He is one of the spirit children*, Morgan had said, with a strange laugh. *He will be among the stars, the Mother will take him to Her—*

And she, Amir's mother, had been pleased at this? She had taken Morgan's words as a compliment to her son?

'*Fool!*' Guenevere screamed, as the force of her seeing hit home. If Morgan had foreseen Amir's death, had she created it too? Had she found a way to use the Saxon hordes as her instrument of revenge? Guenevere reeled. *Of course she had. Why else should he die?*

She turned back to Arthur, flooded by certainty. 'She told the Saxons that you were coming with your son. She led them to you, she bribed them to kill Amir. And she used her magic to make their spears strike home.'

A deathly silence settled on the room. Now, for the first time, Morgan looked afraid. 'Lies!' she screeched. 'All lies!'

'Look at her!' Guenevere could not help herself. She wanted to tear Morgan open, and eat her heart. 'Her guilt is in her face! It was her black art guiding the Saxons there. Her power riding on the point of that spear!'

She killed Amir—

The thought burst like a thunderclap through the small room. Morgan shrank into herself, pitifully shaking her head. 'Arthur,' she appealed, 'listen to me?' She held out her arms to him. 'Remember what we have done! We are the royal kin, brother, born to reign.'

'Born to die, she-wolf!'

Arthur leaped forward, tore Gawain's sword from his hand and made for Morgan, swinging the weapon round his head. *'You killed Amir!'*

Lucan was behind him, his sword outstretched too. 'Die, Morgan!' he screamed, tears pouring from his eyes. 'Before you betray more men!'

Gawain surged into the fray, pulling his dagger from his belt. 'Kill the witch!' he bawled.

Gods above, they had all gone mad now! Kay hurled himself forward and tore at Arthur's arm. 'Sire, hold your sword!'

'My lord!' Bedivere leaped between Morgan and her assailants, barring their way. 'You may not kill a woman! This is wrong!'

Arthur fell back sweating, his face alight with a sickly gleam. He dropped his head, and covered his eyes with his hand. 'Get her out of here!'

'And take her to imprisonment?' Gawain's voice was as harsh as Guenevere could desire. Arthur nodded, his back turned and shoulders bowed.

Gawain strode forward and gripped Morgan by the arm. 'This way, Princess,' he said, with savage satisfaction, as he hustled her out. 'Guards, ho! Form an escort there!'

The sound of tramping feet died away. Lucan fell to his knees and buried his face in his hands. Kay threw an uneasy glance after Morgan and Gawain. A son of the Orkneys was not the man to remember his chivalry where women were concerned. 'What are your orders, sire? What's to be done?'

Arthur shook his head. 'She has done cruel wrongs!' he mourned hopelessly.

'She's a witch,' Kay said shortly, 'a queen of the blackest arts known in hell!'

'Then she must face the course of law,' Bedivere came in.

'And if she's guilty, she'll pay the price.' Kay nodded. 'She'll go to the fire.'

'The fire?'

Guenevere's flesh crawled. Suddenly she saw a black stake outlined against the sun, and flames licking round it, leaping to the sky. A female figure was writhing in the heart of the torment, burning to death. She heard the woman's screams as her hair caught fire, and her skin crackled and burst. The smell of burning flesh choked the air, and now Guenevere was scorching too. Why was she suffering this sight? *'No!'* she screamed. 'Whatever she's done, no woman deserves that death!'

'If she's wronged the King, bewitched him to her bed, killed Amir—' Kay began hotly.

'Then the King will take counsel, when he has come to himself again.' Bedivere's voice was firm. 'And the King will know what to do.'

Arthur shuddered wildly. 'The King?' he said. 'Ahh – the King.' He looked at Guenevere with a wild childish air. 'Will he, Guenevere? Will he know what to do?'

CHAPTER 44

In the throne room of Caerleon, the air was heavy with the heat of the August sun. Every flagstone was filmed with sweat, and the knights' banners drooped from the black beams of the roof. High on the dais Guenevere sat enthroned beside Arthur as he glared down the hall. Her soul gasped for a breath of woodland air, a sweet green space, clean and unprofaned. And a clear call fell softly through her mind: *Come – come away . . .*

In the body of the hall, King Ursien of Gore stood his ground and returned Arthur's gaze unabashed. 'A strange request, Your Majesty.'

Arthur laughed. 'It's not like you to play the coward, man!' he said unpleasantly. 'What are you saying, too rich for your blood?'

Goddess, Mother, what was he doing? Was he trying to give King Ursien offence? Guenevere turned away her head. She no longer knew what Arthur did, or why. But they were still King and Queen, and there was no way out of that.

'Whatever you say, sire.'

Shrewd as ever, King Ursien would not be rushed. He had hurried south as soon as Arthur summoned him, travelling from Gore with all his sons and a train of knights and men. Like a loyal vassal, he was ready to do whatever his lord required. But even Ursien could not have known beforehand what Arthur would ask of him now.

To the left of Arthur's throne, caught in a slanting shaft of sun, Morgan waited under heavy guard. On either side of her, two of Arthur's younger knights stood nervously to attention, overawed by the occasion and the breathless scrutiny of the silent, watchful court. Impassively Morgan stared through them all, a black cloak clasped tightly round her in spite of the heat.

'You'll not find me ungenerous,' Arthur resumed. He glanced at Ursien's sons standing in his father's train. 'Your oldest son is soon to be knighted, is he not? I'll see they all do well.'

Ursien stroked his grizzled beard and bowed. 'Your Majesty is the most generous lord alive.'

And that is not the question, his keen glance said. The question is, why do you seek this service of me now?

He would have heard the gossip, Guenevere knew. Within minutes it had been all round the court: the King's sister, the Princess Morgan, was in the King's bed when the Queen came back!

It did not matter how the tale spread, who whispered it where, who hastened to pass it on, but by the next morning, all Caerleon knew. And by the next day, every ear in the kingdom had heard of her misery and Arthur's shame.

And they would know that no matter how the King begged and wept, the Queen would not hear him, would not speak to him, would not return to his bed, but took to her own apartments that same night. In the weeks that had followed, all the court had to deal with two separate households, the Queen's and the King's. For nothing could reconcile her to Arthur now.

She had listened calmly enough as Gawain told her that Arthur was not to blame.

'You're wasting your time, man!' Kay snapped furiously as soon as he knew that Gawain would speak to the Queen. Gods' blood, couldn't the great fool see that the Queen was not a woman to take an insult, like this?

But Gawain had pressed on. It had all been his idea, he swore on his knees in the Queen's chamber, his and the other knights, to bring Morgan to Arthur while she was away. How were they to know she would turn out to be a witch?

'On the honour of a knight, I beg you to think again, madam,' Gawain said angrily. 'You must forgive the King!'

Kay gritted his teeth. That was not the way to win a woman like Guenevere, and 'must' was not a word a queen would obey. But, for Arthur's sake, he could only hope that Gawain might be right. Against all his inclinations, Kay stepped in to back him up. 'Remember, madam, you never saw the King in his despair.'

His sharp tone left Guenevere in no doubt whom he blamed for that. 'When you abandoned him, we feared for his mind.' He eyed her sourly. 'He beat himself, and tore his flesh till it bled. We had to get whatever help we could.'

'What Sir Kay says is true, my lady.'

Eagerly Lucan and Bedivere added their pleas too. Bedivere wept to remember their fears for Arthur when they rode through the storm to Le Val Sans Retour. 'It took us so long to find the King's sister in the hidden valley that we thought he'd be dead by the time we got back.'

Lucan knelt to her too, just as Gawain had. Guenevere looked at him, and marvelled coldly at what she saw. *Lucan? The Queen's champion, on his knees for Arthur now? God, how these men loved him*! Arthur had deceived his own wife and Lucan's queen, and had taken Lucan's lady for himself. Yet Lucan still set aside his own hurt and loss in the service of a king who had betrayed them both. 'Lady, forgive!' he implored.

But she would not.

She had watched their whole journey in the Lady's seeing-bowl, and she knew they told the truth. But it made no difference, she told them, and she sent them away.

Then Arthur had come, as bleak as a mountain crag, and told her that he would take his life, if she wanted that. But all she wanted was to know how she had lost him to Morgan.

'Did she work on you with spells, with potions, what?' Guenevere had begged in anguish. 'Tell me the enchantments she used!'

He set his jaw like a trap. 'I have sworn an oath never to speak of her.'

'Go then!' she screamed. 'And never speak to me till you can!'

So he kept to his apartments, and she to hers.

Then one night very late he came again, calmer and more himself, ready to break his oath. For her, for their marriage, to set his mind at rest, he would tell her all he knew. Morgan had found him in the chapel, he said, as cold as the stones he was lying on, praying to die.

She had taken him to her chamber, warmed him and stroked his head, and listened while he talked about Amir. She lit a fire there that burned all by itself, and gave off a fume that made his pain seem less. She ordered food to help him to eat again, and fed him with her own hand. She made a potion from wine and rare herbs, and together they drank to the brother and sister Gods.

'And there was more,' he said dully. 'Things she could do. Skills she had, words of power—'

Guenevere could not help herself. 'The skills of the whorehouse!'

Arthur flinched.

Skills and words.

Her skills and words must have been better than mine.

'What can I do,' Arthur had implored her, weeping, on his knees, 'to make you forgive me and love me again?'

And she dismissed him with one word. 'Nothing!'

But his nature would not let him live by that. So he came to her doggedly day in, day out, to do what he could. The least hint would suffice. 'Tell me what to do!'

She could not tell him. Morgan came between them every day. If she was proved a traitor to the King, Kay had said, she would burn. She would burn twice over if she proved to be a witch. But who would send a princess to the fire?

And it came to Guenevere: *she will never be tried for the evil she has done.* Morgan would never be brought to account for her plots against Merlin, against Arthur, against her, against Amir. Arthur was blind with shame at what he had done. He would not have his humiliation dragged out in open court, even though it meant that Morgan would go scot-free.

Guenevere laughed at him then, like a witch herself.

'You offer me your life, which is nothing to me!' she shouted in his face. 'And you spare hers, when she killed Amir!' A murderous fury seethed inside her now. 'If she lives, what will you do with her? Have her living here as the King's sister, just as before?'

'No! Things can never be as they were before!'

'Oh, you see that now, do you?'

The eternal cry of the unfaithful man, too late, too late!

Gods above, why could she not talk to him without floods of tears? 'If you don't know what to do with her, give her to me! She killed Amir! I'll kill her for you. I know what to do!'

'*No!*' Now it was Arthur's turn to weep. 'I will dispose of her!'

'You won't! You still love her!'

'I never loved her! But I will take care of my own flesh and blood!'

The bitter arguments went to and fro. Then one night he came with a strange look on his face. 'If Morgan could be married,' he said slowly, 'into a far-away country, given to a good man, one strong enough to keep her down . . .' He paused. 'There are young knights here I could spare to go with her, to guard her for him – Sir Geras, Sir Accolon.'

Guenevere could not believe it. 'Who would take her on terms like these?'

'King Ursien of Gore,' said Arthur, expelling a heavy sigh. 'He is a widower, and free to marry again. He has growing sons, so he will be looking for ways and means to bring them on. The dowry of a princess would do well for him now. He is an old soldier, and he knows the world. So he will not be tricked into taking Morgan's poison as easily.'

As you did! Guenevere's heart cried.

Arthur swallowed hard. 'And Ursien will be loyal to me, come what may. He has no fear of threats or hot words, so he will know how to keep down a witch! She'll be forced to behave.'

Forced to live in a marriage like a prison? Guenevere thought in horror. Yet what was she doing herself, if not just that? And again and again the call of the woodland sounded in her head: *Come away!*

For the very sight of Arthur tormented her now. She was married to a man she could not leave, forced to endure a husband she could not bear.

Yet Arthur himself presented no threat to her. As a man and a king, the Arthur she knew had died. It was the ghost of Arthur who stalked the corridors of Caerleon and sat beside her on the dais in the hall. And as they played their roles as Caerleon's Queen and King, it was cold and hollow pageantry now that love had fled.

And still Morgan haunted her every waking hour with the everlasting *how* and *why*.

How?

Why?

She thought of the time when Ina cast the runes, and Morgan read how they fell. At the tournament, too, she had known words of power that Guenevere had never heard and, like a fool, had thought that Morgan was only using them to keep Arthur safe.

Where did she learn the art of divination?

Where did she get to know the words of power?

When Arthur tormented her with 'What can I do?' she dismissed him with one command: 'Send to the convent where Morgan grew up.' But if he did, he did not say a word.

Now Arthur leaned forward towards Ursien, a strange look in his eye. 'You'll know everything, never fear!' he cried. 'You won't be asked to buy a pig in a poke.'

Guenevere came to herself with a start. She saw a spasm of rage fleet across Morgan's face. *Goddess, Mother, what now?*

Arthur gestured towards Guenevere. 'My wife,' he said.

She heard him say it, with a distant pain. *Why did he use the word, when the thing itself was dead?*

'The Queen,' Arthur went on, 'asked me to look into the place where it all began.'

He raised his hand. At the far end of the room, the attendants threw open the double doors. A detachment of guards came down the hall with a heavy burden wrapped in ragged cloth, and threw it at Arthur's feet.

Gawain strode in behind. 'Wait outside!' he ordered the men. 'Be at hand in case you're needed.' He bowed to Arthur with an unpleasant laugh. 'As you commanded, sire.' Then he dealt the heap of rags a hefty kick. 'Get up!' he shouted. 'And tell your tale!'

The bundle on the floor stirred, and began to move. Now Guenevere could see the outline of a body, an arm, and a woman's face. Slowly the captive freed herself from the all-enveloping cloth, struggled to her knees, and then to her feet. As well as she could with her hands tied, she adjusted her headdress and smoothed down her habit. Gawain's prisoner was a nun.

She was a nondescript woman of middle height, neither old nor young. But for the fact that her black habit and white headdress were dirty and crumpled from rough handling, no one would have given her a second glance. Only her eyes betrayed her, as Morgan's had. Hooded, a festering green like gooseberries, they throbbed with noxious power. She did not look at Morgan, but Guenevere could feel the connection pulsing between them. And when the newcomer turned her gaze to the throne, her malice fell on Guenevere like scalding rain.

'Speak, witch!' Gawain threatened. He pointed to Morgan. 'Tell us about your sister over there!'

'Sister Ann?' She gave an ugly laugh. 'That's the King's sister, not mine. They took away half her given name to make her sound like a Christian. She and I were only sisters of the cloth. But she was the best of us all. She could have been Queen of the Fair Ones if she'd had a mind. That's why they called her Morgan Le Fay.'

'As you see, Ursien,' Arthur said, in the same high, strained tone, 'this woman is from the convent where Morgan grew up.' He hesitated, then plunged on. 'My father King Uther sent her there, when he married Queen

Igraine. On my orders, Sir Gawain went there to investigate the place.'

A sour satisfaction filled Guenevere. She could not hold her tongue. 'And it proved to be a house of darkness as I thought?'

Gawain hesitated. 'Not exactly, Your Majesty, no.' He turned on the woman beside him, half raising his forearm to strike. 'Answer the Queen!'

Against his great bulk, she was very small. But she was not afraid. Her gaze raked him with raw contempt, then she began.

'It was a Christian convent right enough, and the nuns in there worshipped the Christian God. But how could they call themselves Christians, when so many of us had been locked up against our will?' She snickered without humour. 'And where the Mother Abbess rejoiced in cruel chastisement, and ruled with the rod. My father was the richest king in the west. He had seven daughters, and he gave us all to nunneries, to avoid the dowries if we had found love and married.' Her dull eyes lit up. 'Well, he paid for that, when I came into my power.'

Arthur tensed. 'What power?'

She snuffled with delight. 'The power to kill a man, or destroy him alive. The power to take false shapes that others think are true. To make things fly through the air, and attack those we hate. To lead men as men lead donkeys, by the tip of their tenderest part . . .'

'Enough, you foul-mouthed witch!' Bursting with rage, Gawain broke in to silence the gloating whine. 'Sire,' he began again, avoiding Arthur's stricken gaze, 'she's just admitting what she and some of the others did. It wasn't true of them all. There was a sisterhood within the sisterhood, unknown to the good nuns. They formed a coven in the nunnery, and watched out for those who were resentful or unhappy with the life. Then they seduced them into practising the black arts, while all the others were learning the ways of God.'

The nun smiled gloatingly. 'There was nothing we couldn't do. Sister Ann saw to it that she had the care of the Christian Father John when he came. She made him pay for speaking against the Mother-right. My father died inch by inch, as maggots ate up his flesh. We all had our revenge in the end.'

Her slug's eyes crawled over Arthur, and then slithered on to Guenevere. She smiled, and now her smile was worse than before. 'We could raise storms and fogs to blind the earth. We could ride through the skies on the winds, or escape through a keyhole without being seen. We could hold back a woman in labour, and keep the child rooted in the womb till both child and mother died.'

Guenevere sat up with a start as a new horror dawned.

Keep a child rooted in the womb?

Of course.

Her mind snapped back seven years.

When I was in labour, Morgan held my hand, and the pains I had nearly killed me and Amir. I thought she was praying when she muttered over me, yet however hard I laboured, I could not bring him forth till Arthur took her away.

She wanted to kill Amir. She wanted to kill me too. If I had died then, she would have had Arthur for herself.

'And more. We could do more than any of you dream.'

The nun was still speaking, her green eyes fixed on Guenevere. She had the same look as Morgan when she sat up naked and shameless in Arthur's bed – *and you are next, my lady*, her eyes said. *Yesss, Guenevere, you are next—*

'Sir!' Guenevere was choking with fear. She could not look at Arthur. 'Have you finished with this woman? Has she said all you need?'

Arthur nodded. 'Gawain?'

Gawain grabbed the nun by the arms, and bundled her to the door. 'Guard, ho!' he shouted. 'Get her to the guard-tower, make sure she's secure.'

A clear voice broke the silence. 'Is that a witch?' It was King Ursien's youngest son. 'What will happen to her, Father?'

Ursien's eyes followed the nun as she was led away. 'Oh, she'll burn,' he said. 'Like all of her evil kind.' And he looked at Morgan with a darker gaze.

Morgan stared straight ahead, pulling her cloak even closer around her, her face as tight as a fist. Arthur leaned forward, gripping the arms of his throne. 'Well, what do you say, man?' he growled. 'Take her or leave her. There she stands!'

'Sire . . .' Ursien's hand played on his sword hilt as he deliberated his move.

'It's a royal match for you, Ursien,' Arthur said angrily, 'and she'll come with a royal dowry too.'

Ursien bowed politely. 'I never doubted that.'

'What do you doubt, then? Surely it's simple enough?'

'Sire, marriage is never simple – for man or wife.' He glanced thoughtfully at Morgan again. Then his brow cleared as he made up his mind. 'But the honour of an alliance with King Arthur is not to be refused.'

'It's a match, then!' Arthur cried.

Morgan smiled a smile from the pit of hell. 'Amen,' she croaked. 'Amen.'

Standing at the altar with Arthur and Ursien, head down, still clutching her cloak, Morgan looked like a child between the tall men. The priest muttered, Ursien answered, and in minutes, it seemed, the wedlock knot was tied.

Afterwards there was no wedding feast, because there

was no cause to celebrate either for bride or groom. Night
was coming, and it was a long way back to Gore. On the
steps of the church, Ursien called his men to horse. Morgan
he placed in the centre of a ring of spears with Sir Geras and
Sir Accolon on either side, and the whole train clattered out
of Caerleon with Morgan in their midst.

'Farewell!' King Ursien called over his shoulder, as he
spurred away.

Farewell?

Guenevere stared at the thin, black-cloaked figure of
Morgan till it faded to nothingness.

We shall see, was her only thought. *We shall see.*

CHAPTER 45

*F*arewell.

Night after night she lay awake and wondered how love fled. The same lament ran endlessly through her head.

Oh, Arthur, Arthur—

Every wife has to learn some time that her husband is not the perfect man she dreamed. But not every woman has to go as far as I did down the hard road of truth. When you came, I thought you were a God. But now I know you are only a man like other men, unable to resist the sweet evil of hurting where you love most.

Were you and I foredoomed from the start? Love lifts us all into the garden of the Goddess, and not every paradise fades as ours has into a wasteland of despair. You were the golden lord of all my dreams, and I revelled in the glory our love brought. Now it is gone, and the world is a colder place.

When you came, I thought you and I were destined for each other from the time before time. I thought our union was blessed by the Old Ones who made the world, and by the Shining Ones before them. You shone in my eyes from the moment you dazzled me on the Hill of Queens. But you came with a darkness inside you that I did not see.

For you were not the child of light and love at all. You were born of deception, murder, and adultery. You came to life through

the vicious trickery of a mad and cruel old man. Your life was fated
to be deformed by that deceit. And now mine has been too.

'I should have seen it,' Guenevere muttered, half to Ina, half
to herself. 'He came to me under the banner of the dragon,
the red ravager, and when dragon-power is unleashed, it
lays the land waste.'

'Madam, these are old wives' tales!' Ina protested, with
tears in her eyes.

Guenevere laughed, an ugly sound even to her own
ears. 'Well, we are old wives now, can't you see that?'

For her twenties had slipped by unnoticed as Amir
grew up. Now she was thirty, and looked in the mirror
to see a filigree of fine lines round her eyes and mouth.
She was not to know that they deepened her beauty with
their undying testament of love and loss. Like any woman
she fretted painfully at the loss of her girlhood bloom.

Now it seemed to Guenevere that the cloud-capped towers
and gleaming palaces they once inhabited had fallen round
their ears, and cold winds blew through the ruins every day.
And still the inner battle went to and fro.

I am his wife, I must love him again.

There is no 'must' in love. Love once destroyed is hard to
build anew.

Yet surely it can be done?

When the house is down, where can love hide its head?

It is a duty.

Ah, duty. A cold comforter. Still, it is all you have.

Now in the woodlands beyond Caerleon, the last leaves
of summer hung on the branches before the gales of winter
came to strip them bare. One by one the flowers of autumn
withered as nature drew back all life to its roots. Night after
night Guenevere lay and watched the stars' cold fires as they

flared up towards midnight, then slowly faded to dawn. All the grief had dried up in her now, and she did not weep.

It was strange how soon her body forgot love and its fierce desires, forgot the feel of a man sleeping beside her with all the comfort that brings. She had always pitied women without love, nuns locked up in their convents, especially those like Morgan confined against their will. Now, for the first time, she envied the peace of a house of women, and understood the desire for what she knew she could not have – life without men, or even the thought of them.

But she was aching too, and often hot and restless in her cold bed. Her arms, her heart, her centre, her empty womb were raging for all they had lost that would not come again. She knew she was still mourning for Amir, her whole being dry-weeping for him day and night. But another ache was also gripping her now. A strange longing haunted her pale nights, and came to her in fragments of wistful dreams. *Who? What?* her spirit cried out. She did not know.

Then the great cold came. The hills and valleys drowsed under banks of snow, and the rivers froze in their reedy beds. Ice locked up roads and waterways, till neither man nor beast could safely stir. The poor folk drew their cattle in for shelter, and every dwelling became like a place under an enchantment as men and beasts slept out the winter's sleep.

In Camelot there was nothing to do but wait the winter out. For, like a disease, Morgan was with them still. Arthur's bleak face and sickly air told the world every day that something was amiss. Now he turned more and more to the black-hooded monks who padded around the chapel. He spent long hours among them on his knees, and sent often to London for the counsel of the Father Abbot, which was speedily returned. But nothing could drive the pallor from his face, or take away the anguish in his eyes.

'Has His Majesty been ill?' the King of the Black Lands drew Guenevere aside to ask when he passed through Caerleon to pay his respects.

'I have an old fever,' was Arthur's brusque response to any who questioned him. 'It returns to trouble me.' But all the world knew that he was sick, heartsick from Morgan's poison. In the cold watches of the night, Guenevere feared that he was still heartsick for Morgan too.

But they were still King and Queen, not people who could hide from the world to nurse their pain. So she sat with Arthur in the audience chamber to greet kings and queens, and debate with lords on matters of state. They received the countryfolk who came with their endless grievances, labourers with cruel masters, brothers warring against brothers, and widows and orphans put out of their homes. There was no respite from their struggle to keep the kingdom free.

But the time always came when every dignitary had departed, and all the petitioners had gone on their way. Then Arthur would turn to her and say dully, 'Do you dine alone? Or would you join me for an hour or so?' Every day he would make the same request, and she would turn away as if she had not heard.

Then on a golden day of early spring, something stirred in her heart, and she answered him, 'Tonight, my lord, I will.'

A look of wounded hope leaped in his eyes. That night as she came in, tears stood in his eyes. They feasted on pears and guinea fowl and broth to warm the heart, and as they left the table she went to his bed.

'Ohhhhh,' he wept, 'you're warm!' His body against hers was cold, and filmed in sweat.

She took him in her arms. 'I will try to love you as your wife. Be a husband to me now, love me again.'

But he could not. The loving between them was dead, like Amir. Her body was closed to Arthur like her heart, and she could not force it open to him again.

And he could not come to her. Now that the fire of his lust for Morgan had burned out, he could not feel the heat of their old love. When she held him in her arms, nothing she did could warm him to her now. She took his hand and guided it to her breast, she lay the length of him and stroked his body with loving hands, and still no love came.

The groan he gave then racked his frame and left her trembling with fear. 'She has finished me, Guenevere,' he said hoarsely, his eyes black with terror in the night. 'Morgan has taken my manhood, this is her revenge!'

And she soothed him, 'Hush, never say that, this is nothing, you are a man still, and it will pass,' just as women have always said to men. But neither believed what she said.

Yet still they had to try to live again. Now he slept in his quarters, and she in hers, but she would share his bed for company when his fears were riding him, and the nights were long and cold. They kept up the pretence for the people, as their reconciliation had been the signal for so much joy. By coming together they healed the land again. What did it mean to the people that their union was hollow at its heart?

But still it was not entirely without love.

'I have failed you, Guenevere,' Arthur would say. 'How can I give you back what you have lost?'

Guenevere looked at him. 'Better you give me what I truly need.'

'What do you mean?' he said.

'It does not matter,' she said, and went away.

But she could not forget the night when Morgan sat taunting her in Arthur's bed. *I am the Queen of the Summer Country, and Queen of the Middle Kingdom too,* her soul cried out. *I am Queen of two kingdoms yet no man on earth would raise his sword for me.*

A queen will always have her knights, her mother said.

She was a queen alone, and she knew what she needed now.

One night she went to Arthur in the small hours, when misery is most alive. She found him sitting by a dying fire, staring at the flames. The black-gowned, hooded creature with him rose on silent feet, folded its hands in its monkish sleeves, and slipped away. Guenevere had to mouth down her distaste. *Goddess, Mother, are the Christians everywhere now?*

'Hear me, Arthur,' she said, with all the force at her command, 'your knights serve you, and no man cares for me. I must have a troop of knights of my very own.'

'Poor Guenevere.' His eyes showed he had been weeping, but he was calm enough. 'To give up your home, your country, for a worthless wretch like me – and then to find no man beside you when you need a sword.'

Guenevere brushed it aside. 'I do not need your sympathy.'

He gave a painful smile. 'Would you accept my help?'

'Perhaps.'

'The three Orkney princes are ready to be made knights. Agravain has proved a fearsome fighter, he would die rather than yield. Gaheris is a gentler soul but fearless too, and young as he is, Gareth outdoes them all in feats of arms. They are all as doughty as Gawain, and I dare swear they'll prove as loyal too. Let them be your knights, the Queen's own champions.'

Dear Gods, had he heard a single word she said? 'Arthur,

they are the sons of Morgause! They are your kin! Why should they ever be loyal to me?' She could have torn her hair. 'Don't you see? I need new men, men you do not know – who do not know you – whose only loyalty will be to me?'

He paused. 'I think I know of one.'

'Another of your choosing? I will find my own knights!'

'Not one like this.' He sighed. 'The things they say of him they used to say of me.'

'Who is he?'

'They say no man can match him in battle, and his chivalry never fails,' Arthur mused on. 'His virtue and grace are praised everywhere. He's the finest knight in the land, young as he is, his father says – but then he would, as you know.'

'Know?' Guenevere cried, her nerves strung out like wires. 'How would I know?'

Arthur surveyed her in wonderment. 'Because you know his father, you know them both.'

'Who are you talking about?'

'King Ban of Little Britain. And his son, who has always longed to join the band of the Round Table here with us. I was going to bring him to court anyway, and there's no reason why he should not serve you rather than me.'

'Bring him here from France?' Why was she trembling? 'You mean the boy – the youth?'

Arthur smiled wryly. 'Boy no longer, I think. I mean Lancelot, King Ban's son. How would you like him for the first of your knights?'

She could not help herself. 'Why should I take the son of your old friend? The boy who has been in love with you since the Battle of the Kings? Do I need another knight who will put you above me?' She was madly angry now. 'Understand this, will you? The man I need will come to me by himself.

The knights I want I will find for myself.' She raised her
voice to shout. 'How can I make it clear? Don't send for this
boy, I don't want him, I don't want him here!'

'Go your own way then! I know you will!'

Arthur strode away seething – he loathed it when they
came to angry words. Yet at other times he was gentle and
humble as they struggled to rebuild. 'How could I lose
you? You showed me myself, you made me what I am,'
he said, with enormous sadness. 'All I am, I learned to be
through you.'

'And I you!' she cried. She could hardly speak for
pain.

She was married to Arthur, and she would be till she
died. Yet which of them could endure this marriage to
the death?

Day after day she repeated to herself the promise she
had made to Arthur when they lay together and tried to be
man and wife. *I will try to love you as your wife,* she had said.
And in her heart she was begging him: *Be a husband to me,
love me again.*

And so they came at last to a kind of peace.

CHAPTER 46

He came in a silver sunset at the end of a sweet spring day. The evening star was shining in a pearl-grey sky when the message was brought in. Guenevere raised her head from her papers as the servant bowed. 'Sir Lamorak is here, newly arrived from the Orkneys, and craving an audience with you and the King.'

'Sir Lamorak?' Guenevere cried in delight. 'Come all the way here without a word? Say we shall see him at once!'

How happy King Pellinore would be! Arthur's old friend had never ceased to miss his son. As Guenevere hurried into the audience chamber, the first sight to meet her eyes was King Pellinore leaning on his son's shoulder, weeping openly on Lamorak's neck.

Arthur's pale face looked bright, and for the first time for months he was smiling as he rallied the tall young knight.

'How long is it since we sent you to the Orkneys to attend my sister Queen Morgause? I confess I have forgotten, I forget so much these days. But it has been far too long.' He glanced sadly at King Pellinore. 'It is not good for a man to lose his son. We must have you back at court. You must come home again.'

Lamorak was still clad in his riding wear, encrusted

with the mud and dust of the road. But his time away had lent him authority, and he shook his blond head proudly as he spoke. 'Sire, my home now is at court with Queen Morgause,' he said. A tender light came into his eyes, and he gave an inward smile. 'Believe me, I have taken service with the best lady in the world.' He made a hurried bow towards the throne. 'Except for Queen Guenevere, of course. I could not leave the Queen of the Orkneys now.'

The best lady in the world.

Wild envy swept Guenevere from head to foot. Lamorak loved Morgause more than his father, more than his king, his country, more than his own life. He loved her as a knight should love a lady, putting her above all else. Oh, where was the knight who would feel the same for her?

With an effort, Lamorak brought himself back to the present. He cleared his throat and took an uneasy step forward. 'And it is my lady's command, sire, that brings me here today. A month ago she sent me to Gore, to her sister Queen Morgan, King Ursien's wife.'

Arthur caught his breath. 'Yes?'

'And then she ordered me to come on to you.'

'Well?' Arthur was very pale.

Lamorak plunged on. 'Queen Morgause my mistress sends you royal greetings, and her best hopes for your health and happiness. She is well, and all is at peace in her kingdom and beyond.' He paused. 'Her sister Queen Morgan, the Queen of Gore – her sister and yours, that is, my lord – great news . . .'

He faltered to a standstill, changing colour as he spoke.

'Fear not, son,' said King Pellinore anxiously. 'Say what you have to say, the King will hear you.'

Lamorak took a breath. 'Queen Morgan has been delivered of a son.'

Guenevere wanted to laugh.

A son for Morgan?

She has a son, and Amir sleeps in the sea.

Why did I never think she could have a son?

'A son.' Arthur could hardly speak.

'A fine boy, sire.'

Arthur looked up stiffly. 'When was he born?'

'At Imbolc, my lord.'

Imbolc.

Guenevere laughed aloud.

Truly Morgan is the Queen of Death. Her own day is the feast the Christians call Hallowe'en, our old Samhain when the undead walk from their graves. But how right that she dropped her spawn on the feast of the Black Maiden, the Queen of death and hate!

She counted back to Morgan's wedding last year, and laughed again. 'A seven-month child! Well, he will have a hard struggle, especially being born in winter as he was. Will he thrive?'

'He – he will thrive.'

Arthur struggled to compose himself. 'We must send our good wishes to King Ursien. What has he named his son?'

Lamorak swallowed hard. 'He did not name him, sire. Queen Morgan named him. She has called him Mordred.'

'How?' Arthur's head went up. 'The King not name his son?' A look of dread leaped up in his eyes. 'Why so?'

'You may ask that question of the King himself. King Ursien is coming, he is not far behind.'

Morgan named him.

So—

Guenevere was not listening. Lamorak's voice reached her through a mist of pain. 'I was sent on to break the news to you—'

'The news? What are you saying, man? *What news?*' Then Arthur threw himself back on the throne, and screamed.

*   *   *

In the King's privy chamber, the air was thick with rage, and something worse. The fire, hastily lit, was smoking sullenly on the hearth and the servants had had no chance to freshen the room before Arthur dragged Ursien and Lamorak inside, away from the audience chamber with its wide-eyed listeners and all the gossiping court. But the odour choking them now was not from the room.

Guenevere leaned against the wall, and hugged her empty body in aching arms. *She has Arthur's son, and mine lies in the cold sea.*

Again the wild call sounded inside her head, *Come away*—

Arthur was gripping Lamorak by the shoulder as if he would crush his bones. 'Little hair, you say, and nondescript colouring?'

Lamorak drew a long breath. 'Like all babies, sire.'

'No distinguishing marks to say whose child he is?'

'None.'

'Tell me this, Ursien.' Arthur was shaking in every limb. 'How can you swear the child is not yours?'

King Ursien set his chin and looked Arthur in the eye. 'When I married your sister, my lord, I knew she did not come a virgin to my bed. Any man in my place would make sure that a child of such a woman was his and his alone – and that the world knew this and saw it too.' Surveying Arthur closely, he did not add, *as your father King Uther failed to do when you were born*. But the unspoken reminder hung in the air.

Ursien shifted his solid bulk and picked up his tale. 'Queen Morgan has been confined to her quarters since she came to Gore. She has been attended by her women night and day. All fifty of them will swear that I was never alone with her.'

Arthur clasped his head as if his brain were on fire. 'But why did you not tell me that she was with child?'

Ursien shrugged. 'There might have been no child. Thousands of babies are shed from the womb before their time. Many others are born dead, or deformed, or simple, half-human creatures that only live to die.'

Especially a child of incest, as this was. Another unspoken rebuke rang round the room.

'And so must this one too!' Arthur screamed. 'He must die! Hear me, Ursien! This is the spawn of Satan! He cannot live!'

The only sound was Lamorak's agonised gasp.

'No!'

Arthur paused blindly, beating his head as he surged around the room. 'No, that won't do. Morgan will be too clever for you, she's too clever for us all. She'll send her child to safety and get another to die in his place.' He thought for a moment, his face distorted with wild anxiety. 'Ha! Yes – I know what to do, if we act swiftly now!'

Ursien knew what was coming. His face did not change. 'Sire?'

'They must all die.' Arthur nodded with satisfaction, his face lit by a secret fire. 'All the newborn boys.' He swung round violently, a man possessed. 'Hear me, Ursien. Send for every male child in Gore born this month. They must all be brought to you on pain of death. Then have every one of them put in a ship, and sent out to sea.'

Ursien did not move.

'And scuttle it,' Arthur said simply. 'I want them dead. Him and all of them.'

'Sire?'

'Kill all the newborn?' It was Lamorak, pale to the roots of his hair. 'Sire, I beseech you, do not do this thing!'

Arthur turned on him. 'D'you dare to question a king?'

'The babe has done no wrong!' Lamorak fell to one knee. 'I beg you, sire! He is your own blood kin!'

'Lamorak . . .' Arthur let a murderous pause hang in the air. 'I warn you . . .'

'Sire.' Ursien coughed respectfully. 'What Sir Lamorak says is true. The child is your nephew, the son of your sister's womb. Among some races, a nephew is thought to be closer than a son.'

Arthur did not look at him. 'I have no son!' he howled. *'Then do not take hers too!'*

Guenevere buried her face in her hands. How did these words find their way out of her mouth? She could have torn Morgan's heart out if her rival had been there. But she could not take her child. No woman should suffer as she had for Amir.

She shook Arthur by the shoulders and beat his chest. Now she was screaming too. 'Kill her if you must, but let this baby live. He is your child.'

'Madam, permit me!' Gently Ursien held her and drew her away. 'There is something, sire, in what the Queen says. This is your son, there is no doubt of that. As the child of you and your sister, he can claim both the father-right *and* mother-right of all your lands. Take him and rear him, make him what you want. Pendragon then will never lose its sway.'

'Only a Pendragon true-born comes after me, not the bastard of a whore! Kill them all! I want all the boys killed, not one left alive!'

Arthur burst from the room, his parting scream still ringing in their ears. Above it Guenevere heard from far away the faint, singing cry, *come away, come* – It drew her like an enchantment.

'So!' Ursien breathed out a long sigh of defeat. Lamorak hung his head.

Guenevere mastered herself, and swallowed her distress. 'Forgive me, lords, for this unseemly show. And forgive the King, he is not himself.'

Ursien's voice was hard. 'I hope so, madam. I do not like what I am commanded to do.'

'Nor will the King,' she said tremulously, 'when he comes to himself again. We shall think of another way, have no doubt about that.' A slow idea took shape in her brain. 'Arthur was fostered himself in Gore. Is there any reason why he could not leave the child in fosterage with you?'

'None, madam,' Ursien agreed, his face lightening. 'Or if he wants to send the child away, where better than to his old friend King Ban? The kingdom of Benoic lies far away over the Narrow Sea. And I daresay young Lancelot's mother would be glad of a boy to raise again.'

'I daresay.' Guenevere moved stiffly towards him and took him by the arm. 'Come, King Ursien, let me escort you to your apartments, and see that you have all you want. You must remain here till the King turns from this plan.'

'He will, my lady, won't he?' Lamorak's eyes were suspiciously bright and he looked very young.

Guenevere patted his arm. 'Yes, sir, he will. Come, let us go.'

The low corridor outside the chamber was poorly lit. One sputtering torch burned in a wall sconce, painting the ceiling with streaks of flame like blood. The walls sweated with a cold fever, and the flagstones breathed foul vapours underfoot. Four huge figures lurked at the nearest corner, half shadows, half men. Fear caught in her throat. The first loomed up against the light. 'Lamorak!' he cried.

Lamorak stopped in his tracks. 'Sir Gawain!' He made a courtly bow. 'And your brothers too! Hail to you, princes all!'

Agravain stepped up behind Gawain, his dark face brooding in the flickering light. 'How is the Queen our mother?'

Lamorak's colour rose sharply at the mention of Morgause. His earlier words glanced sideways through Guenevere's mind. *My lady is the best in all the world.* Why did these simple words of knightly chivalry seem so ominous now?

Lamorak bowed to Agravain. 'Her Majesty is well,' he replied courteously. 'She has sent letters and dispatches to you all. Forgive me that I have not yet delivered them. My orders were to go straight to the King.'

'She's well, then, Lamorak, our mother the Queen?' Gareth, the giant baby of the bunch, came bounding up. 'And happy is she, at ease in herself?'

A sweet smile lit Lamorak's lips. 'Never happier, Prince, I promise you.'

'We know we can trust you to look after her.' The quiet Gaheris gently punched Lamorak's arm. 'Well, bring us her letters as soon as you can.'

'You shall have them as soon as may be, my lords.'

'We must await your pleasure then, Sir Lamorak? Well, so be it.' Why did Agravain's every word sound like a sneer?

The torch flared suddenly in the clammy air, bathing Lamorak's face in blood-red light. All Guenevere could see was Agravain leaning towards Lamorak with fire in his eyes. 'When it shall please you – as you please the Queen.'

'Come, Agravain!' Gawain clapped him briskly on the back. 'I am sure that Lamorak fulfils the Queen's every command to the best of his power.'

'He always has!' a beaming Gareth chimed in.

'Look after her, man,' said Gaheris quietly.

The Orkney brothers were now following Gawain away. 'We will have letters ready for you to take back to the Queen when you come,' Gawain called over his shoulder as he went.

'But if you write before then yourself,' Gareth cried, as he strode after them, 'give her our love!'

Come away—
     Come—

The passage seemed very empty when the four great princes left. Guenevere brought King Ursien to the guest wing of the castle, and saw him installed in one of the royal suites. Then at last she was free to answer the call of her soul.

From her own apartments she took a cloak the colour of twilight and fastened it with a crystal clasp shaped like two hands lovingly entwined. She covered her face with a fine veil of silvery tissue, and secured it with a cap of gold and pearls. Then she drifted out of the castle with Ina, down the winding cobbled road from the palace, over the causeway and out of the town.

Dusk was falling, and all the townsfolk were safely gathered inside their houses, dreaming around their fires. Not a soul saw them as they slipped away. She did not know where her feet were leading her. But she knew that she had to go out to the woodland now.

It was cool and dim under the great oak trees, lit with a silvery light. Ahead of them lay a clearing, a perfect circle, an enchanted glade. The call of the night-jar pealed through the quivering air. At first the great shapes shimmering in and out of the undergrowth seemed to come from a dream. Only the soft thud of hoofs on the forest floor told them that the mounted men coming towards them through the trees were real.

'My lady!' whispered Ina in alarm. It was not wise for women to be caught alone in the forest, even so near the town. But Guenevere had no fear.

A light mist lay over the sea of bracken as the horses came breasting through. The night birds fell silent as the strangers approached and the rich scent of the wood fell like incense all around.

Three knights rode through the trees, one in front on a great white charger, and two behind. They drew up in the clearing just ahead. The leader sprang lightly to the ground. He was tall and slender, with broad shoulders tapering to lean, supple hips. He stood at peace in the glade, bathed in its glimmering light. Guenevere closed her eyes in fear of what she saw. But her spirit looked on, and drank in the newcomer.

He wore a green leather tunic set with tiny gilded studs. His short travelling kilt was of the same fine tooled kidskin, embellished with the same small studs of gold. A dagger hung from his leather belt, and a great gold-hilted battle sword swung down beside his thigh. His gold helmet was winged in silver, and set with green guardian jewels like unsleeping eyes. His horse stood gently nuzzling his hand, the weary droop of its neck showing how far they had come that day.

His two companions were also clad as knights of the road, equipped with equal finery but little of his grace. Neither spoke, but the ease between them showed the understanding they shared. They were alike enough to be brothers, but their leader looked like no man on earth. His bright brown eyes burned in the twilight, and the lift of his head had an Otherworldly air. Guenevere stepped forward into the clearing and faced him without a word.

'Ahhh . . .'

His sigh was like a breath from heaven, and she heard

herself sighing too. His eyes never left her face as he fell to one knee.

'Who are you?' he cried.

Who am I? What should she say to him? His voice called to her from the world between the worlds. Now she was crowned with starlight, walking the air, moving among the spheres. She was the lady of the forest, the spirit of love, the Queen of May.

'Surely I know you, lady?' he said, in tones of wonder. His light accent gave music to his words. 'Where did we meet before?' He broke off and gave a self-conscious laugh. 'Or else I dreamed a blessed dream of a lady like you. There is no shame in that.'

He had a knightly air of pure chivalry, the frank bearing of a noble nature free from stain and sin. A light shone in his face as he looked at her. 'You are the lady of Camelot, Queen Guenevere. I have come to serve you, to offer you my sword.' He raised his handsome head. 'I am—'

There was a whirlwind from heaven, and she felt the strong eternal surge of life itself. His voice was calling to her from the time before time. She heard the crying of the waves on the shore and the weeping of the wind in the trees. She saw stretching ahead long days of beauty and breathless nights of bliss.

'Hush . . .'

It was all she could do not to say, *Hush, my love.* She placed her finger on his lips. 'I know who you are.'

CHAPTER 47

His mouth was long and full, and there were little lights at the corners where his lips lifted into a smile. The groove in his upper lip felt sweet to her touch, and the light pricking of his soft stubble stung her fingertips. The closeness of him throbbed like a love-potion through her veins. As she drew her hand away, a tremor passed between them.

He gasped. 'Majesty, I—'

His face had the raw, sharp-angled look of a boy, and there was something tender and trusting in his air. But his eyes had looked out on other worlds than this, and he had not learned in one short life all the power and grace that shone out of him now. He knelt before her in his woodland green and gold, and she could hear his spirit calling above the cry of the nightingale.

A laugh of ecstasy gurgled in her throat. 'You do not need to tell me who you are, Sir Lancelot.'

He bowed his head, and his glossy brown hair swung down past his neck. 'Your servant, my lady.' He lifted his eyes. She was pierced by a violent pain. 'I am your knight,' he said, with simple certainty. 'I have come to lay my sword before you, and offer you my service in the eyes of all the world.'

A poisonous thought struck her like a blow. 'Arthur sent for you!' she cried furiously. 'After I told him not to! I told him I would choose my own knights!'

His eyes flared. 'And so you shall, if that is what you want!' He leaped to his feet. 'But you must know that the King did not send for me!' His head lifted with that Otherworldly air she was already learning to know. 'I follow the life of chivalry. It is written that a knight must serve a peerless lady, the best in the world.' He turned his golden gaze full on her face. 'I chose you.'

He laughed like a boy, and his bright brown eyes lit up. 'Madame, I beg you, do not look surprised! I studied with Aife, the warrior queen of the north. At night round the fire she told us stories of Battle Raven to fire our blood.'

'The Queen's mother?' Ina breathed.

He nodded. 'Queen Aife prophesied that the daughter's fame would grow to be greater than her mother's, and outlast them both.'

Guenevere frowned. 'And did your queen tell you how this would come about?'

Now he looked like a boy again, raw and confused. 'She could not see so far. When she called you up in her seeing mirror and I stood beside her to look into the future, she had no sight of what was to be.'

He drew himself up with unselfconscious pride. 'But do you doubt what I say? It is the word of a queen.' She could feel his temper stir. 'In all the years I served under her, Queen Aife never spoke anything but the truth!'

Guenevere could not help herself. 'You were lucky then, to learn from a woman who never told a lie.'

And she was lucky, she thought a second later, that he did not hear the jealousy in her voice. All the tense planes and angles in his face softened as he gave her his first smile. 'Truly, Madame, I was!'

What could she say? He knelt to kiss her hand, and his two companions knelt at the same time. She trembled at his touch, and tried to suppress it, but she saw that he was trembling too.

He rose to his feet. 'These are my cousins, Bors and Lionel,' he said awkwardly. 'The sons of King Bors, my father's brother – I think you know him?'

Bors the older brother was short, neat and self-contained, with watchful eyes and his father's thoughtful air. Lionel, kneeling beside him, was taller and more unguarded, his ardent gaze fixed on Guenevere.

'*Enchanté, Majestée,*' the two young men muttered as one, and the sound of their accent bound them to her heart. She loved them at once for sounding like her lord.

For already Sir Lancelot was 'my lord' to her. She loved him, and there was no turning back.

Yet how could she say that? How could she even think it? she asked herself madly, as Lancelot set her on his horse and led her back. He was showing her simple courtesy, that was all. He had helped her to mount with the chivalry any knight would have shown any lady, let alone a queen. She had only just met him, he was a stranger to her, just another young man.

How young?

Too young to love with any dignity.

Love a man so much younger – no, Goddess, Mother, spare me that!

The sweet mists of evening rose as the party threaded its way through the trees, across the deep meadowland skirting the forest and back to the town. Slowly her heart revived.

In front of her Lancelot was talking quietly to his horse as they walked along. But his heart was crying, *Fool!* and he cursed himself every step of the way. Aife herself told him no woman likes to hear another praised. How could he have stupidly sung her praises to another queen, still less a queen like Guenevere!

Gods above, fool again! he accused himself furiously. There is no Queen like Guenevere! He knew as if he had known her all his life that this Queen, this wondrous woman, would never be easy to serve, nor to impress. He saw again her huge eyes floating behind their silver veil like moons in a cloud, and his soul burned to relieve the sorrow in their depths.

Her fragrance, sweet and Eastern, played on his senses till his only thought was to be with her all his life, breathing her sweetness like a flower. Yet all he could do was make her jealous of the Queen he had left! Gods above, he groaned to himself, what hope is there for a blind fool like me? She'll hate me soon, if she doesn't already now!

Riding high up behind him on the horse's back, Guenevere could see the growing signs of tension, and her heart misgave. He had come all this way to seek her out, and she could do nothing, say nothing, but show him her ugly jealousy, the jealousy of another woman, which was always hateful to men. Things had to change, she had to do better than this! She must be courteous towards him then, kind but distant, and put all this madness quite out of her head.

So that was it. Who was he, after all? No more than any other young man, she decided, looking down on him as he led her along. She let her eyes play over the bend of his neck under the bright hair as brown as a hazelnut. She watched the hard young hand gripping the horse's bridle, and the taut back and shoulders turned towards her now.

And as she looked, she was lost in love again.

The dew of night was falling on them now. The warm smell of the horse enveloped her, and the rustling sounds of every little creature of the night came with unnatural clarity to her ears. And still her thoughts went madly to and fro.

I love him.

Love?

No, this is not love, it's madness, it has to be. Women who lose a child often go mad, it's well known.

And love?

It's disgusting, ridiculous, even to think of it!

Yes, think if you can, Guenevere, use your mind. You are a married woman, married to a man who can still move your heart. He was your first love, the dream of your girlhood, and the father of your child. You turned against him, and still you found it in your heart to turn to him again, when all feeling lay in ruins and there was no breath of hope.

Love? That is love, not some madness born on a night in summer when the fireflies dance in a stranger's eyes, when the mist weaves its silver ribbons through the trees, and every blade of grass breathes the hope of love anew. And you are a queen married to a king, married to a people and a land—

The thought of Arthur brought on a pain so acute she felt herself tearing inside. How could she think of love for Lancelot?

She could not – she did not, and that was the end, it had to be.

But overhead the stars leaped and danced in the sky, the dark suns sang in their spheres, and the moon soared over the horizon like a bird. *Go, child*, she could hear the voice of the Mother breathing in the soft whisper of the grass, in the sigh of the wind in the trees. *Venture, and you will find . . .*

They slipped back into the palace, the spirit of the woodland clinging around them still. Behind Guenevere walked Sir Bors leading Ina on his horse, with Sir Lionel alongside leading his horse too, refusing in chivalry to ride if his comrades were on foot.

The chamberlain was waiting in a state of high anxiety.

'The King has called for you, madam, a hundred times!' he blurted out. 'And not a soul knew where you had gone!'

'Forgive me, sir,' she began, 'I was delayed encountering Sir Lancelot.'

But already the chamberlain had seen who she was with. 'Sir Lancelot? Oh, my lady, there is nothing to forgive!' He turned to the nearest groom, standing gaping with awe, and boxed his ears. 'It's Sir Lancelot, numbskull, jump to it! Sir Lancelot, is there anything you require?'

Everyone loved him, she saw with joy and pain. She watched in wonderment as the grooms danced round him in glee, bursting to hold his horse or simply to be near him. She had not known that he commanded such acclaim.

But, then, she knew nothing now. Nothing was as it was before. When they reached the Queen's apartments, Ina set her back against the door, her eyes and mouth huge with wonder and delight. 'Ooooohhhhh, madam! Tell me! What—?'

'Ina, please, not a word.'

Guenevere held up her hand and went away by herself. She was lost in a strange landscape of new dreams, and she could not have voiced a single one of them now.

But even the best dreams vanish with the light of day. The next morning she lay alone in bed as dawn stole over the ceiling and across the walls, and watched her hopes and fancies fade away.

What had possessed her?

A spring night in the woodland, a wandering knight, was that all it took?

A sad and lonely woman, a handsome younger man, a story as old as the hills – what must he think?

She clutched her stomach, sick with disgust, mocking her own pain. He was a knight errant, all he wanted was honour and renown. A true knight always sought the lady

he could not have. If he married, he had to give up the life
of errantry and deeds of arms, and stay at home with his
wife. So the rules of chivalry decreed that the queen of a
knight's heart should be a woman he could never possess.

She grinned, and hugged a pillow to her stomach to
hold down the rising pain. Why, he'd told her as much
himself, if only she'd listened to him. *I follow the life of
chivalry,* he said. *It is written that a knight must serve the
best lady in the world.*

And he was only a boy; it was natural that he was
playing by the rules. He already knew she was married,
everyone knew that. For him there would always be safety
in another man's wife, especially one married to a king, as
long as they played the courtly game of love.

And play they did. He was the perfect knight. At
dawn he sent a page to her door to ask how the Queen
had slept.

'And Sir Lancelot swears,' piped the boy gravely, 'that
tonight he will not lay down his head, nor think to close his
eyes, till I bring him word that you are safely in repose.'

'Thank you, sir.' She rewarded the page richly, and sent
him away. She wanted to weep, she wanted to kill herself.
Even at the height of their love, Arthur had never said or
done such things.

'Such devotion, madam!' Ina sighed adoringly.

Guenevere's eyes flared. 'Oh, Ina, it doesn't mean a
thing! This is pure chivalry, it's a game, nothing more.' The
sight of Ina's face annoyed her even more. 'Don't forget
where he comes from! He must have learned these tricks
in the courts of France.' Then another thought struck her,
colder and crueller than all. 'And you must know that I'm
not the one who matters here. He's only trying to please the
Queen because he wants to prosper with the King!'

But Arthur needed no prompting to love Lancelot. He

leaped staring from his chair as she led Lancelot into the King's apartments. 'God bless you!' he cried. 'You are your father come back to me again!'

Was he? Perhaps he was a little like King Ban, Guenevere thought, the bright eyes as bold as a kestrel below the tumbling of chestnut hair, the smile that lit his whole being, not just his eyes. But then she knew that Arthur was wrong, and she was wrong to believe what he said. Because, then and always, Lancelot was simply himself.

Not to Arthur, though. The next morning she found him roaming round her chamber when she returned from her early-morning ride. *What are you doing in my apartments?* she thought coldly. *What makes you think you can invite yourself here?*

'Lancelot – he's myself, don't you see that, Guenevere?' he began abruptly, running his hand through his hair. With a jolt she noticed strands of grey she'd never seen before. When had she last looked at Arthur with the eyes of a loving wife?

She took a breath. 'See what?'

'What they say.' Arthur's voice was lifeless, dull, devoid of hope.

'What do they say?' She was already losing interest. *Oh, Arthur, tell me if you want to, and if you don't, who cares?*

Arthur stood still, and clutched his head in his hands. 'He's myself come back to reproach me – he's all I was, all I ever used to be.'

'Arthur, men of your age often see their former self in younger men.'

'No, it's more than that!' Arthur groaned. 'It's his untainted soul, it shines out of him! And I – oh, God, Guenevere, what am I?'

Yet Arthur shone in Lancelot's eyes too. That evening, for the first time since Amir died, Arthur called for dinner in the Great Hall. As they mounted the dais that night and sat on their golden thrones, as they feasted guests and strangers by the light of a thousand torches, she could see their glory reflected in Lancelot's gaze. And as he looked at Arthur with eyes of adoration, so Arthur revived, and life crept back into him, inch by painful inch.

In the body of the hall Lancelot moved among the courtiers, bowing shyly to ladies and attending courteously to lords. With men he was as proud as a stag in a glen, yet always civil too. But when he spoke to women, even the oldest matron without a tooth in her head, Guenevere had to turn away and bite her lip in pain. The misty glances that followed him from every female eye, and even from old men and boys not old enough to fight, tortured her with a rage she could not explain.

But not all those in the Great Hall welcomed Lancelot. From her throne on the dais she could see that the loyal Gawain rejoiced in Arthur's joy. But then she saw Agravain's stony glare turned on Lancelot in silent calculation, and the flame of his inner darkness seemed to burn higher when Lancelot passed by.

Soon Agravain's harsh, cawing voice was disturbing the evening's peace. 'The King loves the new knight better than our brother now. So much for loyalty, when a newcomer can blind him to the claims of true and faithful men!'

'Oh, come, brother!'

'Surely not!'

Neither Gaheris nor Gareth wanted to hear such a thing. But their troubled looks showed that the idea had taken hold. Frigid with rage, she called them up to her throne with a furious wave of her hand. 'The King is not a child, to find a new friend and ignore the old,' she said icily, staring at Agravain. 'He will never forget true and loyal service – nor hesitate to punish the opposite.'

Agravain stared her out. 'As you say, Majesty.'

In the warm summer evening, Guenevere's skin crawled. What was it about Agravain? In the black depths of his cold gaze, could she see another loveless scrutiny, another mask of hate?

Morgan.

Yes.

It had to come, she knew it. She let herself bury Morgan in her mind because her soul was frantic for respite from the pain. But Morgan was gone, not lost, and some time she would return.

Now the hall was full of light as a thousand candles shone like stars, and a hundred torches leaped flaming up the walls. Outside the windows the pale midsummer night clothed the palace towers in radiance and a silver moon swam in the golden sky.

But when the lone rider galloped madly into the courtyard below, she knew that the darkness was near. And when they were called to the council chamber and Sir Yvain, King Ursien's oldest son, stood before them shaking from head to foot, she knew what he would say.

Arthur stood very still. 'What is the word from Gore?'

'All has been done just as you ordered, sire,' Yvain blurted out, scarlet with grief and distress.

'Arthur, what—?' Guenevere stared in horror and disbelief. When his rage against Morgan had passed, she had thought he was letting events take their course until he knew what to do. Surely he had not confirmed his command to Ursien?

'Yes?' Arthur's teeth were clenched, the veins and sinews standing out on his neck.

'My father called all the newborn boys together, and had them cast away on a sinking ship.' Yvain licked his lips, and his eyes flew madly around. 'But—'

'Speak, man!'

'—but the wind changed, and the ship was driven inshore. It was blown down the coast towards Mona, and wrecked on the rocks of the Welshlands, just above the lost valley they call—'

'Le Val Sans Retour!'

Yvain flinched as Arthur's bellow split the air. 'But who knows, sire,' he babbled desperately, 'if the child lived or died? They found the shore littered with babies' bones. What the sea had not devoured, the birds feasted on. And what could it mean, that the ship was wrecked near Queen Morgan's estate?' He tried a valiant laugh. 'A babe in swaddling clothes could not walk to its mother's home!'

Arthur's skin was glistening with a pale, waxy sheen. 'Unless the mother was there with all her power, to draw him to her.' He fixed Yvain with a killing gaze. 'Tell me your father has her safe under lock and key.'

Yvain's colour ebbed from red to white. 'Sire – she – my father's wife – the Queen—' He dropped his head, and covered his face with his hands.

Arthur screamed, beside himself with a thousand conflicting pangs. 'To horse!' he howled. 'Summon my knights, sound the trysting-horn, we leave at once for Le Val Sans Retour!'

Guenevere ran to Yvain and gripped his tunic front. 'When did she escape?' she hissed like a witch, her face twisted in hate. 'How did she get away?'

He shook his head, gibbering like a natural.

He did not know.

Guenevere turned away. What did it matter? Morgan was free. The darkness was at large.

CHAPTER 48

Never more.

In the dead hour before dawn, Sir Kay stood by the gatehouse and watched the long train of horses gallop out. Torches flared on either side of the causeway to light their way.

Never more would he be one of that blessed fellowship, feel the exaltation at the start of a campaign, know the love that only men can share.

'Farewell!' He limped forward, one arm upraised in farewell, and found himself weeping, though not from the pain in his leg. He had known he would never ride out adventuring again after the wound he took at the hands of the vengeful dwarf. But that did not make it any easier to bear.

And in place of action, camaraderie, and feats of arms, he could only despise the task that Arthur had given him now. Kay threw a cold glance up to the battlements, and the worm of bitterness stirred again in his heart. Left behind to mind the Queen now, no better than the castle cripple, or a poor lady's maid! Well, at least his charge was not so taken up with her handsome new young knight that she'd refused to turn out to wave the King farewell. But dancing attendance on

Queen Guenevere – was this a fit task for a knight of
the King?

High above on the battlements, Guenevere caught Kay's
malignant glance and sighed, feeling the cold air chill her
to the bone. It was not yet dawn, and the air was still thick
with the vapours of the night. Arthur had driven his knights
like a madman, and Sir Gawain and the Orkney brothers,
along with Sir Lucan, Sir Kay and Sir Bedivere, had worked
like demons to rouse all the sleepers and summon as many
men as would come to the sound of the horn.

For Arthur needed good men around him now. In the
dead hour of night, as Guenevere roamed her chamber
sleeplessly and Ina dozed uneasily by the fire, she had
heard a scream outside. A moment later Arthur, his face
glistening and distorted, burst through the door. He was
brandishing Excalibur as he came, wildly slashing the air.

The great sword growled in his hand, roaring for blood.
For a moment she thought that he had come to slash her
to death. Then the agony in his face put that fear to flight.
He came towards her like a man possessed, tears mingling
with the sweat on his face. 'Tell me it's safe!' he howled.

Her stomach lurched. 'What is?'

'The scabbard. Your mother's scabbard, the one you
gave to me.' He waved the naked blade. 'Say that you
came and took it away when I betrayed you, to keep
it safe!'

She shook her head. There was no need for words.

Arthur swung his body madly, like a goaded bull.
'Then Morgan has taken it. That's where it's gone!'

Guenevere closed her eyes and tried to breathe.

*My mother's scabbard, with its power of protecting the
wearer from loss of blood. The finest thing I had, entrusted to
Arthur, and stolen by Morgan now.*

'You had it in your chamber when you slept with her,' she said dully.

'And now it's gone!'

'But why would she want it, Arthur? She doesn't fight, she never goes to war.'

Arthur roamed the chamber, shaking his head in pain. 'To hurt you. To take what was yours. Or to punish me. As if she could do much more to me than she has!'

'No.' Now it was Guenevere's turn to pace the floor. 'No, that's too easy. She must have a reason for this. She has a plan. She means to use it against us somehow – some day.'

'How?' Arthur was gaping like a child.

'Oh, Arthur . . .' All she felt for him festered in her eyes. 'However long it takes, we'll find out. And then you'll wish you hadn't.'

Arthur looked at her like a man under sentence of death. 'I'll get it back!' he screamed, as he ran out.

But she did not believe him. For a long while then, she cursed him in her heart and wished him dead.

Now she shuddered, and huddled into her cloak against the damp early-morning air. Far below, the red dragon on Arthur's banner flared at the head of his troop, fighting the wind as it flew off through the chill half-light.

What would Arthur do if he found Morgan at Le Val Sans Retour?

When he gave her the castle in the valley, he had also equipped it with his knights, and made them swear to die for her. Would he lay siege to it now, and make war on his own men?

And if Morgan's child had survived the shipwreck and was with her as Arthur feared, what would he do then? Kill his own son?

She had told Ina that she would not be disturbed; no

one was to come to her here on the battlements, however long she lingered in the cold. But the footfall behind her now was not Ina's. And there was only one man for whom Ina would disobey her.

She could hear the sound of his breathing before he spoke. His light French accent fell like sweet rain on her ear. 'The King is leaving Caerleon. You do not accompany him?'

She did not turn her head. 'Where the King is going, he must go alone.'

'As you say, Majesty.' Lancelot moved easily to take his place at her side, gripping the stone wall of the battlements as he leaned forward to look down.

Now he was staring at the causeway, watching the horses racing out of the torchlight into the dark. His eyelashes lay on his cheekbones, black and shining as a magpie's wing. A fine scar had left a pale, silvery slash under the smooth tanned skin of his cheek. He wore a loose cloak of green silk over a tunic of darker green, and the hands so near to hers were hard and brown. A sweet impulse swept over her, and almost robbed her of her mind. What would happen if she touched his hand now?

She clasped her hands together and took a trembling step away. But she could not stop her mouth. 'Have you ever been in love?'

A pulse jumped wildly on the back of his hand. 'I? In love?'

Dear Gods, was he a virgin?

'Love? I—'

He tried for a manly smile. 'Every man seeks the woman of the dream.' She watched him closely as his colour changed. 'But the Goddess has not favoured me that way yet.'

Yet.

'How old are you?'

It was the wrong question. His fists bunched, and he drew himself aside. 'I am as old as you need your knight to be.'

Silently she cursed her driven tongue.

Why did I ask? I know how old he is.

If he was fifteen at the Battle of the Kings, he's well past twenty now.

And twenty thinks thirty is old, old old.

Especially a woman past thirty, and worn by grief.

Well, it's nothing at all to me!

She dared not look at him. His light accented voice broke in on her thoughts. 'I beg you, Majesty, do not doubt my faith. When a knight serves a great lady, he will do more for her glory than he could for himself. This is the highest feeling that men have. It makes us noble, though we are made of clay.'

She could not bear it. 'How do you know this?'

He frowned. 'Every knight knows that his lady will stretch him till he becomes worthy of his task. Then, with her image in his heart, he will go forth and do great things. I chose you for my lady, as chivalry decrees. You are bold and valiant, you are the most fair, so you should be the most beloved. You are the Queen – who should I serve but you?'

'Ah, sir.' She bowed her head to hide her face. 'You speak the language of chivalry, such as any lady would be pleased to hear. I am honoured to accept your service, and the good that you will do.'

Again she felt his nearness like an ache. The longing to touch him was almost too much to bear.

'Madame?' he said wonderingly.

She had to collect her thoughts. 'The Gods know how much this poor kingdom still needs good men. You must go forth with my blessing. You must seek out deeds of knight errantry, and do all you can.'

It sounded hollow, even to her ears. But she could not stop. 'So much for chivalry – what about earthly love?'

'Earthly love?' Startled, he looked into her eyes for the first time. 'You mean women's love?' He looked away. 'I do not think to be a married man.'

A pang of fury seized her. 'Oh, all men marry, or what would women do?'

'Ah, lady.' His sigh came from the heart. 'If I married, I would have to stay with my wife till death, for that is what marriage is. I would have to give up the life I have trained for, the only life I know, battles and tournaments and the sport of arms.' He braced himself, as if to repel an attack. 'That is all I can do, and all I want to do. I could not give it up. Therefore to marry would be dishonourable.'

'You will never marry?' A surge of bitter jealousy spurred her tongue. 'So, then, you will take mistresses?'

He stared at her blankly. 'You are my mistress, lady.'

Was he stupid, poor at English, or just pretending not to know? 'Lovers, I mean! Women you take to bed!'

As soon as the words were out of her mouth she knew she had done wrong. How could she have forgotten how young he was?

'To take my pleasure of women, and then leave them by the way?' An ugly red was creeping up his neck. He hunched his shoulders, then straightened his back again. 'No, I could not do that. I have taken a vow.'

A vow of chastity? Or a vow of chastity only until the woman you desire comes along?

Guenevere clenched her fists, loathing herself for all this. But still the inner voice went on and on.

You will never marry, Lancelot?

Perhaps. But you will have lovers, whether you want them or not.

Women will always desire you, to take you to their bed.

How will it be for you then, Sir Lancelot, and your vow? And me?

How will it be for me?

'Lancelot?'

'My lady?'

'I – farewell.'

Abruptly she turned and left the battlements. This was madness, and getting worse. It had to stop. What was she to do?

At dawn the next day all Caerleon was agog. Waiting restlessly in her chamber, Guenevere could hear the servants buzzing like flies as they flew to and fro.

'Orders to depart!'

'The Queen goes to Camelot, she leaves at once!'

'Why, man? Whatever for?'

'Queens don't explain themselves to the likes of me. But hop to it, I tell you! She's on fire to depart, and there's no time to lose!'

Leaning her head against the cold mullion, Guenevere tried to order her thoughts.

How could she tell them why she had to go?

Because the new knight unnerves me, with his hard body and long brown hands.

Because I think of him by day, and meet him in my dreams at night.

She would not be the first woman to run away. Lancelot and she were far better apart. With Arthur gone, there was nothing to keep her here in Caerleon. And where should she run but Camelot? She had only to get him away too.

She sent for him in the dark hour before dawn, and had everything signed and ready for him when he came.

'Sir Lancelot!'

She started as she heard him at the door. Seeing him again struck her like a blow. His eyes were as bright as a blackbird's, his appearance as fresh as the dew on a morning ride. 'What is your will, my queen?'

She handed him the papers, and turned away. 'That you follow the King to Le Val Sans Retour, give him these messages, and remain with him to see how his campaign goes.'

His smile vanished. 'How long will I be from you?'

She waved her hand. 'I don't know.'

'I must obey your will.' He frowned angrily.

She started with sad delight – *he does not want to go.*

'And Bors and Lionel, do they come with me?'

'No, a queen must have her knights. I will keep them here.'

Lancelot drew a harsh breath. 'A queen does not have to explain herself to her knight. And her knight may not demand the reason why.' He gave a curt bow. 'Give me your blessing then, Majesty, for I leave at once. The sooner I go, the sooner I may return.' His eyes were alive with reproach. 'It will be a week at least, maybe a month, before I may come back?' he muttered almost to himself.

'Ah, sir . . .' She shook her head. What would he think when he knew she was already planning to run away as soon as he was gone?

The tension between them stretched out like a quivering thread. They were looking past each other, neither daring to meet the other's gaze. Lancelot caught his breath, brushed a hand across his eyes, and dropped to one knee. 'So then! I go, if you bid me. Give me your blessing, lady, wish me good speed.'

He was kneeling before her, the light shining on his hair. Before she knew it, her fingers reached out to touch the side of his cheek.

He caught her hand in both of his, and pressed it to his lips. 'Adieu, Majesty.'

She could not stop the words. 'Adieu, fair sweet friend.'

CHAPTER 49

Step by step, the horses' plodding hoofs lulled Guenevere's troubled thoughts. Soon the journey would be over, and she could hide herself away in the Queen's chamber, out of reach of prying eyes. It would be good to escape the dark questioning gaze of Sir Bors, and the open bewilderment of his brother Lionel, as they rode with Sir Kay now at the head of the Queen's knights. They only knew that she had sent Lancelot far away, and they made it clear that they did not understand.

All will be well when we get to Camelot, she told herself, again and again. But what would she find in Camelot to save her from these keen pangs of misery, these sharp-edged dreams? What could change for her in Camelot, when things changed so slowly there? That night Guenevere sat at dinner among all the old familiar faces, and felt hopelessness descending like a fog.

'Courage, my lady,' murmured Taliesin, his keen eyes never leaving her face.

'What's that?' demanded King Leogrance, his hand to his ear.

Sir Kay laughed. 'Lord Taliesin wishes the Queen courage, sire.'

'What?' Leogrance leaned forward irritably. 'Why?'

Guenevere suppressed a sigh. 'I am tired, sir,' she said loudly, 'after my journey. I am looking forward to my rest.'

Seated to the right of King Leogrance, Malgaunt gave her an encouraging smile. He was looking well, even handsome, Guenevere noted, his lean face bronzed with action, his tense, wiry body at ease tonight in a fine red tunic girdled with gold. 'Rest, Guenevere?' He laughed. 'You've been away from us too long, if you've forgotten what's coming now.'

'What is it?' Guenevere shook her head. Between the shock of Morgan's escape, Lancelot's coming and her own flight back to Camelot, she had lost track of time. She tried to laugh. 'I hardly knew one day from the next.'

Malgaunt nodded, satisfied. 'You do not keep Beltain in the Middle Kingdom?'

Guenevere sat stock still and absorbed the pain.

Beltain, when April becomes May.

When women become lovers and men become Gods.

When I found the love that cost me my son's life.

And I the only woman in the Summer Country who cannot look for my love.

She took a breath. 'No, the old ways are gone in the Middle Kingdom. We do not keep Beltain.'

Malgaunt's eyes flashed with the familiar sardonic gleam. 'Soon it will be May Day, when all the court goes out Maying, dressed all in green. You must remember – you always used to go.'

Maying – honouring the Great One on Her special day.

Her sight shivered. Suddenly she saw the girl she used to be, dressed all in white riding out of Camelot through the mists of dawn. Her hair was plaited with ribbons of silver, and she was seated on a white pony decked out in gold. Behind her came the other maidens of the town, all gowned in green. They danced and sang as far as the edge of the forest where the white hawthorn, the tree of the Goddess, skirted the wood. And there they gathered great tumbling armfuls of the sharp-scented May blossom, counting each of the bright star-shaped flowers as they rode laughing back.

Could she do that now? Ride out again like the girl she once was? Malgaunt was watching her narrowly. Slowly she nodded.

Malgaunt's eyes flared. 'So, then,' he exulted, 'it's agreed! When Beltain dawns, I'll come for you, and we'll ride out Maying, just as we used to do.'

Guenevere paused. She couldn't remember Malgaunt ever being among the knights and men clad all in green who attended the ladies on their Maying ride. Malgaunt never wooed women, they came to him. He had no reverence for them, using them briefly then casting them aside. And as for the ceremony, Malgaunt had no more faith in the Great Mother than he had in the God of the Christians, or any God but himself.

Something shadowed Guenevere's pleasure, a vague unease. What was Malgaunt up to now? Why did he smile, and smile, as he never had before?

A moment later she was blaming herself again. Why did she always think the worst of him? This bitterness was poisoning her very soul! Malgaunt had changed, the King her father said, and it was clear tonight that he was trying only to be kind.

She forced herself to smile. 'Thank you, Uncle, it's good of you to think of this for me. But there's no need to drag you from your bed.' Malgaunt's face darkened, and she hurried to explain. She nodded at Kay, Bors and Lionel down the table. 'I have my own knights here, they'll be all the escort I shall need. We'll let the maidens go on ahead as they always do, then we'll ride out quietly later on. There'll be no shortage of blossom, and we'll have the whole forest to ourselves.' A sudden longing seized her. 'Oh, it will be good to get out in the greenwood again!'

Malgaunt nodded. Why was he looking at her like that? 'Yet it would be better if you rode out with me. There are dangers in the depths of every forest, and with me you would be safe.'

She stifled a sigh. It was her fault, she knew, but to her eye Malgaunt still had that look of a hungry wolf. 'Thank you, Malgaunt.' She smiled. 'But what can befall the Queen of the Summer Country riding out in her own forest on May Day?'

The laughing band of knights enjoying the evening air on the edge of Arthur's camp did not catch the drumming of the hoofs. But they knew to be silent when Bedivere raised his hand. The quiet voice among louder, bigger men, he often picked up what others noticed much later, if at all. 'Hush!' he said softly. 'We have a visitor.'

'Lancelot!' Arthur cried. His wan face lit up as Lancelot was led in. 'It's good to see you!' He waved a hand round the sparsely furnished tent. 'It's not Camelot, but you're welcome all the same. What are you doing here?'

What indeed? Lancelot asked himself grimly as he stepped up to the makeshift table where Arthur sat. A wild thought seized him – I think your Queen is playing games with me. But there was not the slightest temptation to reveal it to the King. 'Urgent messages from the Queen, sire,' he responded formally, pulling his bundle of papers from his saddle-bag.

'Sit with me, Lancelot,' Arthur urged, pushing forward a camp stool. He looked tired, Lancelot saw, but the warmth of his greeting was undimmed. 'Have you eaten? Bear with

me while I read these, if you will, and then you can tell me
how the Queen was when you left.'

He turned to the nearest page. 'Food for Sir Lancelot at
once, if you please, and wine for us both.' He eyed Lancelot
with feeling sympathy. 'By the look of you, you haven't slept
for days!'

Numbly Lancelot raised his hand to his unshaven face.
He knew that he carried the dirt of the roads on his clothes,
and the stink of his horse through to his very flesh. He was
suddenly seized by a hot wave of shame. How dared he
come before his King like this? Was he already forgetting
his chivalry for the love of the Queen?

The servants were laying a mug of coarse wine before
him, and a plate of mixed meat. For a soldier's meal, the leg
of chicken and thick slice of brawn was as good as a feast.
At Queen Aife's camp, a slab of coarse brown bread and a jar
of ale had been enough for him. But now he pushed the food
aside in disgust. How could he eat, when he felt so bad?

Across the table Arthur was frowning as he perused
the documents Guenevere had sent. Carefully he read all
the pages, then began on them again. At last he laid them
to one side, and turned to Lancelot with a mystified air. He
forced a laugh. 'So tell me, sir, what's all this about?'

To his horror Lancelot could feel his face turning red.
'All what, sire?' he muttered at last. 'I don't understand.'

Arthur reached for the papers and slapped them on the
table. 'These papers. The Queen sends loving greetings, page
after page, but that's all – no state matters, no decision of
import . . .' He paused heavily. 'No reason to send you after
me at all.'

Lancelot found himself choking, as if a hard lump of
the coarse black bread had found its way down his throat.
Arthur's words confirmed all his worst fears. The Queen
was playing with the love he had offered her.

A fury like nothing he had known rose in Lancelot's heart. So be it, he vowed, white-lipped and suffering. If she disdained his love and service, there was nothing he could do. Some knights were content to serve cruel mistresses, who tortured them for love. He knew, of course, that a knight must make no demands. But to become a plaything between the Queen and the King! These letters must surely contain details of the sport, for the two of them to laugh at his expense!

But Arthur seemed oblivious of Lancelot's flushed face and resentful stare. He toyed again with the papers, though his mind was clearly elsewhere. At last a sweet smile lit his lips, and spread up to his eyes. 'Ah, Guenevere!' he said fondly to himself. 'I see what she was up to now.' He turned to Lancelot. 'This is all about you, sir knight!' he cried.

Lancelot's stomach took another lurch. 'What, sire?' he said dumbly, struggling to understand. He felt himself grow hot. The raw colour rose to his face again. What was coming now? What on earth did the King think he knew, when there was nothing on earth to know? And why was he, Lancelot, behaving like a guilty thing? It was only right for a knight to love his queen. It was more than right, it was the duty of every knight.

Gods above! he muttered to himself. If it is your will to sport with me, let me not hurt the King, or injure the Queen!

'Yes, you, sir!' Arthur went on. He leaned towards Lancelot and the rickety table creaked under his weight. 'The Queen knew how much I would want you at my side. So she spared you to me, putting my need above hers.' His eyes misted. 'This isn't the first time, either, that she's done that. What a woman, eh, Lancelot? To part with her own sworn knight for the love of me!'

'Yes, my lord.' Lancelot could hardly speak.

Was this truly the reason the Queen had sent him away? And whether it was or not, if the King thought it was, what chance did he have of getting away again?

Hours later, Lancelot stumbled out into the night. The King had kept him talking over a glass of wine, then another, then another three or four. He could see that the thick red drink with its deep lees and heavy scum was feeding a need in Arthur that mere words and passing company never could. And although he knew he could not keep up with the King in his cups, he had still finished up drinking more than he wanted.

And none of it helped the ache in his own heart. As he pushed back the flap of the tent and came out into the night, he heard himself gasp with a sudden renewal of pain. The Queen had sent him away for no reason at all. Yet now the King said he could return if he wished.

'Go or stay, Lancelot!' Arthur had cried as he bade him goodnight, and directed him to his tent. 'If the Queen can spare you out of love for me, I can make the same sacrifice to her. You can go with me to the lost valley and do battle there, or return to the Queen and support her as she rules the Middle Kingdom while I'm away.'

He shook his head. He did not know what to do.

'Hey, Lancelot!'

The urgent voice from the shadows outside Arthur's tent would have made him jump at any other time. But deadened by drink and distracted by his woes, Lancelot hardly stirred. 'Gawain!' he said, without enthusiasm, as the bulky form hove up. 'What are you doing here?'

'Guard duty, my son!' Gawain grinned expansively. 'Someone has to look after the King while he feasts the Queen's knight!' He laughed uproariously. Clearly Arthur was not the only one in camp who had been drinking that night. 'So while you fed your face, you lucky hound, I was hanging my backside out here to keep you safe.' Gawain chucked his head at the figures of Lucan and Bedivere approaching fully armed. 'A task from which I am now relieved, it seems. And the night has hardly begun.'

He threw a mighty arm around Lancelot's shoulders and drew him across the grass. Carefully he steered him through the lines of tents. 'You'll have your own tent, of course, but first come on back to my mine. I've got some good wine there, both Rhenish and Canaries, take your pick!'

'Thank you, no.' Lancelot tried not to show the distaste he felt. Wrestling with the conundrum Arthur had given him, go or stay, the last thing he wanted was a drunken night with Gawain.

'And that's not all,' Gawain breezed on. 'Look here!' With a brief word, the big knight greeted the soldier at the entrance of the next tent, and pushed Lancelot in. Without enthusiasm, Lancelot allowed himself to be propelled through the door.

Inside the tent, the light was low. The red glow from the brazier showed rough canvas walls, and two simple lanterns shed small pools of gold on the carpet of some sort that covered the grassy floor. The large camp bed in the rear was obviously made up for Gawain or another man of his size. It was covered in fine wool blankets and piled with bright cushions, which picked up the light. And spread out upon the cushions were two further ornaments.

The elder was a woman of around thirty, tall and well fleshed with an open, inviting mouth. Heavy breasts sprawled inside her loose bodice, and her thin skirt outlined a pair of ample hips and monumental thighs. Her dark red hair fell loosely around her face, and her eyes were dilated in the darkness of the tent. She lolled on her elbow and laughed at Gawain as he came in, bringing the point of her full red tongue to the tip of her front teeth. Lancelot could see Gawain's eyes widen in response, then narrow with sharp interest like a dog. There could be little doubt what he was thinking now.

The other girl was the older woman's opposite. Small, thin and fair, she was no more than twelve, a child who had had no childhood, old before her time. A dull fear lit her eyes, and her small work-worn hands lay twitching in her lap.

Lancelot turned to Gawain with a shrug of recognition and reproach. 'Camp followers.'

'To be sure!' Gawain agreed, without a trace of shame. 'Well, men in camp must have some comforts.' He nodded appreciatively at the women on the bed. 'Mother and daughter. An old hand, and a newcomer to the game. The girl has been kept back till she was ripe for it.' He guffawed. 'Or so the old whore tells me, don't you, my love?'

He crossed to the older of the two lying on the bed, and applied a none-too-gentle slap to her full rump. 'Woe betide you if I find you've been telling me tales!' He nodded at Lancelot. 'I can't offer my friend here fresh meat, and find that the child is already rotten goods. She's a virgin, you say? You swear she is? Speak up.'

'I do,' said the woman steadily, staring him in the eye. Again she grinned, and passed her tongue between her teeth.

'How many knights have you told that tale?' demanded Gawain roughly. He slapped her again.

She laughed, unafraid. 'Only you, sir.' She shifted herself invitingly on the bed, and her breasts rolled in the confines of her shift.

'Only me, eh?' Gawain laughed. Lancelot could feel the excitement rising in the thick body, the intensely focused eyes. 'Well, there you have it, Lancelot. A virgin, so they claim, and all yours.' His voice grew thicker as he spoke. 'For tonight at least. Tomorrow I might try her for myself.' He leaned down and gripped the older woman by her forearms, pulling her off the bed and lifting her to her feet. 'But for now, this is mine. And let's see . . .'

With a loud laugh Gawain reached out for the woman's bodice, tore the cross-lacing, and ripped open the front of her shift. The woman bore his rough treatment with the air of one who knew she would be well paid for anything he did. She would have known too that any woman would be proud to show off the breasts that now tumbled out before Gawain's fixed gaze. Long, brown and full, with thick nipples protruding from a wide freckled areola and purple with love bites, they invited handling from almost any man in the world.

But not Lancelot. To buy women who were forced to trade in sex – to steal a girl's innocence, to rape a child – he turned away. Gawain was already burrowing in the woman's neck, one hand kneading her breast, the other struggling to strip her clothing off her back. 'Take the girl then, Lancelot,' he cried, with mounting urgency, 'or give her to the guard, if you're too pure!'

Like a slave, the girl had risen mechanically to her feet, awaiting his command. In her eyes now there burned a light of panic and despair. She is a virgin, the knowledge came to Lancelot, and she will certainly be despoiled tonight. He also knew with equal surety that the poor drab could do worse, much worse, than spend the night with him. He would be saving her from what else would come.

Suddenly Guenevere came into his mind, and he felt lower than the lees in Arthur's wine. Serving a queen, and standing here with a whore.

Yet the Queen had treated him as a male whore, a man of no consequence, to discard and throw away—

He stood irresolute in the door of the tent. On the bed the action had become more vigorous. Gawain raised his head. 'Do what you like with the wench, Lancelot,' he said hoarsely, 'but take her now, go!'

Stay or go.

Lancelot nodded. He reached for the girl, and gripping her thin shoulder, pushed her out into the night. Then, ignoring the grinning guard, he led her firmly to his tent.

CHAPTER 50

A shaft of sunlight was streaming through the hangings of the bed. Guenevere stirred and stretched in a pool of living gold. She had slept long past dawn, and all the palace was awake, the busy hum and stir reaching her comfortably from below. Slowly she uncurled herself among the sunbeams, and lay exploring her troubled thoughts as a tongue carefully probes a damaged tooth.

Every day she awoke with a sense of nameless joy, then the sick knowledge of loving where she should not. But today the dead weight of despair seemed less heavy on her heart, and a dim feeling of duty done brought comfort to her soul. It was wrong to keep him by her, having thoughts she tried to hide even from herself. It was right to send him away, when he had the power to disturb her so.

And now new ideas dropped like stones into the quiet pool of her mind.

If I can rest and restore myself here in Camelot, perhaps things can be again the way they should.

Perhaps. But can you love Arthur as you did?

Perhaps.

Can he love you again in the way of a man?

Perhaps not. But women live with less.

How much less?

He is my husband, and the father of my child. I made him my king, and I owe him that.

Is it enough?

It has to be.

Even at the cost of love?

Love now means banishing foolish dreams of handsome brown-eyed young men.

'Ina!' Guenevere stretched her arms wide, sat up and swung her feet to the floor. 'Have you forgotten we're going Maying today?'

'Why, lady,' Ina was smiling by the window, throwing the curtains back, 'would I forget?'

Guenevere stretched luxuriously, then leaped to her feet. 'Hurry then, there's not a moment to lose. The sun's out, there's not a cloud in the sky, and we should be in the greenwood. I want to be Queen of the May!'

Some days come like pearls on a chain, so perfect that you treasure them ever afterwards. This would be one of those days, Ina promised herself silently as she lovingly robed her mistress all in green, bound up Guenevere's hair with silver braid, and veiled her face from the sun in a cambric of white gold. As always her heart lurched at the beauty in Guenevere's sad face. Oh, lady, lady, she mourned, why did you turn your back on happiness? You lost Amir, you lost King Arthur, why did you send Sir Lancelot away?

At the stables Sir Kay, Sir Bors and Sir Lionel were mounted and waiting, garbed in woodland green. Kay bowed on behalf of them all. 'Greetings, my lady. May we wish you a pleasant day?'

Kay knew his face betrayed nothing of the tumult in his mind. But the fury he felt was not easily appeased. Maying now with the Queen, is it? he harangued himself in disgust. Gods above, we'll be dancing round maypoles next! The pain in his leg was a sharp reminder of his eternal loss. He shifted in his saddle, and sadly relished turning his cruel humour against himself.

No dancing, then, for him. And if he had to endure the Queen's temperaments, at least this was better than standing by watching her stare at Lancelot and startle like a panicking mare. Kay shook his head. What was the matter with her? The lad was well enough, if only she'd leave him alone. Oh, they'd need to lick him into shape before he could call himself a knight of the Round Table, and one of them. He'd shown precious little interest in women, but Gawain would soon take care of that. Still, when he'd taught young Lancelot a trick or two, the boy would be as good as they all thought he was.

But today it seemed that the Queen's tom-fool May Day ride was the duty of all three of them. Kay grinned. Bors and Lionel were no keener than he was for a day in the woods. But they would do their duty and, who knows, there might be some pleasure in the ride.

Beside them two ponies stood ready, snuffling the sweet noon air. They were mild and docile with great liquid eyes, and Guenevere was touched to learn that Malgaunt had commanded the pair himself.

'No turn of speed to either of them, madam,' commented the head groom as he saw to their stirrups, and adjusted the ponies' girths. 'But Prince Malgaunt picked them out for you specially, as nice and quiet for a lady's Maying ride. Where you're going, he said, you'll only need an ambler, and these two fit the bill.' He slapped one mare's neck and lovingly stroked the other's nose. 'This one's Fairylight, and t'other's Merrygold. Sisters they are, and never parted on a ride. They love May Day in the woods, don't you, girls? You can leave it to them to find their way there and back.'

*   *   *

In the heart of every woodland lies a peace not to be found elsewhere in the world. The two small mares forged calmly along the winding paths. Guenevere and Ina passed into the cool shelter of the leaf-laden trees with their three knights in the rear. No one spoke, or dreamed of disturbing the peace. The great oaks were silent, the tall grey beeches murmured and kept their own counsel, and only the silver birches whispered softly and giggled to each other like the silly things they were.

Underfoot, the soft, mouldering loam of the forest floor released its rich, earthy scent with every step of the horses' hoofs. The summer smell of mingled life and decay rose to Guenevere's hungering soul, and for the first time since Amir's death the thought *I might live,* came to her like a prayer. She could feel it now, stirring like a seed, thrusting up a soft green shoot, fearfully trying its tender head above the ground.

I might live—

Deeper they went, and deeper into the wood. May blossom is always at its best round the edge of the forest, she told her knights, where it enjoys sun and rain. Busy matrons, girls who had been unlucky in love, and women without hope of a love of their own would run down to the verge, seize an armful for good fortune, then hurry back again. But serving the Goddess truly called for a ride into the heart of the woodland, to the sacred grove. There lay the place given over to the Mother, where the Druids came at midwinter with silver sickles to gather the golden bough. There she and Ina would make their devotions for May Day.

On the outskirts of the woodland, the doves slumbered sweetly in the midday heat, their heads tucked under their wings. As they went deeper under the leafy canopy, the rays of the sun found it harder to pierce the quivering air. Further still, and the undergrowth grew thicker between the trees, great clumps of whinwood and whortletree dense enough to hide an army in. The wood was dark and still and green now, all the trees silent and slumbering. The horses slowed their pace as they moved through this enchanted shadowland under the forest roof.

Ahead lay a circle of gold, the clearing of the Goddess. The sun poured its dancing beams down into the glade, dazzling their eyes. In a trance they passed out of the shade of the forest. The great trunks of the trees, the solid shapes of the bushes, everything shimmered and dissolved in the molten air. Guenevere loosened her veil, and turned her face up to the kiss of the sun like the warmth of a mother's love. She had come home to the Mother, home to Her unfailing love.

All around lay the stillness of perfect peace. The horses stood without moving, like woodland creatures themselves. Guenevere sat drinking in the copper-coloured air. Never had the forest been so sweet to her, so gorgeous in its Maytime array. Her heart cracked open with a stab of pain, and her being stirred with a new force of life. She saw Arthur, her mother, Amir, and for the first time felt their love as a blessing, not as a loss. Her mind, her soul were greening like the land in spring, bringing life again. Seated on the patient mare, she shook from head to foot. She caught Ina's tender, enquiring look of love, and knew that her face was wet with tears.

Goddess, Mother, take my thanks, hear my prayer.

Perhaps she did not see them because joy was blinding her. Perhaps she did not hear them because her ear was filled by the old May song of her girlhood, the Mother's blessing on all who came to Her, weaving in and out of her thoughts through the still air. She could not stop weeping now, as the healing waters flowed. Closing her eyes, she saw through a burst of golden fire the great circle of earthly love. And she was part of it. She was old in grief, but not in body, and her body was ripe for love.

'My lady, beware! Save yourself, beware!'

It was Bors, bellowing madly as he drove his horse past them into the dark forest ahead. Ina gave a hideous scream of shock. Guenevere started as if waking from a trance.

'Ina, what—?'

But Ina could only point, her eyes bulging with fear.

CHAPTER 51

In the shadows stood a troop of mounted men. Their dark shapes melted into the gloom under the trees. They were as still and silent as the living forest, but they were all armed and helmeted, men of metal without human faces, men of death.

For a second Guenevere yielded to a wild hope – they were one of the fairy troops that haunted the woodland, a lost band of knights enchanted by the Queen of the Fair Ones and never seen in the flesh again. Then she saw the ears of the leader's stallion twitch, she saw his master's iron hand close silently on the reins to keep him still, and she knew they were real and dangerously alive.

'My lady, *go!*' Bellowing his war-cry, Sir Bors rode straight at them, with Sir Kay and Sir Lionel fast behind. 'Save yourself, escape!'

'Ina, d'you hear him? *Ride!*' With a furious scream, Guenevere tore her pony's head round, rose in the stirrups and leaned forward along the short neck. '*Go! Go!*' she hissed madly into the milk-white ears. 'Go, girl! Go for your life – and mine!'

Behind her she could hear the clash of swords, as her three knights took on the stranger troop. Above the brawl rose the sound of Ina's voice as she urged her own mare on, and she knew that if one of the ponies led the way, the other would not be far behind.

'Go! Go!'

The little mares tried, she knew they tried. Two sets of short white legs reached for their longest stride, four pairs of hoofs drummed on the woodland path as the fearful ponies strained their every nerve. But with a gathering dread Guenevere heard again the words of the head groom in Camelot as they left: 'No turn of speed about these two, where you're going there'll be no need of that—'

Behind them now came the sound of horses that could outrun theirs at an easy cantering pace. And above the soft thud of the pursuing hoofs came a worse sound, the low chuckle of the leader as he bore down on his prey.

He let them run for long enough, Guenevere knew, to make sure that the exhausted ponies could not escape again. Then as the mares flagged, the men caught and surrounded them.

'Who are you? And how dare you do this?'

Beside her Ina was snuffling in mortal dread. But Guenevere's anger overrode her fear. 'I order you to let us go, do you hear! What do you think you stand to gain from this?'

The only answer was the leader's muffled laugh as he signalled his knights to force them back along the track. At the sacred grove they came upon the rest of the troop, silently guarding the three companion knights. Surrounded by faceless assailants, a dull-eyed Sir Bors was swaying in his saddle, bleeding freely from a cut on his head, and Sir Lionel's sword-arm was dangling by his side. Sir Kay raised his bleeding hands as Guenevere approached, and she saw that they were bound. Her heart revolted with pity, fear and grief.

Each of her beaten knights was tied to his horse, and

led along. The leader turned his back on the light shining in the sacred grove, and struck off into dark paths never trodden before. The people of Camelot did not venture past the grove at the heart of the forest to the land that lay on the other side.

Where were they going?

Where was he taking them?

And who was 'he' anyway, the helmeted leader, the man with no face?

He drove them till their horses were dropping their heads, and chafing their bits with blood. All around them the sweet day faded into an angry evening, the sky weeping yellow and red like an old wound. But by the time the night birds were roosting in the trees, they came out of the forest and down on to a plain.

Gaunt against the twilight, a black castle stood on the hill-top ahead. Squat and square, it crouched like a toad on the mountain. Still without speaking, the knights hastened forward over the rough scrubland, making for the shadowy portcullis across the dark, stagnant moat. And in the same silence they galloped across the black threshold, and the doors slammed behind them like the gates of hell.

Within the courtyard, sullen-faced grooms and frightened maids leaped to attend them. Tossing his reins carelessly to the nearest lad, the leader vaulted from his horse, and crossed the courtyard to Guenevere. Without ceremony he seized her by the waist, and swung her to the ground. Beside her Ina was suffering the same rough treatment. Across the yard she could see her three wounded knights being dragged from their mounts.

'Where are you taking my knights?' she raged. 'They are injured, they have to be with me, so that I can tend to them!' But she might have saved her breath. With a mocking bow, the faceless leader handed them over to an armed guard, and waved them away.

She and Ina found themselves hustled up a massive flight of stairs, lit by a long window that cast a greenish light on the shadowy realms above. Half-way up the staircase branched, both sets of gleaming oak steps leading to miles of dark corridors hung with banners, swords and shields. Whoever their kidnapper was, Guenevere saw, he followed the knightly way of life. Yet what true knight would so outrage all the canons of chivalry?

At last they reached what looked like a set of guest chambers, behind a stout oak door. A bevy of silent women bowed them in. Guenevere fell on the first of them. 'Tell me at once, who is the leader here?'

Not a word.

'What is happening to my knights?'

Not a sign.

Goddess, Mother, is this rogue knight attended by deaf mutes?

'I demand to speak to your lord! Tell him I await him instantly!'

As if they had not heard, the women curtsied and withdrew, leaving the knights on guard.

'Outside, sirs!' cried Guenevere peremptorily, driving them before her from the room. 'If you must guard us, have the courtesy to do so outside the door!'

The heavy studded oak slammed behind the men with a sound like doom. Ina turned to Guenevere, and clutched frantically at her arm. 'Oh, my lady!' She was weeping without control. 'What is this place? Why have they brought us here?'

'Ina, I don't know.' She tried to make light of her fears. 'Let's see what we can find out, now we're here.'

They were in a spacious apartment finely panelled

with golden oak. High mullioned windows reached up to a ceiling swagged in moulded fruit and flowers. The walls were hung with richly coloured tapestries, and there were enough candle-holders to make the night as bright as day. Great bowls of tumbling musk roses brightened every table and sweetened the air. But one note was discordant with all the rest. The lofty windows were set with iron bars.

Guenevere hurried to the window to look out. Below lay a garden surrounded by old stone walls, cascading with roses whose sunny freedom mocked their imprisonment. A stout and ancient ivy growing right up to their window offered a brief spurt of hope. But they would have to break the iron bars to escape from their cage first.

'Madam, look!'

Ina waved a trembling hand. Through a small archway, a passage led to a whitewashed corridor. To the left were several clean, welcoming sleeping cells for a Queen's attendants, or the knights of her train. But to the right lay a royal suite, and beyond it a queenly bedchamber with a massive bed.

Ohhhh—

Guenevere could not help herself. The coverlet was pure white and gold, and the cool linen smelled chastely of lavender. But, like a ship in full sail, the bed was hung with tapestries depicting amorous scenes of love.

Guenevere could not look. A hunger for Lancelot struck her like a blow. Tears scalded her eyes. She drifted to the window and gripped the iron bars, staring out of her prison to the clear night sky.

'Madam, look.'

Fearfully Ina drew her towards the back wall. Behind the bed was a small inner door.

The room within was fitted out for a queen, with closets of gowns and headdresses, wraps and robes and veils. The dressing-table was a replica of the one in the Queen's apartments at Camelot, laden with boxes and pots and jars. With a dread she could not explain, Guenevere opened one of the boxes and brought it to her nose. It was patchouli, the sweet seductive scent from Byzantium that her mother had favoured, and she loved so much.

Ina was weeping again. 'Why, lady, why?'

The outer door rattled, and a great key turned to lock them in. Guenevere fell into Ina's arms and wept at last.

The audience chamber at Camelot was cool and welcoming after the heat of the day. With Guenevere away it was rarely used, and the cluster of men striding in disturbed its serenity now. 'Where is he?' demanded Malgaunt tensely. He turned on the nearest guard. 'Well, don't hang around, man, bring the fellow in.'

This cursed deafness – Leogrance cupped his hand to his ear, and followed the proceedings as closely as he could. But the head groom's report left nothing to misunderstand. The Queen had gone maying with her maid and her knights, and had not returned.

Malgaunt's face flushed. 'I knew I should have gone with her!' he cried. 'I warned her of the dangers in the wood!'

'Guenevere lost?' said Leogrance stupidly. He could not take it in. 'She can't be, not here in Camelot!'

'She's not in Camelot, she's in the greenwood now! Where others have been lost, time out of mind,' snapped Malgaunt furiously. 'Well, she started from here, so we know where to begin.'

'We must raise a search,' Leogrance said, in the same stupefied tone. Guenevere gone? It simply did not make sense.

'The horses are ready, sir,' the head groom put in,

'and every man in Camelot will turn out to search for the Queen.'

But it won't come to that, was the unspoken thought in every mind. Between the Fair Ones and the wild ones, there's no room in the woodland for lost women roaming by themselves. If we don't find her soon, we'll be looking for her bones.

Yet a search must be mounted, and fast, despite the fading light. Malgaunt faced the men. 'Hurry!' he ordered.' To horse!'

CHAPTER 52

Like Camelot, the castle was as old as time itself. Outside the summer sun played over roses and marigolds and honeysuckle in full bloom. But imprisoned inside the thick, entombing walls, they might have been dead and mouldering underground.

'Who is he, lady?' Ina asked in a dull voice. 'What does he want with us?'

'Never fear, girl,' Guenevere said. 'We shall be rescued, they'll be here for us soon!' But she did not believe her own bold words.

When they did not return, Malgaunt and her father would search the forest, and then give them up for lost. Whole troops of knights had been swallowed up in that woodland, and many a careless traveller had perished without a trace.

Too many in Camelot would readily believe that the Fair Ones had enchanted them, and led them astray. And if the searchers from Camelot could not find them, who else would know or care?

Arthur? He was far away, fighting shadows of his own.

Lancelot?

She clutched her stomach and hugged herself with pain.

The searchers would not find them because they would not know where to look. To know that, they'd have to know who had taken them away.

Guenevere herself returned again and again to this. If it had happened in the Middle Kingdom, yes, she could have understood it. Arthur's land still had all too many rogue knights who would take women at will, steal wards from their guardians, and ravish rich widows on their own estates. But not here – not in the Summer Country, not in Camelot. And what kind of abductor would keep them in doubt as to their fate? Was he holding them to ransom? Would he throw them to the guardroom for a night's sport for the men?

'What does he want?' Ina sobbed.

Guenevere's voice was calm. 'Ina, don't torment yourself, who knows what he wants?' But she could not silence the inner voice that said, *He knows. And you do too. He wants you.*

'Good! Well done! You went well today!'

Leaning forward, Lancelot caressed his horse's neck as he cantered gently up from the field outside the camp. Strange how even a half-hearted passage of arms could lift a wretched mood. And with Arthur's war-party at the peak of excitement now, he was never short of opponents who also wanted exercise too.

Reluctantly his hurt mind returned again to Guenevere. She had treated him badly, and deliberately too, he was in no doubt of that. To send him away to Arthur on a fool's errand had been bad enough. But then to fly off to Camelot as if the hounds of hell were on her heels – there was only one conclusion to be drawn.

She could not bear him. She found him so offensive that she had had to send him away. He could not imagine what he had done wrong. But that was the only explanation, it had to be.

He forced back a sigh. Well, at least it had not made him treat others as badly as she treated him. The young whore Gawain gave him had slept in his tent that night, as she knew she had to, there was no way out for her. But she had slept there chastely, and alone. The next day he had sent her to Caerleon, with a hundred crowns. With a dowry like that, a girl could choose any man. Or she could keep herself tidily on it for a long while. When she left, she smiled at him, an unpractised smile, still timid and untrusting, but it changed her young face. He nodded bitterly. What would it take to make his lady smile? What could put the bloom back on the face of Guenevere?

Could she really hate him enough to send him away? She had not looked at him with eyes of hate. And her last words to him were 'Adieu, fair sweet friend.' Surely that meant something more than courtly flattery?

He groaned. Gods above, what to do? This morning he had to decide, go or stay.

Stay.

Go.

Might as well pick a daisy and let the petals decide! he thought savagely. She loves me, she loves me not—

He rode on moodily towards the horse enclosure, a makeshift corral under the shade of a tree. As he dismounted and threw the reins to a groom, Sir Bedivere ran up. He was moving his head oddly from side to side, as if to shake some dreadful news from his ears. 'The Queen—' was all he could force through his stuttering lips. He tried again. 'Lancelot, the King is crying for you – the Queen's gone.'

Gone.

Lancelot stood stock still.

Gone. Of course.

No wonder she had tried so hard to get rid of him. No wonder she had staged the sudden return to Camelot. She had a tryst, the Queen had a tryst!

One by one the pieces fell into place. He knew about this, it was the way of courtly love. He had seen it in the courts of France often enough. Why did he never think of it before?

Of course a woman like her would have a lover, even though she was married to a king and the best man in the world. An older man, it would be, wise and kind, doubtless her secret love for many years. They would have to snatch their illicit hours together when they could. So the Queen would disappear from time to time, and then reappear covered with convincing excuses, while her knights had been hunting for her high and low.

In the wrong place, of course, or how could she enjoy her lover undisturbed? And the King wanted him to join the search for her?

The King.

Deceived, abandoned, betrayed by his wife.

A huge sadness gathered round Lancelot's heart. He looked at Bedivere. 'Where is the King?' he said.

The summons came when they had almost ceased to care. Guenevere struggled to shake off the lethargy dragging her down. 'Quick, Ina, help me brush my dress, smooth my hair.'

'Yes, madam.'

She could see from the mirror how far she was from the way she ought to look. Her gown was creased now with many days' wear. She would not touch the clothes lining the closet, mocking her fate with their rich splendour. But as Ina settled her coronet over her veil and she felt the smooth green silk of her gown beneath her palms, she straightened her back and held her head up high.

'So, Ina, let me go.'

He was waiting for her in the Great Hall, after a lowering trudge through miles of dark corridors with never a soul but the guards in sight. As the men on the doors threw them open at her approach, the vast empty space gaped before her like a monstrous cave. She had to force herself not to flinch from the fearsome figure straddling the hearth within.

She knew him at once for her ravisher in the forest, the man who had brought her here. He had the lean, hard frame she had first seen in the saddle, and the look of a leader who rewards disobedience with death. His iron-grey hair sprang back from a peak on his forehead like the crest of a hawk, and a pair of fierce eyes of no colour tracked her every move. He wore the short tunic of a warrior, though he was older than most warriors ever lived to be. Half a dozen daggers were thrust through his belt, and he toyed with another as it dangled from his hands. But that was not what made her catch her breath. Around his neck he wore the torque of a Druid of the highest rank.

A cold sweat filmed her palms.

Any knight could be a Druid – Druids were always warriors before they turned to the service of their God, and even in old age they fought for what they believed in, and died for it too. But only one Druid had ever been her enemy, and only he could lie behind this evil Druid now.

Merlin.

Who else would attack her here in her own land?

But was Merlin against her still? Would his hate never sleep, not even now she had lost Arthur and buried Amir? Did he want her life too? She looked at the yellow eye-stone in the neck of the Druid's torque, and almost moaned aloud with fear.

The guards propelled her forward down the hall. The stranger fixed her with a cold metallic glance. 'I am Tuath, a Druid of these parts,' he said harshly. 'You will wonder why you are here, Queen Guenevere.'

He raised a hand. It was horribly maimed from an old sword-wound, the thumb and forefinger missing, the rest of it crabbed like a claw. 'Will you take some refreshment? I will call for food and wine.'

'Food and wine?' Disbelief and fury gave her the words she needed now. 'You dare to insult me with this show of hospitality after all you have done? Where are my knights? I know they were wounded – what have you done with them?'

'They are safe, and well cared for. Have no fear for them.'

'I want to see them, to judge for myself! And I demand to be set free at once. You know who I am – you must know the penalty for abducting a queen!'

He gave a mirthless smile. 'But it is no offence, Your Majesty, to help and advise a queen.'

She was astounded. 'What about?'

He came closer. 'For centuries in these islands, we kept the old ways. A queen would change her consort and take a new king when the time came.' He sighed with a kind of pleasure, and his eyes were brooding with desire. 'The youth the Queen discarded was always given to us, and we gave him to the Gods. For three days and nights we hung him on a tree, then we took his manhood with our golden knives. His seed and his sex made a paste to enrich the earth, and his blood ran down to give the new crops life.' He smiled to himself. 'Every year we made this rite.'

'Sir, all this—'

But he was oblivious. 'Then it became three years, and then seven, before the King had to die. And then queens would spare their consorts' lives, and permit them to live on in the warrior band.' Suddenly his colourless eyes were boring into her. 'And now queens will allow a failing king to live, even when his weakness undermines the land.' He raised his voice. 'And it must not be!'

Guenevere gasped. 'What are you telling me?'

'Your consort has a weakness in his soul. You saw it first when Merlin was lost to him. Without his Druid, Arthur could neither move nor stir. Now he has fallen into the same lethargy again. All his desire is changed to feebleness of heart. Your Arthur is not capable of kingship, nor can you rouse him to his strength as a man. And even for a man in all his power,' his eyes were glittering with Druidic ecstasy, 'the time comes when the King must die.'

She recoiled in terror. 'A curse on you for saying so!'

He was impervious. 'Your mother had her Chosen Ones, and she changed her consort every seven years. You loved your mother, and you claim to honour the Great Mother above all.' His deformed hand flew out like a talon and gripped her wrist. 'Yet you defy Her ways! The law of the Goddess is that you must be championed by the worthiest knight. When one fails in his duty, you have the right to find another – that is your sacred trust!'

She tore herself free. 'I will not set my husband aside because of the weakness he suffers now. I will be strong for both!'

'Why should you cling to a love that is dead, when you should be faithful to the One from whom we all take life? When any woman lives a half-life without love, she wounds herself. When a queen does, her whole country becomes a wasteland.'

'Do not speak to me of my country! I will rule my land as I see fit!'

'To do that you need a warrior, lady, not a shadow man!' He gave a hateful laugh and moved in close again. She could smell the incense of his last ritual on his clothes, and above it the sick, sour smell of mingled blood and seed. 'Answer your own nature. You were not made to be the Christian chattel of a failing man.' He came nearer still. 'You are a daughter of the Otherworld. You are free like your mother to do as you choose. All her acts of love and pleasure she took without guilt, and so should you.'

His loathsome claw gripped her wrist again. He was so close to her now that she could reach out and touch his belt. A cold thought came into her mind. *If I can get one of his daggers—*

'Out! Get out of the way!'

There was a shout at the door, the heavy sound of a mailed fist striking flesh, and the same curse again. 'Out of my way, you fool, open the door!'

The double doors burst on their hinges as a band of knights came through. At their head was the last man she ever thought to see.

'*Malgaunt!*'

She ran to him and threw herself into his arms. 'Oh, Malgaunt, thank the Gods you've come!' She burst into tears. 'I've never been so pleased to see you in my life!'

CHAPTER 53

It was the sweetest moment of his life. *Oh, Malgaunt!* she had cried, and, *Thank the Gods you've come!* And she clung to him as her saviour, and he had gripped her by the waist and pressed her to him as he had always lusted to.

Now he would know those breasts, that body, those long, full flanks he had dreamed of for twenty years. Now she would be his, and all that was hers would be his, and he would be King at last, King of the Summer Country, Malgaunt the King—

Malgaunt grinned in triumph, and clasped Guenevere to his chest. 'So, Druid!' she heard him rasp. 'You have done well, it seems! You've brought her round, have you, she's mine at last?'

'Yours?'

Malgaunt could not contain himself. His savage grin had an elation she had never seen before. 'Yes, Guenevere! My Druid has seen it rising in the stars. You are ripe for a new consort, he says, and all the signs show that you are poised to take another champion and Chosen One. So I had everything made ready for you here, and sent Tuath with my knights to bring you from the wood.'

A flash of the old Malgaunt flickered across his face.

'You have made me wait a long time for this!' He came towards her, and the nightmare came to life.

'Malgaunt, no!' She broke, gabbling, from his grasp. 'I won't change Arthur for another man, your Druid is mad even to think it! I ran to you now because I thought you'd come to rescue me. Just take me back to Camelot, and we'll forget all this. I'll never speak of it again I promise you, only take me home!'

Malgaunt laughed harshly. 'Guenevere, you are home! You are mine now, and this is where you live. I've chosen everything for you, had it all done just as you had it in Camelot. Didn't you see your gowns and jewels, even your own perfume?'

'No!' she whimpered, but he did not hear.

'This is my castle and my estate, you're in Dolorous Garde. Tuath is my Druid, and he brought you here for me.' He looked across at the Druid, and Tuath gave him a mystical smile. 'Mad? Perhaps so. But all he cares about is restoring the old ways. He has forsworn women himself. He longs for the lost days of blood and sacrifice, when queens ruled alone, and he and his kind had the power of death over the finest young men of the tribe. So our purposes came together when I saw my chance with you.'

Tuath's eyes were on her, like iron on fire. 'You are the Throne Woman of the Summer Country. You honour the Goddess when you offer a new man the friendship of your thigh.'

'That will never be!'

The grey voice ground on. 'You have no children. Arthur will give you none.' He pointed his claw-like hand. 'Prince Malgaunt is of the blood royal of our land. Take him, and make a doubly royal child. Take the Mother's way to make yourself a mother again.'

Were they both mad? 'Never!' Guenevere screamed.

Malgaunt's hot eyes were devouring her body as they had all her life. 'You have no choice.' He grinned. 'You're as good as dead to the world – and so is your former husband too.'

'What?' The hairs were rising on her neck. 'My *former* husband? What do you mean?'

He sounded calm, but she could feel his excitement with every word. 'Where do you think I've been while you've been here? I have led the search for you so thoroughly that all Camelot thinks you're dead, or lost with the Fair Ones in the hollow hills. And I've sent to Arthur to tell him you've disappeared. When he returns to look for you, he'll meet some tragic accident on the way.'

He was crowing with delight. 'Then, in a while, I'll find you wandering in the woodland, as if the Fair Ones had set you free. You may have lost your tongue but you'll be alive, and all the world will rejoice.' He laughed again at the look on her face. 'Believe me, Guenevere, I'll cut your tongue out, if I have to, if you cross me now. Your hands too, to stop you telling your story to the world. But you'll see reason, won't you?'

Tuath nodded. 'Of course she will. And all will understand when the Queen takes her saviour Malgaunt as her new consort.'

'Yes!' Malgaunt stared ahead, his eyes dark with dreams. 'And then you and I will join the Middle Kingdom to our own land, claiming it in your right as Arthur's queen. From there, we can even make ourselves High King and Queen of all these islands, as you and Arthur planned.' He laughed to himself, then looked at her sharply. 'And all for one May morning ride!' He reached out to take her in his arms.

'*Don't touch me!*' She leaped away, and spat in his face

He brought his hand to his cheek and stared at her in shock. 'After all I've done for you?'

'All you've done for me? Malgaunt, you can't make me love you, I love—'

Another man, she wanted to say, and choked on the words.

'Arthur?' Malgaunt howled. 'You don't love Arthur! You can't, he's finished now!' She opened her mouth to speak, but he cut her off. 'And d'you think I care if you don't love me, when I've wanted you all my life?' A sour smile split his face. 'I'll take you as I find you, Guenevere!'

She knew that panic was sounding in her voice. 'If you don't care for me, think of yourself at least!' He had to hear this, he had to understand. 'You are the son of a king, a prince of the blood! You're a knight of the Round Table, pledged to honour and chivalry. I'll never love you, Malgaunt. I'd rather cut my throat than come to your bed. If you take me, it's rape! How does that sit with your honour as a knight?'

'Guenevere!'

The face so close to hers was swelling with rage. Behind the narrow lids, the pupils were black dots, shot with pinpoints of light. She trailed off, panting, afraid of Malgaunt now.

'So! Well, choose how you take me, Guenevere, but take me you must. Your choice is now, tonight!'

'Hail Mary, Mother of God, Queen of Heaven, blessed art thou among women, for the Lord is with thee . . .'

The Abbess Placida's lips moved through the familiar convent chant as her wimpled head and large body sailed out of her private quarters into the corridor behind. Truly the Lord blesses His chosen women, and now even my lowly self among them, she marvelled smugly. Praised be His holy Name! To bring such men under the roof of my house! The great days I have envisaged are indeed coming to pass.

'Smartly there, sisters!' she chivvied the trio of nuns who were bearing away the remains of the meal. 'And hurry along with the cheese, and more wine.'

'Yes, Mother!' Heads down, the novices scurried away like mice. The Abbess smiled indulgently. Ah, the beauty of a well-run house of women, when order and discipline triumphed as they should!

She paused for a moment before returning to her guests. An ugly look passed over her face as past events forced their way painfully into her mind. She shuddered. What a trial you inflicted on me, Lord, what a torment for Your faithful handmaid!

She scowled.

To have to learn the truth about Sister Ann. To be forced to undergo the visitation of the King's officers, investigating the coven that that cursed witch had formed inside this holy house. To have to interrogate every single nun, and purge the whole convent of the evil that the wicked one had caused.

The Abbess's fingers twitched at the memory. Her rod had hardly slept all that time. But she had lain down each night with the sense of duty done. And good had triumphed, driving out the bad. Her tireless efforts had restored the convent to a place of peace again.

The Abbess's brow cleared. It had all turned out for the best, praise the Lord. The King's knights had made it clear that the evil was not her fault. Brother John had come hot-foot to confess the nuns and help to restore the right. And now he and the Father Abbot from London were here in person under her roof! That was proof positive of forgiveness of the past.

Such men, such great men . . .

Mistily the Abbess surveyed the future landscape of her dreams. More money, more of everything was coming from Rome, everyone knew that. Monks had been empowered to take on the office of priests, and their tiny flocks were growing every day. There would be bishoprics and archbishoprics and new sees and dioceses, and Brother John and the Father Abbot were the men to take these roles.

And there could not be a better time for Christ's work. God was with them, events were in their hands. Witness the business that had brought the two monks here to break their journey and rest overnight. The Abbess cocked an ear to the even hum of conversation from the room behind. She could rely on the server nuns to keep up the flow of food and wine. Time to rejoin the guests.

'You saw her, of course,' the Father Abbot was saying, as the Abbess slipped back in. After a good convent dinner, his lean face had lost some of its waxen look. But another satisfaction lit his eyes now.

Brother John gave a bitter smile. 'At her so-called queen-making,' he agreed, 'when the harpy screamed at me before all the crowd. A vixen, Father, I promise you. God only knows what King Arthur saw in her!'

The Father Abbot stifled an inward sigh. Would these Britons never understand the ways of men? A monk had to learn to recognise women's sin. Otherwise he could never know how the daughters of Eve preyed upon men, how they dragged them down to lose their immortal souls. Of course the queen was a harridan and, like all the women of the Summer Country, a whore besides. Still, they had to get to grips with that too.

'But a woman of parts, surely?' he prompted Brother John. 'After all, she induced King Arthur to marry her at first sight.' He frowned. 'Thereby adding another decade to our labours – from the very first, I thought we could win him to us!'

'And we shall, Father!' the Abbess Placida put in.

The Father Abbot pressed on, ignoring her. 'And God has shown us that we shall, by these clear signs.' He held up his right hand. 'One, that He struck down the pagan queen, the mother of this one. Two, that He has denied a daughter in the line. Three, that He took the life of the one child this queen has had. And four, that He has now caused her to disappear, leaving Arthur to fall into our hands.'

He paused for a cold moment of concern. Would they be there in time? We came as fast as we could, O Lord, he prayed. Give us the chance to profit from Arthur's loss. For he is ours, he has been ours from the first. He must be ours, if we are to win this land!

He looked up to see Brother John tracking his every thought. He held the monk's gaze, and they shared an imperceptible hope. Under the awed eyes of the Abbess, two minds and mouths moved as one. 'God grant we win the battle for Arthur's soul!'

'Don't touch me, Malgaunt! You won't get away with this. You can't wear me down by keeping me imprisoned here!'

'Imprisoned, Guenevere?' Malgaunt was enjoying himself. 'What nonsense, my dear! You are queen of the castle, and you'll have a new king tonight!'

'Malgaunt, I shall never—'

'Oh, you will. Or what about that maid of yours, Ina? You wouldn't like anything to happen to her, I'm sure.' He turned to the Druid. 'Tuath here has sworn off women for life. But there's a guardroom full of men quite the contrary—'

'My lord!'

A breathless page came flying into the room. 'Prince Malgaunt, they are calling for you on the battlements.

There's a stranger coming through the forest, flying a white banner, riding a white horse.'

Guenevere's blood sang with the beating of her heart. 'Now all the Gods be praised!'

'This way! Over there!'

She could hardly hear the urgent words of the guard. The air on the battlements was as fresh as wine after her long imprisonment, and the evening sun was blinding as they stumbled out. But far off she could see the lone rider spurring across the scrubland, straight and true.

He rode with his visor down. The armoured body, the faceless, ironclad form were that of Arthur when he first came to her. But the lean body lying low in the saddle was not that of the King.

Malgaunt's colour faded, and his eyes drained of everything except hate. But his voice was cool enough when he turned to Guenevere. 'Sir Lancelot!' he said pleasantly. 'What a pity he must die.'

Guenevere laughed in triumph. 'You must be mad, Malgaunt. They'll know in Camelot that he was coming here.'

Malgaunt shrugged. 'But they won't know what happened when he fails to return. There are forty arrows trained upon him now. A hundred swords await him in the courtyard below. When he comes, you'll tell him you're here of your own choice, or my men will hack him piece by piece to death.'

To save his life, more lies.

'Release my knights!' Guenevere cried. 'Have them moved to the rooms next to mine, and I'll send him away and save your wretched life!'

'My wretched life, is it?'

For a second she feared that she had said too much. But,

mastering his rage, Malgaunt turned and, gripping her by the elbow, forced her to descend.

Down they went and down, at such a pace that she feared Malgaunt meant to throw her down the steps and break her neck. By the time they reached the courtyard, she was trembling with the fury of her desire for revenge.

On the walkways above, forty archers were aiming at the gate where Lancelot must come in. On the ground a hundred knights lined the walls ready to greet him at sword's-point. Malgaunt stood on the cobbled yard facing the entrance, his arm resting on Guenevere's shoulders in a loose embrace, but his mailed hand gripping the spot at the back of her neck where hunters kill rabbits with one brutal squeeze. His Druid Tuath stood guard on her other side, and the eyes of the knights never left their leader's face as they waited for the sign.

Oh, Lancelot.

And there he was, she could see him through the gateway coming towards her now. She was afraid to breathe in case she shattered into a thousand pieces from the joy of seeing him, having him here again.

Lancelot.

Banner flying, Lancelot galloped over the drawbridge and into the inner court.

Lancelot, my love.

The white stallion drew to a snarling halt, froth at its mouth, its flanks stained with blood. His sword drawn, Lancelot faced Malgaunt. He did not look at her.

'Welcome to Dolorous Garde, Sir Lancelot!' Malgaunt cried, with false bonhomie. 'The Queen and I are glad to see you. What brings you here?'

'Prince Malgaunt, I know what you have done!' Lancelot was pale, transfigured with rage. 'I am here to call you a traitor to the Queen, a disgrace to the name of knighthood, and a shame to mankind. I challenge you to single combat now. If you fail, I'll publish your dishonour the length and breadth of this land!'

Malgaunt's hand tightened involuntarily on the back of Guenevere's neck. He tried a casual laugh. 'You challenge me, Sir Lancelot?'

'My lord,' Tuath said quietly. 'I raise my hand, he falls under fifty swords. Kill him. Why should he challenge you?'

Guenevere felt the hairs tremble on the back of her neck.

Lancelot stood up in his stirrups, and looked around. On all four sides of the courtyard, the lofty walls of the old castle were broken by windows and balconies and galleries everywhere. A palace like Dolorous Garde housed a thousand ears. Malgaunt's knights and men-at-arms, his servants and maids, his butlers and cooks, washerwomen and scullery-boys would all be listening now.

'I call you a coward, Prince Malgaunt!' Lancelot called. 'And so will every man, if you fail to answer me! Name your time, place and weapon, and I will meet you in the field. But I cannot overlook this insult to the Queen!'

'The Queen, ah, yes!' Malgaunt looked unperturbed, but the cold mail of his glove closed on the back of her neck. 'You have not heard what the Queen has to say.'

'The Queen?' He laughed scornfully. His accent was very strong. 'I pay no heed to what the Queen says!'

She could not draw back now. 'Sir Lancelot,' she said coldly, 'why are you angry? What's the cause of this?'

'Why am I angry?' Suddenly he was a boy again, raw and confused. 'What are you saying, lady? I don't understand.'

Guenevere forced her face into a broad smile. 'I am here as my kinsman's guest. He and I are at peace. I can't imagine what you are doing here.'

'So!' His eyes flared, and he flushed to the roots of his hair. 'You are not here against your will? I thought—' He broke off and bit his lip, looking down like a boy in the wrong. Then he stared straight and deep into her eyes. 'You swear to me – you promise, Majesty?'

'Yes, indeed!' She laughed, a hateful sound even to her own ears. 'I'm afraid you've mistaken the situation, Lancelot.'

She could hardly bear it.

He gritted his teeth. 'Then you and Prince Malgaunt are in accord?' He turned the heat of his brown eyes on her again. 'If I'd known, I would not have—'

She could not help herself. 'You have sworn to be my knight. Do I have to thank you for your good deeds?'

His colour rose again. 'No, lady. Forgive my foolish words.'

The pain now was the worst it had ever been.

CHAPTER 54

'Whatever you say, my lady. Goodnight, and good rest to you.'

Shivering, Sir Bors lay in bed and watched Guenevere's retreating form. He hugged the blanket tighter to his thin frame, and cursed the fever that racked him from head to foot. He had taken knocks and cuts enough before, the Gods knew. It was a mystery why the damned enchantment of the Druid's band of knights had left him so weak and trembling and shamefully prone to tears. It had been bad enough in the dark cell where they had been kept. But he had hated being dragged from his bed to new quarters in the Queen's apartments. He was terrified that being moved would make his wound break out and start bleeding again.

He eyed Guenevere with a hopeless sense of fate. She was trying to help them, he knew, by getting them out of the grim cells underground, and having them housed with her, under her eye. But what if she caught his illness, this wound fever, jail fever, whatever it was?

She meant well, too, with her comforting words, 'My lords, your cousin is here – good news, Sir Kay, Sir Lancelot has arrived!' And it was good to know that Lancelot had come, more than good, the best. But the Queen did not look

pleased when she told them this. Poor lady, she had not slept
for a long while, Bors thought sadly. And the high colour in
her cheeks, the unnatural brightness of her eye, all suggested
that she had a fever already, a disease of her own.

He looked out of his clean white cot in the clean white
chamber and knew that further down the white corridor lay
his brothers in arms, Sir Kay and for Lionel. And he knew,
too, that he had only to call to summon Ina, who had the
chamber nearest to the Queen. Only an antechamber divided
the four of them from the Queen's chamber on the opposite
side of the apartment. Bors shifted his head, and tried to ease
his aching frame. Well, the Queen must be lying easier than
he was, that was for sure. And she would be easier still in
the knowledge that her champion Sir Lancelot was here.

'Leave me, Ina.'

Ina pursed her lips and slipped quietly away. Goddess,
Mother, she wondered, what's wrong with the Queen?
Surely she could not be so distressed about her knights?
Sir Bors had a fever, it was true, but he was young and
healthy, he would shake it off. The others were recovering
well from the cuts and blows they had taken in the wood.
And Sir Lancelot had arrived to rescue them all!

Yet the Queen . . . Watching Guenevere covertly as she
turned down the sheets of the lavender-scented bed, Ina
could not make it out. After all they had been through,
to be crying, shaking, weeping now? From the trembling
in her hands, you'd have thought she had a fever, yet
she would not countenance any of Ina's potions or soothing balms.

'Leave me, Ina,' was all that she would say.

Ina snorted quietly to herself. Leave her here, by the
window, in the cold light of the moon, all weeping and
alone? The Queen her mother would never have wanted

this. Ina gathered her strength to remonstrate. 'My lady,' she began forcefully.

Guenevere's voice was as distant as the moon. 'Leave me, Ina. I'll call you when I want you. Leave me now.'

You must leave me.

She had hurt Ina, she knew, with her sharp rebuff. But she could not help it. She could not help anything now.

For now she felt the force of Merlin's curse, when Arthur had fought Malgaunt to the death. 'If you spare this man,' Merlin had told Arthur then, 'you will suffer for it all your living days. Malgaunt is fated to destroy your peace. He will rob you of your best jewel, and leave a gaudy imitation in its place. All this he will do because you spared his life.'

She had sought to avoid her kinsman's blood on her marriage bed. She wanted to spare Arthur from it as much as Malgaunt, and turn evil to good to bless their wedding day. But Malgaunt's malice had already woven its web. Arthur's peace was destroyed when Malgaunt's actions brought Lancelot here.

She had fled like a child from the fear of Lancelot's love. But the force of fate had drawn him here, and her love for Arthur lay in ruins now.

Her love had been the jewel in Arthur's crown. And what was left but imitation now?

Alone in the bedchamber, Guenevere sat in the window in grief too deep for tears. He had come for her, Lancelot, her lord, her hope, her love. He had come like the celandines in springtime, like the first soft fall of the snow. And she had lied to him, and sent him away.

To save his life?

But did he know that? Would he ever know?

So again he had offered his service, and his trust had

been abused. Would he ever trust her simplest word again? Why should he? Would she, in his place?

She rose to her feet, gripped the iron bars of the deep, mullioned window, and pressed her burning head against the glass. Below her the garden was drowsing as night fell. The scent of the roses was heavier in the evening air, and the warmth of day was leaving the old stone walls. The candlelight from her window cast its lambent glow into the deepening dark. All the world below her was at peace.

The iron bars were cold and rough in her grasp. She groaned. She was still a prisoner, even though Malgaunt had drawn off his watchdogs now that Lancelot was here. Yet this barred room was a place of safety, and she had been glad to take refuge here from the courtyard, refusing to join Malgaunt and Lancelot at dinner in the hall.

But there was no escaping from herself. From this love, this shame, this sickness that she had.

She moaned aloud.

Her only hope was that he did not know.

His head pounding, Lancelot stumbled out of doors. Dolorous Garde! The place was well named.

To come to the aid of the Queen in her distress, and then to find she was not in distress at all – to be treated to a smiling rebuke that was worse than any scorn and then to have to drink and dine with her kinsman, that foul slave Malgaunt. Goddess, Mother, this was not the life of chivalry he had dreamed!

He lifted his face to the moon, letting the cool night air bathe his tormented skin. When he served Queen Aife, she held all her knights in thrall. She was a stern task-mistress, and her knights groaned in her service, she demanded so much of them. But never did they suffer in confusion like this.

A gasp that was half a sob escaped his lips as he wandered on through the castle grounds. He passed under archways and through gates till he came to a quiet garden enclosed within old stone walls. In the centre a great hawthorn sprinkled the grass with stars. He let himself in through the small iron gate and felt safe and alone at last.

From the walls, the scent of June roses drenched the air. High above, the uncaring stars looked down. He tore a rose from a stem and crushed it in his hand. The sharp sweetness of the broken petals stained his clenched fist. He lifted his eyes to the stars, opened his heart, and wept.

She saw him coming, it seemed, from the time before time. First a shadowy figure in the gold and silver light, then the lean shape she loved so desperately. Then the swing of his cloak, the glint of the torque round his neck. And then the dull chestnut sheen of his hair and his long, tormented face. And now he stood in the garden beneath her window, his eyes bright with tears, waiting, she was sure, for her call.

Yet he stood in a silence she did not know how to break. The blood was pounding in her veins, and foolish thoughts ran through her mind. *If only there were someone else here to call him instead of me.*

Wildly she fingered the woodland green silk gown she had not changed since she was captured. *If only I'd worn something better, if only I'd known he was on his way!* Yet would he notice what she was wearing? Would he care?

She lifted her eyes to the distant sky. Far away on the horizon a horned moon was shining and all the heavens were burning with pale fire.

Come—

From the airy mansions of the moon, and the far regions of the world between the worlds, he was calling her. She could hear the soft insistent whisper of life itself.

Come—

She opened the window and whispered, 'Lancelot!'

He started like a stag, his hand unconsciously seeking his sword. Then he stepped into the light from the window, looking up as pale and cold as stone. 'Why did you go?' he began abruptly, staring at her with the hurt eyes of a child. 'I am your knight. Why did you send me away? Why did you leave Caerleon without a word?'

'I thought—'

He turned on her in a rage. 'Why did you lie to me? Lie and deceive?' He flew at the wall, and tore at the ivy in despair.

'I—'

He was climbing now, surging up the massive old creeper with a fearless grip. 'You sent me to the King with a message that was no message at all! You left orders that I was to stay in Caerleon till you returned. You wanted to be parted from me while you were away! Why? Do you have a lover? Another knight?'

Her temper rose to match his. 'If you are my knight, sworn to my love and faith,' she cried, possessed by wild illogic, 'why are you here when I ordered you to stay?'

He had reached the window-ledge, almost within her touch, borne up by desire and pain. 'Because I thought you were in danger – because I had to know what you meant – because I could not bear it without you!'

'Oh, Lancelot—'

He was weeping freely, angrily knocking away great tears. 'You may treat your knight badly, but I am still sworn to you. Wherever you go, I must go!' He reached towards her blindly, like a motherless child.

She could feel her tears rising in answer to his. 'How did you find me?'

He planted his feet in the ivy and gripped the iron bars

with both hands. She could hardly bear his open, wounded gaze. 'Lady, I would have found you in all the world! When I came to Camelot, they said you were lost in the wood. They told me no one was more distraught than Prince Malgaunt. Yet I knew the Prince was next in line for your throne. And when they said he had a castle beyond the forest, I knew where to come. I knew I would find you here.'

'You knew? How?' She leaned on the window-sill. His nearness tormented her.

He shook his head stubbornly, like a child again. 'I knew.' He raised his eyes and locked on to her gaze. She knew she was looking into his soul. His purple-brown irises were flecked with hazel and gold, and his face was wet with tears. She lifted her hand to his lips as she had on the night they met, and let it fall again.

The air was warm, and the tension between them was a thread about to break. His eyes were wide with query, and she answered without words. Furiously he pulled at the bars of the window, till he found one set less firmly than the others in the stone. Then he worked at it steadily, twisting it this way and that, till his forehead was damp with sweat, and the iron was dark with what looked like his blood.

She wanted to laugh, to cry, to dance.

So this is love – welcome, friend, as cruel as you will be, and as sweet as you may become.

Welcome, love.

May we be granted the peace of loving and not losing, of giving and not resenting, may we let this newborn thing grow and flourish between us, and become what it has to be.

Now she could feel herself growing into the woman she had dreamed she might become, moving towards the man who was all she wanted in a man. She could hear his breath rasping in his throat as he wrenched the bar out of its mortar at last. He groaned with the exertion, and she could see the rusty metal had torn the skin of his palms. The veins on his forehead were standing out, and his eyes had an Otherworldly gleam, but no man could have looked more beautiful to her now.

He heaved himself up, and was through the remaining bars, over the casement and into the room in one sinuous move. As he came towards her she saw that his hands were red with blood.

She ran towards him, and reached up to touch his face. The skin of his temple was damp to her fingertips. The hollow by his eyes seemed to have been waiting for her caress, and she wanted to trace the shape of his cheekbones till the day she died.

Her hand found the back of his neck, and he shuddered, but did not pull back. Gently, slowly, she drew his face down to hers, and laid her finger in the groove of his lips. He seized her hand, and pressed it to his mouth. Then he grasped her like a man starving, folded her in his arms and kissed her for the first time.

Outside the window the moon shone down on groves of white hawthorn and roses with silver leaves, making their branches sing. The pale fragrance of apple blossom was in the air. She kissed his mouth hungrily, and felt his hunger rise. She kissed him again, she was starving for him – *oh, my love, my love.*

He gasped and stepped back, only to crush her to him tighter than before. 'The glory of the spring shines in you alone, and the splendour of the stars lives in your eyes!' he moaned. 'You are the woman of the dream, you are the love I have longed for all my life. But you are married, you are the wife of the King! Oh, lady, lady, what does it mean?'

'Hush,' she said. 'Hush, my love.'

She kissed the welling blood from his hand and drew him towards the bed.

CHAPTER 55

They stood by the bed and kissed like people famished for each other since time began. His kisses were hard and hungry like a boy's, and she could feel his passion building with every breath. Trembling, she took his face between her hands. The soft stubble of his chin pricked her fingers, but the skin was as smooth as satin on his temples, and in the tender hollow of his throat.

She wanted to weep as she threaded her fingers through his hair. The back of his neck was as soft as down, and he trembled at her touch. She wrapped her arms round him, and he clasped her to him so fiercely that he lifted her off her feet. 'Ah, lady!' he whispered. 'Is this a dream?'

Sighing, he buried his face in her neck. His lips made a path of kisses round her throat. Inside her gown her skin was pricking for his touch. He brought his hand to her breast, and her body caught fire.

She reached up to her headdress, and cast the gold circlet and veil to the ground. As she raised her face to his, her hair fell down like rain. Gasping, he explored her mouth and she savoured his long full lips, his strong, insistent tongue. Then he lifted her, and swung her on to the bed.

Kneeling astride, deftly he untied the fastenings of her gown. A blistering shaft of remembrance shot through her mind: *Arthur fumbled my buttons the first time he came to me.* Then he pushed back the green silk to her navel, till she was as naked as a lily in its sheath of leaves. She lifted her arms to his neck, her eyes met his gaze, and she thought of Arthur no more.

As the gown slipped down and she lay bare to him, Lancelot made a soundless cry in the back of his throat. His eyes grew bright with tears. Her breasts were white and full, her nipples rosy and sweet as kisses in the night, and already craving his touch. In her body, in her eyes, in every distracted movement and light moan, he could feel her love and need calling out to his own. The sound of his own name dimly reached his ears. She was crooning it almost to herself, lifting her arms to him, wrapping them round his neck.

She was aching for him now, crying out under her breath. He reached out in wonder and stroked the top of her breast. Her nipples tensed in answer to his caress. She reached for his fingers and crushed them against her breast till she groaned in pain. Then she drew him down beside her on the bed, and took him in her arms.

Gently she stroked his back, his sides, and the lean, tense curve of his flanks. Then her hand found the opening of his shirt and her fingers brushed his breast. He started violently, leaped to his feet and, unbuckling his heavy leather belt, tore off his tunic and shirt, and kicked off his breeches and boots.

Naked, he was white and golden like a god. A silver dewdrop glinted on the top of his sex. Gilded by the gold and silver dusk, he was a being from the Otherworld. He leaned over, and peeled away the last remnant of her modesty, drawing the green gown down over her hips. Then he slipped down beside her on the bed, and dropped a rainfall of sweet kisses on her quivering flesh.

The touch of his lips felt like the sun in spring, after the longest winter she had known. Tenderly he explored the dewy triangle at the top of her legs till she writhed under his hand. She felt herself grow wet with joy for him, and a mist of tears came before her eyes. She clung to him in a storm of emotion, of love, of fear, she could not tell. A thought of Arthur passed through her like a knife, and she caught her breath with pain. *What am I doing?* she moaned to herself. *Why am I here?* Then Lancelot renewed his caresses and she could think no more.

Now she was riding the waves of desire as they battered her senseless, pulling her down to the dark rolling depths. He quickened with her till she could not tell where his body ended and hers began. Now they were breathing the same panting breaths, and the need between them could not be contained. She opened her arms and cried out to him from her heart, *'Love me, Lancelot, love me, love me now!'*

And he cried out too, and came into her, and the roaring sea drowned them both.

Afterwards they drowsed in each other's arms. Lancelot held her close, but she could hear the doubt and wonder in his voice. 'When did you know?'

Lazily she traced the fine skin of his eyelids, the tender blue of harebells in spring. 'As soon as I saw your eyes.'

He paused. 'What, the very first time we met, in the forest? When I came with Bors and Lionel?'

'There. I could have lain down for you there.'

He was silent. Anxiety seared her like a flame. He could have had any girl, one of his own age who had never borne children, who did not have the telltale marks of motherhood. Perhaps he hated her body now that they had made love. Perhaps he did not love her, he never had – She forced herself to speak. 'And you? When did you know?'

The silence lengthened and deepened till she could feel

the ground shifting, and a chasm between them opening now. She clutched at him. 'You do know, don't you? Say you know!'

He opened his eyes. 'You knew,' he said gently, settling her back in his arms. 'That is enough.'

And she knew it was not the last time she would feel that pain.

Which of them was it?

Which of her knights was Guenevere's paramour?

Malgaunt circled his chamber like a wolf in a trap, his head thrumming with the same insistent refrain.

It had to be one of them. He had had all night to reason it out, and however many times he passed it through his burning mind, it came to the same thing. Guenevere had a lover, and he had to know who it was.

There was no other explanation of the way things had turned out. Tuath his Druid had seen she was ripe for love. Arthur had failed her, she had to choose again. Yet she had not chosen him.

The familiar fury boiled up in Malgaunt's heart.

He knew why.

Guenevere, damn her, had already made her choice! The new consort seen by Tuath in the stars had already invaded her heart before he, Malgaunt, had even come knocking at the gates!

Why else would she refuse him? Oh, she had always been cold to him, and pretended he was the last man on earth for her. But she knew as well as he did that they were fated to come together, fated to rule together, fated to restore the wrong that the fates had done him by making her Queen, when he should have been King. When she took him in marriage, they would both have what they had wanted all along. They would be lord and lady of the Summer Country, in fate's clear solution to its own whimsical prank. She must know this, it was so obvious!

It was true he had had to give way when Arthur appeared. But that was just another of Fortune's little pranks, to send a raw youth adventuring to snatch the prize from him when he had it in his grasp. He was unprepared for a rival, so almost anyone could have defeated him then. But later he came to see the beauty of Dame Fortune's plan. Once Guenevere had married Arthur, another kingdom was added to her own. Now Arthur had only to meet with an accident, and both countries were hers. And his.

He took a moment to consider Arthur's end. How should he die? Nothing too easy, in memory of Amir. Any man who killed his own son, Malgaunt brooded, who could not save his own flesh and blood from the sea-wolves, deserved the worst of deaths. He should see his death coming, know his life was ending, and understand why. And then Guenevere would be free. Free for Malgaunt, her true partner all along.

Then the blood bulged in his veins and throbbed behind his eyes.

Who was the new consort, the new bedfellow? It had to be one of the three knights in her quarters, the three she had brought with her into the wood.

Not Lancelot then, though it had looked that way when the young fool appeared. No, the May Day ride Guenevere had planned was all too plainly a way of bringing the new lover to a secret tryst. The two other trusted knights would serve both as a cover for dalliance, and as look-outs during her amorous antics in the secret wood. With Arthur far away, Guenevere could indulge herself. She would never have left Lancelot behind in Caerleon if he were the man.

So which one?

Not Kay – too short, too dark, too sarcastic – the

Guenevere he knew would never take a sharp-tongued lover, she had to be adored. Kay was a cripple too: however hungry she was for a man in her bed, he thought brutally, Guenevere would never open her legs to a man without two strong lusty legs of his own.

Bors, then? Not as handsome as Lancelot, but his brown brooding eyes and well-knit body could be to any woman's taste. Bors, yes, maybe.

Still, the most likely one was Lionel. He was made of softer stuff than his brother, and Guenevere would prefer a weaker man. And he had the gold-brown colouring she favoured, with a fine long loose body to boot. Which he was doubtless putting to good advantage now. Unless the sword slash to his arm was much worse than it seemed, he'd have wasted no time. At this very moment, Malgaunt concluded desperately, he must be slipping lustily between the lady's sheets.

The clear image of Guenevere in bed with a lover, her long pale arms entwined around his torso, his body eagerly burrowing into hers, seared Malgaunt's eyes and lit a bonfire in his mind.

'Guard!' he screamed.

A startled man-at-arms almost fell into the room.

'Command a detail to the Queen's quarters!' came the command. 'Get a captain here and six men to follow me for a search and arrest!'

Lancelot fixed his gaze on the crack between the bed hangings, and watched the sky lighten towards dawn. Beside him Guenevere was sleeping as sweetly as a child, her cheeks flushed, tiny tendrils of her bright hair, still damp with the exertions of love, clinging to her face. But he must not sleep, he knew it. He must be away before dawn, and back to his quarters before anyone knew he was gone.

Already a dappled dawn was rising up the sky, painting the chamber with streaks of opal and gold. He had already left it too late to be sure of getting back while darkness still covered his tracks. Go! he told his reluctant body. Go! Or you betray yourself and, worse, you betray the Queen!

He pressed his lips to her cheek, and gingerly started to untangle his limbs from hers. She awoke at once, opening her eyes wide like a child. Then with a sweet smile, she curled into him again, sleepily fumbling misplaced kisses on his chin and neck. The touch of her lips was so unexpected that his flesh stirred at once, and he shuddered with fear and delight. She was the most beautiful woman in the world. She was the most forbidden, and the most irresistible.

Go! ran the last faint whisper of everyday sense. But he was beyond sense. He ran his hand hard down her body, and was startled at the speed of her response.

She came at him with her dewy eyes, her milk-white body and her longing stronger than he ever dreamed women could have. Her shoulders were hot and round and smooth to his touch as he pushed her back among the plump pillows, kicked off the bedcovers and spreading her legs, drove into her till they both knew no more.

Racing through the castle with six guards in his wake, Malgaunt was almost happy. He would catch Guenevere in the act, and expose her for what she was – a married woman with a lover, a queen who lay with her knights.

Why else would she have wanted them with her so badly? 'Release my knights!' she had cried, as soon as he told her how she could save Lancelot's life. She cared for them more than she cared for Lancelot, that was plain. And why should she care for them? Guenevere cared for no one but herself. No, an older woman with a younger man wanted one thing, and only one. Something she was already having, and doubtless had been having all night, hot and strong, while he was condemned to pace the cold floor of his chamber with only rage and jealousy to keep him warm.

Well, not in Dolorous Garde! It would be dolorous indeed for Guenevere when she was caught. Malgaunt's lips contorted in a sadistic smile. For the wife of a king, adultery was treason, and treason in a queen was punished by death. And a traitor's death for a woman meant punishment by fire – treacherous women were denied the swift mercy of the axe and block. So Guenevere would burn, as he had burned for her, for so long, all in vain.

And he would catch her, he couldn't fail. She and her paramour would hardly expect callers at this hour, they'd think they were safe enough at the break of dawn. And with bars on every window, they'd have no chance of escape. They'd both be caught. And he'd be satisfied.

And he would know – *which one?*

As his mind embarked again on the same frantic round, Malgaunt's step quickened to keep pace with his tortured thoughts. And on he strode towards the couple sleeping in the bed.

CHAPTER 56

The clenched hand at the hangings was tearing back the curtains. The dawn light flooded into the dark, safe place, blinding her.

'So, Guenevere! Shall I ask you how you have slept? Not a lot, it seems, from what I can see!'

She grabbed for the tangled sheets to cover herself. Over Malgaunt's shoulder she caught sight of Ina's face. 'Don't blame me, my lady,' she begged in agony, weeping and wringing her hands. 'I couldn't stop them, they broke in before I knew!'

Behind Malgaunt stood half a dozen men-at-arms. Some were staring dumbly at the walls, at the floor, anywhere but at her, others were openly ogling her as she lay in bed. They would all think of this moment, she knew, for the rest of their lives: Queen Guenevere, naked in bed, still warm in the arms of her lover Sir Lancelot.

But Lancelot was not there.

Tears sprang to her eyes. *Goddess, Mother, thanks!*

Where had he gone? With a terrible longing she remembered waking to feel him slipping out of her arms. She had watched him hungrily as he shrugged into his clothes. He had come back to the bed to press a rain of hasty kisses on her hands, her eyes, her mouth, then moved quickly to the window, and slid sideways between the bars. Once outside, he had taken a moment to wedge the loose bar back into place, raised a hand in farewell, then was gone.

Her sharp sense of loss was drowned by a wave of relief. She lay back on the pillows and made her voice harsh with contempt. 'How dare you burst in here like this, Malgaunt? Get out at once, you and your bully-boys! Have my horses prepared. I shall be leaving at once, I and my knights.'

'I doubt that, lady!'

She stared at Malgaunt. With a snake's swiftness, he reached into the bed, snatched the pillow away from under her head, then thrust it triumphantly into her face. 'What's this?' he gloated. 'Does it look as if you slept alone last night?'

The white surface of the linen was smudged and stained with blood. She had a sudden savage memory of Lancelot rearing up over her, driving into her, supporting himself on his hands, without a thought of the cuts he had in his palms.

Malgaunt turned to the captain of his men. 'Get the Queen's knights in here to answer for themselves,' he ordered savagely. 'Drag them from their beds if need be!'

He stood over Guenevere, holding the pillow aloft like a token of victory. 'Leave here, Guenevere? I don't think so, not today! One of your wounded knights has been with you in this bed. You will leave here only in chains, when I take you back to your husband to be punished for your treachery!'

'In here – that's right!'

One by one the three knights were dragged into the room. The sudden exertion had caused Sir Bors's head wound to break out, and beads of blood lay along the raw red scar on his brow. Sir Lionel's eyes were still wide and unfocused from sleep, and as he clutched his injured forearm, the rough dressing was stained with traces of blood.

'So, sirs!' Malgaunt looked at the brothers with a rage that was close to despair.

Sir Kay was the first to respond. His face was jaundiced with pain and fatigue, but he was not afraid. 'So, Prince Malgaunt,' he said firmly. 'What is all this?'

Malgaunt gestured towards Guenevere. 'The Queen has turned traitress to the King!' His teeth flashed. 'Now we know why Her Majesty was so intent on having her knights brought into her quarters, so that she could tend to them.' He pointed a finger vibrating with pent-up spite. 'One of you three lay with the Queen last night!'

Bors closed his eyes. This was madness, it was a nightmare, he must be more ill than he thought. Lionel flinched, and his pale skin mottled with shock. What was the matter with them? Kay thought furiously. Crippled leg or not, it was left to him to challenge Malgaunt now. 'Prince Malgaunt—' he began levelly.

Guenevere's voice rang round the room. 'Malgaunt, demand the truth from these knights on their oath of chivalry. I will stake my life on their word!'

Kay raised his voice. 'Believe it, sir,' he said, with emphasis. 'What you say is false. You wrong the Queen, and you wrong all of us, to accuse us of such foulness and treachery!'

'And I challenge you for that!' added Sir Lionel hoarsely, his cheekbones blotched by two burning marks of shame. 'It's a vile accusation, for the Queen and for us all! Choose which of us you will answer to in the lists, and we shall seek satisfaction from you, prince or no, as soon as our wounds are healed.'

'You talk of satisfaction for the honour of a whore?' Malgaunt cried. 'You'd venture your lives for her? D'you think I'd have accused her without proof?' He grabbed for the pillow again, with its telltale marks of red. 'Queen Guenevere has been unfaithful to the King! Someone came into the Queen's bed last night dropping blood from a wound.'

Lancelot's blood—

Guenevere lay still, and did her best to breathe. In the deep mullioned window behind Malgaunt, the iron bars and the sill beneath were stained with blood. One touch would show also that the central bar was loose. The most cursory search would soon establish which man in the castle had torn the flesh of his hands. Then Lancelot would die too, for treason to his lord.

'I know one of you lay with the Queen last night!' Malgaunt persisted madly. 'Which one?'

She could see from their faces that the blood on the pillow told its own tale. Before, even the cold-hearted Kay had been showing some pity for her shame. Now he was looking at her as men looked at whores in the street. Sir Lionel was shaking his head furiously, his eyes fixed on the ground. But some of Malgaunt's malice had stuck in his trusting heart. And Sir Bors – beneath his tightly closed lids the tears were streaming down, and he was making no move to brush them away. *Oh, Bors,* her soul cried, *don't weep for me!*

Malgaunt watched them all, relishing every sign of misery and shame. *So now you know what it is like to suffer as I have done! Tell me then, lords. Which one? Which one?*

'Who else can it be?' he cried. 'I'll get the answer if I have to keep you here all day! Who lay with the Queen? Who was the traitor she had in her bed last night?'

*   *   *

'Page!'

Lancelot threw open the door of his chamber and peered down the empty corridor angrily. Where was the boy? His own page knew to enquire after Queen Guenevere every morning without needing to be told. But here he had had to summon a household boy, and give him detailed instructions before sending him on his way.

As he had half an hour ago now. What was keeping the wretched lad? He'd never needed more urgently to know how the Queen was.

Troubled and short of sleep, Lancelot prowled his chamber and tried to keep his head.

His love.

And the wife of another man.

He groaned in pain. He had come to Camelot in search of honour and renown. Now he had committed the worst of forbidden sins.

Adultery and treason.

And who was to say which was the worst?

'My lord, my lord!'

The page ran into the room, his eyes staring, his face red with haste. 'My lord, they've arrested the Queen! Prince Malgaunt is taking her to King Arthur to be burned!'

Guenevere stared numbly at the walls of her inner closet. Standing like a statue of herself, she had endured Ina's fumbling attempts to dress her while Malgaunt and his men waited outside. Sir Kay, Sir Bors and Sir Lionel had been taken back to their quarters on Malgaunt's orders, to make ready for the journey to Caerleon, where they would all be accused.

Guenevere bit her lip. There would be a trial in full if Malgaunt had his way. Her kinsman would never forgive her for refusing him now. He would prosecute her and her supposed lover before the King and all the lords of the land.

She was too fearful to allow herself any hope. Any moment Malgaunt or a sharp-eyed guard in the chamber outside might see the blood on the window bars. Then there would be no concealing the truth. If she sent for Lancelot, what could he do? If he came, he might even betray himself. He was young and in love, and in danger himself now, too. How easy would he find it to dupe and deceive, to stay calm in the face of the raging Malgaunt?

'Ready, my lady.'

Ina's dull voice, her pale tear-washed face showed that she, too, had put away all hope. Guenevere nodded. So be it. She clutched her travelling cloak round her and moved towards the door. As she came out into the bedchamber, the cold blast of Malgaunt's hate awaited her.

'The Queen!' he announced sardonically to his men. 'Well, Her Majesty's off to Caerleon now, lads! Let's get her under way.'

In the courtyard below, the whole castle had gathered to see them off. Malgaunt's knights were all drawn up under the command of their leader, the Druid Tuath. Hundreds more eyes watched from the galleries and balconies as Malgaunt led her out.

A covered litter waited by the gate, with an escort of mounted men before and behind. Sir Kay stood ready holding his horse, and travelling chairs awaited the injured Sir Bors and Sir Lionel. Malgaunt pointed towards the litter and offered Guenevere his arm with a cruel parody of chivalry. 'Let me assist you, lady.'

'Hold there!'

On the walkway above the courtyard, Lancelot appeared. From the fresh colour in his face and firm set of his chin, no one would have known that he had not slept. He was clad in a white tunic, and a light coat of mail. In one hand he held a long dagger, in the other a drawn sword.

Guenevere felt the blood rush to her face. But he did not look at her. 'Prince Malgaunt, this is not the behaviour of a knight! To invade the Queen's bedchamber, and insult her in her bed? And to accuse her knights so shamefully – take it back, sir, or I challenge you here.'

'On what grounds, Sir Lancelot?' Malgaunt cried scornfully. 'I have proof that one of these knights came to the Queen's bed. You cannot challenge that!'

Lancelot stood very still. 'I tell you, Prince, on my honour as a knight,' he ground out, 'that none of these three knights lay with the Queen last night! None of these men was with her in her bed! Withdraw this foul scandal now, or prepare to fight. Name the time, the place, the weapons, I am yours!'

'Time, place and weapons?'

Malgaunt paused, considering. Guenevere caught her breath. What was he up to? Would a small flame of chivalry stir at last in Malgaunt's rotten soul? Or did he think simply to kill Lancelot – kill them all? – to cover up his own attack on her?

Fight, Malgaunt, fight, be a man, not a murderer! shrieked her inner voice. As if he had heard her, Malgaunt nodded slowly.

'The time, you say? Why then, let it be now,' he said, with the ghost of a smile. 'As to weapons, choose what you will, I am armed.' In one swift move he drew both his dagger and sword, and stood on guard. Then the wolf in him broke through at the thought of blood. 'And what better place for me to kill you, sir, than here?'

Guenevere stepped forward trembling as the rest of the crowd fanned back. Lancelot vaulted lightly from the walkway and moved to meet Malgaunt in the centre of the court. Guenevere crushed her hands to her mouth to keep from crying out. Not an hour before, she had been so closely entwined with that body, those arms, those legs, that they had made one being out of two.

Terror rose like vomit in her throat.

'A vous!'

'Have at you!'

Malgaunt braced himself, grinning like a man who scents victory, spreading his feet as he crouched low for the attack. Lancelot waited lightly, seeming unprepared for a battle to the death.

Guenevere's senses reeled.

Oh my foolish love!

You could have called Malgaunt to battle in the tournament field, where you would have been armoured and helmeted and protected at every point. But you have nothing, while he is fully armed.

Oh, my love, my love, am I to lose you before I have found you, bury your body before I have known it alive?

Malgaunt feinted left, then right, then leaped up from his deep toad-like squat. As he came up, Lancelot neatly sidestepped the attack, lunged forward, and slipped the point of his sword over Malgaunt's guard and into the side of his neck. Malgaunt could not arrest his powerful upward leap. With his own momentum he drove Lancelot's sword straight down into his heart.

Malgaunt's knees buckled, and he went down grinning as Lancelot drew the weapon out of the wound. Great spouts of blood sprang from the hole in his neck, and his life-force ebbed away. His spirit left his body before his body felt the pain.

Now the thing that had been Malgaunt lay crumpled on the ground, a heap of flesh and chainmail pouring bright blood. His eyes were still glittering with their mad victory glare. He died gloating in the belief that he was seconds away from killing Lancelot. In the world between the worlds, Guenevere knew, Malgaunt would already be boasting of his win.

Lancelot lowered his sword, and the blood ran down the blade. He turned to Tuath. 'Bury your master with all reverence,' he commanded, in a voice Guenevere did not recognise. 'Then leave here, Druid. This castle is mine now. There will be no place for you.'

Tuath gave him a fearsome glare, stood gazing about him wildly for a moment, then bowed his head. Lancelot turned to the four walls of the courtyard, addressing the hidden eyes. 'I have taken this castle in a fair fight, and I claim it by all the laws of chivalry and war!' he pronounced. 'Prince Malgaunt is dead, and I am your master now. He called it Dolorous Garde. From now on it will be known as Joyous Garde, in token of the change. All who wish to serve me will have twice what you were paid before. All who want to leave, will get twice their discharge pay. I will have none but willing hearts about me now!'

The drawn sword-points of the hundred knights had dropped the moment Malgaunt died. All through the castle ran a surge of delight. Malgaunt still lay grinning on the ground, hunched like a vulture gorged on blood. His natural savagery was etched on his face. It would not be hard for Lancelot to be a better lord than this.

'My lord!'

The first of the knights had thrust forward to kiss his hand. 'I am yours, my lord!' he said eagerly. 'As we all are. I captain this troop – forgive me, sir, under our previous orders, we were the troop that captured the Queen – and they call me—'

Lancelot held up his hand. His eyes were very dark.

'You are pardoned, good sir, whatever you did before. And I must beg you to speak to me later, if you please.' He turned on Guenevere a glance of pure rage. 'I shall be busy for a while. The Queen and I have some serious business now.'

CHAPTER 57

He offered her a cold mailed fist, and a glance that was even colder as he led her indoors. Guenevere was struck by a childish pain. *Why don't you kiss me, hug me, smile at me?* Yet she knew they were the focus of a thousand curious eyes. She crushed the foolish longing in her heart.

In the Great Hall for the first time he seemed at a loss. Though he had made himself king of the castle, he did not know where he was.

'May I suggest, my lord,' Guenevere said tremulously, 'that we withdraw to the apartments I occupied?'

As they reached the top of the stairs, Ina came running towards them, laughing and weeping in the same breath.

'Oh, sir!' She was panting so excitedly that Guenevere thought she would pass out. 'Sir Lancelot! *Oh, sir!*'

'Ina,' Guenevere said, as firmly as her voice would allow, 'as you see, Sir Lancelot is lord of this castle now.' She turned to Lancelot. 'With your permission, my lord?'

He bowed. 'As you wish.'

'So,' Guenevere resumed tremulously, 'until Sir Lancelot makes his own dispensations, will you order the household, Ina, and take command? Speak to the stewards, the chamberlain and the butlers, the maids of the chamber and see how it goes. Have some wine and refreshments sent up straight away, for Sir Lancelot will be in need of food. And in the meantime,' she took a breath and dared not look at him, 'see that we are not disturbed.'

Ina attended them back to the apartment and then withdrew, her dancing eyes fixed on the ground.

'Guard, ho!' Lancelot abruptly discharged the man at the door. 'Go to your commander, say I will meet him at the changing of the watch. Until then, tell him, we have no need of you.'

'My lord!'

The man was surveying Lancelot with eyes of open adoration, Guenevere noticed furiously. Why did she hate it so when others loved him too? Why was she jealous of those who could never challenge her?

The guard bowed out, closing the door. Lancelot stood frowning, lost in his thoughts. He stood like a rock, like a stone, while her heart bled for his touch, and her body cried out. She could not restrain herself. 'Why are you angry with me?'

Wordlessly he shook his head. She tried to take his hand, and he thrust her away, closing his eyes. His face was a mask of grief. Her fingers reached out to touch him, and his eyelids were wet with tears.

Fear clutched her heart. 'What is it?'

He tossed his head and his whole body moved like a goaded bull. 'I have lost my honour.'

'How?'

'In loving you!'

A panic so violent gripped her that she could hardly speak. 'But a knight is meant to have a lady. You said you chose me – you said I would inspire you to great deeds.'

He groaned and turned away. 'Loving you as my lady is permitted in chivalry – but lying with my lord's wife is a forbidden sin! It is as bad as killing him – it is killing and castration too. To take his love is to take his manhood, and threaten his life!'

She was weeping with fear. 'Will you give me up?'

'Give you up?' His voice was raw. 'As soon give up my heart, my soul. Oh, lady! I have no life without you.'

She heard him with a surge of savage pride. His answer echoed in her heart's deep core.

He loves me more than his honour, more than his sworn allegiance to his oath.

Here, for once, is a man whose woman is more to him than all the bonds of men, even the love of a king.

All women dream of this.

It is the dream that few ever attain.

It is the bliss, the joy, the love I was born to find.

'Lancelot—' She moved forward to take him in her arms.

But he flinched from her touch and pulled away, pressing his hand to his eyes. 'I am shamed!' He wept. 'Shamed for ever in the fellowship of knights! Gawain and the others would die for King Arthur, and I? I take his wife!'

'Arthur – and his knights?' Guenevere could scarcely contain her rage. She wanted to beat his face bloody with her fists, take his arms and shake him till his eyes fell out of his head. 'I do not belong to Arthur!' she hissed. 'In the country of the Mother, my body is my own!'

'And so is mine, and so is any man's! But I owe faithful service to my lord.'

'The love of a man and woman cancels such debts!'

'How can it, in all honour?'

Honour.

He dare say that to me?

'Understand this, Lancelot,' she cried, 'or you understand nothing at all! Honour is a code between men! Love

has its own honour, far above that of war. Love lifts us to a
better place, burning away killing and cruelty. True lovers
will risk everything for love. So they gain more than they
lose, by becoming better than they were.'

'Do you think so?'

Lancelot's gaze took in Guenevere's flushed face, her
angry stare and parted lips. Below her gown her breasts
heaved with strong feeling, and his desire leaped in response.

He whipped round towards her and took her by the
hips. 'Burn me then. Teach me, lady!' he ordered, lifting
her off her feet and carrying her to the bed. As he tore off
his clothes, she could see he was already erect. He followed
her gaze, and laughed at himself as he stripped off her gown.
'For you see I am ready to learn!'

It was the longest day of all her life. Yet afterwards it seemed
the shortest too. The hours slipped by like pearls on a chain,
and though each was precious, she did not feel them go. All
day, and the night that followed, she had no desire to eat
or sleep. Instead they lay on cushions filled with lavender,
picking at quail's eggs and drinking honeyed wine. She
could not account for what they did with the time. But
the day was not long enough for the love they had to give,
and the night, they both knew, would end all too soon.

Never with Arthur had she loved like this. As a queen,
her life had been ruled by the cares of her own kingdom.
As Arthur's wife, it had been dominated by the demands of
his. Now she saw for the first time why her mother always
chose consorts who had no other life but to love and serve
her. Now she had a lover who would love her so too.

'Madame . . .'

He would not say the simple words of love, and sharply
showed he did not like to hear them too often from her. But
she could see it whenever he turned his head to look into

her eyes, feel it each time he lifted her hands and pressed every fingertip to his lips.

When he touched her she passed through all the stages of the Goddess, from trembling maiden to the radiant fullness of a woman in her prime. The next moment she would be filled with fears, darkness and death, a hateful, shrivelled crone. She could be vibrant with love and cold as the distant hills all in the same breath, green as springtime, blazing with a golden harvest, and then stiff, white and black as the Death Weaver herself.

And he was so young! He had not caught the manly knack of ignoring his feelings, or cutting himself off from her. As they lay on the bed she looked up to see him watching her, his eyes glistening with tears. She turned to him in alarm. 'What has made you sad?'

'Your sorrow,' he said simply. Gently he traced the line between her brows, and the tiny creases at the corner of her eyes. 'And your loss.'

That was the only time they spoke of Amir. But Guenevere smiled and wept afterwards when she pondered it in her heart.

They say that a woman with a younger lover is looking for a son.

They never knew Amir – or Lancelot.

He even loved things about her that he could not have known. 'What were you like when you were a little girl?' he asked abruptly, as evening drew in and they drowsed by the fire. The servants who brought them refreshments had long gone, and she had not rung for candles, so only the firelight lit his thoughtful face.

'What do you think I was like?' she parried lovingly.

He thought for a while. 'I think you must have been the joy of your mother's life, the daughter she wanted for herself and the land. As you grew up, you must have been worshipped more than courted, for who would feel free to approach the daughter of the Queen? So you were lonely a lot, and not understood.'

She pressed his hand in silence. *Yes, you're right.*

A strange sorrow overcame her.

'Don't be sad.' He drew her to him and stroked the outline of her face. 'You must have known you were born to outdo all other women one day.'

She snuggled into him, rubbing herself against him like a cat. 'How?'

'In beauty. In divinity.' He laughed fondly. 'In needing to be praised.'

He stroked her neck, and played with the front of her loose gown. His voice thickened. 'But you do not need to seek compliments, lady, they will come to you.' Roughly he tugged at the fastening, and pushed the soft silk aside, exposing her breasts. 'See, lady, see?' He bent his head, and brushed her nipple with his lips. 'You excel all other women in the glory of the Great One who has made you as you are.'

Her nipples lengthened and hardened under his kiss, and she felt herself grow wet. He reached out his hand to her breast, and she was already moaning for his touch. With a soldier's haste, he pulled her to her feet. 'You are the woman of the dream. Come back to bed, lady, for I want to see you arching beneath me, and have you in my hands!'

CHAPTER 58

G ods, what a woman she was – and she had chosen him?

Lancelot struggled with the mystery at the heart of womanhood as he armed himself and prepared to speak to the men. Lying languorously in bed, supporting her head on her hand, Guenevere watched him with the open interest he still found hard to understand.

'I have to leave you now,' he said gently, 'only to take command of Joyous Garde, to give orders for the night.'

Guenevere nodded moodily. She knew he had to order the men and get to know the guard, to forge the band of knights he had found into a new fellowship. When they had buried Malgaunt, many would leave, out of loyalty to their former lord. Those who stayed would have to be drilled in the jousting yard and tournament field; to learn that Lancelot was their leader now, and worthy of their faith.

As soon as he left, Guenevere found herself as changeable as a child. She could not doubt his love, she was angry at being foolish but she could not stop herself wanting him back at once.

Suddenly she was haunted by thoughts of Lancelot's former mistress Queen Aife. She was sure that he had only loved her from afar. Yet when he returned, she could not prevent herself from questioning him about the Queen and her court. 'What was it like? What did you learn there?'

'She and her maidens taught us swordplay with willow wands.' He laughed ruefully as he threw down his gauntlets and unbuckled his sword. 'A cut from one of those was as painful as any from a blade!'

Guenevere's sight grew faint. Suddenly she saw Lancelot, flushed and laughing, at play in the midst of a group of lovely girls, teasing and sporting together in the abandon of youth. 'What else did the Queen teach you?' she said coldly.

He thought for a moment, and smiled. 'How to use our wits. She used to say that the battle is won in the head, before the sword is ever taken in hand.'

'Oh, a philosopher too?'

His face darkened, but he pressed on, 'Women give new life to the world through the pain they bear, so it's right that they teach men the secrets of both. Women are masters of the subtle arts, because they are closer to the Otherworld. So who better than a woman, who has less strength than a man, to show men how to make full use of the power they have?' He sat on the bed beside her, playing with her hand.

'Yet she must have been strong, if she was a warrior queen.'

He smiled. 'Oh, she was.'

She did not like his smile. 'Was she as tall as me, or taller?'

'Taller. Her legs were longer than yours, and her muscles were well developed, from all the weapon-work she had done.'

Guenevere could not help herself. 'Then she must have been too tall for a woman, and very manly too.'

He gritted his teeth, and ran his hand through his hair. 'She was neither! She was a queen among queens, and a woman far above other women in the eyes of every man. On feast nights, she wore a crown and mantle of gold, and her maidens shone around her like the stars when they greet the rising moon.' He turned on her in exasperation, and took her in his arms. 'But none of them shone in my eyes like you!'

Why could she not be satisfied by that, and stop this madness, this cruelty? Why was she envying every woman who had ever been touched by his shadow as he passed? Was she trying to make him hate her? Dragging him down beside her on the bed, she hid her face from him. 'I am an evil woman!' she wept. 'How can you love a woman like me?'

He shrugged. 'You are what you are.'

'What am I?' she cried desperately.

She could feel him stifle a sigh. 'You are yourself.'

'What's that?'

He thought for a moment. 'You are like the flowers, like the birds in the trees, you are like nature, beautiful and free. So you have the power to find and fulfil yourself, not deny your inner nature to live another's life.'

She settled back, soothed.

But he went on, 'You are a dangerous woman, and love makes you cruel.'

'What?' She could feel the tears rushing to her eyes, the blood stampeding through her head.

'I fear you!' He caught her hand and crushed it painfully to his mouth. 'But I fear even more the loss of you.' He tried to smile. 'Command me what you will, I am yours.'

'I do not command you!'

His smile was even sweeter. 'I am your knight. Who else should you command?'

She groaned, aching with love. 'I want you to command me! Isn't that what love is?'

'Love? Ha!' He tossed back his hair, and laughed. 'Command you? You cannot be commanded! It is against your nature, you yield to no man. And who but a fool tells a woman what to do?' He bowed his head to hide another smile. 'Let alone a queen like you.'

A queen like me? Goddess, Mother, what does he mean?

She had had enough of this. 'Oh, hold me, kiss me, talk about something else!'

'Something else?' He looked at her quizzically.

'You know what I mean!' Her temper flared. 'Think of something else! That's a command!'

'Lady!' He burst out laughing, and moved towards her with purpose in his eyes. 'That you will never have to command!'

For the whole of that day she lived for the stirring of his lean brown length in bed. For the whole night she slept in the comfort of his arms. Then at dawn she awoke in a cloud of hovering dread. For she knew she could not delay their return to Camelot.

He nodded when she told him, and made no other sign. Together they gave orders for their knights and servants, men and maids and dogs. The whole group assembled the courtyard under a sullen sky. Then they rode back to Camelot on a sad and clouded day.

To the boy tending his pigs on the edge of the forest, it was as if the long-lost knights had ridden out of fairyland, and in their midst, all robed in white and gold, the Queen of the Fair Ones herself. Gibbering with fear, he took to his heels and ran. 'The Queen! The Queen!'

By the time they reached Camelot, all the people were lining the streets, cheering themselves hoarse. They wound their way uphill through the dense throng, with girls rushing out to kiss Lancelot's stirrup, and women tossing rosebuds in their way.

'The Queen! The Queen!'

'Sir Lancelot saved her!'

'Sir Lancelot saved the Queen!'

All the bells of the town were pealing deliriously overhead. The cheers of the people had reached a frenzy now. A thin cry rose above the noise all around. 'Guenevere!'

On the palace steps, Arthur was peering forward, white-faced and wild-eyed, King Leogrance and Taliesin at his side. Behind him clustered blackrobed monks, not the two or three he used to have, but a whole troop. 'Guenevere!' he cried piteously, as she drew near.

Leaping down the steps, he reached up to pluck her from her horse and fold her inside his cloak, raining kisses on top of her head. She could feel the eyes of Lancelot boring into her back, and hid her burning face against Arthur's chest.

'Guenevere!' Arthur sobbed openly now as he clutched her, and kissed her on the mouth.

And she wept too, for a sorrow she could not name.

Hours later, Arthur was still marvelling over the tale of Malgaunt's betrayal and Lancelot's revenge. He must have wrung Lancelot's hand a dozen times, while Lancelot stood pale and tense, brushing aside his thanks. Standing behind Lancelot, Bors and Lionel were gripped with the same unease, and Kay's dark face was more enclosed than ever. None of them looked at each other, or at Guenevere. Nothing was said. But it could be no secret from his cousins and his brother knight, Guenevere had to accept, where Lancelot had spent the last night.

But Arthur was impervious to any sense of things moving under the surface of his joy. 'What a miracle you found her!' he was saying fervently to Lancelot. He waved to his silent band of attendant monks. 'I have given orders for a thanksgiving mass. Of course I came back as soon as they sent for me, but I was in despair here, there was nothing

I could do.' He turned to Guenevere. 'See, Guenevere, what it means to have your own knight!' He laughed joyfully to Lancelot, and the sound was horrible to her ear. 'I can never thank you enough for all you have done for the Queen!'

'Do not thank me, sire!' Lancelot protested through white lips. He dared not look at the King. If Arthur truly knew all he had done for the Queen – and to the Queen – and with the Queen—

Oh, it was foul, he was foul, he could not live with this! Lancelot knew he was flaming from head to foot and his brown skin had turned an ugly red with shame.

For all you have done for the Queen.
Goddess, Mother, if only Arthur knew.

Guenevere raised a damp hand to cool her burning face. She saw herself as naked as a willow wand lying in Lancelot's arms, and she thought all the world must be able to see it too.

Lying in his arms – and lying about it now.
Lies upon lies.

She looked around, and felt her stomach lurch. Agravain was staring as if he could read her mind.

'Sir knights, welcome your queen!' Arthur cried ebulliently.

'My lady!' Lucan was the first on his knees, kissing her hand.

'Majesty!' Gawain's big face was bright with happiness.

'Oh, madam, the Gods be thanked who have brought you back!' The tears stood in Gareth's eyes as he spoke.

One by one they all pressed around Guenevere to kneel and kiss her hand. And, with a sudden start, she saw that all three of Arthur's Orkney kin, who had been squires when she left, now wore the gold torque of knighthood round their necks.

She felt an unpleasant sensation she could not name. 'So, sirs,' she said awkwardly, 'Sir Agravain, Sir Gaheris and Sir Gareth now, I see. Congratulations to you all. When did this happen? When were you made knights?'

Agravain bowed, his dark face alight with memory. 'After the battle of Le Val Sans Retour.'

She turned to Arthur, transfixed. 'So you took the castle! Was Morgan there? And did you find—'

'No,' said Arthur, in a strange voice. His eyes were like milk.

'No?' Her nerves were screaming.

Gawain stepped forward, faithful as ever, coming to Arthur's aid. 'The King means that we did not take Le Val Sans Retour.'

Lancelot let out a short laugh of disbelief. 'Why not? If the siege was correctly laid—'

Agravain turned colour. 'You were not there,' he said venomously. 'If you had been, Sir Lancelot, of course we would have won.'

'Won?' Lucan took a step forward, fingering the hilt of his sword. 'Gods above, Agravain, who wins in the Welshlands, especially against a witch?' He turned to Guenevere. 'Queen Morgan raised the worst fogs of the season, my lady, and shrouded the place in mists and drizzling rain. She darkened the sky by her magic till we could hardly see our hands before our eyes!'

'It was hard for our soldiers too.' The shadow in his eyes told Guenevere that Bedivere was still troubled by their defeat. 'The whole garrison there was composed of the King's men, so when we attacked, our troops were fighting their own comrades, men who had been their friends. Cruel, it was.'

Guenevere turned to Arthur again. 'So you did not take the castle?' A huge weariness gripped her bones. 'You never found out if she or her child were there?'

'On the contrary, madam.'

Guenevere's nerve were snapping. *Gods above! Why did Gawain have to answer for Arthur every time?* 'What do you mean?'

'One night there came a terrible black storm, when it seemed all the devils of the earth were at loose in the sky. The next morning the defenders threw down the drawbridge and invited us in. We searched the castle from top to bottom. There was no trace of Queen Morgan at all.'

She looked at Arthur. *Did you find my mother's scabbard, the scabbard I gave you on our wedding day? The scabbard she stole to punish both of us?* surged into her mind. But she knew very well what the answer would be.

She wanted to scream. *Morgan, Morgan, tell me where you are?*

Never fear, the answer came to her. *You will know soon enough.*

'Madam?' Gawain was standing before her, anxiously searching her face.

'Ah, Sir Gawain!' She made a feeble effort to take control. 'No trace of her, you say?' she persisted hopelessly.

'None.'

'Nor her son?'

Gawain nodded bleakly. 'Nor her son. None whatsoever. They are gone, my lady. Gone for good, is my hope and prayer!'

Somehow they made a night of it, feasting the whole court, receiving the courtiers' clamorous welcome home.

'A toast to the Queen!'

'The Queen!'

'And Sir Lancelot, the finest knight in the world!'

And somehow she endured it, knowing that if she could not be with Lancelot, she would soon be on her own.

But as they left the Great Hall, Arthur took her hand and drew her urgently to his side. 'I want you!' he whispered hoarsely, pulling her towards the King's apartments. 'Oh, Guenevere, you must be with me tonight!'

Panic seized her. She threw a glance over her shoulder, and put out her hand, as if to ward Arthur off. 'My lord—'

Behind them the train of lords and knights, Lancelot among them, began to melt away. She opened her mouth, and closed it hopelessly. There was nothing she could do, nothing to say.

'Oh, Guenevere! And to think I nearly lost you!' he muttered, as he hustled her into his quarters, waved away the servants and closed the door. He pushed her on to the bed and started fumbling with her gown. 'Oh, Guenevere!'

Lancelot never fumbled, he seemed to know the way with buttons and bows.

Lancelot – oh!

Don't think of him, don't think of Lancelot now—

She lay unmoving as Arthur clambered on the bed beside her, struggling to throw off his clothes. Then he pushed up her skirt, and his hand closed on her thigh so roughly that she cried out. He stroked the wincing flesh. 'Forgive me, I didn't mean to hurt you – but it's been so long, oh, Guenevere, so long!'

He lay alongside her, fumbling now with her, then with himself. Time stretched between them, and she lay rigid with tension, ready to snap. At last she heard a long-drawn-out, bitter groan. 'It's no good, Guenevere, I'm no use to you, I'm no good at all. You must wish you'd stayed with Malgaunt! He could at least do what a man should do!'

She shuddered. 'Arthur, no!'

He held her very hard. 'We still have something between us, though, don't we, Guenevere? There's still some love left, say there is! I wanted to die when I thought you were gone. You won't leave me, will you, Guenevere? Promise you won't leave.'

'Arthur, I—'

'Swear it!'

'Please—'

A fit of shaking seized him, and he trembled from head to foot. 'Swear! I beg you, swear!'

And she swore. Then he held her and kissed her, and touched all her secret places till he fell asleep.

Then all night she lay and listened to Arthur as he moaned and tossed in his sleep. Her prayers were short, and she had all night for them.

CHAPTER 59

The night was very long. Dawn found her lying stiff and cold in Arthur's bed, as far away from him as she could get. An unwelcome smell he had never had before hung over his sleeping form, and the stink of incense breathed from his tangled hair. As daylight came she edged out of the frowsty sheets and slipped away while he was still sunk in sleep, mumbling to himself.

Hovering like a wraith in the half-light, Ina was waiting forlornly when she got back to the Queen's apartments. 'Oh, madam!' she said. Guenevere nodded. What was there to say?

All she could think of was Lancelot. How could she face him now? But if she could not, how could she survive?

She could not rest for the mad urge to see him *now!* Pacing the floor, she counted the minutes till his page came to see how she had slept, as the boy did every day. Then she could send him back to beg Lancelot to come to her.

But the boy did not come.

'Never mind, lady!' Ina cried, with forced gaiety. 'That means Sir Lancelot will come himself.' Her wan face lit up. 'Oh, madam, let me get you ready, we don't want him to catch us unawares!'

So Ina brushed her hair, and touched up her lips, and

brought some colour to her cheeks. She dressed her in a gown of gleaming silk the colour of foxgloves in a glade. She put on her veil, arranged the silvery lawn under the gold coronet, and tweaked her this way and that a hundred times. And still he did not come.

By noon Guenevere was half crazed with rage and despair. She was afraid to leave her chamber in case he came. But she had to get out of the palace, or else she would go mad.

Now for the first time she felt the cruel illogic of adultery. Spending the night with the husband she had betrayed was a worse infidelity than sleeping with the man she loved. Did Lancelot hate her for it? Did he blame her for her shame?

Walking in the garden under the castle walls, she was soon surrounded by other knights, lords and ladies, pages and squires, and even the dogs that hung around the court. But there was no sign of the man she longed to see.

She could not bear it. At last he appeared far off, walking with his cousins Bors and Lionel. All three drew up to her as stiff as wooden dolls. '*Majestée*?' said Bors.

Above them the sun burned in a cloudless sky. Nearby a blackbird poured out its soul in song, and nodding daisies danced around their feet. Lancelot raised his head, and she could not read his eyes.

'Lancelot?'

The scent of the grass hung heavy in the still summer air. Her hungry heart was ravening for a word from him, a look, the smallest smile. But now he was here, he seemed to have nothing to say. He looked about him distantly, staring over her head. 'Would Your Majesty care to walk?'

He offered her his arm, and they moved away. All around them the smiling courtiers nodded and bowed.

With a piercing shaft of memory she saw his arm as she had last seen it in Joyous Garde, thrown carelessly over the bedclothes. His whole body had been hers to delight in then, from his thick springing hair to the tips of his long bony toes. Now she could not even touch his hand.

His eyes were fixed on the horizon ahead. She remembered last night and Arthur, and felt sick. An aching silence stretched between them like a curse.

She had to speak. 'Why didn't you come this morning? Were you angry with me?'

'Angry?' He gave a brusque laugh. 'No.'

'Then why didn't you come to me?' Her nerves were screaming and it was all she could do not to scream at him too.

He threw a swift glance over his shoulder at the courtiers nearby. Were they in earshot? She did not care. Why was he so cold? His lips hardly moved when he spoke. 'Why should I come?'

'Why? After Joyous Garde – after all we were to each other there?'

Her voice dwindled away. *Goddess, Mother, what have I done to be punished like this?* The last vestiges of control left her, and the tears came like rain.

'Madame—'

She waved him away in a spasm of anguish so acute that she could hardly breathe. 'Go – just go!'

'I did not mean—'

'Go!'

'Lady, listen to me!'

A roar of happy laughter ran through the group behind. Lancelot looked around in alarm.

'Cover your face!' he commanded urgently. 'And hear me now, Madame, I beg.' He groaned in despair. 'How could I come to you this morning? You told me nothing

of how it would be once we were back. I did not know if
I would be welcome to you at all!'

'You? Not welcome?' she murmured, through a haze
of pain.

'You are the Queen of two kingdoms! I'm nothing but
a lowly knight. A knight obeys his queen, a queen obeys
nothing but her will.'

She began to interrupt.

He silenced her angrily. 'How was I to know what I
meant to you?'

'Oh, Lancelot—'

'Or if our time in Joyous Garde was any more than
a woman of power amusing herself with a young knight
who caught her fancy, rewarding him briefly for saving
her life?'

She could not stop the tears. 'Is that what you thought
of me?'

'No!' Furiously he tossed his head. 'But you are the
Queen! It is for you to say – you to command! I was awaiting
your word as patiently as I knew how. I wanted to call for my
horse and ride away. Only my cousins here could persuade
me not to go – or else to put an end to my miseries with my
sword!'

The group behind was almost upon them now. He
dragged his hand roughly over his face. 'Which I will still
do, if you breathe the word. Or I will do whatever is your
will.' He looked round at the laughing courtiers behind.
'They must not see you in tears! Cover yourself!'

She fumbled to draw down her veil over her tearstained
face. 'Oh, my love, my only love – forgive me?'

He snorted with anger. 'There is nothing to forgive!'

'Your Majesty!' came a happy call from behind. She
dared not turn around. 'Tonight I shall be alone,' she whispered. 'Come to me tonight!'

He frowned. 'Walls have eyes.'

She turned away, a chill at her heart, hearing the approaching feet. 'Am I not to see you, then?'

'I will work out a plan. Nothing is safe, if it is not planned.'

'Planned?' cried the nearest knight. 'Tell us, Lancelot, what is being planned?'

His eyes met hers for a second, and he turned away.

'We must celebrate, Guenevere!' Arthur decreed, his sunken eyes in their dark sockets glowing with something of his old fire. 'Let's have minstrels and feasts and jousts, just as we always did. And when we get back to Caerleon, we'll have a tournament – I want the world to know how much joy we have to share.'

'Just as you say, my lord.' Guenevere's lips moved mechanically as her eyes flew to Lancelot, standing with Bors and Lionel at the foot of the throne.

Now the days would be fully occupied, and there would be no chance to see Lancelot alone. And already her whole being was crying and dying for him.

Goddess, Mother, have mercy, do not keep my love from me.

Deceiving Arthur was a daily ache. Loving Lancelot wounded her mortally as it kept her alive. All that was beautiful in their love was cruel and ugly too. All this she saw every moment of every day.

Now she was riding the rollers on a rougher sea than she had ever known. At times she seemed to float on a broad, shining ocean of love, hearing its endless hymn to the Mother and soothed by the signs of sweet love all around. Then, without warning, she would find herself cast up on a harsh and lonely shore, walking the night, weeping to the uncaring stars.

From minute to minute she twisted and turned, like flotsam on the waves. She loved Lancelot now more than her own soul. But how could she love him, when she still loved Arthur?

If she still loved her husband, what was she doing with a lover?

And if she did not love Arthur, what did that make her?

Ina did her best to help. 'In the land of the Goddess, all women have the right of thigh-friendship with the man of their choice,' she said firmly, as she brushed Guenevere's hair. 'And in the Summer Country, you are the Queen. A queen has the right to take a new consort in the seven-year cycle of her marriage with the land.'

Guenevere waved a hopeless hand. 'When I married Arthur, I promised him that I would not take another Chosen One.'

'Ah, lady,' she sighed, 'it seems this promise was not yours to make. The Mother decided otherwise for you. No one defies Her will.'

'Yet to withdraw my love from Arthur, now he is failing . . .'

Ina's voice hardened. 'Now is the time to do it. Soon it will be too late. It is more than seven years since you chose him first. The land is groaning for another king.' Guenevere could hear Ina's voice changing again. 'And Sir Lancelot is a worthy, worthy choice.'

She could feel herself dissolving into tears. 'He is, isn't he, Ina? Oh, Gods above, let him come to me soon!'

Would she come, Gods above, would she come?

Lancelot prowled the woodland clearing, oblivious to the contented snuffling of the horses as they cropped the grass. Nor did he see the soft light filtering through the trees, or sense the anxious glances of his cousins Bors and Lionel watching from afar. It was all he could do not to trumpet his fears to the bright morning sky. Would he ever understand this capricious queen?

A dull colour rose to his face as he thought of the madness of her love. Surrounded by lords and knights, or in plain sight of Arthur's creeping monks, the looks she gave him in the open court, *Come to me!* The rash letters, the messages sent with Ina or his page, all saying the same thing a hundred times a day. And when he sent back, 'We must wait a while, have patience, we must take care,' the next time he saw her it was as if he had hit her in the face, disowned her, spat upon their love.

Her letters and messages were so unguarded that he was in terror she would betray herself.

'Tell your mistress that I cannot write or send as she demands!' he told Ina in anguish. 'Surely she sees that only my care will protect her now!' And didn't she see that he longed for her too?

At last he found a place that would be safe. He chose a time, and sent her word with all the loving care at his command. Her reply was swift. 'I will not come.'

Had she been waiting for the chance to punish him? His blood rose at the thought. Why did she mistrust him? Why did she doubt his faith?

Nothing was safe if it was not planned, she had to understand that! The love they shared at Joyous Garde could not be repeated – why did he have to spell it out for her? There they were private, here at court a thousand eyes watched her every day.

Couldn't she see that they had to behave as if nothing had happened? Only then could they find time to be together without courting death and ruin.

As she was now!

Yet he knew, too, that there was no freedom for those bound by love. There was only endurance, and the faith to endure. So day after day he rode in the tiltyard as always, and won admiring cheers, and night after night he lay in his bed and wept. He went about the court with a firm smile, bowing courteously when Gawain guffawed and pointed out some blushing beauty sick with love for him, or a bold-eyed matron angling for his approach. Left to himself, he would never have noticed the sheep's eyes turned his way, or the pouting, inviting lips. But everything had to be as if he were still the man he was before, whatever the cost.

And it was hard, Gods, it was hard! To be surrounded by adoring women when only one mouth, one gaze commanded his waking thoughts. She – in the midst of his anger he gasped to think that she could love him, that she had taken him to her bed—

She—

Even in the silence of his mind, he could not say her name. But she – he clenched his fists in pain. He had to rule her desires, or she would destroy them both.

And now she said she would not come to him! He closed his eyes and breathed in the warm, clear air. He had forced himself to disregard what she had said. She did not mean it, she could not refuse to come, after all this time.

No, she meant it as a test of his love, a trial of his patience, no more. She would come, she had to, now it was safe at last. For him to ride out at dawn with Bors and Lionel would make no stir. For her to take a pony out much later would be no more than she might do any day. She would set off with Ina in the opposite direction, then loop around once Camelot was far behind. And then they could meet in the deep heart of the wood, where they would be together at last.

If she would come.

He stared through the trees till they began to shimmer before his eyes.

If she would only come.

She would not go!

Flushed with a sudden rage, Guenevere pulled her horse's head round sharply, and came to a sudden halt. What was she doing, riding out into the wood to meet a faithless man?

Behind her Ina pulled up too, her soul already shrinking from the torrent of reproaches she knew would descend. She stifled a deep sigh. No woman in the world ever suffered for a man the way the Queen did for Lancelot. *Ina, do you think he loves me? I'm so afraid. Or was he just using me in Joyous Garde?*

He loves you, lady, you can see that in his face. Every time you come into court, he knows at once you're there. You know he's thinking of you, you can almost hear it, even though he never looks your way.

I know that he tries to protect me, he shows his love that way. But I hate it that he never sends a word of love to me, never writes a note—

Madam, it's too dangerous! And now, see, he's made a tryst at last. He will be there for you, when we go.

Go? Oh, Ina, should we go? I'm afraid I'm making a fool of myself. Can he really love me, Ina, do you think he ever did?

Unnoticed by its rider, Guenevere's horse dropped its head, and quietly began cropping the grass. Under the smiling eye of the sun, Guenevere sat on its back and wept. The same thoughts ran madly round her brain.

She would not go.

She would go back to Camelot.

He did not love her.
Why should she love him, when he did not love her?

She was not coming.

When would their wretched cousin see the truth of this, and go?

Wearily Sir Bors raised his eyes to the scene ahead, and avoided his brother Lionel's troubled gaze. The afternoon sun was slanting through the forest, and the first birds of evening were coming home to roost. Not the Queen, though, thought Bors unhappily. She was not coming. Surely Lancelot knew that by now?

Well, what on earth did he expect? A woodland tryst might suit a milkmaid, but it was far below a queen. Riding out secretly into the wood like this, they were like outlaws driven from court and town.

Yet where else could the pair of them hope to meet? If they found some obscure corner of Camelot, they would be like spies in the Queen's own palace, plotting against the King, her Chosen One. But once they were back in Caerleon, things would be even worse. In Arthur's kingdom now the Christians were growing strong: their love would not only be furtive, but traitorous and sinful too. Could a queen of two kingdoms learn to suffer that? Bors chewed wretchedly on his lower lip. And should a knight like Lancelot, who all his life had prized honour and nobleness, consent to live like this, even for the sake of his love?

No – it was madness and dishonour twice over. How could he do it? Bors's plain mind shrank from the question, knowing that he could not understand. Things had been bad enough at Joyous Garde, knowing that Lancelot had lost himself in love for the Queen. Surely they knew that what had happened there should have ended there too.

His mind began to clear. The Queen was a woman

blessed with a sense of duty and a strong mind. She would have seen all the difficulties, foreseen all the griefs, and decided that this tryst was wrong. And the same must be said of their love – it was dangerous, it was cruel, it was bad for two good men. In short, it must not be.

Bors cast a fearful glance through the trees. The lone figure still stood hunched in the clearing, tensely watching the woodland track. How long had he been there now? How many hours?

Beside him he heard Lionel sighing heavily, and knew that they shared the same thoughts. It would be grief beyond words for Lancelot, they both knew, when he accepted that the Queen had broken off their love. They'd have to take him away, as far as possible, back to Little Britain to join the struggle against France. Or further still, to fight in the Turkish wars, or to join the struggle in the Holy Land.

Acre, Jerusalem – yes, love could be buried there, and honour reborn. Bors heaved a sigh, and felt some relief. He nodded to himself. That was what they must do.

And all would be well. Bors soothed his faithful heart, it would be for the best in the end, even though Lancelot would suffer terribly on the way. Queen Guenevere was a woman out of his sphere, a love that was beyond him in every way. By saying farewell now, she would leave him an untainted dream to carry all his life. And not only Lancelot, he swore to himself. He and Lionel, too, would help Lancelot to honour her name, and keep her memory green. Every battle they fought, every victory they won, they would dedicate to her.

So be it. Now he must say all this to Lancelot, or some of it, to begin. They would leave tomorrow, there was no time to be lost. Bors straightened his back, and his fingers flew unconsciously to the throbbing scar on his head. 'Lionel,' he began.

Lionel raised his hand. His eyes were fixed on the distant woodland ahead. To their right Lancelot had frozen in position, staring furiously through the trees. The birds had hushed their evening songs, and the whole forest seemed to hold its breath.

The sound of horses' hoofs floated towards them on the warm, night-scented air. Framed against the setting sun, Lancelot was straining like a falcon poised for flight, its earth-bound body fretting for the sky. In the glimmering light, a slender shape was to be seen making her way slowly towards him through the trees, while another waited with the horses behind. Lionel turned to Bors, his eyes glowing. 'The Queen!' he breathed ecstatically. 'It's the Queen!'

CHAPTER 60

Jubilate Deo, Deo Jubilate – Rejoice in the Lord, O be thankful in His name . . .

The voices of the monks rang gravely round the chapel, weaving in and out of the old stone tracery of the roof. Arthur raised his head and sighed with joy. She was back, Guenevere was safe! He could feel his eyes filling with tears at the thought of losing her. Had he really believed she was gone from him for good, lost for ever in the wood? He did not know. But even the dread void of unknowing he had endured was a place of terror to his memory now. To be without her, or even in fear of life without her, was a hell of its own.

Kneeling at the rail before the altar, he bent his head and tried to pray. Above him a flood of glorious sunshine poured through the stained-glass windows and shattered on the flagstones in sharp fragments of red, blue and gold. What a day to be back in his beloved country, King again in his own castle – on top of this, to be playing host to the finest tournament Caerleon had ever seen! A fleeting hope of happiness brushed Arthur for the first time in a long while, and his bruised soul lifted to the sound of the chant. O give thanks unto the Lord, for He is gracious, and His goodness endureth for ever . . .

At the altar, the priest-monk in charge was disposing of the remains of the communion breakfast. The morning service would be over very soon. Arthur eyed the busy monkish back thoughtfully as the robed figure chanted and prayed and solemnly swallowed the last of the bread and wine. In his hour of suffering, this holy father had been one of many Christian voices telling him that Guenevere was lost and must be given up for dead. And they all knew why God had taken her from him, as a punishment for his sins.

Well, they were wrong, Arthur mused, without rancour. Guenevere had come back. Oh, she was still strange to him, huge-eyed and silent, her gaze always roaming round the court, and always on the verge of tears. But after what she had suffered in Malgaunt's cruel grasp, was it surprising she was still nervous and distraught? And given that Lancelot had saved her life and protected her from worse outrages than Arthur cared to think, was it strange that she seemed to want him rather than any other man near her all the time?

Serve the Lord with thanksgiving, lift up your hearts . . .

Arthur bent his head. Have I sinned, Lord, he asked humbly, in too much sorrowing for Amir? My sin was grievous when my pride in him cost his precious life. But did I then fall into a worse offence, the sin of despair? I despaired when I lost Amir, and even more when I lost my queen. But she has found it in her heart to forgive. May I now forgive myself a little too?

He looked along the altar rail and suppressed another sigh. He had to hope – despair was a dreadful sin. Kneeling beside him he could see Gawain and Kay, and at his back, he knew, were Lucan and Bedivere and all the rest of the Round Table fellowship. There was comfort there. He still had the unswerving love of all his knights. Nothing had changed that.

'Bring your joy unto the Lord,' the treble voices of the choirboys purled through the air, 'and come before His presence with a song.'

Outside the chapel, a lark rose singing in the sky. The stewards and groundsmen would be down at the jousting field now, overseeing the last touches for the tournament. It would be wonderful to be out there. How long was it since he had gone tilting or jousting with his knights?

'The grace of our Lord Jesus Christ,' intoned the priest, 'be among you and remain with you, now and for ever more. Go in peace, and serve the Lord.'

Two lines of black-clad monks rose from the choir stalls and led the way out of the church. Arthur rose from his knees, and his knights followed him. How pale they all looked and dejected, like men who expected nothing and hoped for less! Looking round the well-known faces, Arthur felt a surge of grief for them, and impatience with himself. He had not led these knights as a king should. The signs of neglect were on every one of them, plain to see. Gawain's great shoulders were hunched, and Kay's sallow face looked sick with inward grief.

Kay—

Arthur paused. Kay was not himself. He'd been strange for weeks now, ever since he got back from Joyous Garde.

Why had his old friend and foster-brother been so afflicted by his time in Malgaunt's hands? Was it the injuries Kay had taken when he and the others had tried to defend Guenevere? Was it the misery of imprisonment and the daily fear of death? Or was it constant grief for the loss of his fighting strength now that he was crippled by a withered leg? Whatever it was, Kay never spoke of it. Since Joyous Garde it was as if he dared not speak of what happened there.

Arthur looked up at the sky. It was a clear forget-me-not blue, dotted with clouds as white as a rabbit's tail. Poor Kay. Only time, trust and love could hope to drive his clouds away.

An odd odour rose faintly to Arthur's nose. It was the smell of incense hanging in his clothes. He looked at himself in wonder. How long had he worn this dreary, fusty black? Time for a change! Well, at least he'd have fine new robes for the tournament, Kay would have seen to that.

He turned to his knights, and threw his arm round Kay's neck. 'To horse, lords!' he cried. 'The field awaits us, let's ride out as we always used to do! Come on, Kay. And where's Lancelot?'

Where indeed?

Kay did not know he could contain so much bitterness and live. He could feel his face yellowing, his eyes bulging with tension, his mind shaping a venomous retort as his mouth bit it back.

God Almighty, he cursed, as he stood on the chapel steps. What a position to be in! He could have wept. Why should he protect the Queen? Concealing her adultery from the King made him guilty of the worst disloyalty a knight could commit against his lord. But to tell Arthur would be to break another faith, betraying Lancelot, a blood brother, a fellow knight of the Round Table whom he had sworn to defend.

Yet Arthur was his brother before Kay was a knight – before Lancelot came, before everything. What should he do? What was his duty to his king and brother now? Yet to do nothing was a kind of cowardice too.

Kay could feel the bile rising at the back of his mouth, the pain gnawing at his innards as he puzzled on. After all, young Lancelot had been only half of it, the whole thing at

Joyous Garde. What about the Queen? Whatever she had done, she was still Arthur's queen, and every knight of the Round Table was sworn in loyalty to her too.

A fit of rage shook him, as a dog shakes a rat. He dared not look at Gawain or any of the other knights, for fear his face would give him away. If they knew about the Queen, if they had any idea of what had happened at Joyous Garde, he couldn't begin to think what they might say or do. Lancelot would very likely lose his life. At the least he would be banished for ever, and the King would surely put away the Queen. And did he, Kay, the closest of all to the King, want to destroy the fellowship of knights, and bring down Arthur's house of love? No, he could never say a word.

And who was he to judge? Sourly he struggled with his dislike of the Queen. The great Guenevere, in her own eyes at least, was not just Arthur's queen, but the queen regnant of her own country, where women chose their men. So she believed that she had the right to a new consort when she pleased, and a duty to take the best of her fighting men. And who could be better than Lancelot?

'Where's Lancelot?' Arthur cried again.

Bitterly Kay looked at Arthur, and felt his heart rending. 'Where's Lancelot, my lord? I don't know. Shall I send for him?'

'Don't go like this!' Guenevere reached up from the tangled bed and tugged at the edge of Lancelot's tunic as he dragged it over his head. 'Oh, I'm sorry, I know you have to, it's just—'

She threw herself back on the bed. Loving this man was like doing battle with the ghostly spirit of herself, the spectre of the one she hoped to be. The first time they had come together, the furious fire of their love burned out their old selves, and fused one being out of two. And then they shared a bond closer than their skin, too close to live with, too hard to live without.

Now they seemed to sigh on the same breath, and if he wept, her eyes would fill with tears. When she found a sword scar on his shoulder, she felt the pain in her own arm as she traced the silvery seam. When they were in public she watched his face for every passing thought, and when they were alone, he sensed her every mood. And when he came into her, every time they were one.

She reached out her arms. 'Kiss me before you go.'

Lancelot did not look at her. He knew he was lost if he even threw a glance her way. 'You know I have to hurry,' he said brusquely, grabbing for his boots. He glanced out of the window and read the time by the sky. 'Gods above, it's late! The King will already be out on the jousting field!'

Lancelot's heart burned as he turned his back on Guenevere, cursing himself for yielding to her desire. They should not have come here, slipping through the corridors to one of the disused guest apartments, snatching a forbidden hour together while Arthur and the court were all in church.

Boots, sword-belt, go!

How often could it go unnoticed, after all, that Sir Lancelot had taken another of his 'dawn rides', while the Queen remained behind in the palace, 'indisposed'? Especially as she would now appear in the viewing gallery within the hour, radiant with health and beauty, for the tournament – the tournament that was surely beginning now, even as she lay there naked in the bed begging him to stay?

And among the contestants the King would want to see one Sir Lancelot, he thought desperately, pulling on his boots. Arthur was expecting their best efforts from them all. The competition would be fierce, as the finest knights from many countries would be there. Among them would be such proven warriors as Arthur's old friend King Pellinore, with his brother King Pelles from faraway Terre Foraine. Every one of Arthur's own knights too could give a fearsome account of himself when his blood was up – Lancelot flexed his right shoulder ruefully, still feeling the bruises from his last bout with Lucan when the champion of the Summer Country had almost had him down.

Almost, but not quite. Without vanity, Lancelot knew he was the best of them all. He knew that he could turn aside the worst of their assaults, and pierce the most desperate defences in a way given to no one else. And he knew that his skill and spirit would be much in demand today. Reaching for his helmet, he ran a desperate hand through his tousled hair. The King was probably calling for him all over the court. And he was still here, lingering in my lady's chamber, with – with—

Her unmistakable fragrance assailed his nostrils as he turned to say goodbye. She lay propped on the pillows, her eyes huge, her bright hair tangled with love-knots and spilling wantonly over her nakedness. He could see her breasts beneath the tumbling locks, her full nipples pink and engorged from their love-making, from the passionate touch of his hands and lips and teeth. Instantly he wanted her again, for all the world as if he had not only just emerged from between her long, strong thighs.

She held up her white arms in a last appeal. 'Lancelot!'

Turning from the door again, Lancelot threw down his sword and went back to the bed.

CHAPTER 61

Gods above, were the Great Ones smiling on him at last?

Arthur reined in his horse and turned up his face to the sun. He felt like a prisoner released from confinement underground. His fine new robes were sweet and silky on his skin, and he had forgotten the vibrant pleasure of colours like this royal red and blue.

It came to him with the gentle pain that accompanies the first recognition of a loved one's shortcomings that his new God did not have much to say about days and events like this. The faith of the Christians dealt in guilt and grief, sweating tears and blood over sorrows of the past, and seeking to avoid eternity in Hell.

But the Great Ones saw the trembling beauty of the present moment, the feathery difference of every blade of grass, the serene, unending wisdom in the world of nature, so much more noble than anything made by man. He nodded with sad recognition. Yes, it was true. He had been too long in low cells and dark chambers, on his knees in dank chancels, prostrate before cold and remote high altars – too long indoors.

Now the jousting field opened before him, a dazzling expanse of emerald green and gold, spangled with a glittering array of banners, swords and shields. He sighed with satisfaction. This would be a tournament that all those here would remember all their lives. No, more than that: it would be remembered after they were gone. Other hands and voices would honour their memory on high days and holidays still to come, when those as yet unborn sang the lays of great heroes and their brave deeds of yore.

A sour voice at his elbow brought him back to earth. 'She's late! On a day like this, with royal guests from far and wide, she makes kings look like fools by being late!'

Arthur frowned. Even Kay must not speak of Guenevere like that. 'The Queen was not well this morning, she sent word. You know she hasn't recovered from all she suffered in her imprisonment.'

And what was that? Kay felt a bilious urge to demand. The close attentions of young Sir Lancelot would not be called 'suffering' by many females, that's for sure!

'But her waiting gentlewoman promised that she would be here,' Arthur continued placidly. As he spoke, a great roar rose from the throng crowding the railings all around the field. Arthur smiled. 'And, indeed, here she comes.'

At the far end of the jousting field, a slender silken shape in white and gold flickered briefly in the viewing gallery as Guenevere appeared. Burning like a candle, she raised her arms to acknowledge the applause, and took her seat. Then she leaned forward, and a scrap of white lace fluttered to the ground. Arthur's voice rang out, and the heralds and trumpets sprang to life: 'Let the tournament begin!'

Leaning forward on her throne in the centre of the crowded viewing stand, Guenevere raised a hand to her flushed cheek and tried to look like any other woman at a tournament, with the sun shining down and the court all around. But she knew she was wearing the heavy-lidded, amorous look all women have when they come from their lovers' beds. Thank the Gods that the midday heat gave her reason to wear a veil.

Lancelot was concealing his part in their tryst, she knew, by galloping madly away from the town. He would find a place of shelter, equip himself for the tournament, and return to the jousting field by another route. But even this simple plan was risky, because he was so well known. Only the fact that all Caerleon was at the jousting field would save him from recognition, and protect them both from worse.

Yet what could be worse than living like this, both together and not together, and so often apart?

'Let the tournament begin!'

The trumpets flared again as all the contestants set off round the field. Mechanically Guenevere noted the fluttering banners, and prepared to greet the lords and kings passing by the gallery. At the head of his men, Arthur's old friend King Pellinore rose in his stirrups and doffed his helmet with a courtly bow. 'Your Majesty!'

'King Pellinore!' she cried, with pretended gaiety as she waved, but her heart shrank at the sight of his thinning hair and aged, sun-speckled pate. How old he was – and so suddenly too, it seemed. What had become of the King Pellinore she had known?

Beside him another rider rose to greet her too, taller than Pellinore and thinner, but still recognisably his kin. The light of devotion shone from his pale eyes. His thin white cheeks showed the ascetic spirit of those who mortify their flesh. As she watched him, Guenevere recognised him from long years ago.

At the Battle of the Kings Pellinore had presented his brother, she remembered now, the good Christian King Pelles of Terre Foraine, who believed his daughter was destined to give birth to the greatest Christian knight. Had he brought the divine daughter with him Guenevere wondered, with a sharp pang of jealousy. Or was she still locked up in the castle of Corbenic, cherishing her precious virginity under her father's anxious guard?

Rank upon rank of knights were surging past her now, as they followed their lords and kings in formation for the joust. Behind the lesser knights came the heroes all the people loved and longed to see, Sir Gawain, Sir Lucan and Sir Bedivere, riding alongside those who had come to answer the challenge from far and wide. With a stirring of pain Guenevere saw many whose names she had all but forgotten in the trials of recent years. The King of the Black Lands and the King of Belle Isle were among many who rode past, saluting as if they had last seen her yesterday. As she waved to them the years fell away, and her hurt spirit was bathed in the air of love and goodwill.

'To the lists! To the lists!' The heralds were signalling the first contestants into the ring. Laughing, Arthur slammed down the visor of his helmet and rode forward to open the jousts. At the far end of the field a number of riders milled around in front of the knights' enclosure, each claiming the honour of the first passage of arms with the King. The chosen contestant would ride at Arthur, bow and feint, then ride past. By knightly tradition, a bout in which neither rider was unseated would bring good luck on the contest and all who took part.

So the opening joust would shed no man's blood. The sun put a glittering edge on the long lances and sharp spears massing for the fray, and in spite of herself, Guenevere felt a sudden shaft of fear. Beset by sorrow and hag-ridden by his monks, Arthur had not ridden in a tournament for a long while. He could not hope to withstand a full bout now. And even the young and fit were known to die falling from a horse, when the weight of the armour broke their bones and crushed their insides.

If only Arthur still had the scabbard I gave him, my mother's scabbard to keep him alive.

Don't think of it, it's gone, don't feed on bitterness.

Her eyes raked the knights lining up for the first bout. Well, Gawain was there, and Lucan and Bedivere, they would all take care. All the knights knew the low state Arthur was in now. There was no need to worry.

All would be well.

She sighed.

If she could only forget the last tournament, when Arthur nearly died—

Enough!

She must learn not to fear.

'King Arthur!'

Till the last day of his life, the chief herald swore that the first anyone knew of the child was when the tiny figure stood up in the middle of the jousting field and cried Arthur's name. Some said he must have dropped from the clouds, others that he had sprung alive from the earth. What was certain was that no one saw him come.

Yet there he was, facing Arthur in the field, absurdly small against the ranks of mounted men. He was a thin child of no more than four or five, with black hair and white skin, clad in a diminutive black tunic with black breeches and fine black leather boots. His childish face had an old-young look, and he stared strangely at Arthur straight ahead.

'A boon, my lord king,' he piped, 'I ask a boon! My master Sir Ganmor craves the honour of the opening bout with you.'

'Sir Ganmor?' Arthur smiled in delight at the strange child and his old-fashioned ways. 'Who is he, boy?'

The child made a courtly bow. 'He is a knight of the Lost Lands, sire. He has travelled many miles to break a lance with you.'

Arthur laughed. 'With me, but not on me, I hope, little sir? I am out of condition, I trust your master knows that.'

'He knows.'

A sudden tremor ran through Guenevere. The piping voice was not young, nor old, nor like anything that she knew. The sound seemed to worm itself inside her mind, and she shook her head in an attempt to silence it. Then a black premonition seized her. The sunlight faded, and from nowhere she heard her own voice raised in a mad inner cry, *Kill him! Kill the boy!*

The next second she was gripped with scalding shame. How could she think that way about a child? A little boy, no older than Amir. She groaned. *Amir.* Was that why this boy unnerved her so?

Below her Arthur was sagely nodding his head. 'Sir Ganmor, eh? Well, we are honoured to welcome any stranger knight. I accept your lord's challenge for the opening bout. Let him approach.'

'Thank you, sire.'

The boy turned away from Arthur, and began to walk back up the field. He moved with an eerie poise far beyond his years, calmly looking this way and that. As he drew level with the viewing gallery, his gaze swept up to meet hers.

His eyes were a hyacinthine blue, and their unwavering stare was unnaturally old. Under the bird-like plume of blue-black hair, his pale face was immobile, and Guenevere felt a cold rash of terror dew her skin. Then he was past her, stepping out sturdily on his short legs. As he came towards the knights' enclosure at the far end, he raised one arm in salute, and bowed.

'Approach, Sir Ganmor!' he cried. 'The King awaits you now!'

A huge black horse bearing a rider armoured all in black cantered out from behind the wooden walls, and loped down the field. Twenty paces from Arthur, the rider drew to a halt and bowed his helmeted head. A black lance rose in salute, and Arthur nodded, intrigued as he scanned the banner depicting a misty terrain. 'A knight of the Lost Lands, eh?' He gestured towards the distant figure of the child. 'You are well served in your small squire, sir. He's a fine, well-spoken lad.' He smiled, and Guenevere could see the shadow on his face. 'Your son, by any chance?'

The stranger knight inclined his heavy head.

'He shall sit at my right hand when we feast you afterwards,' said Arthur, a shade too heartily. 'And you, sir? May we see your face?'

Slowly the black helmet shook from side to side.

'No?' Arthur smiled. 'Perhaps you have sworn an oath?'

The black knight made a gesture of assent. Arthur gripped his lance. 'Well, sir, a knight will always honour another's vow. You are welcome to our tournament, and most welcome to take the opening bout with me.'

Arthur raised his lance, and brandished it over his head. 'Sound, heralds, for the honour of the fairest lady in the land!' he cried. 'And let the tournament begin!' He lifted his eyes to the gallery, searching for her gaze, and for the first time Guenevere noticed what he wore on his sleeve.

It was the silk rosette he had sported the first time he fought under her colours as her champion. The old favour was crumpled now, but in the depths of its creased and battered folds she could still see the same cornflower blue as the day it was made. The iron hand of memory crushed her heart. *I loved you so much then.*

'A vous!'

'Have at you!'

Afterwards Guenevere felt that she must have known all along. She heard the words of the challenge, as she had done a thousand times before, then events began to drift sideways as in a dream.

'*Prenez garde!*'

'On guard!'

'At your will, sir!'

'Come on!'

The stranger knight began to move forward at an easy pace. Then without warning, he jabbed his spurs in his horse's side, and in a second the creature was charging down the field. Now the black rider was spurring his mount on till the huge beast was straining forward and screaming in agony.

The stranger was thundering down on Arthur twice as fast as any normal knight, faster than any man could safely feint or stop. Arthur came on towards him as steadily as if he could not see the furious pace, or the glittering spear-point driving towards his heart. As the horses drew level, Arthur feinted and raised his lance in a knightly salute. At the same moment his opponent couched his own weapon in its rest, and drove the iron point squarely into Arthur's chest.

As lightly as a doll, Arthur flew backwards off his horse. The hole in his breast-plate was already seeping blood as he thudded to the earth with enough force to kill him. More blood was running now between the joints of his ruined armour, and oozing from his ears and mouth. A silence fell like night upon the field. Then the cry began. '*He's dead! The King is dead!*'

CHAPTER 62

From a mile away, he could hear the roar of the crowd. The distant sound only added to his despair. The tournament had begun, just as he feared. Gods above, would he ruin himself for this woman, betray all his knightly vows for this enchanting queen?

Lancelot groaned, and urged his horse on towards the jousting field. The whole town had been deserted when he galloped through, and out here, too, not a soul was to be seen. All the world was at the tournament except himself!

Even the breakneck pace he was setting could not lift his sense of shame. He should be there now, he should have been there an hour ago. Never before had he failed to appear along with his lord and his fellow knights for the start of a tournament, to ride in the procession under the banner of the King. And now – Gods above! – and now—

He dared not think of now, still less of *then*, when he should have gone and had not been able to leave the Queen.

The roar of the crowd sounded louder as he drew near.

'The King! The King!'

What were they howling for? Seized with a sudden dread, Lancelot spurred his horse over the last half-mile, and galloped through the outlying tents towards the jousting field.

Another rising cry assailed his ears. What was going on? Standing up in his stirrups, he craned over the heads of the screaming masses pressing against the rails. And then he saw it. Far off the body of Arthur lay on the grass, while a black knight on a black horse stood triumphing over him.

Without conscious thought, Lancelot thundered through the knights' enclosure and straight out on to the field, ploughing through the figures already running to Arthur's aid. As he passed the viewing gallery he had a brief glimpse of Guenevere's white face, her mouth open in horror for a scream that did not come. He spurred forward over the endless expanse of grass. At the far end he saw the black knight lift his head from gloating over the body at his feet, and turn his horse to meet him as he came.

A black lust for revenge filled Lancelot's heart. '*A vous!*' he howled. 'Have at you, stranger knight! Prepare to defend yourself!'

Ahead of him the black-helmeted head shook slowly from side to side, in amusement, in disbelief he could not tell. Blind fury drove him on. '*A vous! A l'outrance!* To the death, Sir Knight!'

The black knight gathered up the reins, set his lance in battle readiness, and urged his horse into action again. The black beast screamed and leaped straight into a gallop, eager for the kill. The furious drumming of its hoofs reached Lancelot through a mist. Transported by the thundering of his own charge, crouched above his horse's withers, poised for the attack, he was exalted, transcendent, with only one purpose now – *kill – kill – kill*—

They came together with a clash mightier than human power. Feinting sideways, then dropping low over his horse's neck, Lancelot dodged below the stranger's spear and brought his lance up under the black knight's guard to catch him squarely in the chest. The next second he was almost out of the saddle, falling forward with the force of his own blow. For his thrust encountered no resistance, passing straight through his enemy's armour as if it were thin air.

The body of the black knight flew backwards off his horse and floated lightly to the ground. Overhead the sky darkened, the clouds convulsed, and a clap of thunder split the air. Tossing its head, the riderless mount ran screaming down the field. As the foaming beast neared the knights' enclosure, a squire ran forward to catch its trailing reins. The black stallion broke its stride for a brief moment to recoil into its steaming haunches, then rear up in the air, and strike down the youth as it dropped back to earth. Then it was out of the field and away before any of the bystanders saw where it went.

'The King! Attend the King!'

Already Guenevere was out of the viewing gallery and half-way down the field. Sir Gawain and the other knights were clustering round Arthur now too. Lancelot checked his own horse's mad forward charge, slowed to a walk, and hastened back to join the group gathering in the centre of the field. There would be time enough to see how his enemy had fared. Lancelot's only thought now was for Arthur.

Arthur still lay as he had fallen, covered in blood. Twenty yards away the armoured body of the black knight lay unmoving on the grass. Guenevere knelt beside Arthur on the ground, careless of the mud and blood staining her light silk gown, cradling his head in her lap. Her face was stained with tears, and a smudge of blood already darkened one cheekbone where she had pushed back her veil.

To Lancelot she had never looked more beautiful, not even the first time she had given herself to him, when she lay in his arms tender with desire. Her fingers were struggling with the metal fastenings as she vainly tried to get Arthur's helmet off. 'Oh, my love, my love,' she was sobbing. 'Arthur, don't leave me, don't go!'

Lancelot knelt stiffly at her side, almost winded with pain. 'Allow me, Majesty,' he muttered, reaching past.

Freed from the heavy headpiece, Arthur's face was pale but unmarked. There was no sign of any wound, and the blood that had covered the visor had not come from within.

'Not a wound to be seen, for all this show of blood?' Gawain started forward, his eyes almost leaving his head. 'May the Gods preserve us!' he muttered superstitiously. 'There's been some witchcraft here!'

'What, man?' cried Kay sharply as he came limping up. 'Witchcraft? Let me see!'

'Here, go easy now!' Behind Kay a squad of soldiers under Lucan's command was arriving at a run, carrying a square wooden pallet to bear Arthur away. Roughly Lucan ordered Kay and the others aside. 'Out of the way! We must get the King back to the castle and into the doctors' hands. And then—'

Lancelot rose blindly to his feet, and took a few wild paces to and fro. Guenevere was crooning to Arthur, wordless cries of entreaty and desperate love.

Lucan stepped forward. 'Your Majesty, forgive me, we must move the King.'

Guenevere raised her stricken gaze to his. As she looked up, Lucan found himself back on another long-ago jousting field, with Guenevere cradling another unconscious body in her arms, while he wept for the Queen and cursed the day he was born. The droop of Guenevere's body and the grief in her ruined face were the same as they had been then. *Again?* her eyes asked him. *Again?*

The soldiers lifted Arthur on to the stretcher and turned

to go. Lancelot moved forward to where Guenevere still knelt in the dirt, her head bent, her arms cradling her empty lap.

'Majesty?' He reached down with a formal bow to offer her his hand. An hour ago I had you in my arms, he tried to tell her, without words, half frantic with grief and love. But the look she gave him in return was as wild and strange as that of a deer in a snare. He drew back, and bowed again. 'Will it please Your Majesty to return to the palace with the King?' he said, and waited without hope.

Guenevere turned her head oddly, as if she had not heard. Tears were running unchecked down her face. She sank down in the dirt, her dress bright with Arthur's blood. 'The King,' she said, weeping, 'the King—'

'Come, my lady.' It was Bedivere, with a white-faced Ina on his heels. 'See, your gentlewoman is here, we will take you to the King.'

Guenevere did not hear. She reached out, plucking at Bedivere's arm. 'The child. What happened to the child? He came with the black knight, what became of him?' Her voice was trembling, and she cast a wild glance around. 'He must be frightened, and there's no one to look after him.' She was flooding with tears. 'We must help him, I must take him in. He's lost – he's alone—' The unspoken name took shape in all their minds. *Amir, Amir, Amir.*

Bedivere shook his head. His soft brown eyes burned with pain. 'He's not lost, Your Majesty, that little boy. He disappeared in the confusion when the black knight fell. The child came with him, and vanished with him too. Come now, come.'

Between them, Bedivere and Ina raised Guenevere to her feet. Bedivere's soft voice carried no conviction at all. 'All will be well. Let us bring you to the King.'

Lancelot stood unmoving and watched them go! 'Oh,

my love,' she had said, and she had not meant him. Arthur was her love, as he had been all along. In an instant Lancelot saw the peril and the pity of it all, the true darkness at the heart of love. Too late, he knew, to understand this now. He had chosen this path. There was no way back.

'Lancelot?' Lucan called. He was standing by the body of the black knight. Lancelot moved over to the still form of his opponent feeling the sick stirring that always assailed him at the fall of an enemy.

Lucan gestured to the dead knight on the ground. 'Who was he, anyway?'

Lancelot shook his head. With a brief word of prayer, he knelt to remove the black helmet to see the black knight's face.

'Aagh!'

The battle-hardened Lucan leaped back with a scream of fear. Lancelot rose to his feet, and set the stranger's helmet down on the ground. Steadily he gazed at the thing lying at his feet, as if his eyes could make sense of what he saw. Where the head should have been there was nothing. The armour was empty of whatever had animated it before.

Lucan looked at Lancelot. The blood drained from his face, and his body began to quake. He brought one finger to his lips, and shook his head wildly from side to side. 'It can't be—' he gasped hoarsely. 'Not after so long?'

A raucous cawing filled the air. Perched on the top of the viewing gallery, a black raven stretched its wings, and performed a little preening dance. Then it took wing and began a wide, low circuit of the jousting field. As it came near, Lucan grabbed for his sword. 'Damn you, you thing of evil!' he screamed. 'I cursed you once, and I curse you again! Come to me now, and see what you get for your love. Only come to me, damn you, come to me, come to me!'

With a mocking laugh, the raven sailed easily through

the flashing movements of Lucan's circling sword. Evading his wild rage, it flapped and beat at his head till he ducked and fell to his knees, screaming in fear. Then it rose to the sky, still cawing in triumph, and flew straight into the sun.

Gently Lancelot crossed to the weeping Lucan, and helped the stumbling knight to his feet. 'It could be, brother,' he sighed, wishing to the depths of his soul not to have to say this, 'and indeed, I think it was.'

CHAPTER 63

Arthur lay on his great bed of state, slumbering as if he would wake at any time. The baffled doctors had come and gone, professing their bewilderment just as they had with her mother so many years ago. Watching them handle Arthur's big body, lift the muscular arms and flex the well-shaped legs, filled Guenevere with feelings she could not name. Once she had loved to see him naked like this. And he was still as good as ever to look on, only her feelings had changed.

Oh, Arthur.

She turned her eyes away from the figure on the bed and felt her guilt again like a living thing. It was inside her now, eating her up, a gnawing, exquisite pain. She clasped her arms across her stomach and leaned forward to hold the grief down. *How did it happen, this madness, this cruel love? Cruel to me, cruel to Lancelot, but most of all to this man?*

Arthur, you were my husband, my first love, the father of my child. You were the man who came to me in the white and gold glory of our early days, you were my partner in the springtime of our love. How did that fail? How did our love grow cold? And why did I punish you by taking another man?

She could not weep. Dry-eyed, she rose to her feet and walked the chamber as she had ever since the accident, night after night. Sooner or later, she knew, her body would succumb, and she would drop like a mayfly at the end of its one brief day.

But not yet.

Forgive me, Arthur? she implored the silent form. *Forgive me and love me again? Can you renew the love you had for me? Lancelot loves you as I do, he will give you this gift from his heart. He will want nothing so much as to see you live again.*

Her wanderings had brought her to the window within sight of the setting sun. The day was dying in fiery pink and gold, and the first soft dews of evening were weeping from the trees. She fell to her knees at the open casement, drinking in the sweet-scented air.

Goddess, Mother, hear my prayer, grant me this, I beg you on my knees. Give Arthur back his life, let him wake and live again as he used to do. Help him shake off the sickness in his soul. Heal his wounds now, both within and without, and make him whole again.

She took a breath, and nerved her soul for the last leap.

And in return, I will send Lancelot away, and lie with him no more. I will forget the dream I dreamed, and the joy I had with him. I will kill that love for him, if you give Arthur life.

Now her whole body was melting into fathomless pain. She held her breath as her prayer left her and took its flight. *Hear me, Mother,* she willed it on its way. *Hear me, and grant my prayer.*

On the far horizon, a white moon sailed up into the sky, bathing the earth with light. She could hear an owl calling from the nearby wood, and the soft cooing as the doves nestled down for the night. The clouds parted, and she saw her mother walking lightly through the world between the worlds. She turned and smiled at Guenevere, and when she smiled, she had the Lady's face.

May you awake from your dream, the Lady said, *and be that which you have dreamed.*

Guenevere buried her face in her hands. *Long ago I dreamed of a knight all in gold who came to rescue me from the peril I was in then. And with him I dreamed a greater dream than that. We shared a vision of these beloved islands all at peace. I dreamed of a man to rule with me in my kingdom, and he came to me. He is my dream, and he must be so again.*

For only I can keep him alive, can give him his life again.

And if that means death for me and for my love, then it has to be.

There was a soft knock at the door, and she raised her head. Darkness had fallen, but the moon was high.

'Sir Lancelot,' she heard the attendant say.

She drew herself up. 'Show him into the next apartment, I will see him there.'

She seemed taller and straighter to Lancelot than he had ever seen her before, pale, lofty and composed. The glowing red silk of her dress flowed down over her body like wine, and her bright hair caught every glint of gold in the dying light. Her mouth, her folded pose, made her a rose to him again, waiting to be opened, waiting to be kissed. But she was looking at him with her deer's eyes again. She had the look of the woodland, wild, free, and strange.

She stood in the centre of the chamber, and Lancelot knew what she would say. He felt himself falling through time and space. As he moved stiffly forward his body was not his, and his voice was not his own.

He reached for her hand, and brought it to his lips. 'So, lady,' he said huskily, 'I must go, it seems. The time has come upon us. We must part.'

She saw the cliff ahead, and her soul fell spinning into the chasm beyond, the void of darkness without him, without his love. 'You know I do not choose this for myself?' Her senses spun.

'Ah, lady!' He sighed. 'We have no choice.' He straightened up, and seemed to grow and tower in the room. 'The Gods command our lives – we must obey.'

'The King—' She was choking now, and had to fight for breath. Her resolution faltered under a wave of pain. *He talks of leaving me, it can't be true—*

Then, like a broken thing, her mind came limping along behind. *You have made a vow, your love for Arthur's life. It must come true, and you must make it true.*

He looked into her eyes, and read her mind. With infinite sadness he took both her hands in his, raised them to his lips, and kissed her fingertips one by one.

Guenevere's heart swelled till she could hardly breathe. 'It is for Arthur – you know that – not for myself?'

Lancelot moved away. 'So?' he said, almost to himself, shaking his head in disbelief. 'We must part?' He covered his eyes with his hand. 'Well, perhaps the Mother knows better than we do. Perhaps—' He broke off.

'What do you mean?'

He turned to her again, with the ghost of a smile. 'We have been lucky, lady, to escape discovery. We have been in danger since the time at Joyous Garde. There will be nothing to fear if we are apart.' Except being apart, he thought, with a sick lurch, but did not say the words. He nodded to himself, turning away. 'I never thought to leave you. But now I see I must.'

'Oh—'

He tossed back his hair, and his eyes were very bright. He reached for her hands again. 'My queen, let us make a good farewell. We shall have a long time to remember it.'

'Oh, my love!' Her breasts, her lips were aching for

his touch. Never had she wanted him more than now. *You must forget me, find another woman, one you can marry, who can live with you as I could never do*, she wanted to say, but knew she never would. 'You will forget me,' she said sorrowfully. 'You will find another love.'

He took her in his arms. 'There is no other love for me but you.'

The force of all she was losing struck her again, and she wept at last. 'With you I lived and loved for the first time.'

He gasped. 'Is that true?'

'You gave me back the life I lost when Amir died.' She checked herself – *enough*. 'Where will you go? What will you do?'

'Oh . . .' He raised his head, and let out a baffled sigh. 'Something – anything.'

'What shall I do?'

He took her in his arms and rested his chin tenderly on the top of her head. 'Wait – wait and hope. Hope on, and keep the faith. Wherever I go, you will be always there. And wherever you go, my prayers will be there before. What we have between us is stronger than life, older than fate or time.'

'Lancelot—'

He put her away gently, drew a ring from his little finger, and slipped it on to her finger. 'Wear this for me?'

It was a pure-water moonstone, a mysterious silver-blue, in a thick band of antique gold. He held her hand and gazed into its depths. 'I chose it for the colour of your eyes. I was keeping it for the right time.' He brought her hand to his lips, his lashes glinting with unshed tears. 'I did not know it would be this.'

Guenevere looked down. Her mother's wedding ring

gleamed on the finger next to the moonstone, a thick twist of old red gold. She tugged it off and threaded it on to his hand. She saw the love light in his eyes again, and tried to fix the image in her mind.

He raised his hand, and brushed the ring against his lips. 'So.' He took her gently in his arms again. 'Remember this!' he commanded huskily. 'As far as I go away from you, that is the measure of my love. It is a sign of the power you have, and the power to draw me back to you one day. If the quest leads to the ends of the earth and beyond, I shall return. If I die, I will come back to you after death. And then we will never be parted, for my soul will be with you always, till you join me in the Otherworld.'

'Oh, my love, my love.'

He folded her in his arms, and gave her the sweetest kiss of their lives. 'I swear by the Maiden, Mother and Crone, by the Three in One and One in Three, I will keep faith with you. Till the sky falls, till the seas drown the shore, till the earth swallows me, I am yours. You are my holy thing. You are my three in one and one in three. You are my love, you are my life, and there is nothing else.'

She was beside herself now. 'Lancelot – oh, don't say that, don't.'

'My lady!'

There was a tapping at the door, and Ina's low voice. 'Madam, the doctors are here again to see the King.'

Lancelot met her eyes. There was no need for words. Outside the window the evening had come down, and the last faint fingers of light were stealing through the glass. In the thick greenish light, he looked very ill.

He tried to smile, and she lost the last trace of self-control. 'Come, my queen.' He kissed her again, but on the forehead, distantly, as if they were already strangers now. 'The Gods weave sorrows into the loom of life only to increase our joy. We must believe that this endless winter will give way to spring. One kiss, and then we part.'

CHAPTER 64

Dressed like a king, not like an invalid, Arthur lay motionless on the great bed. His body was sleeping, but his mind was never more alive. He had heard Guenevere order his attendants not to swathe him in the garb of the sickroom like a dying man. Marvelling, his soul flowered with the sweetness of it, for he knew it spelled her longing desire to bring him back to life, and restore him to what he had been. And he knew now that she was back in his chamber again, sitting at his bedside where she had been all along.

He should stir himself, he knew, and tell her that all was well, that there was nothing wrong with him but this sleepfulness. Yet while he was dreaming so blessedly, he thought, he would sleep a little longer yet. The dreams that had come to him in this time of waking sleep had made him sing to himself with joy, and cry to dream again.

He had dreamed of his boyhood, when he had roamed with Kay through long summer days that never seemed to end. He saw himself on his first day as a squire, a tall boy of fourteen leaving off the short cloak of a page for a full-length red mantle with a royal trim. He had served King Ursien of Gore then, and the King's banner floated through all these dreams. One by one his thoughts retraced all the steps that had brought him from squire to knight, and then at last to king.

And at his side through it all moved the thin flickering form of the one who had been more than a father to him, more than tutor, more than life. He saw Merlin again as the old man used to be, the rare visitor to the court of Sir Ector where he spent his childhood in happy ignorance of what he truly was. Merlin would arrive on a beast as strange as himself, a tall white mule with one brown eye and one blue. He would be closeted with Sir Ector for a long day or a night, while the two men exchanged news, Merlin's of the outer world and the country at large, Sir Ector's, as Arthur learned later, a loving report on the details of his foster-son's life.

Then the dream changed again. With Merlin at his side, he rode for London, and relived the glory of when he was proclaimed. Once more he fought under Caerleon's battlements, took his kingdom and came into his own. With his enemies on their knees at his feet, he saw again the purest of all human sights, the joy on the face of the vanquished when they know their lives will be spared. 'Go in peace!' he heard his own voice echoing through the dream. 'And make war no more!'

Now he dreamed of a high green hill under a smiling moon, and a queenly young woman standing bathed in white and gold. He could hear her soul calling to him as he plunged towards her, breasting a sea of fire. She held out her arms and he came to her, and they were one. They grew together like trees in a forest, separate yet intertwined.

But deep in the roots of his tree he could feel something stir. With the blind eyes of sleep he looked down through the earth and saw a great scaly thing uncoiling its loathsome body beneath his feet, and slowly thrashing its hideous forked tail. In the branches above his head, he could hear a raven cry. With a mournful clattering of its wings, it took to the air and circled round into his view.

As the great black bird flew down he could see that it clutched a small child in its claws. Black-haired and white-faced, it was the child from the tournament who came as herald for the black knight. Passing Arthur, the boy turned his head and looked full at him, and Arthur shook with the force of his stare. Once already he had seen the odd, lustrous, hyacinthine eyes. But now for the first time he saw in the child's face the mirror of his own.

The raven set down the child on the jousting field, and circled away with a hideous cawing behind the viewing gallery at the knights' end of the field. Moments later, the black knight rode out on to the field. And now Arthur was forced to relive his charge down the lists. Again he was thundering towards a black lance that would not feint away. Now he could feel the agony in his chest as the point brought him down, now he crashed to the ground with the heavy armour mangling his every joint, now his life blood oozed from him as he lay in the dirt.

And he saw what he knew no one else could see, the helmet of the black knight part from its iron collar and gape open to the air. Through the crack came a black beak, a black head and a dead blue-black eye, then the raven was free and away and circling up through the air. She winged her leisurely way to the end of the field where the child stood now watching the sky. Unnoticed by all, who were running madly down the field to the fallen King, she wheeled down, picked up the child, and soared away to the clouds.

A loud mocking cry filled his ears as she went. Arthur shook like a willow and a pale sweat bathed every limb.

Now he knew why the child had begged the boon for the black knight. Now he knew why the black knight had come to challenge him. Now he knew who it was.

He had to wake now, he had to, the fear was too intense. But he could not stir. Instead he watched in agony as the spirit shadow of Morgan hovered above him and took shape. In a sick parody of their love, she began to strip him of his clothing, piece by piece. She stripped him as she had when she seduced him, and he lay naked in a welter of scalding shame.

And, as always, she took him further than he meant to go. Now she led him on further still, in spite of his resistance and his pain. Taunting and abusing, she still set herself to arouse him and he watched in helpless horror as his flesh answered her call. Now he was lying naked and erect, but unable to cover himself, his hands and feet pinioned in the torpor of the dream.

Now he was drowning in shame like boiling oil.

And still she had not finished with him.

'See, Arthur see!'

The deadly hissing was all around him now. A sickness gripped his stomach and he felt a stirring at the root of his being, deep in his loins. Then to his terror, his whole sex juddered and a blue-black eye emerged at the very tip. First one eye, then another, then a blunt questing head, and as he watched a grown snake emerged to the light of day, crawling inch by inch out of his shuddering member.

Arthur looked on, trying to force himself awake, trying in vain to scream. The snake sat coiled on his chest now, hissing lightly, surveying him curiously. Its scaly body was black with red markings blotched like blood, and black wattles swung from its neck as the head swayed ominously to and fro. But the eyes assessing him so coldly were not black or red but a deep hyacinthine blue. The snake that had issued from him was the boy on the jousting field. And the boy on the jousting field was—

'Aaaaghh!'

As Arthur's mind closed round the terror, the snake reared, spat and struck. He felt the stinging venom in his eyes, then sharp fangs sinking into his throat. Thrashing like a sea-serpent, the snake was tearing his windpipe out. The thing that had sprung from his own loins was going to take his life.

'Aaaaghh!'

'Arthur, Arthur! What's the matter, oh, my love!'

Arthur burst into consciousness, weeping with terror and clutching at his throat. Guenevere's face was above him, her warm arms around him, her whole being alight with love and anguished concern.

He tried to speak, but no words came from his mouth.

'What is it?' she implored. Then her face cleared and a light of joy shone in her eyes. 'Oh, Arthur,' she whispered, wide-eyed, 'you've come back to me, you're awake again, you're alive.'

Arthur shook his head, too weak to speak again. A cup of strong liquor was at his lips now. 'Drink this,' urged Guenevere.

The fiery liquid seared its way through the gag of dust and cobwebs blocking his mouth. He grabbed at the cup, and drained the cordial down. Then his hands plucked madly at Guenevere's arm. 'Morgan,' he husked. 'She was there, and—'

'And Mordred.' Guenevere drew away from him, he saw with a stab of agony, at the very mention of the name. 'Yes, she has come back to plague us once again.'

Arthur fell back on the bed, seeing it all. Morgan the black spirit, who had come as knight and bird. Mordred the terrible boy, the old-young offspring of a force that existed before time began.

Raw evil from ancient times, already abroad and looking for fresh meat when he stepped in its way. And in the folly of his own young manhood, wounded by love and dragged along by insatiable desire, he had made more evil out of the evil that was. He had let loose another Morgan in male form to darken the years to come.

He looked at Guenevere hovering over the bed. Her once-lovely eyes were purple with suffering, and her face was as wild and fierce as a haggard of the rock. She was paying too, he realised with blank dread; she would pay for Mordred in times to come, and so would Kay and Gawain, Lucan and Bedivere, so would they all. He closed his eyes. Tears as big as hailstones escaped from his lids and ran down his face. 'I should have died,' he said.

Guenevere leaped to his side. 'Arthur, no!' She took his hand. Her grip was cool, and as she leaned in to him she smelled as sweet and wholesome as the blossom on the trees.

'Yes,' he persisted stubbornly. 'For all I have done – done to you.' He gave a rusty laugh. 'And to Morgan too, and to him now, the little one.'

'Your son.'

Arthur shuddered.

'Your son,' Guenevere repeated as steadily as she could. 'Mordred. He lives, we know that now. We have to say his name.'

Arthur turned his head aside.

'Say it. Arthur. He has to be recognised.'

He closed his eyes. 'Mordred,' he heard himself say.

'Your son.'

He paused. 'My son.' He opened his eyes and paused. Could he say this? He had to. 'My second son.'

Guenevere flinched. Arthur pressed on. 'First Amir, then Mordred. Is this the end, Guenevere? In your country queens may change their consorts when they need a better man. Even in mine, a king may live alone. I will do whatever you want that will make you happy now.'

'It will not make me happy to be alone.'

A dull spark of hope lit Arthur's eye. 'Could you ever think of being with me again? Could you ever forgive?'

Could she? She took his hand. 'Hear me, Arthur. When a marriage fails, there is fault on both sides. Morgan could not have taken you from me if our love had been strong. No woman can steal a man who is truly loved. I failed you then.' She took a fragile breath. *Do not speak of Lancelot*, her heart urged, and she heard its voice. But something had to be said. 'And I have failed you since. You talk of forgiving. But you, can you forgive?'

'Oh, Guenevere!' He drew her down to the bed and took her in his arms. He felt a surge of love for her so powerful that the blood burst through his body and rushed through his loins. Tenderly he kissed her eyes, her forehead, and the soft skin of her face. After so long, he dared not approach her mouth. But he wept softly with joy when he felt her kissing him.

My love.

Arthur, my love . . .

She took his face between her hands and kissed his lips as she had not done for a long time. With confident hands she unfastened his tunic and parted the shirt underneath.

Without haste she set about renewing the love she once felt for him. Gently circling, kissing and caressing, she rediscovered his long length, and made much of his every limb. A languorous warmth suffused her as she played him like an instrument, wringing from him groans of pleasure and tiny stifled cries of disbelief and joy.

Waves of desire seized Arthur, racking him from head to foot. He felt himself grow strong and flourish as he had feared he never would again. He tossed Guenevere back on the bed, and fumbled with the fastening of her gown. Laughing softly in her throat she pushed his hand aside and slid herself out of the bright silken sheath.

Naked against the cloudy folds of silk, she was like the creamy stamen lying at a poppy's heart. Arthur's senses swam. He passed a trembling hand over her warm heavy breasts, feeling himself quicken again at the sight of her nipples urgent for his touch. Awe and wonder held him back, and a moment of blind panic almost had him weeping with fear – *what if I lose this again?*

But her hands on his body were all the reassurance he could need. She stroked him slowly and tenderly, and her every touch told of love awakening from its long sleep. And when she kissed him deep on the mouth and drew him into her, he knew he had come home.

CHAPTER 65

Kay hurried through the lower courtyard, cursing his leg as he went. Not for the pain, that hardly troubled him, he was used to that now. No, the problem was that getting about was so damnably hard these days. Dragging a lame leg meant that strolling about was a thing of the past.

So it would not look casual when he came across Bors and Lionel down at the stables. But Kay was past caring now. If it was true that Lancelot was leaving, he wanted to hear it from the horse's mouth.

And they should be down there with the horses, Lucan said. He had heard Lancelot tell them to make ready, they were leaving at once. At this time of the night? Kay cocked a dubious eye at the evening sky. It was a warm enough evening, for sure, and every knight had slept under the stars often enough to have no fear of it.

But no one set out at nightfall by their own choice. Something had sent young Lancelot packing post-haste, and Kay fervently hoped that the 'something' was the Queen. Gods above, if only Guenevere had come to her senses at last!

He hurried on, trying not to let his hopes overtake the truth of what he knew. There was more to this whole thing, he conceded grudgingly, than he had first thought at Joyous Garde. The Queen was no trollop, nor some bored, loose-sided woman looking to lie with the first handsome young man in sight. No, what had drawn her and Lancelot into bed was something more than he'd ever dreamed.

Oh, gratitude perhaps at first – after what the Queen had suffered at Malgaunt's hands, a few nights of midsummer madness might have been excused. For the love of the King, Kay had devoutly prayed that it would be only that.

Kay sighed. Had he known even then that the feeling between those two was too strong to be put away? That the time in Joyous Garde did not slake their appetites, but created instead a hunger that had to be fed? A hunger so great that they were ready to ruin the life of King Arthur – for all his errors the best man any of them would ever know – in the drive to satisfy their love? Kay frowned. No, not love but lust, like farmyard animals in the spring, goats on heat or a pair of rutting dogs.

By God and all the saints, what was he thinking of? Kay struggled to put away the visions that accompanied such thoughts, for he was not a lewd man. And when he remembered the look Guenevere wore whenever Lancelot was not in sight, he felt a pity for the two of them greater than he had ever known.

But it could not go on. He stumbled on the cobbles, turned his leg painfully, and swore. It should not have started. It should have ended where it had begun, in Joyous Garde. It should never have dragged on in Camelot and Caerleon, everywhere they went.

He swore again, and not for the pain in his leg. How they thought they'd keep it to themselves, the Gods alone knew! Oh, they would have known they could trust him, that he would keep silent for Arthur's sake. And Bors and Lionel were Lancelot's own men and would die for him. But back at court, the very dogs could have nosed it out by now! There were always eyes at court, always watchers like Gawain's brother, that damned Agravain. Sooner or later they would betray themselves, and their secret would be known to the whole world.

But if Lancelot were leaving – if he would just go away—

Gods above, what a relief that would be! Not that he had anything against Lancelot, Kay reminded himself sharply. He was a good knight and always one to have on your side. And losing Lancelot would sadden Arthur. That would be bad. But sometimes one bad thing led to a greater good. Arthur's happiness would be greater, Kay knew in his heart, when the man who was the Queen's best friend and the King's dearest enemy was far away.

Through an archway in the distance he could see the faint glow of a lantern and hear the low hum of voices exchanging a few subdued words. He hurried along, ducked through the low arch, and came out in the stableyard. Bors and Lionel stood beside their horses, methodically loading the saddlebags. Farther off, tethered to the wall, stood a third horse, Lancelot's white charger, fully laden and ready to go.

Kay came up to them awkwardly, unsure what to say. He chucked a thumb at the horses and raised his eyes. 'You're leaving?' he asked unnecessarily.

Bors nodded, and did not meet his eye. His neat fingers were busy closing flaps, fastening buckles and tightening straps. 'Time to be off!' he said lightly.

'It's a bit sudden,' Kay ventured, feeling oddly ill at ease. Once there had been no barriers between him and the two French cousins, and they had talked freely about everything under the sun. But things had never been the same since Joyous Garde. Keeping Lancelot's secret had put lead weights on all their tongues.

Bors smiled, and looked Kay in the eye. 'But not a moment too soon.'

Kay saw Lionel drop his head and suddenly bury himself in his packing, the colour mounting up his neck to the tips of his ears. These two were no happier than he was at the turn of events. He could have laughed, except it was not funny. Well, too late to commiserate with one another now.

'So!' said Kay with forced enthusiasm, rubbing his hands. 'Well, you're off, then! Where will you go?'

Lionel raised his head, looking happier for a moment. 'Back to Little Britain.'

Bors glanced fondly at his brother. 'Yes, we go back to France,' he said. 'We have not seen our country for a long time. Lancelot has had many letters from his mother the Queen, begging him to return. She longs to see her only son again.' His expression softened. 'And, truth to tell, Lancelot longs to see his mother too. She is a rare lady, the Queen. Any son would be happy to have such a mother, and they rejoice in one another, they have done all their lives.'

'So, our Queen has given him leave to depart the court?' Kay probed.

'Queen Guenevere is leaving the court herself,' said Bors. 'She is taking the King back to Avalon to complete his return to health. The two of them will be the guests of the Lady to rest and walk and take the waters, until King Arthur is himself again.' Bors paused and remembered Guenevere's face as he would always think of it. '"Going home," she said to me as we left. "We are going home."'

The words hung sweetly in the air between them. From the woodland above, a nightingale called through the night, 'Going home, going home, going home . . .'

Bors straightened up, his face brightening as he spoke.

'So we're off again, taking to the road as we did when we were boys.'

Lionel grinned. 'Just the three of us, the way it used to be!'

Kay's spirits lifted in sympathy. 'And when shall we see you back?'

'Ah!' Bors's dark eyes searched the star-encrusted sky. 'Do not ask. We are knights-errant now, wandering where we will. As soon as Lancelot has bidden farewell to the fellowship of the Round Table, we are on our way. You would see him yourself if you were up at the castle with Gawain and the rest.'

Lionel came forward, his arms outstretched. 'Farewell.'

Kay felt the pang of parting, and feebly tried to stave it off. 'But you will return?'

Bors first shook his head, then nodded, and finally shrugged his shoulders helplessly. He tried to smile. 'Before we die, we hope. But not soon. Not yet.'

Kay forced an answering smile. 'Well, then, some of us will have to travel over the Narrow Sea,' he said stoutly, 'and challenge you to a bout of arms for the honour of the old days.'

Bors stepped forward and took his hand. 'We count on it,' he said. His smile was very sweet. 'Until then, old friend, wish us "*bon voyage*"?'

Kay took him in his arms. 'Till we meet again, brother,' he said. 'Till we meet again.'

Merlin lifted his old hawk's head, and sniffed the air. Was there a greater joy on earth than to be out and about on a morning of green and gold?

He cackled with delight till his whole frame shook. When Uther died, he had been forced to run for his life, but now he rode like a king, just as he had before. They had hunted him then, but those days were gone. He had come back to the palace and taken his place again, even though they had all laughed at his 'boy'.

Then there had been his own world of crystal, his healing cave, his safe, sacred place. And now he was well again, he was free, he had the world to himself, he could go where he pleased.

A skylark rose singing from the wayside, and his spirits soared. He checked his horse, to savour the moment in his mind. But the canny native pony took the bit between his teeth, plodding on serenely down the arched greenway. They were deep in the heart of the country, with no other soul for miles. Overhead the midday sun spangled the leaves with fire, and the mayflies danced like broken motes of light in the shafts of gold pouring down through the trees.

Merlin's heart shifted as if squeezed by a giant hand. There was nothing he would not do for this land – this tiny sea-girt island, lying where the Gods had tossed it through the mists of time to its place on the edge of the world.

He saw it now through the eyes of a high-flying hawk looking back in time. Queen Igraine of Cornwall – yes, an outstanding woman, rare and beautiful. And her husband Duke Gorlois was a fine man, it was true.

Merlin sighed. It was a pity that theirs had not been an arranged marriage, devoid of any passion except dislike. Or that they could not have had a union of the ordinary kind, in which love so gradually gives way to indifference that neither party misses it when it is gone. But they had loved one another, Gorlois and Igraine, and that was bad. He could remember that he had felt some pity for Igraine, for them all.

But it had had to be.

And the sorrow had not ended there, it could not. Real grief is never done. The mother's suffering had become the daughter's and their vengeance was still to come. Madam

Morgan was still at large, and her huge sense of grievance would never die.

Merlin shifted uneasily in his saddle, and felt the future coming on. There were other troubles ahead, too, that he could only dimly see. But he knew they were there waiting, he could smell their approach as rank as any fox, hear the drumming of their hoofs like rutting stags in spring. They could not be avoided. Whatever was coming was already in the stars.

Well, so be it.

All this, too, would have to be.

For all this had been needed to give Britain a High King.

But for Arthur, the Saxons would be at the gates of London now, breaking down walls, burning the city, crucifying women and toasting babies in the fire. Without Arthur, all the petty kings would be slitting one another's throats, and the land would be crying out from its open wounds as all countries do in time of war. King Lot of Lothian would still be the self-styled High King, squatting like a toad in the Middle Kingdom, making widows and orphans, hounding bards and dream-readers and those who walked the world between the worlds, as he had hunted Merlin when Uther's day was done.

King Lot of Lothian, Lot the loathsome, Lot the loathed.

Everything had been worth it for that death alone.

Merlin sighed.

And Arthur's work was not done. And because of that, neither was his own.

On your way, then, old fool!

With a self-mocking cackle Merlin heaved up his trailing robes, and tucked them under the backs of his thin shanks, resettling his scrawny buttocks on the saddle and lifting his keen eyes to the road ahead. There was much to do, and only he could guarantee to bring about what would be needed in times to come.

A good thing he was fit again now, the spirit poison of Morgan's enchantment well and truly shaken off. A good thing he had had Nemue to take care of him on the Sacred Isle. She was the best Maiden of all Avalon for healing the mind's sickness and the spirit's decay.

He cackled softly to himself. Nemue was still a fine woman, and she would be for many years. He stroked his bony hands and thought of her small, firm body, her clear eyes and unaffected stare. One of these days she still might be his, as he had hoped from the first. Life was long, like his patience, and the man who waited got most of what he wanted in the end.

He hunched forward in the saddle, his ears pricking forward like a dog's. In the meantime, he had the glory of the open road, the sweet secret greenways like this, the sunlit highways, cool dark forests and at the end of the road, the ever-open sea. And the world would know that Merlin was on his way again. Know the old man was about, busying himself for the good of the land.

He drew a breath of the sweet rich air deep into his lungs and humbly thanked the Gods. Life was good, he had been blessed, and there was more to come. The Gods were on his side, on Arthur's side, weaving the future They had granted him the gift to dream. While there was blood in his veins then, strength in his limbs and fire in his heart, Merlin would do Their will.

He would repay.

'May the love of the Great One and all your Gods go with you all the way!'

Arthur reached for Guenevere's hand. Together they left the Lady's house with her blessing still ringing in their ears.

In the world outside, the dawn was breaking in a cloudless sky. Behind them lay a long, loving night of talk and prayer and tears. In the safety of the Lady's house they had found what had been long lost between them, the truthful dialogue of loving souls.

Arthur lifted his face to the faint warmth of the sun. The pale light gilded his wide forehead and strong jaw. 'She was very good to me,' he said quietly.

'No more than you deserve.' Guenevere stroked his hand. 'She loves you.'

He shook his head. 'She loves both of us.'

Hand in hand they walked away from the house, taking the path up the hill. The island was still hushed and dreaming after its sleep, and the dew lay silver on every blade of grass.

Arthur put his arm round her shoulder. 'It's good to know that Merlin is free again.'

He fell silent, but Guenevere could read his thoughts. 'Never fear, Arthur, you have not lost Merlin. You will see him again. Believe me, he will appear when you least expect it, to help and support you as he always did. Till then, you have to grant him the freedom to roam. He has been out of the world for a long time.'

'You're right.' A look of fond memory crossed Arthur's face. 'Merlin is Merlin. The old hawk must fly when and where he wills. Oh, Guenevere,' he squeezed her shoulder feelingly, 'it's better than I dared to hope that he is well.'

Guenevere pressed his hand. 'I could say the same about you.' She was almost afraid to tempt providence with the words. 'Oh, Arthur, you are truly yourself again!'

'I'm glad you think so,' he said humbly. He gave a tired grin. 'But I hope we don't have too many more nights like this. I'm not the man I was when I came to your queen-making on the Hill of Stones.'

A golden image dropped through Guenevere's mind. She saw Arthur stepping towards her through the fiery dark, her Beltain love, her lord of fire and light. Then she saw him hag-ridden and haunted with the curse of Morgan's love, then ill and wasted, lying in his bed.

But now another Arthur stood by her side, the great frame scarcely changed in the ten years since they met, his fair hair only lightly touched with grey. Leaving the Lady's house, he had walked with a firmer step and there was no trace of the beaten Arthur she had hated, the man in thrall to his monks. She brought his hand to her lips and kissed it tenderly. 'No, none of us is the same.'

Into the silence between them fell the memory of all that they had shared – Malgaunt, Amir, the days of love and pain. Throughout the night the Lady's murmuring voice had led them back through the labyrinths of old rage and grief to a new beginning, a tremulous fresh start.

It would not be easy, they knew. The shadow of Morgan still hung between them, and would walk with them always now. There had been no trace of her or her son since she had fled from King Ursien. But neither of them believed that she was gone from their lives.

And Amir – Amir was dead, but they still had the life of a child between them, the countless memories of his sweet small body, his trusting eyes, his loving ways. The sturdy seven-year-old would remain more fresh to them, she was sure, than many a child who lived to become a torment to his parents, or simply passed into adulthood before their eyes.

Guenevere gripped Arthur's hand and suppressed a sigh. Unknown to Arthur, another spirit shadow would be with them always too. Guenevere knew with the ache of a fresh wound that Lancelot would walk with her all her days. She would not punish Arthur with the knowledge of what had passed. But she would carry the burden of it from now on. Now every tall slender man seen at a distance, every bright brown enquiring eye, every lift of a head turned a certain way would set the spirit of lost love free to roam again the mansions of her mind, mourning its flight from paradise.

She nodded to herself. *So Arthur and I are one. Both of us have suffered the cruel loss of love. We share a common currency of pain. We can help each other through the times ahead.*

She looked up. Arthur was watching her with a look of anxious concern. Behind his head a cloud of white blossom was breathing out its sweetness to the world. 'It can never be the same,' she went on, 'but it can be different, we can make things good again.'

His eyes filled with tears. 'I love you, Guenevere.'

'And I love you.' She paused, nerving herself up. *Do I have to do this?* But it had to be said. 'Morgan loved you too, Arthur, I can see that now. She must have loved you from the moment you first met. She had been starved of love for all her life. I'm sure that she's fated to love you for ever now.'

Arthur stopped, and took her in his arms. 'Can you truly forgive me?'

Can you forgive me?

'Oh, Arthur . . .' She folded him in her strongest embrace. 'I already have. I was wrong too. I—' She broke off, sighed, and began again. 'I lost sight of what we are to one another – I – I did not – keep faith.'

She could feel in the answering sigh that escaped him an acceptance of her words. For a moment they cradled one another, suspended between wounded love, and a longing for better things.

'Oh, Arthur . . .'

She raised her hand to his face. The back of his head was soft to her touch, the downy hairs tender to her fingers just as they used to be. She caressed the strong, sinewy column of his neck, and traced the smooth, warm outlines of the bones of his cheek.

He shuddered. 'Oh, Guenevere, can we . . . ?'

'Hushhhh.' She drew down his head and kissed him on the lips. 'Beloved, you have punished yourself enough. We have to try to forgive ourselves now. And we have much more in our lives than past memories. We have each other. And we have the land.'

Arthur's eyes took on the bright gleam she remembered from their earliest days. 'We have done some good in our reign, haven't we?' he said fervently.

'And we will do more.' She turned and looked back down the hill. 'See there.'

The new day was breaking over Avalon in a haze of gold. In the distance the white towers of Camelot beckoned through the mist. Guenevere took Arthur's arm and pointed the way ahead. 'Come, my love!' she said.

THE CHARACTERS

Abbot, the Father Head of the abbey in London where Arthur was proclaimed, leader of the Christian monks in Britain, implacably opposed to the worship of the Great Mother, and supporter of Merlin and Arthur against the Lady of the Lake

Agravain Second son of King Lot, brother of Gawain, Gaheris and Gareth, nephew and later knight to Arthur

Agrisance, King One of the six vassal kings of King Lot, holding Caerleon illicitly at the time when Arthur was proclaimed

Aife, Queen Warrior queen of the north, leader of a college of women where young men were taught the arts of war, and teacher of Lancelot

Amir 'The Beloved One', only son of Arthur and Guenevere

Arian, Dame Wife of Sir Ector, mother of Sir Kay, and Arthur's foster-mother

Arthur Pendragon, High King of Britain, son of Uther Pendragon and Queen Igraine of Cornwall, husband to Guenevere

Ban, King   King of Benoic in Little Britain, father of Lancelot, older brother of King Bors, ally to Arthur in the Battle of the Kings

Baudwin   Knight of Caerleon, old servant of Uther, supporter of Arthur when he reclaimed his throne

Bedivere, Sir   Knight to Arthur, one of his first three companion knights

Black Lands, King of the   Vassal to Arthur

Boniface, Brother   Monk at the abbey in London, sent as emissary to the Lady of the Lake on Avalon

Bors, King   King of Benoic in Little Britain, younger brother of King Ban, father of Bors and Lionel, ally to Arthur in the Battle of the Kings

Bors, Sir   Son of King Bors, brother of Lionel, cousin of Lancelot, knight to Guenevere

Brangoris, King   One of the six vassal kings of King Lot holding the Middle Kingdom illicitly against Arthur, and later his enemy in the Battle of the Kings

Brangwen   Wife of Sir Niamh, a knight of Guenevere's mother, and a staunch defender of the Mother-right

Carados, King   King of Northgales, castellan of Caerleon, leader of the six vassal kings of King Lot

Castle on the Rock, King of the   Ally of King Lot in the Battle of the Kings

Cormac   Bard to Guenevere's mother in Camelot and Guenevere's first love

Cradelle Haut, Sir   Knight to the court of the Summer Country

Damant, Sir   Knight to the court of the Summer Country

Dinant, Sir   Knight to King Arthur

Ector, Sir   Foster-father to Arthur, father of Sir Kay, knight to Arthur

Epin of the Glen, Sir   Knight to the court of the Summer Country

Excalibur   Sword of power given to Arthur by the Lady of the Lake

Faramon, King   King of the Green, friend of Arthur

Gaheris   Third son of King Lot, brother of Gawain, Agravain and Gareth, nephew and later knight to Arthur

Gareth   Fourth son of King Lot, brother of Gawain, Agravain and Gaheris, nephew and later knight to Arthur

Gawain, Sir   Eldest son of King Lot, Arthur's first companion knight, brother of Agravain, Gaheris and Gareth

Gorlois, Duke   Champion and Chosen One of Queen Igraine of Cornwall, father of Morgause and Morgan, murdered by Uther and Merlin

Griflet, Sir   Knight to Arthur

Guenevere   Queen of the Summer Country, daughter of Queen Maire Macha and King Leogrance, wife of Arthur, lover of Sir Lancelot and mother of Amir

Helin, Sir   Knight to Arthur

Igraine, Queen   Queen of Cornwall, wife of Duke Gorlois and beloved of King Uther Pendragon, mother of Arthur, Morgause and Morgan Le Fay

Ina Maid to Guenevere

John, Brother Monk, leader of the Christians in the Summer Country and father confessor of the Abbey of the Holy Mother where Morgan Le Fay was placed as a child

Kay, Sir Foster-brother of Arthur and knight of the Round Table, one of the three companion knights of Arthur from the time he was proclaimed

Ladinas, Sir Knight to Arthur

Lady of the Lake Ruler of Avalon, priestess of the Great Mother

Lamorak Son of Sir Pellinore, knighted by Arthur after the Battle of the Kings, later knight and Chosen One to Queen Morgause of the Orkneys

Lancelot, Sir Son of King Ban of Benoic, knight of the Round Table and lover of Queen Guenevere

Leogrance, King King of the Summer Country, first champion and Chosen One to Queen Maire Macha, and Guenevere's father

Lionel, Sir Second son of King Bors, brother of Sir Bors, cousin of Sir Lancelot and knight to Guenevere

Lot, King King of Lothian and the Orkneys, one-time ally of King Uther Pendragon, husband of Morgause, father of Gawain, Agravain, Gaheris and Gareth, and later usurper of the Middle Kingdom and enemy of Arthur

Lovell the Bold, Sir Champion to Guenevere's mother before Sir Lucan

Lucan, Sir Champion to Guenevere's mother and her Chosen One, later Arthur's knight

Maire Macha, Queen   Guenevere's mother, Queen of the Summer Country, wife to King Leogrance

Malgaunt, Prince   Younger half-brother of Queen Maire Macha, uncle to Guenevere

Marhaus, King   King of Ireland, friend of Arthur

Merlin   Welsh Druid and bard, illegitimate offspring of the house of Pendragon, adviser to Uther and Arthur

Mordred   Son of Arthur and his half-sister Morgan Le Fay, cast adrift in a boat off the coast of Gore and lost

Morgan Le Fay   Younger daughter of Queen Igraine and Duke Gorlois of Cornwall, placed in a Christian convent by King Uther, her step-father, under the name of Sister Ann, Arthur's half-sister and lover, wife to King Ursien and mother of Mordred

Morgause   Elder daughter of Queen Igraine and Duke Gorlois, given as wife to King Lot by King Uther, Arthur's half-sister, mother of Gawain, Agravain, Gaheris and Gareth and later lover of Sir Lamorak

Nemue   Chief priestess to the Lady of the Lake, courted by Merlin

Nentres, King   King of Garlos, vassal of Lot

Niamh, Sir   Knight, early champion of Guenevere's mother, husband of Brangwen and defender of the Mother-right

North Humber, King of   Ally of King Lot in the Battle of the Kings

Palomides, Sir   Knight to the court of the Summer Country

Pelles, King   King of Terre Foraine and the castle of Corbenic, brother to Pellinore and father of Elaine

Pellinore, King King of Listinoise, ally of Arthur

Penn Annwyn Lord of the Underworld in Celtic mythology

Placida, Abbess Mother Superior of Christian convent where Morgan Le Fay was placed as a child

Rience, King One of the six vassal kings of King Lot holding the Middle Kingdom illicitly when Arthur was proclaimed

Sagramore, Sir Knight to Arthur

Solise, King of Ally of King Lot at the Battle of the Kings

Taliesin Chief Druid to Queen Maire Macha and the Summer Country, staunch supporter of Guenevere

Tor, Sir Knight to Arthur

Tuath Druid of Dolorous Garde in the service of Malgaunt

Ulfius, Sir Councillor to King Uther, later supporter of Arthur

Ursien, King King of Gore, overlord of Sir Ector, the foster-father of Arthur, and later husband of Morgan Le Fay

Uther Pendragon, King of the Middle Kingdom, High King of Britain, lover of Queen Igraine of Cornwall and Arthur's father

Vause, King One of the six vassal kings of King Lot illicitly occupying the Middle Kingdom when Arthur was proclaimed

Western Isles, King of the Ally of King Lot in the Battle of the Kings

Yvain, Sir Eldest son of King Ursien of Gore

LIST OF PLACES

Avalon Sacred Isle in the Summer Country, centre of Goddess worship, modern Glastonbury in Somerset

Bedegraine Forest on the borders of Gore in the north of England

Caerleon Capital of the Middle Kingdom, formerly the City of the Legions during the Roman occupation, seized by King Lot after the death of King Uther, held by a force of six vassal kings of King Lot, reclaimed by Arthur in a surprise attack, modern Caerleon in South Wales

Camelot Capital of the Summer Country, home of the Round Table, modern Cadbury in Somerset

Canterbury First base of the Roman Church in the British Isles, and site of the first archbishopric in England

Cornwall Kingdom of Arthur's mother, Queen Igraine

Dolorous Garde Castle of Prince Malgaunt, taken by Sir Lancelot, later Joyous Garde

Gore Christian kingdom of King Ursien in the north-west of England where Arthur and Kay were raised

Hill of Stones Ancient burial site of the queens of the

Summer Country, location of ritual queen-making and site of the feast of Beltain

Iona Island on north-west coast of England, site of first settlement of Celtic Christianity in Britain

Island of the West Modern Ireland

Listinoise Kingdom of King Pellinore, modern East Riding of Yorkshire

Little Britain Territory in France, location of the kingdom of Benoic, home of King Ban and King Bors, modern Brittany

London Major city in ancient Britain, capital of Christian colonisation of the British Isles

Middle Kingdom Arthur's ancestral kingdom, lying between the Summer Country and Wales, modern Gwent, Glamorgan and Herefordshire

Orkneys, Islands of the Cluster of most northerly islands of the British Isles, and site of King Lot's kingdom

Saxon shore, the Site of invasion by tribes called 'the Norsemen', raiders from Norway, Denmark, and east Germany

Severn Water The Bristol Channel, estuary of the River Severn, dividing the Middle Kingdom from the Summer Country.

Summer Country Guenevere's kingdom, ancient centre of Goddess worship, modern Somerset

Terrabil Castle of Queen Igraine of Cornwall, defended by Duke Gorlois, taken by King Uther in battle where Gorlois lost his life

Terre Foraine Kingdom of King Pelles in northern England

Tintagel Castle of Queen Igraine of Cornwall

Val Sans Retour, Le Estate of King Ursien in Gore, donated to Arthur, presented to Morgan Le Fay and the base of her power

Welshlands Home to Merlin, modern Wales

POCKET
B O O K S

GUENEVERE I
The Queen of the Summer Country

Rosalind Miles

Across the many kingdoms and islands of ancient
Britain, Arthur begins his quest to become High King.
But even as he battles to reclaim his birthright, an
impassioned and beautiful woman is waiting to claim
her destiny.

Guenevere, daughter of Queen Maire Macha and King
Leogrance, will soon take the throne in the Summer
Country, following the sudden and tragic death of her
mother. From the swirling mists of Avalon, she will
survey the heroic exploits of the new High King. And
then summon him to her side...

With a rare and intuitive magic, acclaimed novelist
and historian Rosalind Miles vividly brings to life a
legendary woman's greatest and most glorious time,
revealing Guenevere's bravery, passion and inner
torment as she ruled a truly ancient kingdom.

ISBN: 0 671 01812 4
Price: £6.99

POCKET
B O O K S

This book and other **Simon & Schuster** titles are available from
your book shop or can be ordered direct from the publisher.

0 671 01020 4	**Ramses: The Son of the Light**	Christian Jacq	£5.99
0 671 01021 2	**Ramses: The Temple of a Million Years**		
		Christian Jacq	£5.99
0 671 01022 0	**Ramses: The Battle of Kadesh**	Christian Jacq	£5.99
0 671 01023 9	**Ramses: The Lady of Abu Simbel**		
		Christian Jacq	£5.99
0 671 01024 7	**Ramses: Under the Western Acacia**		
		Christian Jacq	£5.99
0 684 86073 2	**The Black Pharaoh**	Christian Jacq	£9.99
0 671 51673 6	**The Sanctuary Seeker**	Bernard Knight	£5.99
0 671 51674 4	**The Poisoned Chalice**	Bernard Knight	£5.99
0 671 51675 2	**Crowner's Quest**	Bernard Knight	£5.99

Please send cheque or postal order for the value of the book, free postage
and packing within the UK; OVERSEAS including Republic of Ireland £1
per book.

OR: Please debit this amount from my:

VISA/ACCESS/MASTERCARD ....

CARD NO ....

EXPIRY DATE ....

AMOUNT £ ....

NAME ....

ADDRESS ....

....

SIGNATURE ....

Send orders to:
SIMON & SCHUSTER CASH SALES
PO Box 29, Douglas, Isle of Man, IM99 1BQ
Tel: 01624 675 137, Fax 01624 670923
www.bookpost.co.uk
Please allow 14 days for delivery.
Prices and availability subject to change without notice.